I0825263

The Arkis Tales
Volume II

All The Devils Are Here

Renée Tamsin

Cover Design by Sarah Winningham
Edited by Kendra Savage

ISBN-13: 978-1-961872-03-5

To Robert Louis Stevenson and his good buddy J.M. Barrie, for each setting yet another stage for me.

Much appreciated, gentlemen.

Contents

Part One

Part Two

Part Three

Acknowledgements

I've always considered *The Arkis Tales* a bit of a group project—one where I do all the writing, but a wide assortment of people contribute ideas and strong opinions. It's what makes this series so personal for me. It's what's given a unique sense of life to the characters. From patient coworkers forced to spend full shifts learning lore and workshopping plot holes to close friends and family who have been cheering me on, fully invested from the first draft.

Each installment I publish is for you.

Rereleasing these newly revised editions has reminded me that I was never actually alone in my journey to create tangible versions of my work. All of you helped me bring this into fruition and I am eternally grateful for each and every one of you.

"HELL IS EMPTY, AND ALL THE DEVILS ARE HERE."

~THE TEMPEST, WILLIAM SHAKESPEARE~

Prologue

Every individual seeks fulfillment in their own way. For some, fulfillment comes from obtaining power. For others, it comes from falling in love. Some seek after superficial accomplishments, while others seek after more sentimental core values, such as virtue or family. And then there are those who care less about glory, rank, or respect and instead seek blatant material gain. It is quite common, in fact, for individuals to care more about their own temporal benefit as opposed to the character acquired during the journey itself. Silly things, such as riches and treasures, can corrupt even the most secure individuals. I'm sure by now you know that faults are quite universal in existence; shortcomings spare no man nor woman.

Greed, in my personal opinion, is one of the most ordinary as far as faults are concerned. Such cupidity is a common, yet impactful little thing. It can instigate selfishness, betrayal, and ultimate destruction. It can build a man up only to tear him down. It can inspire an utterly inexperienced adventurer to risk his life just at the mere prospect of getting his hands on desired wealth.

In the city of Bristol, on the coast of England, Squire Trelawney sat contentedly dining in one of the seaside town's best inns. He was quite pleased with himself. He had made arrangements so quickly with the captain of the ship intended to take him to the location of a treasure chest.

In his suit coat was the treasure map given to him by Dr. Livesey, who had recently "acquired" it from a young boy, Jim Hawkins, or something like that. The three were now business associates. Being the patron for the expedition, it was decided that Trelawney was to keep the map, for safekeeping of course, and all would set sail for this so-called Treasure Island and return as wealthy as kings. Squire Trelawney may have been a fool, but he was a fool with a map.

Having finished his meal, he rose to leave when he noticed a rather beautiful woman lingering in the foyer. Her rusty locks spilled over her shoulders in perfect curls, half of them fashionably pinned atop her head. Her fierce eyes curiously watched him from afar. She was the sort of woman whose face was just generic enough to blend into a crowd, but with enough intrigue to draw you in. She was quite petite, with a sophisticated air about her, and wore stylish clothes.

"Good day, miss," Trelawney smoothly bowed as he approached her.

"And you, sir," she grinned.

"Pray, what is that lovely accent?"

Bashfully, she chuckled. "Galway."

"Charming." Trelawney kissed her hand without taking his eyes off of the lady. "And how do you like Bristol?"

The woman giggled girlishly at the kiss. "It's damp, but not too terribly different from home."

"Well, it is much brighter now that you're here, I'm sure."

"My, my, you are quite the charmer, sir." She playfully nudged him with the fan in her hand, making him blush. "Words like that are in danger of sweeping a girl off her feet."

"I'm certainly endeavoring to, miss." He stepped a bit closer to her in an attempt to establish further physical contact in his technique. Just then, however, this little dalliance was interrupted.

"For your sake, I hope not," a threatening voice growled from behind Trelawney. The hopeful squire suddenly felt a crushing defeat upon seeing the tall, fair-haired gentleman staring down at him.

"I...I beg your pardon, sir," Trelawney stammered. "I-I was only..."

"Attempting to woo my fiancée?" his competitor challenged.

"Your—?" the squire glanced back at the woman. "Fiancée?"

The woman shrugged, unmoved by the jealousy of her betrothed.

"Erm, my apologies, good sir. She is a very fine lady, if I may say so—"

His clumsy attempt to make amends was cut off by the flare of the gentleman's temper. The man pinned him against the wall with terrifying rage in his eyes. The small handful of patrons occupying the tables of the inn's dining room all froze, watching eagerly as the tension unfolded.

"My love, my love," the woman scolded, taking her man's arm. She gently guided him away from the frightened squire, patting his hand soothingly. "The gentleman meant no harm; he was only being friendly. Be at ease, darling." Once the fires were extinguished, she apologized to Trelawney with sincerity. “Please excuse my fiancé's temper. He's a very passionate man.” She then lowered her voice lewdly. “Makes me both fearful and eager for our future years of wedded bliss,” she winked.

The squire blushed at her implication and at her closeness. With coy ambition, the woman kissed his nervous cheek and turned to leave with her tense fiancé. As flattered as Trelawney was, he did not envy the gentleman's apparent need to keep a close eye on a woman such as her. The conniving couple exited the inn, arm in arm, and made their way down the crowded cobblestone street.

When they turned a corner, the man mumbled to the deceptive beauty, “It wasn't the moron's heart that was supposed to be stolen.”

She gave a devilish chuckle. “Oh come on, darling,” she prodded, her accent completely faded back to her slightly more English persuasion. “A lady needs to stay in practice, you know. Don’t you worry,” the vixen teased, wrapping her arm tightly around his. “I only have eyes for you.”

“Hm,” his scowl softened. “Until you pay him a visit.”

She stopped in the street and cupped his cheek in her palm. “Only to pay my dues, love. In any case, I’ve kept you too long. When you give the rat the map, be sure he knows who got it for him, love.” She kissed him affectionately on the mouth, then grabbed his chin earnestly to look into his eyes. “Now go clean up your own mess, and we'll be seeing each other again soon.”

Trelawney met with his new captain, as planned, and was introduced to Captain Smollett's first mate, Mr. Arrow.

The squire gave his new colleagues a complete briefing of the adventure thus far, assuring them that he understood all a voyage such as this would entail. He told them of Dr. Livesey and young Hawkins, explaining their itinerary. When Captain Smollett asked for proof of this treasure map, Trelawney proudly reached into his pocket; his face fell when he felt that his pocket was empty and the oilskin pouch that contained the old map was now missing.

That blasted man at the inn! Trelawney suspected that the jealous fellow must have lifted it from his pocket during their scuffle.

Filled with a mixture of panic and anger, the squire did not once suspect the wiles of the beautiful woman. Few do. A beautiful face could get away with murder–some already have.

If you remember, dear reader, I warned you about this one.

Part One

Roses From Ashes

1

Heads Will Roll

Thirty magical years since their jaunt through the realm of the Great King Arthur, Ben and Stella Caverly lived a life filled with more adventure and heroism than any I have ever seen. Every realm the pair entered felt the full effect of such a powerful Keepership.

The Scarlet Pimpernel was no different.

The war-torn realm was nearly beyond salvaging; even the presence of the Pimpernel and his crew of Regent Keepers was not enough. A story in which so much disdain and blood-lust is woven into every word has very little hope for revival. The French Revolution was indeed one of the grisliest and most gruesome events in the history of Middangeard–your own world, that is, dear reader–but to have it immortalized in a realm of its own does not inspire the possibility of saving.

Even so, a great author once stated that no book is so bad that there is not something good in it. Even a setting with so much hatred and death can contain something as good as a Regent. Or even three or four.

Yes, this was Yonas' design: to raise heroes as roses from ashes, to prepare them for even more crucial destinies. And it was now time to pick those roses. Ben and Stella were given the task of gathering them. Sadly, Korbl, as always, was only a step behind them.

Sir Andrew sat in the filthy prison cell, surrounded by rats and the weeping noble blood of the French landscape. He had served alongside the Scarlet Pimpernel since the start of the French revolution. The heroism, the personal fulfillment, the adrenaline–their cause was as enticing as they come. While he did not know the Pimpernel's plan, he was confident one existed. Then again, he considered, Keepers were killed all the time. What made him so special while the lives of others were frequently a priority?

A horrid peasant woman hacked phlegm from her throat as she lumbered along the row of cells, mockingly tossing stale bread crumbs at the prisoners. She spewed out insults and crude retorts about misfortunes falling upon the well-deserved. When she approached Sir Andrew's cell, she aimed the bread directly at his face, hitting her mark with a cackle. Taking a torn handkerchief out of her apron pocket, the hag blew her nose uncouthly and proceeded to throw the wrinkled linen at Sir Andrew as well.

Recognizing a gleam in her sky eyes, Andrew took the dirty rag and noticed it was embroidered with a symbol—a small scarlet flower. A pimpernel, to be exact. A signature that held promise. Promptly, the prisoner gathered the enchanted crumbs from the dusty floor and quickly swallowed them. By the time the soldiers came to collect their next batch of victims, the enchanted dough had settled in Andrew's stomach, slowly taking effect.

In moments, his skin paled and broke out in a cold sweat, he lost his balance and collapsed right before the prison entrance.

Frustrated by the inconvenience, the attending soldier gave Andrew's pulse a cursory check and tossed his body out of the way of the other prisoners boarding the cart that would lead them to their death. As the loaded cart was pulled along to its appointment with Madame la Guillotine, two dingy citizens rode up in their own cart to collect the dead prisoners.

Another guard loaded the back of the wagon with shabby coffins of prisoners who had died before meeting the great blade. One of the two drivers noticed Andrew's limp body on the ground and rolled his eyes.

“Is it too much trouble to put these things in a box or something?” he grumbled.

He gestured for his partner to help him lift the body into the back, and the two argued through the labor, each man thinking he knew the most effective way to carry a corpse.

After securing the bodies and coffins in their rightful place, both men assumed their seats in front, the first man taking the reins. They rode the cart through town and made it all the way to the West Gate of Paris before being stopped for inspection. As was the routine, the shrewd Sergeant Bibot insisted on checking papers and inspecting the cargo.

"You're more than welcome to rummage through those coffins," the second undertaker snickered. "But I will say, the prison has had a bit of an outbreak. Dunno what it is, but speculation says it could be the plague."

Any interest Bibot had in testing these unsavory suspects disappeared the moment he heard the word *plague.*

"Just to be safe," the first undertaker contributed, "we're takin' them outside the walls, to burn 'em before it can spread."

"Hold on," a familiar voice intervened before Bibot could wave them through. Bastien, who had only recently entered the realm, stalked over to the cart. "Let me take a look; I have a remarkable constitution."

He kept a wary eye on the two drivers as he circled the cart, carefully peeking under the sloppy lids and sampling a whiff of the smell of death. Only the top layer of coffins were subjected to his scrutinous inspection, however. Giving only a slight pause, Bastien nodded his approval to Bibot.

"Carry on," he allowed, wearing a cryptic but content smirk.

And so the cart rolled along the dirt path which took it further from the gates of Paris. As soon as they reached a safe distance, the two undertakers met up with their patient cohorts in a gathering of trees.

"Lookin' good, handsome," Stella, freed from her phlegmy alter ego, greeted as her horse approached the cart.

The first undertaker's makeup masked his face so successfully; even Bastien could not recognize him. Ben wiped off his disguise with the bottom of his dirty shirt, makeup now smeared over his visage and nodded respectfully to the beloved Scarlet Pimpernel at his side.

"That was a very clever save there with the plague," Ben applauded.

Sir Percy Blakeney grinned in satisfaction as he hopped down from the top of the cart. "Every time. It's a strategy we have used before, isn't that right Tony? One would expect those Frenchies to have learned their lesson the first time."

Stella's riding partner chuckled in agreement. Sir Antony Dewhurst dismounted and congratulated his wise leader. "They never learn. Well done, Percy."

"Come now, let us free dear Andrew." Percy waved to Antony, and together they moved the top layer of coffins aside to reveal an open box and a drowsy Andrew lying within, just beginning to regain consciousness.

Their rescued colleague inhaled quickly to fill his lungs with fresh air. "Well that took longer than I had hoped," Andrew coughed.

"Oh, be grateful we even came for you," Antony chided with a grin.

"Suzanne, is she—?"

"She is perfectly safe, Andrew," Percy assured him. "Caverly was sure to see to that."

Andrew gave Ben a grateful nod, but the Keeper did not see. He was preoccupied, lifting his precious wife from her horse. Even a quarter of a century of marriage could not fade the couple's newlywed gaze. Stella made some funny comment regarding the convincing stench of Ben's disguise, at which he rolled his eyes in amusement.

"Caverly," Percy called to him.

"Hm?" Ben answered.

"What is our move, my good man?"

Ben shed the first grubby layer of his costume, hoping to shed the smell in the process. "Chauvelin has been given orders," he started. "If he knows anything about Korbl, he's not going to give up those orders so easily. I think it best that we return to England, fetch Suzanne and Marguerite and leave for the Arkis."

"You think we're in the clear?" Stella questioned. She readjusted the bun atop her head, allowing strands to fall subtly around her face.

Time had treated both Mr. and Mrs. Caverly quite kindly. Inter-realm travel has that effect, to be sure. Stella's once soft, round face was hardly sullied with wrinkles or anything like them. She had lost the youthful fat from her cheeks, giving her elegantly defined cheekbones that still managed to enchant. No one could imagine she was any older than forty years of age.

"If I'm right, we should have just enough time to make it to the coast. Of course, I have been wrong before," Ben replied.

He had a strange look in his eye that greatly troubled Stella, but she said nothing. The Aerest Keeper knew very well that he was never the only one to have read the book. Their enemy was rarely ignorant.

"And you shall be wrong again," that eerily familiar voice crowed.

Dark soldiers, more sullied and stained than the French revolutionaries, surrounded the rescue party on all sides, perched on their black steeds. The darkened skin around each set of eyes brought a more harrowing sense of being in a cage than Stella would have liked. She no longer tended to worry for very long, however. Time had been a marvelous tutor and Ben Caverly had planned for this.

"This realm suits you well, Bastien," Ben blandly commented. "Resentful and smelly." Stella chuckled at this, nudging Ben's arm in agreement.

"You are too sweet, Keeper," Bastien hummed in a low, snide tone. "Forgive me, I've only just arrived, but I assume these gentlemen are the Pimpernel and his boys. No more need for secrecy, Blakeney. Your realm has betrayed you."

Antony and Andrew glared, but their leader grinned with irony. Amongst those who knew his secret identity, Percy was famed for his bravery in the face of danger; he had a peculiar sense of daring which Stella found especially relatable. When presented with any adversary, his masterfully crafted mask of fop and folly came out to play.

"What is it that your colleagues say?" Percy jived, heightening his tone and slowing his words, so as to appear as simple-minded as they come. "Tou-ché?"

A soldier behind Bastien chuckled until receiving a silencing glance from his superior.

"If you don't mind, we have an appointment in Paris that I would hate to miss," Bastien stated succinctly.

"Oh, I don't believe that is completely necessary," Percy countered, shaking his head. His posture lightened, his movements becoming careless. "I think we could better sort this out here and now, like gentlemen. After all, we are civilized beings, however assorted."

"How very English," Bastien rolled his eyes. "If a kindly escort is not an appealing enough method for you, we are more than happy to use brute force. In fact, we prefer it."

Right on cue, the dark soldiers behind him aimed their muskets, invoking an equal reaction from the Keepers they faced.

Joining the Pimpernel and his men in their defense, Stella drew her own concealed weapon, but something in Ben's countenance brought hesitation. He did not draw his weapon. He did not react. He merely watched with that same strange look in his eye.

There was no antagonism in his voice, only diplomacy, as he said, "Paris it is."

Percy, Antony, and Andrew glanced quizzically at Ben. They all knew the escape plan, should they find themselves captured, but they did not expect to go into such a situation so willingly. Their confusion was nothing to the questioning in Stella's big sky eyes. Ben sensed the uneasiness and turned to his wife. Tenderly intertwining his fingers in hers, his expression told her to trust him. Which, of course, she did.

"Percy, I'm sure you've heard the phrase '*live today, fight tomorrow*.'" Ben shot him a knowing glance, and the Pimpernel holstered his pistol.

"Indeed." Percy nodded to his men, who followed suit.

The Aerest Keeper and Companion, along with the League of the Scarlet Pimpernel, were peacefully ushered back through the gates of Paris. Like many storyfolk villains, this realm's primary antagonist, Citizen Chauvelin of the French Republic, was an easily recruited Scada agent. Incidentally, the misguided theories of the Revolution aligned quite well with the Scada credo. They claimed what they thought was freedom, but only opened themselves to disturbing vulnerability. Naturally, this made Bastien's assignment quite manageable. Chauvelin gave him all the information he needed and offered his unconditional loyalty.

Upon arriving at Chauvelin's office, Bastien ordered Chauvelin's men to stand back as the Scada agents searched the prisoners for weapons. Pistols and small daggers were quickly confiscated from the subdued Regents.

"Wait," Bastien barked, just as one of his agents moved to search the Arch Keeper. Smoothly, the dark general moved between Scada and Keeper, looking Ben Caverly directly in the eye. "Your sword."

Ben could feel Stella tense beside him, anticipating his assumed rebellion. He wasn't often one to stray from expectation, but his decades of marriage to the wily Towson girl had an effect on his nature, it seemed. Our Keeper maintained eye contact with Bastien as he reached behind him, where, underneath his conduit leather jacket, he was able to conceal Caliburn with remarkable discretion.

Bastien grinned as he took the sword from Ben. His arrogance began to rise as he examined the Keeper's sword. "I'm much obliged, Keeper. Thank you for your cooperation. And now, that jacket of yours."

Ben's head cocked to one side as he clicked his tongue. "That, I can't do."

Sighing, Bastien tucked Caliburn in his own belt in acceptance. "Very well. Your magic would prove to be ineffective here, in any case."

As he spoke, Chauvelin's men clamped abnormally polished silver cuffs around each captive's wrists.

"Those must have fetched a pretty penny," Ben commented, as casually as one might comment on a fine pair of wing-tipped shoes.

"Extraordinary how the right craftsman can take something as forgettable as a Queen of Avalon's ring and turn it into a handful of Keeper-proof shackles."

"Which Queen?" Stella softly asked, but her question fell on deaf ears.

Ben's mouth lightly curled into a strange smile, distant and pensive. "Timo's certainly outdone himself."

Bastien's smile exceeded the Keeper's, reaching both of his ears as he stepped back and watched the Regents exchange defeated glances. Their leader kept an unwavering eye on Bastien.

Chauvelin took the reins of taunting the prisoners, gloating, "It seems your quest to save the realm has failed."

"It was worth a shot," Stella shrugged and glanced at the Scarlet Pimpernel. "You were right, Percy. The French are just too clever."

Percy chuckled, his witless mask held tight like a shield. "Sink me, they may be monstrously ill-dressed, but they do seem terribly efficient."

Chauvelin strode over to the Pimpernel with a smug expression on his face. "Oh, don't play the fool on my account, Sir Percy. There is no bumbling your way out of this."

"Maybe he just likes saying *Sink me*," Stella suggested, imitating the comical manner in which Sir Percy would wield his flamboyant facade. While Sir Antony appreciated the humor, this only resulted in her being the receipt of Chauvelin's contempt.

"While we value opinions in our new Republic, yours is as good as aristocratic, madam," the Frenchman sneered. The fair lady merely took her husband's hand and sneered right back at her opponent, in that endearing way she does. "There is no benefit from retaliation. You have lost the realm, Keepers."

Ben quietly looked to Bastien with a knowing glance. "You know we aren't here for the realm," he murmured, loud enough for the dark general to hear.

Bastien pressed his lips together thoughtfully as Ben went on, gaining volume. As before, Ben's tone was even and without antagonism.

"The realm is beyond salvaging," the Keeper claimed. "That was never the intent."

Bastien studied Ben's expression before shifting his gaze to the Regents. "The Keepers," he mused aloud to himself. "It was all for the Keepers. My, my, Myk must have something quite serious planned for these fellows."

"It's a shame that we won't figure out just what that is," Chauvelin contributed. "For you will all be dead."

Sir Andrew missed Ben's cautionary glance and spoke up too soon, with too much audacity. “You think you can succeed in bringing down the League of the Scarlet Pimpernel?” Andrew scoffed proudly. “Not with the Aerest on our side, sir. I'm afraid you will be the one to fail.”

Citizen Chauvelin may have been a small, seemingly weak man, but his ruthless nature knew no bounds. In a swift but deadly movement, Chauvelin reached for his own pistol from its place on his desk and pointed it at Sir Andrew. He glimpsed back at Bastien, awaiting a nod of approval. Bastien paused for a moment, taking in the situation.

“It seems your expiration date has long passed, Regent.” Bastien gave the nod, and Chauvelin pulled the trigger.

Sir Antony shouted with fury, unable to control himself as Chauvelin’s bullet tore through Andrew’s chest. The League that was so famed for its control, stealth, and calculation was now falling apart. Percy held his friend back, struggling to contain his own anger. Stella joined the men in their outrage, but before any of them could act, Ben gave his orders.

“Stop,” he said firmly, his voice far steadier than one would expect. He then looked imperviously toward Bastien. “We are not incapable of admitting defeat.”

“Attaboy,” Bastien applauded.

“But, perhaps, we could end this with a compromise. Sir Percy and I will surrender peacefully if you release Sir Antony and Lady Stella.”

“Ben,” Stella started, but he silenced her with a squeeze of the hand.

Bastien considered the proposition. "I could just kill the four of you right now."

"But you won't," Ben challenged.

Bastien slowly paced the space in front of the captives, before responding. "Lucky for you, those weren't my orders." Abruptly, he stopped directly in front of Ben. "I'll agree to that, Keeper. No harm, I suppose. Besides..." he leered in Stella's direction, "...there's something my master would like the lovely Mrs. Caverly to see, and she can't see it if she's in here, now can she?"

His timbre toward Stella made Ben uneasy, but the deal stood. Ben knew what he was doing. After all, reader, he planned for this.

Stella, however, was not quite so at peace with the arrangement. When Bastien's man attempted to grab her arm and escort her out, she pulled away. "No, I'm not leaving. What are—?"

"Stella," Ben cradled his wife's face ever so gently. He had that look in his eye again, that strange look. "Everything is under control," he whispered and kissed her lovingly. It was the sort of kiss one would give a lover before a long separation. It was tender, yet passionate, and sadly short. "I love you."

Her sky eyes misted over. Ben would think of something. He always did. He was a strategist. He adapted plans as needed, and that was all he was doing. She kissed him back and stroked his cheek. "I love you back."

Obediently, she followed Antony and the dark soldiers out of Chauvelin's office. The moment the door closed,

Bastien nodded to the Scada standing closest to him and watched him follow shortly behind the freed captives. Ben knew Bastien wouldn't keep his word. It was the Scada way, and he expected as much. Bastien would have Stella and Antony followed by his men; Ben assumed this was to see that Stella was at the right place at the right time to see what Korbl wanted her to see, but he trusted Antony to keep her at a safe distance from the enemy.

"Bind the Keepers," Bastien ordered, crossing his arms in front of his chest. When his wish was granted, he flippantly gestured to Chauvelin. "Well," he said, "you've hunted the notorious Pimpernel long enough. He's all yours."

Bastien waved him off. With the help of his soldiers, Chauvelin saw to it that Percy was roughly hauled through the door and into the next room, leaving Bastien and Ben alone.

In a very different tone, Bastien narrowed his attention to Ben. "I think you're familiar with your options, Caverly."

Scada agents are required to offer Keepers alternatives, given a chance. Claiming physical victory in killing a Keeper is not nearly enough; real success comes when a Keeper is led to corruption. An Arch Keeper is a particularly grand victory, and one that has never before occurred.

But Bastien knew better. Arch Keepers were not elevated to such a rank if they ran a risk of being easily corrupted. It's simply not how Myk operates. Bastien knew that Benjamin Caverly would never succumb to whatever offer might be made, no matter how tantalizing. Rarely is a

Keeper's assignment as simple as it seems—and their dark counterparts are no different.

"I urge you to consider something," Bastien masterfully began. "Greater than you have found themselves on my list of targets. I've hunted Companions, Keepers, even Creators."

"*Hunted*, yes. You've done your best," Ben murmured.

"Even so, no execution will give me more joy than that of the Aerest Keeper, I can assure you."

If the thought affected Ben, he did not show it. He did not reveal any emotional distress or concern. Instead, he stood a little straighter, still and controlled, and responded with cool observance. "You haven't been paying attention."

Bastien raised his brow curiously. "Is that so?"

"Killing me will only usher in the next one. I can assure *you* that your Master is unprepared. I've kept the chaos at bay for quite some time now. Unappreciative as you are now, you'll soon learn that, of the final three, each one will be more problematic than the last."

"Hm, shame," Bastien muttered. His words taunted, but his tone tensed at the Keeper's warning. "The poor little Creator's name was next. And she will soon be without her Keeper. My assignment is becoming so simple, it's almost unfair. It won't have to end like this, of course, if you have our protection..."

"No, thank you," the Keeper declined politely.

Bastien sighed; his favorite part was coming. "Then I suppose it is your turn first."

A gruff French soldier shoved Ben into his prison cell to await his impending doom at the guillotine the next morning. Percy was thrown into the neighboring cell, bruised and beaten. Chauvelin had taken a more physical approach to his obligatory offer of alliance to the Regent. Percy was a strong man. He could withstand the unspeakable with nerves of steel. It was what made him such an acclaimed hero in his now deteriorating realm. It was what made him a Keeper. And it was why Myk needed him extracted.

That night, the two heroes slept on the cold, stone floor. Well, Sir Percy slept—Ben leaned solemnly against the wall of his cell. He was troubled, and he knew Stella suspected it. He was unsettled and couldn't bring himself to close his tired eyes. Percy also sensed Ben's restlessness. He lifted himself from the floor and peered through the metal bars that separated them.

"What is it, Caverly?" he inquired of the Aerest.

Ben's head snapped up at him, startled. "Oh, I'm just... pondering."

Percy sighed. "It will all work, Ben. We planned for this."

"Yes, it will," Ben replied confidently. He then turned slowly to face him. Percy noticed his expression and was immediately alarmed. "I need you to do something for me—without question or argument, Percy. And...I understand...if you are unwilling. It is almost too much to ask of you."

Percy stared into Ben's soberness and nodded with soft but sincere conviction. "Caverly, I will do whatever you ask."

What makes a grand Regent is noble submission. Something in Ben's eyes brought hesitation and uncertainty. But, Percy was a unique sort of hero. He understood without knowing. Percy trusted his calling, he trusted Ben's calling. So, with commendable devotion, Percy straightened his back and urged the Keeper to proceed.

Dutifully, Sir Antony kept Stella at a safe distance from the men he knew were following them. They found shelter for the night in a run-down boarding house in town. There they slept, and waited, anticipating the original escape plan to be already in motion.

The next morning, soldiers with eyes darkened by an oath beat against the door with such force that the landlady didn't dare question their intrusion. Stella and Antony were found and taken into the streets. The men made minimal physical contact, yet they seemed very resolute in their herding. Once they were positioned precisely in the center of the crowd surrounding the guillotine, the soldiers stepped back.

“How considerate of them to take us where we needed to be,” Antony mumbled.

“Yeah...” Stella agreed. She suddenly felt anxious, but couldn't explain why. “Don't worry, I think we should be seeing them soon,” she said, more to herself than to Antony.

The crowd around them cheered loudly as the cart of victims arrived. On a usual day, those filthy aristocrats would be led to Madame la Guillotine, for justice to be served. Today, only one victim rode in the cart. The poor figure wore a hood over his head, shielding his identity from the onlookers. The crowd fell to a curious murmur, watching intently as two French soldiers led the unfortunate soul, like a lamb to the slaughter.

"Wait." Stella grabbed Antony's arm.

This was the part of the plan in which Percy and Ben were to have switched places with some unsuspecting French soldiers. But the faces wearing the uniforms were unrecognizable. And there was only one hooded man.

"Something's wrong," she breathed.

Antony understood her fears and warmly hugged her shoulders, bracing her for whatever was to come. The dark general himself strolled to the guillotine, insisting on doing the honors. He lifted his hand and tore the hood off of his victim's head.

Stella's heart fell harder than she could stand. Ben's face was flushed from the heat of the hood, and he searched the crowd for her sky eyes. He didn't want them to see. When his eyes met hers, he found them swimming in confusion and pain. He couldn't bear it.

"No, he's not..." Stella struggled. Antony attempted to restrain, but she fought back. Fortunately for Antony, his reinforcement came briskly. Percy appeared beside them, to hold onto Stella's shoulders firmly.

"Stella, Ben knows what he's doing," he tried to calm her.

But the storm wouldn't calm.

In her hand, Percy placed a small, pressed rose petal—the very rose petal Stella had given to Ben before his first quest all those years ago.

She was broken.

Her fist tightened around the petal. Her sky eyes filled with clouds like a dark curtain. Mists rolled in and a thunder grew within her. She fought to get away from the Pimpernel, trying to move to the guillotine stand.

She had to stop Ben.

She had to.

Bastien complacently forced Ben's head under the blade. "You were quite a feat, Caverly. But...at last...another one down."

And the demon released the blade.

The devil himself grinned. It was only fitting that Korbl personally attended the execution of one such opponent. His dark, mighty laugh echoed through the crowd. He may have been unseen, but his terrible presence was felt.

The depth of the devil's victory could only be rivaled by the agony of dear Stella's scream. Her throat tore with anguish. Percy and Antony surrendered their hold on her, allowing her body to crash to the ground as she wept.

The crowd no longer cheered. Even the wicked of the realm could feel the newfound chill of loss.

Adrenaline coursed through her broken body; her heart plummeted to her gut. Stella attempted to stand and run to Ben's body, but horror attacked every fiber of her being.

As he so faithfully promised, Percy took Stella in his arms and guided her to safety. Her flooding eyes were closed so tightly, she hardly noticed when they returned to the Arkis.

She felt safe, in the way a soldier having just lost a limb and soul feels safe in the infirmary. She sobbed until her shredded throat forbade her to continue. The rose petal in her fist moistened and crumbled. Fighting his own sorrow, Percy held her close, letting her drench his shirt in tears until a new comforter came to relieve him.

Myk delicately took Stella into his arms, calming her with his steady heartbeat. He stroked her blonde hair with a soothing hand, hushing her fears.

"He knew what had to be done," he whispered. "It was time. He was ready."

Her breathing steadied, but her face remained buried in his garments. Myk looked up at the two noble Regents who stood before him and gave them a small smile of approval. They had done what they were meant to do. They had proven themselves.

"The war is great and tragic," he went on, addressing all three of them. "It has cost the best blood throughout time to save these ruined worlds."

A small hand wrapped itself around Stella's and squeezed. Stella pulled Alice in closer to her and desperately latched on to her for dear life. Yonas stood quietly over them, lending his soothing presence to the mourning angel. He didn't need to speak for Stella to know he was there.

But, of course, he did anyway.

"This Keepership has not met its end, my love," he told her. "The bond of Keeper and Companion may be shaken by death, but never broken. There is still much work for you to do."

After a moment of silent communication between the Galdere, Myk finally added, "Stella, if you're afraid of not being cared for—"

"I don't want anyone else," she interrupted emphatically. She kissed the top of Alice's sweet head, swallowing her tears. "Could I stay here?"

"Your assistance is very much needed, Stella," Yonas said lovingly, "but in your homeland, to raise up the winning generation."

Stella frowned in confusion. She had been rendered barren since her first encounter with Korbl and had abandoned any hope of bearing children, particularly with Ben now taken from her. "I don't understand...."

"I promise," he assured, fervently. "You will understand soon enough. Korbl has not seen the last of you, my dear."

Yonas cupped her face in his great hands and smiled. He then gingerly took the crushed rose petal from her hand and held it in his. In an instant, as he winked at her, white sparks returned the petal to its perfectly preserved state.

"Not all stories have to end."

As per the Aerest's orders, Percy had managed to smuggle the Keeper's jacket out of the realm and rightly returned it to Myk. Percy received high accolades for his service in Ben Caverly's League of Regents. His role as second-in-command had hardly been christened, but his worthiness was beyond confirmed.

Myk himself accompanied Sir Percy in the retrieval of Marguerite Blakeney and the remaining members of the League. Once all were reunited, they were promptly relocated to a more gothic venue, where they were to await further orders.

Meanwhile, Alice took Stella to find something to eat.

When Myk returned to the Arkis, he sunk into his usual armchair by the fireplace in the common room. Moments later, Yonas appeared in his own armchair opposite Myk's, watching his son thoughtfully.

Myk studied the flame in front of him and sighed, regretfully. "We're getting closer."

Yonas nodded. He understood the melancholy in Myk's expression. The Galdere are a fascinating race; the omniscience they gain in their individual progression does not negate the grief that overcomes them amidst tragedy. Ben's death was not a thing of celebration, even if one knows its necessity. The weight is not quite so heavy when on the shoulders of the most ancient of the Galdere, but Yonas' empathy for his son was far from removed.

"Your brother can feel it as well, despite all he's forgotten" Yonas replied gently. He reached for the tea kettle from the table to the right of his armchair, pouring himself a cup. "Ignorance can be more dangerous than knowledge."

"Of course," Myk muttered solemnly, biting his thumb pensively.

Yonas crossed one leg over the other, leaning into the arm of the chair nearest Myk. "Korbl will continue to fixate on Stella until his eyes are forced another way."

Abruptly, Myk stood from his armchair, adjusting his shirt as he did so. "Let's make that force as swift as possible, shall we?"

Yonas smiled and delicately lifted his teacup. "Give Anne my best."

2

Open Promises

Oxford was never the same.

Aside from the thirty years of change it had endured, there was now a new emptiness to it. Only half of a Caverly returned in the summer of 1993. As if the warm, humid air were not suffocating enough, Stella felt as if she hadn't drawn breath since the guillotine. Myk's steady arm around her was the only thing keeping her on her feet.

When her father had passed on, Caverly Manor served as a hopeful, albeit unexpected, sanctuary from grief. Upon her many returns from assignments with her Keeper, it continued to provide that same sanctuary. But now, with unbearable heaviness in her heart, she approached the door with dread. Inside was no longer comfort and peace from the weight of their calling; instead, two soft hearts were waiting to be broken.

Patricia saw the two arriving from the window, and she opened the door eagerly. Two footsteps later, she caught sight of Stella's tear-stained cheeks. And no Ben. She knew. From the day Patricia found and read Albert's journal, she knew it would come to this. No one plays war without risking death, and even magic couldn't stop that.

Myk held the same bearing as the commander who once brought Patricia the news of her late husband after the only other war she could remember. And Stella bore the same expression she once bore herself. Shivering in shock, Patricia slowly stepped back into the house, not stopping until she came to the sofa, upon which she collapsed with her hands in her face. Her sobs mirrored Stella's feelings startlingly. Myk moved to console Patricia's shaking shoulders and glanced up at the Arch Companion with an understanding nod.

"Go to her," he told her. Stella stood motionless for one numb moment before following his words.

Grief can be so blinding. Stella couldn't remember how she made it to the top of the stairs to Anne's bedroom door. But there she was, looking in at her aging mother-in-law with dense clouds in her eyes.

Anne Caverly sat comfortably in the rocking chair in the corner of her room, her hair casually gathered to the top of her head and her reading glasses perched on the tip of her nose. In her hands, she held a carefully bound family copy of *The Scarlet Pimpernel*. Any good mother does everything in her power to know her children's whereabouts at all times—particularly when one's child lives the life of a Keeper.

She would have liked to accompany them on their adventures, but a woman nearing ninety is often slowed by ailments associated with age. And so she sat in her armchair with her son's latest assignment in her hands, studying every word. Just as she had every other time.

But this time, Anne's eyes met Stella's, and slowly the book was lowered to her lap. She exhaled arduously. Before Stella could attempt to speak, Anne shook her head.

"It had to be this one," she said. Her hands shook as she closed the book. "When he told me which book was next....there was something in his voice."

"You knew?" Stella whispered.

"It was time, my dear," Anne beckoned her to the chair. "If I knew it, you can bet Korbl knew it. He may be a snake, but he knows what he's doing. Benjamin was just too good for him." Stella allowed a little smile as she took Anne's hand and sat on the floor beside her.

There is something to be said for the strength of a matriarch. Anne Caverly faltered in dark moments, but when the light of another was in jeopardy, she became a great beacon. She stroked Stella's hair gently, freely showing all the motherly love Stella had never known.

"How did it happen, Stella?" Anne quietly and delicately pressed.

Stella cleared her throat, maintaining composure. "Bastien....Bastien got him. The, um....the guillotine. H-he, um....wanted me to see it."

"That devil," Anne growled. A tear rolled down her cheek, but she angrily wiped it away.

"I'm so sorry, Anne," Stella mumbled.

"No, no, sweetheart. I am much closer to seeing him again than you are. Do you know what this means, my dear? Bastien could not have done this had Ben not allowed it. They would have never caught him. He was always so good at making difficult decisions." Anne's back straightened with confidence as she assured Stella. She did not raise her son to be a man so easily beaten.

Stella wiped her face with her hand. "Yeah, he was. If he hadn't been, I'd still be stuck in Boston."

Anne chuckled. "That's my girl. He always knew what he was doing. Perhaps that's what made him so valuable to your Myk." As she spoke his name, Myk appeared in the doorway as if on cue. Anne's eyes met his, unmoved by his presence. "When will we receive his body for burial?"

Myk's eyes deepened. "I assure you, Mrs. Caverly, that he will be given the utmost respect. The situation is quite delicate."

Patricia stepped in from behind him, her face puffy and red, to see Mrs. Caverly's response. The old woman's eyes closed as she nodded.

"Well at least we don't have to bother with a funeral," Stella contributed optimistically. Anne patted her hand and opened her eyes with a small smile. Within a few moments, her eyes restfully closed again. "Don't you go dying on me now, Anne."

"I can promise another day or two, but beyond that, I cannot say," Anne smiled again.

"No promise is necessary, Mrs. Caverly," Myk assured. He looked to the remaining Aerest with a faithful smile, inspiring Stella to stand and step just a bit closer to him. "Stella is more than capable of pushing forward and standing strong because she'll have to."

The frown on Patricia's mouth straightened into something a little less devastated as Stella leaned into her, lightly rubbing her arm in consolation.

"Benjamin's life opened the final stage of this war," he went on, "and now his death has sealed his purpose. There's only more death to come, I'm afraid. They're beginning to unleash their worst, and there's no stopping it." For a moment, Myk's eyes fell to his hands. And Stella noticed. Before she could reach out to him, however, he quickly lifted his head and continued. "What I can promise is that, though terrible things will continue to unfold, it is all by design. Our forces will be just as unstoppable. We have strategies in place that will not fail. Longevity favors the true, after all. Korbl will not win."

With such a promise, Anne's face lit with pride. "Good. Someone needs to keep that beast damned. Ben's turn is over....who's next?"

Myk smiled, lightly shrugging. "Someone Benjamin would have proudly fought beside in another life, to be sure."

And in vague confusion, he left them. But Stella was not satisfied. She hurried down the stairs and stopped him before he reached the door—as if he needed a door. He turned just as he knew she'd be approaching.

"I want to meet him," Stella demanded. "I should meet the next Keeper."

"No, Stella," was the simple answer.

"Why not?" she argued.

Patiently, Myk sighed. Heartache could not quell her gumption. "I promise you, Stella...."

"You've said that before."

"And have you not believed me?"

She fell silent, correcting herself, as he expected.

"Stella, it will not be long before you and the next Keeper are more intimately connected. But, for now, the worlds must wait for their next hero, just as you will."

"Is he not ready yet?" she questioned. "Time shouldn't be wasted, Myk."

He laughed. "My dear, I am certain he will be ready when we have need of him. The waiting is good for both sides, believe me. Sometimes it's best to let the enemy celebrate and get comfortable in his own arrogance. Arrogance is laziness and laziness is weakness. We need weakness right now. He was growing desperate after his loss those years ago, so we must encourage his inflated ego for the time being."

Stella made a face. "Yes, speaking of those promises you keep making...."

"Stella."

Those rain clouds in her eyes misted over again, just enough for a few traitorous tears to slip down her cheeks. "You took the child, and then you let them take Ben away from me too. Shame on you, Myk."

Her voice had no trace of spite or bitterness, only sadness. Despite her words, Stella knew that everything Myk did was by careful deliberation. And his promises were always kept.

Myk took her by the hand and kissed it tenderly. "All will be set right, my dear. Ben's time will return, and the child is being tended to. Your chance to nurture will come. This will not be the last you see of me."

Stella forced a smile. "It better not be."

He returned the effort. "I'll be around so often that you won't have time to miss me." He lightly kissed her forehead and, before turning to leave, he added, "Take good care of Anne, Stella. Your mother-in-law does not have much longer. Her passing will be the start of that outpouring of fulfillment for which you've so patiently waited."

"Do you mean—?"

"Just wait a bit longer. It's happening rather quickly."

He winked and disappeared, leaving Stella with a small smile she no longer forced.

3

The Changing of the Guard

Alice is a curious soul. Legs crossed, she sat on the floor of a shelved room in the Arkis with her chin in her palm. Myk and Yonas had been gone for quite a while. She wondered what in all the worlds could be taking them so long. Clancy bustled to and fro, carrying on his duties as usual. Occasionally, he peered over the edge of the platform he stood on at the crestfallen child in concern before bustling off again.

"I really like Ben," the girl said, sadly twirling a golden blonde curl.

Clancy frowned in sympathy. "Oh, Alice. You know that—"

"Yes, I know," she sighed dramatically.

Seeing Ben and Stella pass through the Arkis, on their way to save another world, brought Alice such a thrill; she always wished she could go with them. Clancy looked down at the book in his hand and cleared his throat.

"Why don't you help me organize these?" he suggested.

With another Arch Keeper's reign ending, it is customary for an Arkis caretaker, such as Clancy, to organize said Keeper's adventures. Of course, it is an unending task—as you can see, I am still transcribing. The legend of the Keepers is nearly perpetual, but as the baton is passed, the former Arch Keeper's story is chronicled in his own special wing of the Arkis, where Alice now sat pouting.

"There are quite a lot of them," Clancy pressed.

It was no exaggeration, in fact, that Ben Caverly had a very extensive resumé of successful ventures. While he was, by no means, the longest reigning Arch Keeper, he carried the war forward more than almost any other Keeper thus far. There are countless volumes to support this statement.

Just as Alice stood to assist Clancy, her ears perked. Footsteps approached down the hall, so the child eagerly bounded to the nearest sliding bookshelf, exposing the door that led to the rest of the Arkis. She peered down the corridor to sneak a peek at the happenstance causing such a fuss.

Two Arkis attendants were supporting the limp weight of a young man, perhaps no older than thirty years of age. Gently, they guided him down the hall, toward the infirmary, though no apparent injuries were visible. His brown bangs flopped across the side of his face and Alice's eyes lit in recognition.

"Declan!" she cried out.

Clancy stood behind her, placing a silencing hand on her shoulder. He followed her eyes and frowned. "They found him," he whispered in relief.

"He could be the next one, Clancy," she mused.

"No...no, Alice. After what that witch has done– unfortunately, I think Declan O'Leary's days in the field are over." Clancy's shoulders fell.

The loss of a Keeper comes in many forms, some more damaging than others, but all tragic. They watched the poor Regent delicately carried to a room of care from which Clancy doubted he would return.

"He'll be back out soon." Alice's arms crossed and her back straightened. She was always so certain.

"If he is, Alice, I'm afraid he'll be quite mad."

"We're all mad here, Clancy. That's how I like it best. He can still...." she trailed off as another voice captured her attention.

It was Yonas's soft hum in the other room, heralding his presence. Her eyes widened in excitement as she bounded to the next chamber. With exasperated responsibility, Clancy followed. Alice was his charge, and Myk never let him forget that.

"Did you get him?" Alice blurted the moment she entered. Myk and Yonas sat in those grand armchairs, counseling quietly with one another, legs crossed and fingers pensively intertwined, as wise men do. They fell silent when they heard her pattering little feet.

"Did we get who, petal?" Yonas vainly inquired.

The adorable blonde creature climbed onto his lap and attempted to melt the information out of him.

"The next Keeper," she sighed, knowing that he knew precisely what she meant. "Who is he? It's Declan, isn't it?

He's just down there, and he'll be just fine soon, in any case. He'll do. Clancy says it can't be Declan, but I think Clancy's wrong—Declan's going to be mad, but he's not broken."

Yonas chuckled heartily. "No one is truly broken, little one."

"I'm sorry, sir," Clancy began the apologies. "I tried to keep her occupied, but...."

"It's quite alright, Clancy," the great Galdere smiled. "She's only eager. I'm sorry, Alice, but we haven't retrieved him yet."

"But you know who he is," she assumed.

"Of course he does," confirmed Myk. His hands were gathered in his lap, fingers interlocked with contemplation. He bore the same solemnity as he had the last time he sat in this armchair.

"And you know where he is...." Alice continued to dig.

Yonas grinned again. "Yes, we do." In a flicker so fast I nearly missed it, his eyes led Alice to the aged copy of *Treasure Island*, which sat on the shelf nearest the door to the hallway.

A mischievous beam dashed across the child's face. "Why aren't you getting him now?"

Yonas patted her cheek affectionately and shook his head. "It won't be quite that simple this time, my dear."

"Why not?"

He gazed down in amusement and a hint of veracity. "I'm afraid this one will have to come to us. It will take patience."

Myk gave a small smile and stood to search the shelves, pacing slowly from one corner of the room to the other. “Perhaps you should go back to helping Clancy, Alice. Time will pass so quickly; you'll meet the Keeper in minutes.”

Alice pouted, as little girls do, but she obediently slid down from Yonas' lap and lumbered to take Clancy's impatient hand. Perhaps not all little girls are the same, but in my experience, there is far too much rebellion lurking beneath the surface for them to ever be truly content sitting on the sidelines. Obedience can often be a subtle way of describing the patience feigned until rebellion bursts.

Alice’s rebellion happened to bubble to the surface the moment she caught sight of Ben's jacket, lying across the back of Myk’s armchair. The very jacket which held Albert’s journal, tucked away in the interior pocket. They were practically begging her to take them.

She twinkled at Clancy, who responded with an admonishing expression, before she quickly snatched the jacket. Lunging toward her target, dragging her reluctant guardian with her in the process, she flung open the book and they both disappeared between the pages.

“Oh no, wait,” Myk observed with lackluster concern. He tucked his hands in his trouser pockets and glanced at his father to commiserate. “Whatever will we do?” he shrugged.

The old Galdere's lips curved into an inscrutable smile. “Sit here in a tepid state of panic, I suppose.” Thoughtfully, he paused. “This will be quite good for him, I think.”

“You think so?” Myk chuckled at the understatement. “Let us wait for Clancy to see it that way.”

"He will, in time," Yonas mused. "He knows what's at stake. And being at odds with the Assassin could earn anyone the wrinkles he yearns for."

Myk reached an arm toward the nearest bookshelf, retrieving a story of ornate lamps and cryptic genies. "Finding the Keeper will make that much easier, I'm sure. The target on Alice's back brings out the hero in everyone."

"And thank the heavens—but," Yonas pointed at his son, "our Keeper will need much more incentive than that."

"Yes, well." Myk crossed one leg over the other and opened the book across his lap. "Every little bit helps, doesn't it?"

Meanwhile, our rogue travelers landed rather inelegantly within their destination. They were both unaccustomed to this form of travel.

Lucky for Alice, Clancy broke her fall.

Unlucky for Clancy, his face soon became the surface upon which her little hand pushed to launch herself to her feet. Tousled and flustered, the scribe scrambled to his own feet and exhaled sharply.

"Now, why would you do such a thing!" Clancy scolded, his hands waving around to exhibit the damage she'd done in pulling them from the safety of the Arkis.

"How terrific!" Alice giggled. "We did it. We did it! We're in *Treasure Island*!"

Weather-worn peasants bustled past them through the streets of eighteenth-century Bristol, England. The coastal town was adorned with them, along with the waste of their horses. The ocean spray barely rinsed the dirt, grime, and sweat that the city produced. Townspeople struggling in trade and attempting to exploit local merchandising hardly noticed those with whom they so rudely collided.

Clancy dusted his grey Arkis robes several times before groaning in frustration. Their clean, outdated attire should have caused them to stand out, but I suppose a port town frequented by strange foreigners would learn to glance over certain anomalies.

"Well, it definitely smells."

By this, dear Clancy did not necessarily mean the manure, nor the sweat—no, not even the salty filth from the ocean. Clancy had so seldom left the Arkis that his olfactory senses only recognized the aroma of the pages which surrounded him. *Treasure Island*'s pages were entrenched in the scents of the realm–the scents which would be recognized by travelers as the side effects of local living conditions.

"So what do we do now?" he shrugged.

Alice slipped her arms into the oversized sleeves of the Keeper's jacket before placing her tiny hands on her hips and grinning from ear to ear. "Find the Keeper, of course."

Of course. Clancy released a heavy sigh, saturated with dread. "And how do you expect us to do that? Just how familiar are you with downtown Bristol? Wait—" he stopped. His accusing finger pointed at her once again, but this time in confusion. "What's...what's happened to you?"

Alice frowned. What on earth could he mean? Curiously, she looked down. Her white slippers and dress had gathered dirt from the road, but that was hardly worth the alarm. Clancy gingerly reached his hand to touch a stray curl from Alice's head.

"Your....your hair, Alice." He tugged the curl to show her the darkened ends. Her golden crown had changed to a crisp shade of brown.

Alice's frown deepened. "Oh dear..." she sighed. Her wide eyes stared at him in distress. "I don't look much like Miss Stella anymore, do I? Are my eyes still blue like hers?" She widened them even more to give him a better view.

Tensely, the scribe shook his head, even stepping back as if looking upon a ghost. "No, they've darkened too."

"Oh?" Alice's eyebrows perked right up. "Like the great Queen Rena."

Clancy lifted a brow. "I'm sorry, who is that?"

"Rena. Clancy, I mean Rena. I met her in–oh, never mind. She was before your time, I think."

The scribe's eyes rolled as he sighed. "Before my time? I'm quite a bit older than you, Alice."

Ignoring his claims, Alice caught sight of her reflection in a nearby puddle. Her voluminous curls and their new rich, chocolate hue made her grin. "I could be a Creator."

"What? No, you couldn't."

She wrinkled her nose in frustration at his failure to see her potential. But she soon relaxed as she tipped her head from side to side, letting her new locks dance across her shoulders. "Well, alright. But I always did look like Rena. This is wonderful."

"Is it?" Clancy sharply questioned. "Or is it rather an omen that we've been cut off from the Arkis and we're in terrible danger?"

"No, no, Clancy," her small hand brushed him off. "We can go home whenever we want—but we can't yet. We have things to do. Now, we must find that new Keeper. It shouldn't be too hard. Let's pretend we're reading the pages—oh no! There's no hope of this staying white, is there?" Her grin abruptly turned into a frown as she looked at the filthy state of the hem of her white dress. "Oh my...."

"Alice, Alice, Alice," he shook his head. "I think it's safe to say that our Arkis garments aren't going to stand much of a chance here at all. Might as well give up hope of anything for now. We should probably change...so that we don't stand out quite so much."

"That's not something I like doing," Alice furrowed her brow.

"What—changing clothes?"

"Giving up hope. And since I'm more experienced in things like this, I think I should be in charge, Clancy. Myk would agree, I'm sure," the child confidently assumed. She regarded Clancy as the subordinate she believed him to be and began formulating a relatively uninformed strategy.

Pensively, she looked down at her feet against the cobblestone street. Those reliable little things had never steered her wrong before—or at least, not too terribly wrong. So, with gusto, she let them and her intuition be her guide.

Clancy raised another eyebrow, seeing Alice take confident strides forward. "Myk wouldn't want you here in the first place," he corrected. "And where are you going?"

Alice waved her hand at him again. Her efforts to focus on direction were starting to fail her, but she refused to show Clancy any sign of discouragement. She got as far as the closest dock entrance before Clancy stopped following and quietly watched. Assuming he could no longer see her, she tightened her lips in disappointment and planted herself down on the side of the road with legs crossed.

"I can't seem to remember where to go," she shook her head. "I know I've read it in a book once, but I just can't remember where. If only the book had been called *Where To Find a Keeper*...then I would remember it." She propped her elbow upon her knee and cupped her chin in the palm of her hand, continuing to ponder aloud. "Well, every pirate story has ships. The Keeper is bound to be on one of those, right? Although, I shouldn't assume—it confuses me terribly and makes me look silly. Well....what is it that Myk always does when looking for Keepers? In all of those books, there has to be something. What would a Keeper be found doing in a realm like this?"

"What indeed," Clancy contributed, strolling up behind her. His nose was in the air, curling in response to the putrid air. "Well, if he is here, then he'd do what every Keeper does—even if he isn't officially a Keeper yet—after all, it's in his nature. *Follow the heroes.*"

Alice sat up straighter. This was a novel idea; she briefly chuckled at her silent pun. "But...who are the heroes here?"

Clancy's shoulders tightened as he crossed his arms across his chest. He looked down his nose at her, scrutinizingly. "It was on your list. You didn't read the book, did you, Alice?"

Her hands went to her hips defensively; her nose wrinkled. "Clancy, you know I did my reading—I just forgot!"

"Of course you did," the scribe rolled his eyes. "I suppose I'll summarize on the way."

As Clancy reminded little Alice, the well-known adventure of this particular realm is the quest to find an island containing treasure. The realm's narrator, a boy of twelve or thirteen called Jim Hawkins, came upon a valuable treasure map after a mysterious pirate, whose name was Billy Bones, stayed at his family's inn. When Bones died, following his reception of the Black Spot—a dreaded omen of death amongst pirates—young Jim escaped with the much sought after map and joined forces with the local doctor and a country nobleman. Dr. Livesey and Squire Trelawney, respectively, believed it profitable to take advantage of the resource they beheld and so the three of them arranged a voyage to Treasure Island.

That is how it was written. Like every story, even the slightest external influence has the potential to change settings, affect seasons, and provide opportunities for the native folk within to choose paths varying from that which was otherwise written. The nature of Treasure Island was forever changed from the moment the Galdere set foot inside, and even more so since becoming a neutral territory for both sides of this war. Nonetheless, this brings us to our current page.

But first, a slight deviation from these two lost seekers...

4

Two Truths and a Lie

What would a Keeper be found doing in a realm like this?

The answer to little Alice's inquiry is quite simple:

Our prospective Keeper was in a jail cell.

Awaiting a hanging.

He lay flat on the floor, staring at the musty ceiling with iron bars and armed guards standing between him and his freedom. Inhaling deliberately, he rolled onto his stomach and retrieved some folded parchment and a small piece of charcoal from his pocket.

The two men who shared his cell were in varying degrees of lethargy. The large, lumpy one sat slumped in the corner, his head resting on his propped knees. The smaller, leaner one reclined with his torso angled toward his doodling colleague and his eyes lazily followed the movement of the charcoal.

"Five people will die tomorrow. This charcoal is horrible—too rough," the doodler said slowly, in a studied tone. "And I'm profoundly bored."

The lumpy one groaned in exasperation. His balding scalp moved slightly, but he refused to lift his head and honor the doodler with a response. The lean one, however, exhaled thoughtfully. He was just a bit younger than his cellmates, of a pale complexion, and with the most absorbent eyes. His tight mouth held secrets, none of which were telling him the answer to the doodler's riddle.

When he took too long to reply to his game, the doodler nudged. "Come on, it's your turn. Which is the lie?"

"You still drunk? I'm not playin' your blasted game anymore," the lumpy one grumbled.

"I wasn't talking to you, Booth," was the low response. The doodler chuckled for a moment, not once losing track of his charcoal sketch. "Go on—unless you're afraid of losing. Eck, this is terrible." He crumpled the parchment and tossed it across the cell, rolling onto his back.

"Loon," Booth, the lumpy one, groaned again.

The lean one, called Ryder, smirked. "Well, Hastings, I think that narrows it down a bit. I take it the charcoal one was the truth." He straightened his back, reclining fully against the cold ground. "That leaves *five people will die tomorrow*, and *you're really bored*."

"*Profoundly*," Hastings corrected, running a hand through his black curls.

"Apologies," Ryder waved a hand graciously.

"Well? *Profoundly bored* or *five dead*?"

"I don't..." he trailed off, pausing to gather a general headcount of the hall and all the cells within.

"You're bored," a voice answered from across the hall.

Of all the sleeping or unconscious prisoners in this local jail, one of the few still lucid sat in the cell across the way, her legs propped up in front of her in an attempt to hide her face with her knees. She wore a filthy cloth head wrap, holding most of her hair atop her head. Her hair, however, was just as mussed as the cloth which contained it, giving what could have possibly been dark blonde locks the appearance of a darker, musty hue.

When she saw that her contribution was heard, she cleared her throat and gathered her hands nervously in front of her.

Ryder sat up quickly. “What was that?”

“What was that?” Hastings repeated.

“The lie. It's that you're bored,” she explained.

With keen new interest in the game, Ryder moved closer to the bars of the cell to get a better view of the lady. “But, you also said that five people will die tomorrow. There are eight people in this jail-house. And she doesn't really know you well enough, to be fair. You're always bored. So I think I win....”

“Hang on,” Hastings stopped him, intrigued. “Let her finish.”

The woman tucked her legs under her and sat a little taller, squinting at Hastings in confusion.

“Watch yerself lass,” lumpy Booth briefly glanced up, coughing violently for a moment before properly exhaling. “He's mad.”

She lifted a brow, but would not be deterred. Shifting her weight, she carefully considered. “Well....you've been awfully interested in the game—you can't be both interested and bored. Sorry—*profoundly* bored." Her accent was uneducated, but her logic was sound; Hastings crossed his arms in amusement.

"But, I have no way of knowing that exactly five people will die tomorrow. Who's to say that that wasn't the lie?" he challenged.

"It was a bit vague," she established, her confidence rising. "Any five people could die anywhere in the world tomorrow. If you meant only in the jail-house....you never said that *only* five people will die—simply that five will. The other three don't matter much, then, do they? All of us will most likely die tomorrow, but saying at least five will wouldn't be wrong, would it? The law's guaranteed you at least five bodies."

Ryder shrugged. "Well, I give up. Seems you've gone and won the game. Happy, Hastings?"

"Fantastic," Hastings grinned.

"Lovely, now shut yer mouths. Yer aching my head," Booth grunted, returning his head to his knees. "Wake me up for the hanging—I'd hate to miss them readin' off my offenses."

Creative minds never cease; I suppose that's the cross to bear for brilliance. Brilliance and experience leave one's mind in a consistent state of unrest. Thomas Hastings rarely met a full night of sleep. When darkness fell, not three hours later, Booth filled the cell with snores while Hastings sketched his demons away. His attention faded from his parchment to the heavy steps of a man seeking vengeance making his way to the cell of the intuitive young woman across the way.

Whoever he was, he was a large man with a dark face, framed by dark curls that fell to his shoulders. He dressed like a rough-and-ready sailor, with a dose of class in his appearance, and he wore a shiny pocket watch across his breast pocket. His piercing ice blue eyes bore down on the young lady with sincere intent, but the smirk on his face offered anything but sincerity.

"Hmm," he hummed. "This is unfortunate. For you."

At the sight of the visitor, the woman rushed to the bars that contained her, reaching for his hand. When she spoke, her voice was tender and earnest, as if speaking to a lover. "Please, please, I didn't think you'd –"

He swiftly grabbed her wrist and pulled her closer. That was when Hastings noticed that the man's free hand, which was now held threateningly against the woman's porcelain neck, was not a hand at all.

It was a hook.

The man's dark face grew darker as he coarsely grumbled, "I'm not here for you."

Her face fell, but her eyes grew wide. "I-I don't...."

"I want it back," he smoothly growled. Hastings heard something that sounded like a whimper, but he couldn't be sure. The woman was hesitating.

"But....you gave it to me...." her voice choked.

"You took what wasn't yours. Bad form," he chided.

Gruffly, the man clutched the woman's thumb and ripped off an over-sized, gaudy ring that had been struggling to stay on the delicate fingers that wore it. With a wicked gleam in his eye, the man smugly lowered his voice to taunt her.

"I'll not be so easily drawn in next time. Though, I doubt you'll see a next time. You should have known better, woman. Should've known what you were getting yourself into. There are some places you just don't belong. Best of luck with the noose."

As he turned away to leave, the woman pressed her body against the bars, desperately reaching for him again. "James—James, please! You said we'd both see this to the end—please don't leave me here!"

Her tears fell fast and hard; the farther the visitor made it out of the dank hallway, the softer her desperate cries became. The poor woman backed herself against the stone wall and slid down to the cold floor. She knew what was coming. She hugged her knees and quietly sobbed, with her face hidden from the eyes of her spectator.

The cruel visitor, Hastings presumed, was her former partner— apparently the only one who escaped the arrest—and was so coldly willing to leave her there to die. A lack of sympathy, lack of any emotional connection, was shown to the woman. There had been a heavy dose of malice in his tone.

Perhaps he had been wronged by the woman in some way. Perhaps she had made a mistake, the consequence of which was her impending death sentence. Perhaps the man felt justified in leaving his foolish partner to rot while he moved on to find a more worthy cohort.

Whichever the case, Hastings watched the woman weep and felt a sharp sting in his otherwise hardened heart.

"A wise friend once taught me that every tear cried by a woman is a curse to the man who caused them," he contributed, attempting to console her.

Now realizing her loss had a witness, the woman lifted her head and sniffed away a few tears, wiping the moisture on her filthy sleeve. "Thank you," she eventually replied. "But, I fear the gallows aren't gonna let me see that curse carried out."

"What are you in for?"

A tiny smile tugged at the corners of her mouth. "Bein' stupid enough to get caught. 'Course he managed to get away," she added with a tearful grumble. "At least I'll die knowing he'll always miss this." She held up the man's shiny pocket watch, wrapped around her fingers. This made her smile again, which brought a grin to Hastings's face as well. "Angry people don't pay attention much, do they?"

"Clearly," he laughed.

"What'd they get you for?" she posed, looping the chain around her hand with mild contentment.

"Hmm," Hastings leaned his head back contemplatively as if mentally listing his offenses and deciding which to claim. "Piracy. That's the general term for it, I suppose."

"You're a pirate?"

There was no fear in her voice. Something told Hastings that her previous partner was of a similar occupation. Thievery wasn't simple thievery if it was done on the dangers of the high seas. The skin of a pirate was said to be thicker than that of a petty criminal. Thomas Hastings, while not quite as ruthless as most pirates of the age, had a roguish air about him that made the law's claim seem credible in the woman's eyes.

"So they say," he smirked.

"What's your name?"

"Hastings."

Her smile grew a little, in a sweet and comfortable movement. If she had to die, at least she would die next to a friend.

"Well, Mr. Hastings...looks like your truth earlier was right. We'll be amongst the five."

Hastings sighed lazily. "And what do they call you?"

"Lorelei Musgrove. Some call me just Lorelei. He used to call me Lori...but you can call me whatever you want, I 'spose. Obviously. I prefer Lorelei—but I wouldn't be angry if you called me Lori. It'd be awfully petty to be angered so easily when we're dying in the morning."

He chuckled at her rambling and tipped an imaginary hat in her direction. "Well, Lorelei, it'll be an honor to face the gallows with you."

5

An Aimless Voyage

"Line it up! Sort 'em out!" the jailer shouted.

The prisoners were filed out of their cells like cattle and separated into two lines. A freshly sobered Hastings reached across the stone floor to nudge his more corpulent cellmate, but Booth's head merely slumped further to the side with no sign of movement. The entire cell lacked signs of movement, as a matter of fact. While one cellmate had gone limp, the other had simply gone. Hastings hardly noticed Ryder's absence for longer than a moment, however, as it was apparently a fairly regular occurrence.

Hastings gingerly touched Booth's swollen neck and felt no pulse. Ship fever had claimed so many unsavory and unhygienic associates that Hastings wasn't the least bit startled.

"So long, mate," he whispered with vague respect. "Your place in this realm was not entirely a waste."

Neglecting the dead and dying, the jailer herded the able-bodied prisoners down the corridor. Gruffly, he then announced that some were to be transported to the jail near the gallows to await their execution while the remaining five were to be taken to the gibbets along the coast.

"But...gibbets ain't been used in this town for years," one of the five voiced.

"Our–our sentence was hanging, not...." Lorelei stammered in panic. Anxiety welled within her and spilled through her eyes in misted tears.

"Well, it seems the judge has changed his mind. Now shut it with the questionin', the lot of ya!" The jailer impatiently forced them into their respective execution carriages.

Hastings watched Lorelei wring her bound hands as she sat solemnly across from him in their carriage of death. He felt the nagging urge to comfort her, to put her at ease. He knew better. Nothing was comforting about the gibbets. Hanging is quick and over before you know it—provided, of course, you don't miss the neck breakage and find yourself slowly strangled to death.

A gibbet is a cage fashioned in such a way that you live the remainder of your shortened life in a very uncomfortable position to endure starvation and exposure until you've wasted away entirely.

"I thought....I thought they waited until after you were dead," Lorelei muttered. Her eyes were wide but vacant. Fear was making her numb. "Am I wrong?"

Hastings leaned forward in his seat on the bench, resting his elbows on his knees and looking up at her. His expression was more pensive than comforting, but his calm demeanor was enough to inspire slightly steadier breathing in his new friend. "Gibbeting criminals alive is not unheard of... unusual, but not unheard of. Typically takes days to prepare proper gibbets, though...."

"Typically," she repeated.

"Nothing about this is typical."

"We don't deserve this."

"They're taking us closer to shore," another of the five condemned commented. "Hm, the more elements to tear at us the better."

Lorelei stared at the man who spoke. Sallow eyes and moldy teeth suited a man with such confidence in his own death. "Why you?"

The man chuckled. "The law doesn't much like it when robberies involve young casualties or the wives of magistrates." His two accomplices smirked, giving Lorelei a rush of goosebumps.

Hastings sat back in disgust. "They don't deserve this, do they?" he asked her. She turned her horrified eyes back to him, and suddenly they were no longer vacant. The numbness of fear was wearing off, promptly replaced by pure terror.

And this is where paths crossed.

Executions of any kind are bound to attract crowds. There was some thrill in seeing despicable criminals facing their proper end. Nearly everyone in Bristol gathered near the coast to witness the unusual gibbeting, and that includes the native heroes our lost Arkis travelers sought.

Clancy and Alice stayed along the docks, hoping they'd come across the *Hispaniola*, which was presumed to be the vessel on which young Hawkins and his guardians would be traveling to their intended treasure. As is appropriately convenient, our lead characters in this account were all drawn to the same coastal execution at the very same moment. Just as little Alice neared the gathering crowd, without seeing the focus of the audience, she caught sight of a face she recognized.

"It's them!" she shouted, out of Clancy's reach.

The winded scribe struggled to keep up but eventually joined her amidst the hoards that congregated around the rocky cove. Neither Alice nor Clancy were quite tall enough to see above the heads of onlookers, but crawling atop Clancy's shoulders gave Alice the ideal vantage point.

"I found them! Jimmy Hawkins and that doctor—they're just down there!" Alice pointed a short distance eagerly ahead of them, nudging Clancy's shoulders, nearly falling from her perch. Consumed with frustration, however, Clancy was unmoved. His failure to respond to her would simply not do. "What is it, Clancy? What's the matter with you?"

"Ow," he grunted. "Well, how can you be sure it's them?"

"I recognize them from the book, of course. I'm quite good with faces, you know–oh!"

"What? What is it? What's happened?"

Suddenly, the girl's excited tone softened into nearly a whisper. "I know who it is, Clancy."

Tugging at her leg until she allowed him to pull her to the ground, Clancy resisted the urge to roll his eyes. "I can hardly hear you." He held her shoulders still in front of him so he could look directly into her eyes. "Who is where?"

Alice sighed with great heaviness–far more heaviness than an apparent child like herself would be expected to sigh. Slowly, she raised a finger and pointed to the shore. "He's there."

Clancy squinted. All he could make out were the gibbeting poles that were securely built in the water just a stone's throw from the shore, the temporary scaffolding where the gibbets awaited their victims, and the small boats that transported the doomed criminals.

"Jim Hawkins?" he asked.

"The Keeper."

Clancy buried his chin against his neck, staring down at her with condescension. "You can't possibly see the Keeper from here. You don't even know who he is."

Her expression of deep thought morphed into indignation. "I do, in fact. You're not the one wearing the jacket." She lifted her small arms to show him the enchanted conduit leather that still consumed her frame, the long sleeves hanging over her hands.

Clancy blinked a few times at her claims, but chose against continuing the debate. It wouldn't prove to be the most productive use of their time, and the sooner they could return to the Arkis the better.

"Alright, alright," he conceded. "First things first, though. Show me where those heroes are."

With only a brief moment's hesitation, Alice darted far enough ahead of Clancy to tug at young Hawkins's arm, startling the poor lad. Her onslaught of questions would have been overwhelming had Jim Hawkins not been an eagerly curious soul by nature. Though initially alarmed by a strange child drilling him for information, he was quickly intrigued by how much she assumed he knew.

"Where's the map? Have you met any pirates yet? Did the Keeper find you already? I've seen him already too, but Clancy says we must speak to you first...." Alice babbled.

"Alice, don't bombard the poor boy," Clancy chided.

As he approached them, Jim Hawkins' temporary guardian, Doctor Livesey, stepped protectively closer.

"Easy now," Clancy assured him. "She doesn't mean any harm; she's just...persistent."

"What is the meaning of this?" Livesey questioned, eyeing the little girl and her ridiculous questions.

Alice crossed her arms in front of her chest. "Well, did you find the treasure yet? Are you working for the Keeper?"

"Alice, they've only just started, or they wouldn't be in Bristol," Clancy corrected.

"Curse that squire," Livesey muttered. "He can't just lose a map, but he also has to spread word about the treasure while he's at it."

"Wait, wait," the scribe held up a hand. "The story's already been tampered with? You've lost the map?"

Livesey raised a brow.

"He didn't lose it. Squire Trelawney did," Jim told them.

"Jim," Livesey scolded.

"Well it hardly matters now, does it?" the boy reasoned, crossing his arms. "Squire Trelawney lost the map—it was stolen—and he's drunk himself into a stupor because of it."

"The voyage is off, good sir," Livesey finished for him, taking Jim's arm to turn them away. "I'm sorry to disappoint."

"I–I think I know what happened to the map," Clancy stopped him.

"What?" Jim asked curiously. "What happened to it?"

"Well," Clancy paused. "I think I know who stole it... though I can't think of why."

Alice sighed in exasperation; how could Clancy not know? "To ruin the story, of course, Clancy. You know that."

"I'm sorry, sir, but who the devil are you?" Livesey demanded. His hands aggressively moved to his hips.

"Believe it or not, we're here to help you," was the scrambled answer. Clancy weighed the situation hesitantly before justifying himself. "I actually...I was actually once a friend of the boy's mother, as well."

Jim's eyes snapped from Alice to Clancy. "My mother? How do you know my mother?"

Livesey crossed his arms, waiting for Clancy to explain himself. Clancy cleared his throat, deliberating his next words.

"I knew her too," Alice contributed. "She was in the Looking Glass when I watched this story before. She used to sing to you when you were just a little baby. I used to listen to her all the time."

"Her name is Isla," Clancy spat out, covering Alice's mouth. "She has brown hair and green eyes. She married a man called Matthew Hawkins and currently runs an inn."

Jim's face was brighter than the sun; he had no idea who these strangers were, but the way Alice spoke of his mother brought a strange sort of familiarity to their words. Livesey, however, stared warily at Clancy. Accurate though the man's claims may have been, there was something he found quite curious about these two.

"I think she's telling the truth," Jim told Livesey. The doctor looked down at the boy with a skeptical brow lifted.

"Do you happen to know who might've thwarted us then?" Livesey challenged. "I'd assume whoever has stolen the map is after the treasure."

"Oh no, you're probably wrong," Alice shook her head. She glanced over to Jim, who would more likely see reason. "He's probably wrong. Scada don't really think about the rich stuff. Only the magic stuff."

"Doctor Livesey—" Clancy started.

"How do you know my—?"

"You and little Jim here still need to embark on your voyage to Treasure Island. Believe me, it's necessary."

"I don't see how that's possible, seeing as we no longer have a map, a crew, or a ship," the doctor posed.

"None of that matters, silly doctor, we just need the Keeper to help us," Alice contributed. She pointed to the gibbets and jumped up and down. Even following the path of her finger didn't answer Jim's burning questions, but her enthusiasm was contagious. Jim peered over at Livesey with an eager expression, but the doctor was still warily watching Clancy.

Clancy watched those gibbets lower closer to the rolling water below and shook his head, doubtfully. "Whatever you say, Alice."

6

Silver Lining

Crowds dissipated by nightfall. The show was over; the criminals had been lifted into their bird cages, dangling precariously close to the crashing waves beneath them. The excitement was as dead as the spectators hoped the criminals would soon be. Patience is entirely necessary when viewing a live gibbeting. It's not the edgy thrill-ride of a hanging or guillotine decapitation.

Those morbid enough to find interest in a gibbeting would be the first to inform you that the true entertainment comes more from the state of the dead criminals before their bodies are trapped in their eternal enclosures. The live victims leave far too much to chance and timing. The starvation. The potential hypothermia. The aggressive predatory birds awaiting the fresh meat. There was no knowing just what would take them.

Lorelei was sure it would be the tide. The skies had shown no previous signs of a storm, but the ocean chose to crash violently down on them all the same. The waves were remarkably high enough to not only reach the height of the gibbets but to completely envelope them. As if swatting the curious buzzards wasn't terrifying enough, the stinging salt water hit her like a swarm of bullets. For whatever reason, her gibbet hung slightly lower than the others, exposing her more easily to the harsh waters. The loud crashing masked her sobbing and heaving, but her agony did not go unnoticed.

"Just kill me."

During moments of relief from the waves, Hastings could hear the poor girl whimpering and whispering to herself. Her head wrap was long gone, and her soaking hair stuck to her face, making her all the more pitiable. He shouted to her, to offer some comfort, but she could not hear. Suddenly, he saw a lone rowboat slowly paddling its way toward them. In it sat a huge man, with a parrot on his shoulder, and a gaunt, wiry man with an eye patch.

"Lorelei!" Hastings called, his hope in comforting her having been renewed. The waves began to settle. "Lorelei, look at me," he said, softer this time. His voice carried over the tide. Terrified, she obeyed, clinging to the bars of the gibbet for dear life. "Hang on! We'll get out of this."

His promise was only briefly calming. It was his friendly call to the rowboat that brought true comfort.

"Now, who said I needed your help, Silver?" Hastings quipped.

The larger man in the rowboat, Long John Silver himself, chuckled as they approached. "Yer always so keen on welcoming death like its yer best mate. This time I need ya, so death'll have to wait in line."

Hastings rolled his eyes. "Of course you do."

The large sailor nodded to the wiry man and signaled him to climb. And he did just that. Expertly he lunged himself out of the boat and wrapped his limbs around the secure pole which held the gibbets above the water. Between his teeth, he bit a thick keel hook, which he carried with him to the top of the scaffolding. After perching himself directly above Hastings's gibbet, he then began to use the hook to pick at the previously weakened bolts and chains, ignoring the empty deals and pleadings offered to him by the two murderers still conscious.

"You must be exhausted from all that charm and bribery." Hastings leaned lazily against the back of his gibbet as he waited. "Takes quite a bit for a judge to be so sloppy with an execution."

Silver only chuckled. "Sloppiness makes fer an easier escape, Hastings. Charm and money are all that's needed."

"And you have plenty of both."

"Hm, a man can always have more."

As he said this, the top bolt of Hastings's gibbet broke and fell into the ethereal waves below. Lorelei gasped and cried out, but Silver and his cohort only laughed. As planned, the gibbet hit a rock below, further weakening the already rusted metal. His edgy audience watched and waited until he finally burst through the still water. He had broken through his cage, scraped and bruised from the fall, and pulled himself into the rowboat.

Lorelei exhaled deeply, leaning back against the bars of her gibbet in relief.

"Excellent attention to detail," Hastings coughed. "Replacing the gibbets with your own."

"Well, sturdy metal is much harder to break open, innit? Couldn't have that," Silver chuckled. "So lucky for you, eh? So lucky you might even feel indebted to me..."

"What do you want?" Hastings grumbled, wringing out the bottom of his shirt.

"I've recently...acquired a means of reclaiming somethin' rightfully ours."

"Hm, and what would that be?"

"Hastings...I know where Flint's treasure is."

Hastings stopped. "What? How?"

"A new acquaintance of mine managed to get his hands on a certain map. All we need is the ol' crew," the pirate grinned hopefully.

His old colleague merely laughed at him. "You're mad. What difference would a map make if you're cursed the moment you step foot on the island?"

Silver scoffed. "Yer the only one who believes that, mate."

"I know what I saw," Hastings solemnly pressed.

Silver chuckled lightly and shrugged his shoulders. The reward outweighed the risk. "My new employer has the means to overpower whatever cursed swine voodoo you reckon lives on that cursed island." When Hastings frowned at this, the pirate pushed, "What say you, man?"

"Silver, I don't...." Hastings shook his head, but suddenly he considered something. "How did you know which gibbet would be mine?"

"I didn't."

"So you replaced all of them," he assumed.

"It only made sense."

Hastings glanced up at Lorelei, who had quietly resumed her hyperventilation. "Save the woman, and we'll get your treasure."

Silver cocked his head upward, giving Lorelei a quick and curious bit of scrutiny. He didn't quite understand—the woman was marginally attractive, he supposed, but beyond that, he couldn't see the value. Nevertheless, he shrugged and signaled for his man to climb over to Lorelei's gibbet, thus repeating the procedure, and watched her gibbet follow Hastings's into the ocean below. The moment the metal hit the waves, Hastings jumped in after her. With quickness and exactness of strength, he broke Lorelei free from the rusted gibbet and pulled her to the surface.

Once both were safely in the boat, Silver chuckled in amusement. Hastings attentively brushed Lorelei's wet hair out of her face, gently cradling her in his arms as he calmed her hysterics.

"Yer gonna need some trousers to cover curves like hers," the pirate ogled. "If she's part of our deal, she'll have to be a bloke. The rest of the crew aren't as....gentlemanly as I am."

"Just get us out of here," Hastings grimaced.

"And the others?" Silver teased.

Hastings glanced up at the criminals still hanging. "Let them rot."

7

Alice's Choice

The Wanderer was not an especially large ship; it was only slightly smaller than *The Hispaniola* itself. It was enough to suit Spyros's purposes. This assignment would be quick and easy, in theory, so there was no need for extravagant resources. His one redeeming quality, in my opinion, was his determination. For good or bad, Spyros was not one to intentionally waste time —his idiocy did occasionally impede his progress, but that is beside the point. His alliance with Silver proved to be a rather beneficial one; the two stood on the deck of *The Wanderer*, watching as each crew member prepared and boarded, receiving their assignments and settling into their bunks on the forecastle.

"Fetched as many of Flint's old crew as I could," Silver reported, nodding amiably to the passing crewman. The parrot squawked, both in agreement and at the acknowledgment of her own name. Long John Silver named his parrot after his cursed and deceased captain. "Lost some to the raid at *The Admiral Benbow*, but not much loss there. I assured the rest o' them that they'll be adequately compensated." It was less of a report and more of a confirmation. As friendly as he was, Long John Silver was not one to be cheated. “Couldn't help noticin' most the crew bein' of your....kind.”

“Well, it is my expedition, Silver,” Spyros scowled, in his usual way.

He sourly leaned against the side of the ship, setting his metal leg to the side, only inches from Silver's wooden equivalent. Two one-legged men standing side-by-side on a vessel was a somewhat humorous sight, I must say.

“Oh, naturally, sir. And they seem like a decent sort of fellows, to be sure. Likely more competent than old Flint's boys. Where'd you happen to find 'em?”

Spyros inhaled deliberately and almost smirked. “When you've traveled as I have, you pick up a few things. But, rest assured, they are all competent sailors. They'll do.” Spyros then added with smug surety, “I anticipate a smooth journey.”

“Hm,” the pirate cleared his throat. “Whatever you say, mate.....”

Off in the distance, Silver noticed a small cluster making their way to the docks. The young Hawkins and his temporary guardian, Doctor Livesey, followed by a little bouncing girl and a short blonde man, possibly a decade shy of middle age. They were a curious sight, but he could guess their purpose. Waving off his employer, Silver waddled off the ship to meet the group halfway.

“Well if it isn't Jim Hawkins and the good doctor,” Silver greeted them on the docks. “Come to rejoin the voyage?”

"You seem to have bearings," Livesey acknowledged. "We mean no trouble, and we'll pull our weight."

Silver sized up Clancy and Alice, making a strange face of doubt. "Hm, very well. Welcome aboard then. And...tread lightly." He added a wink in Jim's direction.

When Silver turned to limp back to his duties, Clancy lunged behind a large stack of wooden crates, dragging Alice with him. Jim and Livesey looked at each other in confusion, but then soon hid with them.

"But, why are we hiding?" Jim whispered.

"Because he's a villain," Alice explained, pointing to the one-legged man who had caught Clancy's eye. "Clancy, he's got a lot more people than we do."

Clancy pressed his lips together without answering. He recognized more stained eyes than he cared to; the place practically reeked of Scada.

Spyros seemed to have been given his choice of priority Scada to assist on this assignment—whatever it was, Clancy feared it was quite dangerous. A noticeable character strolled past their hiding spot with his messy brown hair, colorful tweed cardigan, and beady eyes, standing little more than four feet from the ground.

"Hm, naturally," Clancy scoffed, watching the dwarfish nomad swagger his way on deck to claim his place in the crew.

"We have to get on the ship, Clancy," Alice tugged his arm. "We have to. The heroes need to find the treasure like in their story."

"Yes, yes. But there are other ways. We need to find the Keeper."

"What's a Keeper? Is he Myk?" Livesey asked.

"No, he's the one who's going to save the heroes," Alice said shortly. These were all elementary details, and they didn't have time to waste. "But where could he have gone?"

"Well, I...." Clancy shrugged with a helpless sigh. He didn't even know where to start. Finding the heroes first didn't seem to have worked as easily as he hoped it would. Providentially, however, his eyes darted around cluelessly and happened to flick over another familiar face.

Walking only a stone's throw from the crates was our very own escaped convict, and his disguised accomplice. The two moved through the staggered clusters of sailors getting their affairs in order, and made their way onto the deck. Once they were out of earshot, Alice released a soft giggle.

"Well, that was fast. I found him again," she declared. "Shall we go get him now?" She vainly posed the question, only to stand upright, ready to take action without waiting for a response.

"What?" Clancy tugged at the bottom of her dress and gestured for her to crouch back down. "No, no, no," he said firmly. His expression was suddenly very solemn; it alarmed the girl.

"What? Why not? It's him."

"The Keeper, right?" Jim clarified.

Alice sighed and cocked her head to one side. "Yes, Jimmy. Do keep up."

The boy graciously held up his palms in apology and returned to being a silent observer. Livesey chuckled at the young girl's tenacity.

"Alice. No. Just trust me," Clancy pressed earnestly. "That man is not a Keeper. He's very likely Scada, an evil man, and I think we're looking in the wrong place. It could be anyone else—it could even be James here."

"Me?" Jim spoke once again. Alice's mouth twisted and she rolled her eyes at him.

"No, it's not you, Jimmy. You're just a boy. A Keeper has to be a man. Maybe when you have more hair on your face, but not now. It's him. It's the man with the beard. I mean, it is rather short and only faintly scruffy, but a beard is a beard. I know it's him. I can feel it. We have to talk to him, Clancy. We just have to."

Clancy kept his wary eye on Hastings, losing his resolve against Alice by the second. "Oh Alice...." he said quietly. "You haven't read his story...."

"They're all looking."

"No one is looking."

"Won't someone be able to tell?"

Hastings sighed. "No one will suspect because they have no reason to."

Lorelei uncomfortably adjusted the head wrap underneath her hat. Her breasts were hidden under an oversized linen shirt and vest, and the shapeless masculine trousers sheltered her slender legs. From a distance, one would assume Lorelei was merely a prepubescent young man, eager to prove himself on the high seas. It was bad luck to have women aboard a ship, you see—as well as dangerous—shielding her fair gender seemed the obvious solution.

"I'm sure you've done something like this before," he assumed.

She released a half-chuckle and lowered her voice. "I'm really not that sort of criminal. I'm a thief, but I sneak in and out—I don't usually stick around long enough to...well, you've seen what happens when I stick around too long. I'm no good at pretendin' to be someone else–I'm hardly good at bein' myself. But especially not a boy; it's just not natural."

"You'll do just fine," Hastings promised her.

They spoke softly in an empty corner of the deck. All of the other crewmen moved quickly past them to their designated areas. No one bothered to eavesdrop; there was far too much to be done. Hastings gave her an encouraging pat on the shoulder and leaned in to provide further instruction:

"Your name is Alfie. You've been on a handful of voyages before. Your father was a sailor, and your mother was a midwife. You're standoffish and despise people—so don't get too chatty. Just keep your head down, and avoid trouble. If anything should happen, I'm Silver's quartermaster; I'll be the one to handle it."

Lorelei smiled and sighed with self-assurance. "Okay. Thank you." Her tone then lowered, after ensuring there were no curious ears. "You know....you could have just left me there."

"I know," he nodded. "But I didn't."

"What makes you think I didn't deserve it?" she posed.

Hastings looked into her sea green eyes, finding fear and anticipation that told him that every fiber of her being had expected him to leave her behind. Her previous partner had done so without so much as a blink of hesitation. So what made our hero bother to turn back and see that she was set free?

"My gut," he replied.

Traditionally, when a new Keeper is chosen, Myk would personally bestow the jacket upon the appointed; the new Keeper would then put on the jacket, accept the call, and continue the work of saving realms.

I am sure this goes without my saying, but Thomas Hastings was not a traditional Keeper, in any sense of the word. And Alice was far from the usual bestower.

Her guardian, however, was not so keen on what he believed to be her uninformed assumption. Clancy kept a grip on her arm, preventing her from running to the scoundrel's side. He was a well-studied scribe, to be sure, but logic did little to smother the excitement in Alice's eyes.

"He's not the type," Clancy insisted.

Watching the scene transpire from a distance and never once suspecting Alfie of being anything other than what Hastings publicly claimed, Clancy and Alice remained hidden. Young Jim Hawkins was sent below deck to retrieve the necessary garments for Clancy and Alice to sneak aboard The Wanderer and be properly unrecognizable.

"You haven't said one word to him, Clancy." Alice was growing impatient. What she knew to be true and what Clancy refused to accept was beginning to form an obstacle for which they simply didn't have the time.

Jim scurried back to their side, garment bag in hand. "Got them," he said, out of breath.

He handed Alice the bag, and she began to rifle through her options, picking the most convincing attire for the powder monkey she would become.

"Thank you, Jimmy," she beamed. "Clancy, I think you should wear this one. Although, you don't really look good in rough linen....you're more of a soft cotton sort of fellow. These are certainly more ruddy than your Arkis robes, but you could probably still look sort of good. Of course, we'll need to get them much dirtier if we want to be convincing. Swashbuckling heroes don't usually bathe as much as we do...."

"We need to rethink this, Alice. Stop what you're doing," Clancy took the clothes out of her small hands. Capturing her attention, his mouth tightened with his nerves, preparing for his admonition. "We don't know that the Keeper will be on this ship—"

"Yes we do," she crossed her arms defiantly. "He's right there."

"Alice." His gaze hardened.

She was immovable. Her stare was more intense and resilient than his.

"Alice...." he sighed.

She kept staring, turning the corner of her mouth downward with adamancy—a trait she picked up from years of Stella's influence.

"Alice...I'm telling you...."

Jim noted Clancy's disparity but couldn't help but be impressed by Alice's willpower and joined her in her stubborn stance. He knew very little about the conflict, but something told him that Alice was in the right.

"I can't do this, Alice," Clancy continued to fight. "You don't know him. Not like I do."

Arms still crossed, Alice's face softened. "Let's pretend you don't know him at all. Let's pretend he's brand new—just like Ben was. Let's pretend no one has ever written his story until now. It's his turn, Clancy." She lowered her arms. "It wouldn't be fair if he didn't get it."

"Her reason seems sound," Livesey put in. Clancy nearly forgot the doctor's presence, and the Alden's grimace wished he'd be forgotten again.

Clancy thought of the many reasons they should ignore all fairness and return to the Arkis, waiting for the next one. But, he couldn't return to the Arkis. Not without Alice. And he knew Alice would not concede. In frustration, he clutched his new clothes and hurriedly changed into them, muttering incoherently to himself. Alice giddily followed suit, while Jim modestly shielded them from potential onlookers.

"What's that?" Jim peeked, noticing Clancy adjusting a leather vest over his new linen shirt. He didn't remember fetching it for him.

"Conduit leather," Clancy grunted. His focus was reluctantly aimed toward fitting into the uncomfortable breeches.

"Were you always wearing it?"

"Always."

"In the Arkis he usually wears it under his robes; it gives him magic," Alice explained.

"Is the Arkis where Myk lives?"

"Yes, it is. And I have my own room there. It's much bigger than Clancy's," Alice informed him, carefully adjusting her clothes. "It has loads of good fun—stories and talking paintings and—"

"Clancy lives there too?"

"It's where a lot of us live when we're not having adventures like this one."

Jim leaned forward intently. "Did my mother live there before she came to England?"

"No, no, your mother lives in the inn. I just saw her in the Arkis."

"How's that?"

Alice sighed. "Jimmy, what do you think Looking Glasses are for? So I can watch stories all the day long and see heroes win." Before Jim could aim another question, Alice spun to face him and posed proudly with her hands on her hips. "How do I look?"

Her hair was pulled back and tied with a small rope, with a hat casting a shadow over the top of her face. Much like Lorelei, an ignorant observer would easily mistake her for a young boy.

"Like a swashbuckling hero," Jim smiled, accepting that she was done answering questions for the time being.

Alice beamed in satisfaction. She had always wanted to be a swashbuckling hero—being a pirate seemed like such an exciting adventure. In contrast, Clancy inhaled deeply and waited too long to exhale. His breath was unsteady and anxious. He didn't know what to say to the man, or how to say it. Sensing his anxiety, Alice gave his back an encouraging pat.

"I'll get the Keeper and then we're ready for an adventure," Alice smiled, carefully folding the Keeper jacket she had just taken off and tucking it under her arm.

Clancy grabbed her shoulder before she could dart away. "No, no, no," he scolded. "You will not be approaching that man."

Wrinkling her mouth to one side again, Alice placed a hand on her hip. "Then you will do it." She held the jacket out for him to take.

Only a moment of vain resistance passed before Clancy sighed once more. "Fine."

Carefully, he folded the robes and stashed them with Alice's dress in the crates in front of them, before taking the Keeper jacket.

Tightly gripping the Haeleth's mantle, Clancy walked hesitantly toward the ship. Panic was rising within him; if this went badly, he would have exposed himself as an Alden on board a vessel inhabited by Scada. The danger was alarmingly apparent, and Alice's inability to understand that fueled a frustration inside of him.

Hastings walked the perimeter of the dock, ensuring that everything was in order to set sail. As quartermaster, Hastings's duties revolved primarily around the crew itself—personnel management, as it were. He spoke personally with each crew member before allowing them to board, waving off the young powder monkeys and allowing Alice and Jim to slip past him with ease. Clancy stopped in front of him and leaned in close, lowering his voice so that only the quartermaster could hear.

"Thomas Hastings?" Clancy began, his voice shaking.

Hastings raised his eyebrows. "Yes?"

"I, erm, I don't know if you recognize me," he whispered, "Clancy, from the, um, from the Arkis." Hastings took a step backward. "I'm told by an obstinate source that you're the next owner of this."

Clancy pulled the jacket from behind him and held it subtly between them. Hastings's stance became defensive, his back straightening and shoulders tightening. Within seconds, Clancy fully expected the man to draw a dagger or pistol and finish him off.

A man's bearing can tell his story. A soldier, for example, tends to hold himself in vigilance while absorbing his surroundings. When a threat presents itself, one may spot a soldier by his readiness to act. In this case, of course, Clancy had read more than this man's bearing—though that may have been enough to put a tight shock through his spine. Contrary to expectation, and to the relief of the flurried scribe, this particular soldier left his weapon untouched.

"I thought you Alden were smarter than this," Hastings smirked stiffly.

Clancy's muscles tensed, but his pride wouldn't allow the slander. "I resent that—we're a lot smarter than you, Scada. And a lot more efficient as well, as a matter of fact...."

"I'm not Scada," Hastings suddenly seethed, pulling Clancy's collar closer to him threateningly. "I'm not anything. And I'm sure as death not a Keeper. Get someone else to fight your battles."

His harnessed aggression intimidated Clancy, bringing the tremble back to his voice. "But, the Haeleth Keeper must —"

"I. Don't. Care," Hastings enunciated, thrusting the jacket in Clancy's direction. He stepped back and held his hands up carelessly. "I don't care. Just find a new one, like you always do."

Clancy huffed. "Well, all right then," he scowled. He glanced around for Alice and Jim, only to see them already situated on deck with the other powder monkeys, with Livesey shadowing them nearby. Hastily, he bounded to inform them of the change of plans.

"Alice," he whispered, once he was close enough.

"Lewis," she corrected.

He frowned. "What?"

"I'm Lewis now. Girls can't be powder monkeys. And Captain Silver told Jim he could use me for errands. I can't be an errand boy if I'm a girl, now can I?" she rambled. "And you must be Ronald now. Clancy is not a pirate name."

"Ronald is not much of a pirate name either," Clancy pointed out.

Alice considered this and looked to Jim for support. Jim just shrugged—his experiences with pirates were only slightly more than hers. What did he know about pirate names?

"Well, it's too late because I've already called you Ronald," Alice supposed. "It suits you well enough."

"It doesn't matter, because we're leaving," Clancy said firmly. Before she could protest, he went on vehemently, grabbing her hand. "He doesn't want it, so we're leaving. We're going elsewhere.....to find someone who will treat the calling as sacredly as they should, instead of shoving it back in my face and mocking it...."

"Oof, sorry," a disguised Lorelei clumsily squeezed past them.

Once she was out of earshot, Alice pulled her wrist out of Clancy's grasp and exhaled sharply. "We can't leave yet." Her tiny fists took their place at her hips. "We barely tried. We have to give him another chance. Sometimes people are mean when they're afraid, Clancy."

The child was right. Again. And, as in many tales of fallen and tragic heroes, the path to redemption can be even more powerful than the clear road of consistent heroism. It was a formula with which the little one was most familiar, though her exposure to tales such as these had been somewhat filtered as needed. The logic may not have entirely sat well with Clancy, but I, for one, remain hopeful.

8

MIND YOUR BUSINESS

Much like the other crew members, Clancy, Alice, Jim, and Livesey were given their assignments before the ship set sail.

Livesey and the newly christened "Ronald" were given regular duties commonly assigned to the deck crew. Jim, as was appropriate, was snatched up by Captain Silver as his personal errand boy—according to the manner in which their creator wrote them, Long John Silver and Jim Hawkins had a peculiar close connection that combined mentorship with, at times, rivalry.

Now, little Alice—who carried on referring to herself as "Lewis"—did not receive the position she anticipated.

Instead of joining Jim in running Silver's errands, she was sent directly to Spyros's cabin. She was charged with passing communications between Spyros and Captain Silver, as well as delivering Spyros's personal meals, and anything else that suited his fancy. This concerned Clancy greatly, who noticed, from afar, that her star-like glow was slowly fading the more she was in the presence of such darkness.

To maintain her light, Alice sought the company of Jim during their moments of respite since Clancy was kept adequately busy. When errands were temporarily scarce, the two of them sat idly on a couple of wooden barrels and swapped childhood stories.

Well, I suppose I should clarify that Alice did the storytelling—she had much more experience in childhood, you see. Jim spent his early youth working in his parents' inn until his father died and a strange pirate pulled him into this adventure. Alice, on the other hand, had more stories to share than her tiny body could contain. As they were on a pirate ship, she felt it necessary to tell Jim how experienced she was with such tales.

"....and I once knew a girl who met mermaids—though they were not very kind to her. They tried to drown her. They were nothing like another little mermaid I read of—she was so kind, but she was tricked with her legs and nearly turned to sea-foam. She would have liked Wendy, even when none of the others did. And the pirates Wendy met were very rude too. They usually tried to kill her friend. But I think he may have been quite a troublemaker himself, so maybe the pirates weren't entirely wrong," she told, amidst her stories of Keepers who fought off pirates and scoundrels to save the day.

The silly girl didn't consider the possibility of danger coming to those who mention the heroism of Keepers, while on a ship run by Scada. It's common with storytellers—and even readers—to go somewhere else entirely when the story envelopes them.

"I would like to meet a mermaid," Jim mused. Everything she recounted appealed to him—a young boy who, not so long ago, was fearful of leaving his family's inn.

"You shouldn't, they don't much like men." Lorelei had been leaning a short distance from them, listening to some of their conversation, and she couldn't help herself. Jim looked at the newcomer strangely.

"Why's that?" he questioned, suddenly disappointed. "What have they got against men?"

Lorelei shrugged. "That's just how they were made. They sit on rocks in the ocean all day long, singing and luring men to their deaths."

"That's horrible," Jim shook his head.

Lorelei considered this. "Yes, it's quite boring, I imagine."

"Well, let's pretend we will meet one on this adventure," Alice suggested, brushing the danger and potential boredom aside. "A beautiful mermaid who likes men a great deal. Her name is probably something very elegant and smart. Like Angelique. Yes, I like Angelique very much. I might've met her before, but I can't remember which story. She sounds lovely and funny, anyway. Those are important things for a mermaid to be. Unless she's a mean mermaid, like my friend Wendy met. Those are surely the ones Alfie knows. Singing and killing and such things. But, she doesn't sound very mean...Angelique sounds like she would like me quite a bit. And, of course, she would like you both too, when she meets you. She'll probably ask you if she's pretty—and if you say yes, she'll grant you three wishes. It is always three wishes, isn't it? What would your wishes be?"

"Lewis, boy!" Spyros barked loudly from around the corner. Clancy, who was swabbing the deck across the way, flinched at the sound of Alice's alias. Spyros's clattering metal limp gave Alice a rush of fright and sent Lorelei to hide around the corner. "If I have to call your name one more time..."

"N-no, sir," Jim spoke up. Instinctively, he stood up and stepped between Spyros and a puzzled Alice. "I was distracting him. We didn't hear you call because of me."

Spyros furrowed his crusty brow and grunted. "So it's you who gets the beatin' then, eh?"

"Um, I—"

"I'll be the judge o' that, mate," Silver interceded. He had limped himself over to the situation when he heard Jim speak up. "He's my cabin boy, and I'll see to it he's reprimanded."

Spyros had too much weight on his already strained mind, so he had no interest in pursuing any form of punishment. Indifferently, he grunted again and waddled back to his cabin. With a wink of his eye, Silver leaned in toward the two children.

"Consider yerselves reprimanded," he chuckled, in unison with squawking old Flint. "And it'll never happen again, eh?"

Jim smiled and thanked him. It doesn't take much effort to win Alice's good graces—and even an individual as disreputable as Silver managed to do so in a matter of seconds. While trust is relative, inspiring hope in one's character can be everlasting. Especially for a girl like Alice.

A man like Clancy, in contrast, takes much more convincing. Our simple scribe was not meant for the labor required of him on a ship such as this. Among many things, when swabbing the deck, he had clumsily whacked a couple of crew members in the head with the mop not an hour into the job; while assisting in the repair of a torn sail, he stabbed the tailor three times with the needle; and, when "Alfie" asked for his assistance lifting a crate on top of three other boxes, he toppled the stack on top of Spyros.

That was the proverbial straw that broke the camel's back. Unfortunate Clancy had drawn too much attention to himself, and not the pleasant sort. Unwittingly, Spyros had had entirely too many interactions with the resident Alden agents, and they were not making his assignment an easy one.

Much to the surprise of Clancy, however, Spyros was cut off once again before his punishment could be administered. A bottle of rum in his hand and his old friend Ryder appearing at his side, Hastings observed the interaction and exhaled in exasperation.

"Come on," Ryder nudged Hastings's arm. "Clancy's a good one. Terribly stuffy, but probably good." He slipped his hands in his pockets and smiled. "Just a bit sheltered."

Hastings grunted, taking a swig from the bottle. "I may have improperly assigned this one," he finally spoke, sauntering toward the conflict and leaving his impalpable friend behind. "He may be better suited as the ship's entertainer. He seems the type to whistle a few tunes and make up pointless stories...."

"I beg your pardon. Pointless stories...." Clancy crossed his arms, defending himself against Hastings's condescending tone.

Hastings tightened his lips. "Then it's settled. You'll be assisting the cook during the day, and entertaining the crew in the evening."

As the small audience of onlookers dispersed, Clancy bitterly thanked Hastings. "Why did you do that?" he interrogated.

Hastings's expression was complex. Clancy couldn't discern if he was softening or deliberately putting up barriers. "I'm going to assume the little chatty one is with you, too. *Lewis*, is it?" Clancy stuttered but ultimately nodded in acknowledgment. "Look, I'm not on anyone's side, but I won't give you away. Just keep your heads down from now on, leave me be, and we'll be just fine."

Pan flute music filled the lower level of the ship, or forecastle as they call it, where the crew ate their slop and laughed too loudly at jokes of minimal substance. It took very little, on Clancy's part, to entertain the uneducated pirates. Scada need only hear themselves jabber on, and the native sailors need only laugh at the Scada.

Those who weren't on duty had decided to muster up some games, gambling away portions of their share of the potential treasure. Had Hastings been with them and not in a private meeting with Silver, no one would have dared speak of such games, as gambling was traditionally against the pirate code. Then again, with so many Scada and little scruples or conscience, perhaps Hastings's presence might not have made much difference.

Lorelei volunteered to take watch up on deck when the games began. The overdose of competitive masculinity was motivation enough to seek solitary in a tedious duty—and with any luck, the gambling would distract anyone else from offering to relieve her for quite some time. She savored the salty air and the rush of the sea. Her hands were resting on the railing of the ship, her eyes closing as the sea clamored for her attention—an onlooker would assume she'd found a sort of peace in the crashing of the waves. But her jaw clenched. Her muscles tightened. Her fingers gripped the railing for dear life.

The average onlooker would be blind to this, but Hastings was not. She hated the sea, that much he could tell. Her willingness to stand so close to the edge of the ship gave the impression of bravery; our Keeper suspected a touch of masochism in her.

"Does she look a bit familiar to you?" he heard Ryder's voice muse beside him.

Hastings cocked his head to one side, ultimately shaking his head. He was careful not to verbalize his response, for fear of startling her. Before long, however, as Ryder's presence left, Hastings could hear Lorelei mumble to herself. It was soft, but steady, as if in conversation.

Curiously, he took a step toward her, achieving what he had previously avoided. Startled, Lorelei jumped slightly, even releasing a frightful gasp.

"Easy, Alfie," Hastings assured her with a chuckle. "Your nerves'll betray you. Who were you talking to?"

She sighed in relief and leaned against the side of the ship. "Talking?"

"You were whispering."

"Just...to myself, I suppose. Makin' your rounds between bottles, eh?"

He nodded and leaned beside her. "Making sure you're doing your job," he said, ignoring her jab.

"Mhm. Everyone else is busy—"

"I know," he interrupted.

"Are you gonna stop them?"

He shrugged. "Don't have to if I don't catch them in the act."

His indifference made her smile. It seemed, to her, like sound logic. In her unmistakably feminine way, she leaned in slightly closer to him. "You know, I would have never guessed you to be a pirate. You're too clever. And kind. In my experience, pirates are nothin' but scoundrels."

"I completely agree. Scoundrels, all of them. And you are right: I am entirely too clever to be a pirate," he dallied with a playful smirk.

She giggled softly, covering her mouth with her dainty hand. "So...you're not a pirate? What are you then? You seem a bit like a soldier to me. The way you carry yourself and such. You seem to know how to keep men in line. A captain, maybe?"

"Oh no," he chuckled. "Never a captain. I've just worked with enough of 'em to know how it's done."

"So you were a soldier?" His shrug gave her the answer. "Which war then? Did you fight the French?"

His mouth tightened with memories. "The English," he sighed.

Lorelei's eyes squinted in confusion. "The English? But, how could that be?"

"Ireland's war for independence."

"But they are not independent."

Hastings wryly raised his eyebrows. "Not yet. Not here. But we will be. We'll have a rather violent future because of it, but that's not really my problem anymore." He shook the memory of Ryder's face from his mind and cleared his throat.

"I don't think I heard much about this war."

"It hasn't happened yet. Not in this world. But in my time....where I came from....it's where I started."

"In your time?"

He didn't answer.

She narrowed her eyes again, eager for an explanation she would not easily gain. "Do you still call yourself a soldier?"

Hastings laughed to himself and lightly shook his head. "Not in the least."

"Then what are you?"

He stared at her for a moment and shrugged. "I'm just an ordinary sailor with rather dubious connections, I suppose. I'm not really anything. I'm just here."

A short pause later, Lorelei pointed at him. “You're not really anything.”

“Hm,” he nodded, humoring her. “That's what I said.”

“No, that's the lie.”

He looked at her strangely at first and then remembered their jailhouse game.

“You are here, and you most definitely have dubious connections—though they do come in handy. You're not really anything is the obvious lie. Though, I don't think I quite understand. You seem the sort that is very much something. Something important.”

“And what gives you that impression?” he leaned in teasingly.

“Your eyes,” she decided. “You've seen things, but they're too bright to be so....empty. I think you believe it's a truth though–that you're nothing. My question is....why is someone so special throwing away his lot with good-for-nothing pirates?”

Disregarding her praise, Hastings sighed deeply. “Yes, well, this is just a way to make ends meet, minding my own business.”

Lorelei wrinkled her nose in thought. “Mm,” she hummed. She turned around to face the ocean, sparking Hastings's curiosity. She took out the stolen pocket watch and examined it idly, flipping it open and then closing it.

“What's that?” he pressed.

“Well,” she began, choosing her words carefully. “Pirating isn't minding your own business, though, is it? I mean, you're interrupting other people's lives.”

"Sometimes you have to do what needs to be done."

"Then why are you doing this now?" Her question was innocent enough, and there was no accusation in her eyes.

"To pay a debt."

She raised an eyebrow. "I think you could've gotten yourself out of that gibbet. I said you're a clever one. Why does Silver need you?"

"Some years ago," he explained, "Silver and I worked for a man called Flint. The whole crew was cheated out of a rather sizable treasure, which Flint hid for himself. Silver's determined to get it back, and he wants to bring the crew back together."

"And what about your share? Is that motivating you to do this too?"

He frowned with consideration. "Well, it would be enough to be a sort of final hurrah. I could retire and hide away somewhere."

"Mmm, where would you go?" she leaned in again. When he took too long to answer, she began musing aloud. "I think I'd go somewhere dry—England's too damp for me. Ireland seems nice, but thanks to you, now I know to steer clear of it for a while. Perhaps the Mediterranean."

"You'd take your share of pirate booty?"

She peeked at him from the corner of her eye. "Well...if it gets me out of here then, why not? As you said, some things need to be done to survive. I don't think the ocean is far enough to escape my problems. It takes money to go farther."

"You think your old partner will come looking for you?"

She shook her head. "He doesn't want anything to do with me anymore," her grin faded quickly. "But he's not the only demon I'm running from." She inched closer to him, so their arms touched along the railing. "Doesn't matter now, though. I'm getting farther away from the rest of them. And I feel safe here."

She looked down at her hands until he lightly took one of them in his. Jaded though our hero may be, a great fool he was not. The parts of his heart previously privy to heroic stirrings were still kept well alert and barred with walls that would make any artisan envious. I can attest, however, that the trust of a lovely woman is enough to make even the hardest of hearts soften. There was no need for armed guards or walls here. He craved neutrality, and her very presence satisfied that hunger.

9

Impostor Syndrome

The sound of Clancy's pan flute soon faded and was drowned out by cheers and clamoring around a rousing game of Liar's Dice. A circle of pirates and Scada leaned around overturned cups, which hid the clusters of dice that determined their fate. Each scoundrel took a turn placing a bid on how many of a given number was upside underneath all of the cups. Clancy was horrible at this game. After every failed bid, a player lost a die. Poor Clancy was on his last. Without completely understanding the game or the ramifications of the gamble, he frowned in discouragement, for his pride was quickly beaten down.

"It's all right," Alice assured him.

"I've lost nearly my whole share," he complained under his breath.

"You should probably stop then," she suggested, in a hushed tone. She put a hand on his arm, subtly urging him to step away. "We're not here for the treasure anyway. Where did the Keeper go?"

"I don't know. He has other duties to attend to. He could be anywhere." Clancy's contribution was only half-hearted. He was far too intelligent to be so taken by Scada fools. As he scrambled to find possible explanations for his loss, an intimidatingly massive pirate reached across the Scada with the eye patch to aggressively strike the greedy dwarf across the face.

"You knocked it over!" the large one shouted. "I had it right—and you changed the number, you short bas—"

"Hey! I did not!" The dwarf defended himself.

Apparently, the large one had placed a bid on the number of fours on the table, and the dwarf knocked over a die to change the outcome. His defense was in vain, as the large pirate had already charged him. The other men in the circle began scrambling over one another, throwing fists and curses. Clancy and the eye patch Scada sitting next to him stepped away from the rumble while Alice hid behind a wooden chair some distance from the excitement.

"Did you see him knock it over?" The patched Scada, Havelock, asked Clancy. His concern was absent and replaced by curiosity.

Clancy shrugged. He knew the dwarf to be the nomadic rapscallion, Riddock—and he had no intention of defending the likes of him. The two men had very little previous interaction, but Clancy had seen enough of Riddock's traipsing in and out of the assignments of other Keepers to have developed a strongly negative opinion of him—amongst Clancy's many other prejudices.

Faithful to his duty, Hastings was below deck within minutes of the loud disruption, which had carried throughout most of the ship. Lorelei quietly lagged behind.

The quartermaster made two attempts to catch the miscreants' attention, but the large pirate was narrowly focused on doing more damage to Riddock than possibly necessary. He felt understandably cheated, but Riddock, the physically incompetent and minuscule opportunist he was, put up very little defense, including flailing his arms wildly in an attempt to block the blows.

Seeing his intervention going nowhere, Hastings cleared his throat subtly and stepped in between two onlookers. Lorelei slipped in beside Clancy and Havelock, taking no notice of Alice hiding near her legs. They all watched as, in one swift movement, Hastings pulled his pistol from his holster and expertly fired a shot, hitting the large pirate in the arm. The forecastle fell silent, aside from the large pirate's moans of pain. Riddock's eyes widened, fearfully staring at Hastings's relaxed figure.

"Have we finished, gentlemen?" Hastings inquired. The large pirate muffled his cries; that masculine inclination to swallow pain to save face failed to work in his favor. He stumbled to the floor beside Riddock, and all eyes snapped to the quartermaster.

"He shot a man," Clancy whispered in horror.

"Least he didn't kill him," Lorelei whispered in half-hearted defense. Catching herself and her feminine voice, she added in a deeper tone, "After all, he's got to keep order."

Clancy wrinkled his eyebrows but returned his attention to Riddock's cowardly response.

"Oh yes," Riddock nodded quickly to Hastings. "We've just finished up, actually. All is right again."

Hastings holstered his gun. "Hm. No more problems, then?"

Riddock held up an affirmative gesture and slowly propped himself back up. The large pirate, however, would have none of it. Yet another masculine inclination prevented his struggle to contain himself from lasting more than a few moments before he burst again.

"He cheated me! This ain't over!" he insisted, firmly.

"I see," Hastings nodded. "It'll have to be continued at the next port, I'm afraid. Unless you want your other arm to match."

Lorelei smirked while Clancy's face twisted in distaste.

"No," the pirate rose from the ground. "I won't wait. I'm finishin' it now!"

And the scuffle resumed. In such an enclosed space, the confusion was tremendous. Not even the innocent spectator was immune; bystanders anxiously moved along the wall, dodging dangerous arms and stumbling victims. The threat of wounding the other arm had become moot. Hastings couldn't shoot the arm of every offender, or he'd have no crew left.

Watching the ridiculous dogfight unfold, he quickly formulated solutions to end the conflict and resume business as usual, allowing him to continue minding his own business. None of these solutions were peaceful, of course. Personally, I would've much preferred the route of a stern talking to, but I suppose that's why I was never destined to be the quartermaster on a ship of ruffians. Our quartermaster's approach was far less passive.

His mind was made when he spotted the presence of several clashing wristbands of a familiar stain. He drew his weapon once more and fired three shots in the barrels of rum, which hung on racks above them. The golden liquid rained down, soaking those beneath. Before long the fight ended and all were scrambling to preserve the remains of the alcohol. Hastings barked for the mess to be cleaned before dawn, or there would be hell to pay. Briskly, he slipped back to the main deck as quickly as his legs would allow.

His stubbornness and bitterness toward Clancy aside, Hastings was now inclined to see the need for a Keeper.

Silver had colluded with Scada. Neutrality was a farce, but one to which Hastings clung with every ounce of energy. Uninspired was the fool who claimed Thomas Hastings a hero. It was Plato who said: We can easily forgive a child who is afraid of the dark; the real tragedy of life is when men are afraid of the light.

Hastings was such a man. And yet, there was growing within him a renewal of understanding, however embroiled in cynicism it might have been.

Long after the excitement of the previous night had simmered, the crew returned to their daily routine: Clancy to the kitchen, Jim to cleaning Silver's cabin, Lorelei to swabbing the deck, and Alice returned to running errands for wicked Spyros.

It's a curious thing, Alice's story.

Most human children I know aren't quite so strongly affected by the mere presence of evil. Children, while impressionable, are still capable of blissful ignorance of such wickedness. Make no mistake: children of any kind are incredibly susceptible to the influence of darkness and need fervent protection. The literal wilting caused by shadow, however, is not necessarily a human trait.

Indeed, it is a more common trait in precious flowers who crave sunlight.

Little Alice has more in common with bright flowers than bright humans. She absorbs all around her—the good, the bad, and the informative. Like a sunflower, she is drawn to light. The Arkis provided her with a copious amount of Light magic amongst which she flourished. Out and about in other worlds, darkened by ambiguity and the influence of Scada magic, Alice was beginning to fade. Her skin had taken on a more greyish complexion as her energy drained. Spyros's presence clouded and suffocated her. Alice was a flower without a light source.

Alice's workload was tiresome—even more so when considering her diminishing vigor. Clancy had helped the cook make Spyros's meal and prepared the tray for Alice to deliver. Seeing her vacant expression, Clancy offered to deliver the meal himself, but Alice merely sighed and assured him she was perfectly capable.

She weaved through working crewmen on the way to Spyros's cabin. The closer she came, the more her stomach curled. She always worried he knew what she was and that he had horrible plans for her and Clancy, but then she would remind herself that, due to the rarity of their leaving the Arkis, it would be doubtful that Spyros would recognize her.

Dear Alice tends to overestimate people, including herself. She thought she could carry the tray of food and rum to the cabin with ease, but as she approached his door, she began to sway. The Scada guarding his door was idly glancing away when she slipped past him and into the dark room.

Scada thrive in darkness. Only one candle and a small window lit the cabin, shedding just enough light for one to move around without knocking over furniture. It was sparsely furnished with a chair and a small desk in one corner and an unkempt cot in the other.

There was a heaviness in the air.

The highest in ranking amongst Korbl's hierarchy ordinarily had that effect on a certain atmosphere; when there was no necessity to hide their true identities, their core shade would unravel and proudly overtake their surroundings, smothering any and all light.

While considerably high in rank, Spyros's power, in this regard, was nothing compared to another, even darker force—with whom we will eventually reunite. In any case, Alice felt the pressure engulf her.

Alice sought relief through the food in front of her. She placed it carefully on the desk, staring at it longingly.

"Oh dear," she sighed. "I don't know if I'll have the strength to walk out of here. Especially if I can hardly breathe. Two sandwiches are a bit much for a grown man, anyway. And besides, I am a growing girl, after all. Sort of. And Jim distracted me through breakfast. I am in need of a midday snack. How else should I get the energy to help the Keeper? Myk depends on me to help the Keeper, and I can't be caught sleeping around—he'd lose all faith in me. Yes, I think I should have at least a bite of one."

And with that reasoning, Alice snatched one of the sandwiches from the platter and took a bite. She had a tendency of helping herself to anything she could find. It got her into quite a bit of trouble in the past, but not all lessons are appropriately learned, I suppose.

Alice happened to pass by Lorelei, on her way to Spyros's cabin. Ever since the row on the forecastle, Lorelei thought it best to keep a closer eye on those who deliberately avoided the conflict. A keenly observant and intuitive woman, she saw something in "Lewis" that she also saw in herself—a female pretending to be something she very much wasn't. Auspiciously enough, Lorelei spied Alice sneaking past the guard and sensed she would get herself into trouble.

Lorelei, thinking quickly, engaged in an argument of a somewhat boisterous nature with the cabin's guard. By the time Spyros returned from his meeting with Silver, regarding their impending stop in Tortuga, Lorelei had stood strategically in his way.

"Eck, just move," Spyros grimaced, shoving her aside. He limped into his quarters with eyes squinting from the sun.

Alice suddenly found it much harder to swallow her bite than before. Spyros stumbled over to her with a penetrating glare, caked with fury. He had had just about enough of little Lewis. He grabbed her roughly by the collar and pulled her face closer to his. Abruptly, the ship began to sway more powerfully, being shoved by larger waves. Spyros was not fazed.

"And what d'you think you're doin'!" he demanded.

That's when Lorelei slid into the rescue. Before Alice could choke down the sandwich and gather a reply, the lady thief spoke up, dragging the Scada guard behind her.

"It's his fault, sir," she said, deepening her voice. "He let the boy in and gave him free rein."

Spyros's mouth was twisted. It was safe to say that he could be easily influenced by strong suggestions; original thought was not a strength of his. Spyros turned his glare from Alice to the unfortunate guard, who stood with a red face and wide eyes.

"Is that right?" Spyros growled. He advanced toward the guard, just as Lorelei smoothly took Alice's arm, slipping her out the door.

While Spyros shouted at Lorelei's victim, Alice got a closer look at Lorelei's face. When they were behind the closed door, Alice whispered to her, "For a pirate, you're awfully pretty."

Lorelei's cheeks went pink, and she chuckled nervously. "Well....thank you. And you should be more careful. You're bound to get found out with habits like yours."

Alice's mouth spread into a wide smile. "And you're one too!"

Lorelei hushed her, pulling her around the corner, hidden from the possibility of the guard coming out and pointing fingers. "One what?"

"A girl," Alice whispered.

The impostor sighed. She supposed the girl would figure it out whether she confirmed the suspicion or not. "Just keep it to yourself, okay? Otherwise, we're both in for trouble. Don't tell a soul—not even your little friend in the kitchen."

Alice promised. She could've sworn she knew the woman's face. It gave her such joy to find someone she knew who didn't terrify her. Or someone she thought she knew; she couldn't quite place her.

She must have read about her in the Arkis. Why else would she be so pleasantly familiar?

What story was she from? Was she a princess? A poor serving girl? Her hands were rough—though she looked like a princess, a serving girl was much more likely.

Perhaps she was the heroine of her story and happened to fall out of sorts in another realm. Maybe she needed the Keeper's help. He had smiled more around her than anybody else.

Could that mean something? He probably knew she was a girl all along.

Oh, all of these questions had Alice bursting at the seams. How could she keep this from Clancy when she could have so easily found the Keeper's Companion?

10

Drunken Secrets

"Well, it certainly took you long enough."

"Oh shut it." Spyros loudly belched. He slammed his tankard of rum on the wooden table and spat in Bastien's general direction. "It was a journey from Bristol—and Tortuga's a blasted freak show. And it smells...."

"You don't have to sell me on it; I already thought you'd fit right in," Bastien munched on some tough meat.

"Shut it," Spyros repeated a little louder. "Did you bring him or not?"

Bastien leaned back in his chair, casually glancing around them and pausing just long enough to elicit the desired grunt of exasperation from his colleague.

"Of course I brought him. He put up very little resistance after watching Caverly's head tumble. Decapitation tends to dampen spirits." He sighed smugly, resting his joined hands on his stomach. "You know, these things seem to come so easily to me—this assignment of yours should be a breeze."

Scowling, Spyros cleared his throat. "Where are you keepin' him?"

"Don't worry, someone's keeping him close for me." Bastien sipped his rum.

"And the map?"

Bastien reached into his trouser pocket, just where Ava had left it, and slid a folded piece of parchment across the table, for which Spyros eagerly reached. Bastien pulled back teasingly. "And I take it you have what I need as well?"

Spyros snarled. "Are you ever gonna do your own dirty work? Seems Ava and me are pulling all the weight, as of late."

Smoothly, Bastien exhaled, almost with humor. "Now, now. I brought you what you wanted. I could've left him with those Frenchman. This is called cooperation, Spyros—Alden would even call it camaraderie, though I'm sure that's far beneath you."

"Eck," the rat snorted. "I'll let the woman give you your share of camaraderie. You're just restless because you failed at that last hit of yours." Spyros jutted his chin at him. "Caverly was child's play."

"Try killing a Creator sometime...." Bastien muttered. "Instead of gathering trinkets."

Satisfied with the nerve he struck, Spyros snorted again. For a moment, he thought it prudent to take advantage of Bastien's lapse in composure and attempt to snatch the map. He was mistaken; Bastien only slapped the top of his hand, leaving a stinging red mark.

"Despite what the witch tells you," Spyros hissed. "I'm more competent than I look. Now—give me the map and the prisoner!"

Bastien shook his blonde head slowly as if correcting a child. "Hm, I'm afraid I can't do that. Not without supervising. Tell me: what's the next step in your scheme?"

Grunting again, Spyros spitefully shifted his weight in his chair; he felt surrounded by insubordinate idiots. "The Englishman will get it for us—we just have to get him to it. That's what the map's for, obviously."

Bastien nodded, humoring him. "Very good. Of course, that's assuming he's still suitable by the time we get there...."

"Why wouldn't he be?" Spyros suspiciously snapped.

Bastien leaned over the table between them, his voice smooth and chiding. "You should've clued her in. She's much better at this preservation nonsense than you are."

"Now you look here," Spyros pointed at him, "I don't need that little harlot telling me how to do my job. I've been doin' this long enough without her input."

Bastien leaned back and raised an eyebrow aimed to the rim of his mug before sipping. "Your plan's good; she could've perfected it—"

"I said I don't need her!"

Bastien nodded again. "All right then. You don't need her."

Excluding the third member of their trio would bring about sorry repercussions, but he was all too willing and eager to see Spyros fail miserably. Coordinated efforts were never as amusing as singular failure.

"Where has Ava been, anyway?" the rat spat.

Bastien took a gulp and deliberated his report. "The Alden recovered that O'Leary boy. She had to rearrange some assets and...check in."

Spyros grunted again; it was something he frequently did. The unintelligent tend to have very few arrows in their quiver of retorts.

"I'm sure we'll soon hear all about her great successes," he added in a high-pitched, mocking tone. "Of course she went to see him first, as she does, yeah?" He loved to watch Bastien squirm, and reminding him wherein Ava's interests lie was one of the most effective instigators.

Bastien chugged the rest of his rum, swallowing hard and rolling his eyes. He wiped his face with the back of his hand before he stood. "Well, if you're done with your drink, we should be loading that cargo into the brig."

While docked in Tortuga, the crew of *The Wanderer* did what any average crew of sailors would do when at port, spend part of their pay on beverages and other leisurely pleasures until they were required to report back to the ship. Amidst the to and fro of those who bustled into the dank city, Clancy attempted to keep a close eye on Hastings, intending to eventually revisit the issue which nagged the both of them.

As luck would have it, not only did the diligent scribe lose track of the reluctant quartermaster, but he seemed to have misplaced young Alice as well. His shoving through putrid pirates amid crowds leading to local taverns became more frenzied as Alice disappeared into the throngs. She was his one charge. If he lost her, he would never forgive himself, and he feared Myk would never forgive him either. Alice had an extraordinary place in the Arkis, a place which cannot be altered—

"Oof!"

"Hey, watch it!"

"I beg your pardon!" Clancy retorted, brushing the incivility from his clothes.

The dwarfish pirate recovered from the collision and took a step back to get a better look at him. "Oh no, I was afraid it was you. Hopin' I was wrong," he whined.

"Nice to see you, Riddock," Clancy acknowledged dryly.

Riddock suddenly froze; his eyes flickered about in dread. "Is it just you—or is the Big Man with you?"

Sighing, Clancy's shoulders fell. As much as he personally despised Riddock and his fickle nature, he was secretly relieved not to have to be his pirate persona for a time. It was getting tiresome. "Just me, and...Alice," he added, still searching the street with his eyes.

"Is that right? The kid never leaves home," Riddock exclaimed casually. "Can't believe Mr. Keeper allowed it."

Clancy bowed his head. "He didn't. He...he isn't... anymore..."

Riddock's face fell with Clancy's. He understood. He'd seen it before, and he would no doubt see it again. The flighty stooge had survived many a Keeper's reign, and always feared the end of each and every one.

In the not too far distance, they could hear the ethereal yet mournful tone of a woman singing in the streets. She sat on a small stage, a book sprawled across her lap and vacancy in her eyes. An attendant sat beside her, collecting coins from passersby. Her melancholy song felt as though it were sung for Ben Caverly himself.

Riddock paused for a moment, nodding to the attendant in recognition before hanging his head and turning back to Clancy.

"I'm sorry. He was a good one." His sincerity surprised the scribe. "I liked him—that's why I helped him quite a bit."

"You were also against him quite a bit," he corrected.

"Yes, but I've always been taught to remember the pleasant memories of the deceased." Riddock stepped to the side, away from the path of incoming rum bibbers, and Clancy followed suit. "So...." Riddock went on, "how about the missus?"

This sudden compassion was incredibly uncharacteristic of him, according to Clancy's knowledge. It only seems fair to point out that I've never been the only one partial to Stella Caverly. She and Ben were favorites of many but Stella herself had touched some of even the most unreachable souls.

"She's...coping," Clancy hesitated. He regretted not having visited Stella before this adventure. The last he had seen of her was in the Arkis, and he didn't quite know what to say to a woman who had just lost everything. He left the consoling to Alice. "She's doing better, I believe."

Riddock nodded in reassurance. "Good, good. I liked her best. Who's the new one?"

If the casualness of this conversation hadn't alarmed Clancy before, it certainly had now. Riddock could sense Clancy's loss. He knew just as much as he did, or so they both thought. Hearing Hastings's voice vaguely pass them, Clancy's eyes widened, and he sought him out. Riddock understood this as well and even guffawed aloud.

"Yeah, I doubt that," he managed to say between breaths. "Doesn't seem like the type, but what do I know?" Considering this, he held up a finger. "Although, there is always an off chance that he'll work out, ain't that right? That's what heroes do—they work out. He killed a troll once, didn't he? Single-handed with only a handkerchief at his disposal. Keepership will be a breeze."

"Dragon," Clancy corrected. "And he didn't use a handkerchief."

"Agree to disagree," Riddock nodded. "So, anyway, I think I'll be going now..."

"Good heavens," Clancy rolled his eyes. His arms dropped to his sides in aggravation. "You'll willingly sail with Scada for treasure, but the remote possibility of a Keeper aboard and you weasel out?"

Riddock shrugged. "Basically, yeah. Keeper means trouble. *King Solomon's Mines* for me. I hear it has treasure and no Keeper. My odds of survival are much higher there, my friend. And I'd rather not run into my brother and his lot."

He pointed over his shoulder at the singer and her attendant. "I owe him a favor I'd rather postpone repaying."

Clancy watched him slither through the crowd to his next destination. Continuing his previous quest with renewed determination, Clancy pushed on to find little Alice. His gut told him to follow the direction in which Hastings's voice traveled, but he quickly discovered he had no idea which direction that was.

Aimlessly, he wandered by every tavern that showed even a hint of *The Wanderer*'s crew. Alice surely would not have gone anywhere without Jim or Hastings. Would she?

Finally, a sharp anxiety pierced his mind, telling him to walk into the next tavern he passed. Sure enough, who could be seen sitting on a stool next to fellow shipmates but Little Lewis.

Clancy scurried to her side, taking the cup of rum out of her hand. She was alone at the end of the table while the other sailors loudly assembled at the other end, flirting heavily with one of the barmaids.

"What do you think you're doing?" he demanded.

She looked directly into his eyes, and something was wrong. Her big, bright eyes were hazy and confused. Her tiny frame seemed to have shrunken slightly and withered even more since they left the ship.

"You should try this, Clancy. Though it tastes rather... strange. One of those fellows just left it sitting here without finishing it...can you imagine that? It was half-full and everything." Her speech was slurred, unable to focus on much more than what he had taken.

"Alice, Alice, look at me," he coaxed.

"What else would I look at?" she mumbled. Her eyes widened and narrowed on the cup in his hand. Predictably, she lost her balance and toppled over on him. Clancy propped her up carefully, slamming her cup of rum on the table before lifting her off the chair. Rum was a vile drink, but even more so for a child—especially a child with the sensitive quality of absorbing all around her. She was reacting horribly to the alcohol; her body tried, with every fiber of its being, to mend her, but the calamitous beverage was working against it.

"Let's get you back," Clancy decided. He lifted her in his arms and pushed his way through to the exit.

The curious meeting between Spyros and Bastien did not go unnoticed by inquisitive ears. Long John Silver was perfectly capable of slipping his presence into conversations without being realized.

After handing Jim a list of errands to perform while in Tortuga, Silver followed casually behind Spyros and positioned himself strategically some distance from the rendezvous point. He was just far enough to go unnoticed, but close enough to gather what he was after. He didn't trust Spyros—few do. But, with Spyros's obvious resources, he served as the best ally in regaining Silver's lost share of Flint's treasure. The moment he learned a sliver of Spyros's ulterior motive, his mind began recalculating his plans of action.

Shrewd and silently scheming, Silver archived every piece of information he could process, storing it for future purposes as they arose. He had only previously known Spyros from his frequenting the Spy-Glass, but Silver's keen judgment of character had been at play ever since.

He and Clancy happened to start for the ship simultaneously, stepping across one another's path. Seeing a drunken "Lewis" limply hanging from Clancy's arms, Silver raised a concerned brow and continued his whistling stride.

"Need any help there?" he offered.

Startled, Clancy stammered with little articulation. "Um...no...it's okay. He, uh, got a hold of some rum," he said, once words finally formed.

Silver gave an understanding nod and sauntered beside him. He had a warm smile that calmed Clancy, despite Clancy's knowledge of the original text. His written description was as accurate as they come; he excelled in making others comfortable and trusting. With casual friendliness, Silver made conversation while they trekked to *The Wanderer*.

"Did ya watch the duel? Heard there was some trouble aboard."

Clancy shrugged. "Yeah, I suppose. There was no duel, though. They both seemed to go their separate ways, as it were."

Silver nodded again, lifting his hand to feed Flint on his shoulder. "Hastings didn't say much about it. Hearin' the juicy details is always good fun. Did you see what happened?"

"Um...you know, I didn't quite catch what happened," Clancy countered too quickly.

"Not even the big rumble, eh?" Silver probed.

Naturally, even in her wrecked state, Alice felt it necessary to be a part of the conversation. Before Clancy could bumble another lie, Alice garbled loudly, "It was fun, but a little scary—"

"Shh," Clancy hushed softly, trying not to draw Silver's attention.

"Scary, huh?" whistled Silver.

"Uh huh...but he could've stopped it all...if the Scada had gotten too horribly naughty..."

Silver raised both of his eyebrows this time. Sizing up Clancy, no one would believe him capable of stopping even the smallest of brawls. Clancy laughed it off and quickened his step, cutting the conversation short.

Much to his fear, Silver's interest had been piqued by the mention of Scada. Thankfully, the pirate was smart enough not to push his new well of information and allow the supply to flow naturally. So he changed the subject until he helped Clancy put Alice safely in her cot.

11

Lorelei's Likeness

Unlike the rest of the crew, Hastings had supplies and mild mending to oversee on the ship before he could retire to his preferred watering hole. Lorelei did what she could to assist with the restocking of the supplies and then lingered until he finished his duties. The two then followed the current of sailors to the tavern that would suit their thirst.

Many taverns were the same; if you've walked into one, you've walked into all. Thomas Hastings was somewhat of a connoisseur of worthwhile establishments. Being in the realm as long as he had, he had stepped foot inside more taverns than he could count. After all, filling the well-hidden void in his heart with rum was a favorite past-time of his.

Uneasy, and exceptionally self-conscious of concealing her long hair and girlish figure, Lorelei was sure to keep a very minimal distance between herself and Hastings. Fears sprinted through her mind, but as long as she could see Hastings, she was safe. He protectively guided her to the best tavern in Tortuga, the name of which is irrelevant, and to the most reclusive table, which bore a single leftover mug still containing a few gulps of rum. He promptly ordered two more tankards and retrieved his new makeshift sketchbook from the leather pouch on his belt, as well as a thin piece of charcoal—much better quality than his previous utensil, might I add.

"You've been here before," Lorelei guessed.

"Mhm," he mumbled, focusing heavily on the parchment propped carefully in his hand.

"Oh...that's good, I suppose."

Her eyes darted everywhere, soaking in the rowdy drunks and convening pirates. She made a face at the bar wenches throwing themselves at every pirate who came through the door, trying to understand them. When they began to make her uncomfortable, she turned her gaze to Hastings. Unbeknownst to her, as soon as Hastings inhaled the final drops from the used mug, they were soon joined by his old colleague. Young Ryder propped his feet up on the table and carefully watched as Lorelei peered over Hastings's parchment.

"What's that you're sketching?" she asked curiously.

"Hm?" He was too focused to notice anything else around him. It mattered little to her; she merely sat up straighter in her chair to steal a peek over the top of the parchment. He meticulously sketched beautiful features, luscious locks, and inquisitive eyes.

"You're spot on with those eyes, mate," Ryder commended.

"Is that me?" Lorelei questioned. Quickly, he turned the parchment over and looked at her accusingly.

"I wouldn't say that so loudly if I were you, or someone's bound to make a connection," he teased. She blushed and cleared her throat.

Ryder moved his feet to the floor and leaned closer to his friend. "Don't tease the girl, Hastings. You can tell her she's beautiful without selling your soul."

Hastings brushed him off. When he hesitated to answer her, Lorelei smiled wildly. "It is me, isn't it? Can I see it?"

After checking the possibility of prying eyes, he cleared his throat and handed her the sketch. To his surprise, she frowned. "What?"

"I don't look like this."

"What? The proportions are exact, down to the last detail," he defended with authority. "To be fair, you probably haven't seen a mirror in—"

"My cheekbones are slightly more pronounced than this. And my lips are more upturned here," she pointed. "Also, I have a freckle right there—of course, not that I expect you to be looking that closely at my face...but it is there."

Doubtful, Hastings scrutinized the sketch and then her face. After a few moments of analyzing his apparent mistake, his face fell, and he leaned back in his chair in defeat. "Hm," was all he said. They were such minute details, but he scolded himself for carelessly overlooking them nonetheless.

"But, the rest is a nearly perfect likeness," Lorelei encouraged.

"Nearly perfect," he repeated. The corner of his mouth twitched with antagonism.

"Well," she considered. "There's only so much that can be done on paper, right?"

He munched on a piece of bread from the basket on the table. "I suppose you're right."

"Sorry for the wait, lads," the barmaid apologized. "We've been overrun."

He nodded and waved her away politely. Lorelei stared at her cup with wide eyes. It was a relatively large serving of rum for a young lady of her size. Before daring to take a sip, she watched Hastings guzzle the first half of his own whiskey.

"Well, cheers," she commented with surprise. Suddenly aware of her eyes on him, he finished swallowing and set the tankard down on the table. When he returned the stare, Lorelei decided to take the chance and try her own drink. She choked it down but managed to polish off the entire serving. "Oh my," she breathed.

He pointed at her with what was left of his piece of bread and noted, "You're going to want something more substantial to eat with that."

So he stood to fetch her more bread. On his way to the galley bar he brushed past a startlingly recognizable band of women. Clad in dark, form-flattering clothes and stern expressions, there was one among them who did not match the trademark darkness they carried. Bringing up the rear was a flicker of red locks, capturing his attention as she fluttered past him and took her place toward the front of the band heading out of the tavern. Her eyes were still bright, her expression carrying a lightness to it.

He stared for a good long moment before being reminded of the unguarded party he left back at his table. Hurrying back to Lorelei's aid, Hastings thanked the barmaid and returned to his seat. Another round of drinks still followed, which Hastings drank more slowly with each serving.

Lorelei, however, knew no better and gulped each cup too quickly, finally quitting after her third. The barmaid made her final delivery and made a special effort to wink at young "Alfie," lightly rubbing her arm as she walked away. Just as she left, Hastings's old friend pulled up a chair and sat quietly, shooting a sharp gaze at his mug.

Lorelei's reaction to the flirtation was a mixture of nausea and confusion. Hastings laughed.

"She does think you're a man," Hastings muttered, loud enough for her to hear, as he sipped his last tankard. "I guess you can't help being such a pretty little thing."

"You think me pretty?" she slurred, her tipsy ears suddenly perked.

"Careful there, mate," Ryder warned with a grin. "That's a loaded question."

He laughed again, taking another sip. "I really shouldn't answer that in public—people will start to talk."

Lorelei giggled until she fell off of the chair, spilling what was left of her rum. Sensing she had reached her limit, Hastings set his cup down and tucked his parchment and charcoal back into his leather pouch.

"All right," he said to her, as he lifted her from the floor. "Time to go back to the ship."

Smoothly dodging her flailing arm, he supported her weight on one side while she limped clumsily with him out the door.

"Good luck to ya, Hastings. She'll keep your hands full," Ryder saluted, remaining comfortably in his chair as he watched them depart.

Hastings had dealt with his share of drunks, as he had frequently been in their position before, so he handled her compromised state with ease. She was significantly lighter than the last colleague he carried safely back home. He distinctly remembered assisting a drunken Captain Flint back to *The Walrus* before their final voyage together.

It was a strange memory and one that Lorelei snapped him out of with an alarming gesture. Her limp arm was wrapped around his neck, and she thought it best to take advantage of the opportunity and attempt to kiss him. Thankfully, she had waited until they were close to the ship and out of sight of passersby.

"Whoa." He backed his head away from hers. Chivalrously, he held her at a distance while still supporting her weight. "I think you've definitely had enough."

As if unaware of what she had done, she stared at him in confusion. "What...what did I do? Do you not like me?" Her words were still warbled from the rum, her eyes still blurry and unfocused.

"No, I do," he assured her. "It's just not the time to express it. Not when you're like this. You shouldn't...."

Hastings trailed off, distracted by a belligerent set of feet. Our beleaguered Arkis scribe led with a heavy step. Clancy was not the least bit happy to see Hastings. He had just seen Alice to her cot and was prepared to exchange words with the infuriating quartermaster.

"You," he pointed with venom. "Do you know where Alice is right now? Sleeping off a drunken stupor, thanks to you."

"Thanks to me?" Hastings resented.

"This—this is why I didn't want it to be you," he added a violent flare to his finger wave as he marched toward him. "Irresponsible. I told her, but she insisted. She was so determined it was you that she followed you all the way into town, only to get lost in a tavern. How dare you! Of all the people to harm in your indifference, it had to be Alice. As a Keeper, her safety is your responsibility."

"I am not a Keeper," Hastings finally retorted, shrugging Lorelei to his other side, out of the line of fire. "Your little friend is your problem, not mine. You are her guardian so you should have watched the girl more carefully. I told you both to leave me be. Now, if you don't mind, I have my own drunkard to deliver."

He left Clancy standing alone and furious. What little faith the man had in this new Keeper was now gone. He would never be a Keeper, he thought. And good riddance.

12

Mister's Jacket

Both of our lovely ladies awoke with blinding headaches and sore eyes. Little Alice, with disposition restored, was physically unchanged; her countenance remained withered. It didn't take her long to notice Lorelei's hungover demeanor as well.

"Does your brain hurt, too?" Alice asked the first thing that morning. She found her new friend leaning against the railing of the ship, her hands covering her face. The ship was beginning to set sail, and the shouting and exchanges of orders were ringing in Lorelei's ears.

"Mhm," she grunted. Lorelei rubbed her face, her fingers glossing over a thin, white scar across her jawline, which Alice had never noticed before. It was along the contour of her jaw, hardly seen except at a certain profile. Lorelei lifted her face from her hands and suddenly looked right at Alice. "You had rum? How could you reach the table?"

Alice giggled at the joke, but the laugh faded. "It was an adventure. I never did it before, and I won't ever again."

Lorelei chuckled humorlessly in agreement. "Here, here."

"Lewis!" the ship cook called. It was time to serve the first meal to the prisoners in the brig. Holding the side of her head, Alice reported to him obediently.

As she left, Hastings strolled over, and Lorelei's heart sank. The little she remembered of the previous night was enough to incite a rush of shame. "Sir," she called to him until she was close enough to speak in a softer tone. "I am so, so sorry. I've never...I've never done anything like that before—it's just not–"

"Relax," Hastings said calmly, giving her arm an assuring rub. "I've seen much worse."

She sighed in relief. "Right, pirates. Though, any other pirate would not have been so chivalrous," she pointed out with a grateful smile.

"Any other pirate would not have known what to think if a young sailor made advances and would have likely clocked you in the jaw," he pointed out with a smirk.

"Very true," she chuckled. "How lucky for me. Are you always such a gentleman, or only when rum is involved?"

"Rum is always involved," he winked, before cutting the interaction short and resuming his duties on the other side of the ship.

A dutiful Alice staggered down to the clammy cells below deck with a food tray in hand. The orders were to feed the lone prisoner: Bastien's mysterious captive. He had been tossed in the farthest cell in the narrow brig.

He was a scrawny fellow, with pitch black hair and a sallow face. His eyes were so wide in terror that all other features were overshadowed. Alice sensed his fear from the other side of the corridor. She quickened her pace, fixating her attention on the stranger.

Alice crouched down to the floor, reaching the man's level. He was curled up in the corner of his cell, breathing unevenly and biting back tears.

"Are you from here?" Alice stated, trying to hand him a piece of bread, her hand still unsteady.

The young man shook his head and rocked slightly back and forth. "No."

He was English, Alice was certain. But his clothes didn't seem quite right. Almost immediately, Alice recognized the distinct leather belt around the top of the man's pants.

"Well, then, what's your name?"

He shook his head again, this time in refusal.

"Did Ben give you that belt?" Alice pointed.

The man's eyes snapped up at her and held her gaze, but he refused to answer further.

"I know he did. And Regents are supposed to talk to me. I'm quite helpful." Alice was growing very irritated. He was not very cooperative, and she was not one for patience.

She plunked down the bread back on the tray. “Alright, then. If you won’t answer me, maybe you’ll listen to the Keeper.”

As she stood to storm away, the young man mumbled. “He’s dead. I watched him die.”

This made her stop. “There’s a new one,” she whispered. “You’ll love him. Perhaps. Just wait here.”

Suddenly driven, she set the tray on the floor before his cell and darted back upstairs with eagerness.

Alice seemed to have regained some of her energy. She finally found something the new Keeper could do to prove himself. He could instill new hope in a lost Alden. She skated across the deck to find Hastings delegating assignments to other crewmen. She impatiently stood beside him and tugged at his shirt.

“Mr. Hastings,” she nagged. “Mr. Hastings, sir. Mr. Hastings.”

After ignoring her for a few moments, he eventually snapped down at her. “What?”

“I should learn your first name. Mr. Hastings is too much for me to say,” she said thoughtfully.

“Hastings is fine,” he murmured.

“All right then. I shall give you a first name,” Alice decided. “For now, Mister will have to do.”

“What do you want?” Hastings sighed, crossing his arms in front of his chest.

“There is someone who needs you to talk to him downstairs,” she quickly explained. “He’s new and in a cell all by himself and he’s scared, and he needs to know there’s a new Keeper.”

"Wait." Hastings held up a hand to stop her. "There's a new prisoner? Why wasn't I informed?"

"He didn't tell me his name, which is awfully impolite... but he's a Regent Keeper, and he's from somewhere else. I don't know that either, but I'm sure of it."

Hastings smirked, but that smirk faded as he noticed a change in her. The aftereffects of the rum had left Alice dull in complexion and spirits, but in the presence of the one meant to be Keeper, her thirst for light was gradually satisfied.

"Take me to him," he said. His suspicions of conspiracy grew. First the presence of Scada, and now a misplaced Alden.

On the way down to the brig, Hastings stumbled across yet another addition to the ship. The Scada, Bastien, with the familiar leather vest akin to the one he once wore himself. The two men stopped and studied one another. Bastien stood a few inches taller than Hastings, and he seemed to make himself taller in order to size up the quartermaster.

Both wore skeptical stares, but Hastings's narrow eyes heavily scrutinized him. He recognized Bastien's vest but not his face. They had not met before, and yet something about him pulled a painful memory to the surface. His eyes were stained, just like Spyros and the other crewmen. He had a trademark darkness to him that Hastings had seen many times before, pushing himself to suppress the unwanted memories.

"You must be the quartermaster," Bastien presumed.

"Hm," Hastings nodded, self-consciously tucking his right hand in his pocket. In the same movement, he stepped in front of little Alice. "And you?"

"Visiting," was the glib answer. Bastien cleared his throat and quickly moved past him. Hastings warily watched him walk away.

Alice took his hand. She had been hiding behind him, as Bastien terrified her more than Spyros, but resumed her initial mission the moment he stepped away. She led Hastings down to the brig and pointed at the frightened man in the far corner. He moved her aside while he slowly stepped toward this stranger.

True to his nature, he took in every detail of the fearful man. He wore revolutionary garb, most likely French, but his mumbling was undeniably English. He didn't fit, as expected. The closer Hastings came to the cell, the more he realized the Englishman was not in a state to be reasoned with.

The Keeper took the set of keys out of the hands of the sailor assigned brig duty and moved forward. Carefully, he inserted the correct key and unlocked the Englishman's cell. Of the few in the brig, his authority was all that mattered—no one higher in rank could question his intrusion, and he preferred to keep it that way for as long as possible. The prisoner simply stared at him with those fearful eyes.

"Easy, mate," Hastings held up his hand. "I just want to know what realm you're from."

"Scada!" the prisoner accused.

He viciously lashed out and snatched the dagger from Hastings's belt, attempting to defend himself. Hastings wrestled him to the ground to retrieve the knife but the helpless man cut a rather large hole in Hastings's jacket before he was apprehended. Hearing the jacket tear, Alice scrambled back above deck.

"Hey, hey, hey," he said. "I'm not Scada–I'm not anything. I'm not gonna hurt you."

The man's breathing slowed to a steady pattern, and he released the knife. Hastings propped him up against the wall and began to interrogate gently, watching his every twitch for silent answers.

"What's your name?"

"J-Jackson," the man stuttered.

"Good, good. Good name. You're English?"

Jackson nodded.

"And where did you come from? Don't say England."

Jackson was at a loss. "I...I don't...."

"Who did you work for?"

"The Scarlet Pimpernel."

"Hm." Hastings touched his fist to his lips, deep in thought.

"And...and the Keeper, before...he's gone and they found me."

"Why did they take you? Why didn't they kill you?" Hastings inquired. Jackson's eyes widened again. He had considered death an option but never thought that he was being held for something much worse.

"I...I...don't know."

Realizing he had once again spooked the captive, he waved a reassuring hand once more. Then, much like Alice before him, he noticed Jackson was wearing that notable thin leather belt around his waist. "You're a Regent."

Jackson nodded again. "Yes, sir."

Hastings's eyes wildly calculated the new information and his face squinted in contemplation. "Hm." He turned to walk away, about to shut the cell door behind him, when Jackson stopped him.

"Wait—if you're not a Scada, then what are you?" Jackson asked heavily.

"I told you," Hastings responded over his shoulder. "I'm not anything."

Hastings had gambled with Silver for enough years, he knew his tells. He had very little to worry about Silver. The man had his schemes, without doubt. From a personal perspective, regardless of how much Silver understood, he was harmless to him. Their employer, however, had quickly lost whatever trust Hastings feigned to have in him. Spyros was a Scada leader—that much was easily perceived from the moment Hastings met him, though he pretended not to notice.

With the arrival of the Regent Keeper and yet another prominent Scada, there was very clearly more to this voyage than the acquisition of treasure. There was a dark agenda in which he had no interest being involved. His conflict came when his impressive intellect insisted on understanding every facet of such an agenda. It was yet another puzzle he had to unravel.

Waiting on deck for him was a grinning Alice, holding the Keeper jacket in her arms. She looked at the deep tear in the jacket he wore and then merrily held up the jacket she knew would change him. Few words were exchanged because there was very little need. Hastings glanced down at the rip, remembering the hysteria in the Regent's eyes. He couldn't deny knowing that the jacket was his best chance at escaping this mess—however briefly he intended on wearing it. Ambitiously, he promised himself a temporary involvement. And so our anti-hero reluctantly shed his own broken covering, replacing it with the enchanted leather.

"Only until this is over," were his only words as he donned what many Keepers before him had proudly borne. And, to his chagrin, it fit him perfectly.

13

The Curse Onboard

"Scada always take care of our own," Spyros recited. Captain Silver sat across from him in the captain's cabin, skeptical. He rolled his eyes and handed his parrot a pinch of bird seed on his shoulder. "Not only would there be a share of treasure in your future, but also protection from what is to come. So, unless you want to die, I'd suggest you accept my offer."

You, reader, have heard his speech before. Many years earlier Stella did not fall for its weak argument, and neither would a man like Long John Silver. Crooked as he was, Silver acknowledged his freedom to be such, unwilling to give that freedom up even to the most enticing of offers.

"He's not falling for this," Bastien discerned. He stood in the corner of the room, picking at the end of his dagger, idly listening in on the negotiations. "He knows you're not going to kill him."

"Who says I'm not!" Spyros challenged.

"Captain, do you have any interest in making an oath that ensures potentially unending power and protection from a source greater than yourself?" Bastien asked the pirate. He was growing bored and impatient.

"No, thanks," Silver shook his head.

"Well, Spyros. Go on and kill him, then."

Spyros hesitated, scowling viciously in Bastien's direction.

"He won't kill you, Silver. Do you know why?" Bastien posed.

"Because I'm still more valuable alive. You still need to get to the treasure, and that map is only gonna get you so far," Silver answered. "If you wanted to trap me into an oath, you ought to have done it after my usefulness ran out."

"He ought to have, surely," Bastien criticized, though slightly amused. "He's not the greatest at planning ahead, is he?"

"Shut it, dog," Spyros grumbled.

"He is right, however, in needing some assurance that you won't turn to betrayal," Bastien continued, idly pacing the room. "I think you can probably sense our urgency in this voyage, and you should understand that—despite whatever my colleague here is lacking in intimidation tactics—we will not hesitate to kill you, should we feel you...stray from fulfilling our needs."

"All right, fancy man, that's what I said," growled Spyros.

"Understood," Silver nodded to Bastien.

"We won't just be taking you at your word, pirate. We're gonna need some insurance," Spyros insisted.

Silver looked to Bastien, who only shrugged in compliance. "Very well. You can have the crew. If I make one wrong move, you can kill me whole crew."

"The crew?" Spyros scoffed.

"Some of my closest friends are in this crew, mate."

"You can't fool me, Silver. You'd sell out your own wife if it meant saving your own neck."

"He would...but maybe not his crew. Not this crew," Bastien granted. "I noticed the boy Jim Hawkins is on board, along with his friend Doctor Livesey."

Silver stiffened slightly and cleared his throat. "The boy is my lackey. I see no need to harm him."

"Hm, sweet," Bastien nodded. "Clearly he's a matter of valuable collateral."

"We have an...arrangement."

"Oh, and that quartermaster of yours," Bastien led.

"He's been with me since Flint's crew. I reckon he'll be as useful to you as I am. He was there when we buried the treasure, and he's countin' on bein' there when we dig it back up."

Bastien sheathed his dagger and tightened his mouth. "Hm, and did you know anything about the man before he joined Flint's crew?"

"Didn't need to."

"Very well."

"What does that mean?" Spyros demanded.

"It means we can take his crew as collateral," Bastien sighed. "At least the boy and the quartermaster."

Almost as if on cue, a knock and a call came from outside. "Silver!"

Bastien acknowledged the knock. "Hm, well look at that. Here he comes now."

Silver excused himself from the meeting, giving Bastien a solemn nod. Hastings stood just outside the door, arms crossed and eyebrows pulled together in a tight scowl. His shoulders were tense and everything about his stance told Silver he was learning too much.

"This isn't what I signed up for," Hastings took him aside and whispered.

"What is it that's troublin' you, mate?" Silver feigned ignorance.

"You know exactly what's troubling me. You have no idea what you're getting involved in," Hastings asserted. Men like Silver don't easily heed warnings unless they come from their own gut, but Hastings cautioned him just the same. "I've played this game before, Silver. It doesn't end well for either side. Get out of this at the next port, or I will."

"I don't think leaving the voyage early would be very beneficial, Quartermaster," Bastien contributed. He had left Spyros alone to fume in the cabin while he surreptitiously lent an ear to Silver's business.

"Mr. Bastien has a lot to offer us. We'd be smart to stick it out," Silver encouraged.

"Bastien," Hastings repeated. He knew the name. That painful memory returned, even clearer and more distinctly this time before he could suppress it.

Bastien straightened his back, instinctively puffing his chest as Hastings spoke his name. "I don't quite remember learning your name, quartermaster."

Hastings gave an antagonistic raise of the brow before walking away. "That's because you didn't."

Unsettled, Jim watched from afar, standing behind a crate and listening to Silver disregard Mr. Hastings's warning. It all made him quite anxious. Clancy and Alice were nowhere in sight.

"They should probably know," he whispered to himself.

"Who should probably know what?" Lorelei joined him behind the crates. Lorelei saw no use in lowering her voice to Jim, as his voice was almost as high as hers.

"How long have you been there?" Jim asked, startled.

"Well, I saw the tall fellow talking to Hastings and the captain," she explained.

"There's trouble starting here," Jim shook his head. "I just know it."

"And you think the little girl should know about it."

"How do you know about—?"

Lorelei smirked. "Oh please. I think we're all on the same side here. You're a savvy one, though—is it Silver you don't trust or the tall one?"

Jim watched quietly as Hastings walked away and left an unsatisfied Bastien to scowl. "I think the tall man shouldn't be trusted."

Lorelei followed his line of sight and nodded thoughtfully. "I think you're right. See, you are savvy....is it Jim?"

Jim turned to her and offered an introductory handshake. "Jim Hawkins."

"...Alfie." Lorelei shook his hand but withheld her identity. As undoubtedly good-natured as this boy appeared to be, she had no desire for anyone else knowing her true gender unless absolutely necessary.

"Oi!" a fellow pirate shouted at her. "Move along, there! That deck ain't gonna swab itself!"

Her lack of response prompted him to advance, suddenly motivated to shove her into submission. When he laid his hands on her chest, they both immediately lunged back in bewilderment.

Her face went white.

He knew.

His expression twisted from shock to excitement, and that terrified her. He moved toward her again, but she dodged his arm and slipped out of his grip. He shouted at her once more, chasing her across the deck. When others found themselves involved and soon figured out the cause of his zeal, she found herself pinned against a wall, each pirate wanting her for himself, pushing poor Jim to the side.

Thankfully, her feminine shrieks caught Hastings's attention. He sprung to action, shoving men out of his way and barking orders and threats.

In the midst of determined sea-dogs, Hastings used much more brute force than necessary. Realizing their quartermaster was the one stopping them, most of the crew backed down, disappointed. There were a small few, however, who refused to give in so easily, even resorting to drawing their weapons.

Hastings stepped in front of Lorelei just as a bullet blasted toward her and ricocheted off of his jacket. A miraculously subtle, but incredibly revealing defense, which only two pairs of eyes witnessed amidst the pirates' mania.

"Get back to work!" Hastings barked. At last, all obeyed. He turned away, and the owner of the first pair of eyes grabbed his arm.

"That...what was that?" Lorelei whispered in awe.

"What are you talking about?" He brushed her off, but she only stepped in front of him.

"Some kind of magic or something?" she continued. "Are you a sorcerer—"

Before she could utter another word, Hastings grabbed her by the arm and pulled her aside with force. "Not a word," he threatened. For a moment, something in those curious sea green eyes of hers prompted a pause.

"Oh no," she shook off his hesitation. "No, I wouldn't dare. It's far too spectacular to share with these morons. But you are...aren't you?" She grinned, burning with curiosity. He didn't even have to answer for her anticipation to grow. "I knew you were something different. You're too brilliant not to be."

The compliment mildly took him aback, but he quickly regained his wits. "Yes, well, there are those who would disagree. You need to swear to me that you'll never breathe a word of this."

She nodded loyally. "Of course. But...what exactly are you? And don't try denying it."

He considered this. "I don't really know." He only knew what he was not.

"Are there others aboard like you? The little girl? What is she, a sprite or something?"

"She's something," Hastings chuckled. The concept of magic excited Lorelei, and there was no end to her questions. "Under normal circumstances, I would welcome your attractive desire to figure this out, but there really aren't enough answers for me to—"

Spyros's door slammed open, causing all on deck to jump. The rat-faced man limped heavily out of the shadow of his quarters and demanded the attention of absolutely every man (and woman) aboard. "Where is he?!" he bellowed.

Havelock, who had been guarding his commander's cabin, happened to be that second pair of eyes who witnessed the protection of Hastings's peculiar jacket. He had informed the limping leader, who knew it could only mean one thing: there was a Keeper aboard.

The chaos was enough to make any witness unreliable, however. A bullet ricocheted off of someone's jacket, to be sure, but Havelock couldn't quite place the wearer. Was it the quartermaster or the storyfolk pirate standing beside him?

With overwhelming fury, Spyros shouted for all hands on deck and carefully ran his dark eyes over each and every face.

"Where. Is. He?"

His curtness struck terror in the hearts of each crewman. Clancy and Alice hid behind taller sailors, shielding their faces from the Scada. Lorelei stepped instinctively closer to Hastings. She suspected Spyros was looking for the sorcerous quartermaster, but she was the last soul on board who would expose him.

"There is a Keeper here," Spyros went on. Bastien leaned lazily against the outside of the cabin, amusedly watching his colleague conduct this witch hunt. "There is no use in hiding any longer; if he does not reveal himself....there will be dire consequences."

Every living being remained silent. Those who did not understand the meaning of the word *Keeper* simply glanced from one to another in confusion but thought it wise to keep their lips sealed, regardless. Spyros paced up and down the deck, wearing his most intimidating grimace but to no avail. Finally, he decided to prove his sincerity.

"Bastien," he barked. "Gather Silver's boys!"

Bastien did so and gathered the native crew members, lining them up in front of the captain's cabin. All of them, save the Keeper himself. Bastien just so happened to pass over the one man he suspected, quietly anticipating his colleague's thrilling search for a hidden target. Once the natives were displayed before the crew, Spyros's grimace twisted into a wicked grin which caused his right eye to scrunch into a thin, crooked line; it was a common expression worn by the rat before he had the pleasure of taking a life.

"So be it," he decided aloud.

His saunter back down the line made Clancy hold his breath. He was familiar enough with Scada methods, through the many misfortunes he had read in the Arkis, to understand what was happening next. Bastien, in his casual observance, was equally aware of his comrade's methods.

And, as both spectators predicted, Spyros took a pistol out of his holster and fired a shot into the chest of the unnamed crew member standing closest to him.

Everyone flinched except Bastien. Jim and Alice squeezed their eyes shut as if not seeing would prevent the evil from happening. When the pistol was cocked for a second execution, Jim's eyes flew back open in time to see the gun pointed at Doctor Livesey.

"Please no!" Jim stepped in front of the gun. "Stop!"

Spyros lowered the pistol and peered curiously at the youth. "Why's that, boy?"

Jim fell quiet. "I....please. Please don't." He didn't know quite what to say. His protests came quicker than his fear of the gun.

"Oh please, please don't," the fiend mocked. Bastien rolled his eyes as Spyros held the gun inches from the boy's face.

"How do we know the Keeper isn't you?" Silver spoke up. With all of the magic Spyros had allowed him to witness, for the duration of their entire voyage from Bristol, he had suspended all disbelief.

Spyros snapped his head over his shoulder toward Silver. "Excuse me?"

Silver limped forward, Captain Flint lightly hissing as her master stepped closer. "You do have magic, sir. Many of us don't understand the difference—how are we to know you aren't the Keeper who is oh-so-dangerous?"

"I'll have your guts, Silver," Spyros seethed in offense. "I am no Keeper. But he is here. And I will find him."

"What if we toss the woman over? Lure him out," the large pirate, who had previously lost a gamble to Riddock, piped up.

He and many of the others would have done anything to cast suspicion from themselves. Whatever a Keeper was, they would certainly not be accused of being one.

"Woman?" Spyros repeated with disgust.

The large pirate quickly grabbed Lorelei and shoved her to the front for all to see before Hastings could stop him. Not that he put forth any outstanding amount of effort. Generally respectable as he was, self-preservation was a well-learned trait of his.

Spyros paused suddenly and raised a filthy finger to his lips. "Mmm...chivalry. The curse of every Keeper, it seems. Put the girl on the plank. Isn't that how things are done here?"

He glanced back at Silver, who merely shrugged passively.

It took three men to wrestle Lorelei onto the plank. She put up quite a fight, kicking and throwing fists at anything within range. By the time she reached the plank, the men had managed to not only tie her wrists but strap a cannonball to her ankles upon Spyros's orders.

"Alright then, Keeper," Spyros spoke up again. "This is your final chance to come forward. Unless you want this lovely lady to fall to a watery grave."

Lorelei glanced in Hastings's direction to see his conflicted distress. Subtly, she shook her head, urging him not to surrender on her behalf. He was inclined to do just as she urged, but there was something inside him that yanked his gut in an entirely different direction, compelling him to step in to stop this.

This woman did not ask for death.

She did not ask to be involved in this war, and now she would become a casualty.

He could not allow that. As fortified as his heart was, she had somehow stumbled her way inside.

Spyros approached the plank with consideration. He frowned at the sight of his victim and then chuckled darkly.

"Oh no, this won't do." With a wave of his hand, a dark smoke untied her wrists and disposed of the cannonball.

Ever so briefly, Lorelei sighed in relief, thinking she had obtained her freedom.

And then Spyros clarified. "Just watching her fall off the side of the ship won't quite do it. But maybe if there was more to see...."

Spyros raised a hand, gripping the air with such strain that his muscles tensed. As he raised his hand, Lorelei was slowly lifted in the air, clutching her slender neck. Her throat was enclosed by his magical grasp, squeezing tightly. Her free hands gripped the air around her neck, desperately clawing for relief. Even the brutish pirates aboard flinched at the horrid sight of Spyros's violence. Bastien set his gaze idly in Hastings's direction, unamused and expectant.

"How about now, Keeper?" Spyros taunted.

At last, the compelling force was bursting from Hastings in a way he could no longer contain. "Stop!" he finally roared, making those next to him move aside.

So many expected some spectacular display of power to challenge Spyros's cruelty, something unbelievable and terrifying. But nothing came. No blast of light, no powerful eruption of energy. Just rage.

Had Hastings brought himself to lift a single magical finger to stop Spyros, it would have been to no avail.

Something else had beaten him to it.

Yes, something else caused Spyros to be so dumbfounded and distracted from the revelation of the Keeper that he couldn't take his eyes off of the struggling woman before him. Surely, he heard Hastings's verbal outburst, but a verbal outburst was all it was.

No, what captured his attention was the woman's resistance. A powerful resistance which gradually pushed his strength and magic aside. For once, he was speechless. The fool's eyesight was not his greatest sense; he hardly noticed what Bastien looked like—only how he smelled and sounded —not that he cared to look at him much. However, what he was beginning to see before him made him feel even more foolish than Bastien believed him to be. And that was infuriating.

All eyes were on Spyros. All except Hastings's. What had silenced the boisterous ogre? What, indeed. Hastings followed his angry glare to the culprit.

Lorelei's strangled expression was softening with relief. In her eyes, there was no more panic, no more fear or dread.

Instead, she now grimaced with vengeful confidence.

"Curse you, Ava! Curse you!" Spyros's hand shook, fighting against the unseen retaliation.

In exhaustion, he sharply dropped his arm, in effect, dropping her to the ground. Bastien's ears perked at the sound of her true name. Suddenly, they had his undivided attention.

Lorelei's face darkened as if a shadow were cast upon it. Her soft features sharpened, her tanned complexion lightened, her bright eyes became stained, and her dark blonde hair became a wild, rusty red.

It didn't take long for Alice to finally remember why Lorelei had been so familiar to her before. She once knew her by a different name.

The poor little girl frowned and looked to Clancy for assurance, but the scribe was too gobsmacked to offer much of anything. All he could manage was a dropped jaw and alarmingly wide eyes. Livesey and Jim both looked to him for an explanation, only to be left in confusion.

"You moron," Ava spat.

She stepped back onto the plank and casually strolled over to face him. "If you put forth some thought before carrying out business, you probably wouldn't have been so quick to kill the only woman on board," she corrected, tearing off her head wrap and letting her flaming hair fall past her shoulders.

"Well, if you had let me in on this assignment of yours, perhaps you wouldn't have been in danger of me killing you," Spyros frothed. "Though, I make no promises I won't."

Ava scoffed. "Oh, a threat. Adorable. I think, though, that this whole endeavor of yours would have run much smoother had you consulted me before setting out. This harebrained arrogance is going to get you into trouble someday. You didn't even know there was a new one, did you, you silly clout?"

Ignoring this, he grumbled, "What were you doing with the Keeper anyway?"

A devilish grin came upon her face. "Hm, you should ask the Keeper that question. You screwed everything else up. Go on; you might as well screw up the interrogation too."

"I was trying to get him to be Prince Charming and save the day, therefore exposing himself—which he did, might I point out."

"I've never been one for Prince Charming. Now, why don't you take control of the situation like a man? Or would you like me to show you how?"

After more grumbling on Spyros' part, he gestured for Bastien to shove Hastings against the side of the ship so that he could get a better view of this new threat. Only after receiving an approving nod from Ava did Bastien obey.

One would expect an enraged outburst of betrayal and pain. It would be understandable, to be sure. However, this Keeper's response was strange. He naturally tensed with anger, but his eyes narrowed, and his head cocked slightly as he read the situation.

Many Keepers before him have made the mistake of acting impulsively when encountering a trickster such as Ava. Had Clancy felt a bit more objective toward Thomas Hastings, I'm certain he would have made note of a phenomenon such as this new approach.

"And what do they call you, Keeper?" Spyros began.

"Not Keeper," was the uncooperative response.

Spyros struck his backhand against Hastings's face and repeated the question. "What is your infernal name?"

"Thomas Hastings," Bastien contributed, scrutinizing the Keeper.

His interrogator sighed. "Of course your name is Thomas. Englishmen from Middangeard have such little imagination. James, Albert, John, Richard, Henry, Thomas, Ben...you're all the same."

"I'm Irish."

"Well, there's that," Bastien muttered.

Spyros shrugged. "I suppose I should probably kill you now," he said.

Ava clicked her tongue.

"Or perhaps keep you alive a bit longer," he then amended. "But, you can't be in my way, so it looks like we'll be making a little stop here."

Purposefully, the ship was passing a minuscule island with very little vegetation. It was here where Spyros planned to dispose of our heroes.

"At least there you won't be a nuisance."

Backing away, Spyros muttered some orders to Silver and another crewman, giving Hastings a clear view of Ava's smug expression.

"How did you even find me?" he furrowed his brow.

"Wasn't as hard as you were trying to make it, handsome," she said snidely. She crossed her arms and stepped toward him. "The damsel in distress card is a classic. There aren't many who don't fall for it." At the corner of his eye, Hastings could see Bastien turn his head away from her claims. "You Keepers are always the heroic type. Just throw in a bit of vulnerability, and you're taken."

He chuckled lightly. "Oh, you really didn't get to know me that well. I'm not the heroic type."

Ava pouted her lips condescendingly. "Mm, maybe repeating that to yourself will actually convince you of it someday." Then, over her shoulder, she added, "I'd throw in his friends too, if you don't want any more trouble."

Spyros turned his head back to her. "The Keeper already has friends?"

"The little one parading as a cabin boy and that short one. Though, for good measure, darling," she added, "I'd include little Hawkins and the handsome doctor. Better get them out of your way as well."

Following this suggestion, Hastings, Alice, Clancy, Jim, and Livesey were filed onto the plank for the marooning.

Clancy held a steady glare on Hastings, formulating just how many ways this dilemma was the new Keeper's fault.

"Why are you letting this happen?" Jim asked Hastings innocently. He hadn't intended for Ava to hear him, but nothing was quite going the heroes' way.

"Because he's a coward," she answered for him. She stepped in front of the Keeper and lightly grabbed his face. His eyes still narrowed, his mouth couldn't decide if he was furious or intrigued. "Aw, but look at him. No one that handsome should look so dejected."

From behind Clancy, Alice mumbled sadly, "It is a shame she's an evil one; I liked her."

14

Fair Play

The Wanderer floated adrift some ways from the island, taunting the marooned heroes. Peering over the side of the ship, watching them with a sneer, Ava munched on a crisp apple. Bastien was at her side, after ordering the crew to return to their duties. The sun was setting, giving the despair of the Keeper and his friends such a satisfying glow. It was always the little cruel things that gave Ava the most pleasure.

"Are we in any danger of the Keeper and his friends using magic to leave the island?" Bastien asked her.

Ava's lip curled into a knowing smile. "I think you're too accustomed to the last one." He chuckled because she chuckled. "No, no," she went on, "This one isn't remotely ready to consider that an option. He'd trust his intellect before he'd trust his magic again. And intellect won't get him off that island."

Spyros then joined them, grunting as he propped his metal leg up on a small crate. "He'll stay where he is then. Good. Makes my job easier."

"You need all the help you can get," Bastien commented.

"I will have you know that this assignment is of top priority to the Master," he defended. "Certainly a better use of time than tracking down people you can't even kill."

"That is true," Ava contributed, eyeing the apple before taking another bite.

"Ah," Bastien pointed. "But, how many Arch Keepers has he killed?"

"Yes, how many, dear?" Ava stroked her chin derisively with her right hand, subtly displaying two dark rings tattooed around her fingers.

Spyros wrinkled his nose in distaste. Arch Keepers were admirably tricky marks. Unfortunately for Spyros, his strengths remained elsewhere. "I'm given more....pressing assignments whenever there's an Arch ready to die."

"That could be a sign of trust," Ava pointed out, antagonistically. "And, you know, you did fail to kill the Aerest the first time, love," she frowned at Bastien. "It took you a few attempts."

"Exactly," Spyros agreed as if it were his idea. "It took you a few attempts because you failed the first time. You failed with Towson too, if I recall. Needed Ava to finish that job for you."

"He's not wrong, darling," she clicked her tongue. "He was even an easy one. No Companion in the way—he was practically begging for death. Though, you were still rather fresh." She gave his arm an encouraging rub, excusing his misgivings.

Bastien rolled his eyes. She never properly chose sides; he loved when she took his, but she just as quickly fed Spyros ammunition, which he did not love. She laughed at him, in that way that drove him mad, and slowly backed away from them. He took the apple she left on the stack of crates and threw it at her. Playfully, she caught it and giggled, taking one more bite.

"I'll be checking on Silver. Make sure there's no conspiring down there," she winked before leaving them.

After she was out of earshot, and Spyros was sure there was no chance of her returning, he nudged Bastien's arm. "Hey...how's she done so far?"

Tearing his eyes away from where Ava had left, Bastien raised an eyebrow. "You mean before you blew her cover?"

"How was I to know the Master would sic her on an Arch? She's never been set on one directly before...and I'm beginning to see why. Think she could still pull it off or might we behold her first failure?" Spyros snickered like a weasel.

"Ava doesn't fail," Bastien stared at his hands. "Despite your best efforts, her plans are unending."

"Are you telling me she foresaw my interference?" he scoffed.

Bastien smirked. "Are you telling me she didn't? She's too clever not to have a contingency plan."

"And of course you would be privy to all the, erm... intimate details of that plan, eh?" Spyros picked, hoping for a telling response to report to his master. "That's why you let her just toss your target on that little speck of sand without putting up a fight on your part. The little girl was a Storyteller, you know. She's on your list."

Bastien gave him no such satisfaction. He merely twiddled his thumbs and chewed on his lower lip in contemplation. "Powers of observation would lead one to assume a greater scheme than just wearing a disguise and batting her eyes. No need for inside information—this is Ava we're talking about. Know your allies, Spyros. She's not one to waste resources, and we both know of recent...assets she's acquired. There should be no doubt she'd use her latest catch. And your blunders are so predictable, she most certainly planned to use them to her advantage. And as for my new target...Ava and I frequently intertwine."

"By intertwine, I'm sure you mean she gets her way, and you just become content with her besting you so easily, conceding that her assignment is the most important. Her well-trained mutt."

"Mutt beats rat," Bastien retorted throatily.

With another snarl forming in his face, Spyros had no rebuttal, so the two stood in silence for close to twenty minutes, just staring and ignoring one another. When Ava returned to this mini-conference, she grazed her fingers along Bastien's arm, cruelly teasing him. The look on her face was self-satisfied, inflicting more pain. So, Bastien did what Scada do best.

"You know, Spyros...that map Ava gave me to give to you was not the true map. She slipped me the fake one just before leaving me to...check in."

Ava took a step back, silently asking the reason for the betrayal. But she was not surprised. It was the Scada way, after all. Spyros and Bastien both stared at her expectantly, waiting for her to produce the real map to Treasure Island.

Scowling, with a hint of mischief, Ava reached into her shirt and pulled out the genuine copy of the map of Treasure Island. Spyros snatched it maliciously out of her hands, continuing to glare. The intensity of his gaze and the passiveness of Bastien's caused a mildly concerned expression to overtake her coy grin.

Part Two

Such Beauty & Such Evil

15

Woes of the Marooned

"Well this is just fantastic," Clancy muttered, wringing out the hem of his drenched shirt. They sat, defeated, on the beach of the deserted island, wondering what had gone wrong.

"At least we found the Keeper," Alice pointed out, optimistically. "Lost the ship, but kept the Keeper. We can still win."

After checking the well-being of little Jim Hawkins, Doctor Livesey stood with his hands on his hips, glaring down this Keeper Alice found. His eyes were accusing and demanding. He didn't know what had just happened, but he felt Hastings was to be held responsible.

"An explanation would be most helpful, Mr. Hastings," he spat, lightly brushing the sticky sand from his pants. "Answers of any kind? What exactly is that devil Spyros? What did he want with you? And why did he count us among your allies?"

"Which one was Spyros?" Jim quietly asked Alice, helping her brush the wet sand from her shirt and pants.

"The fat one," she answered. She patted her head to feel her hat had sadly gotten lost in the swim to shore. "With the funny nose and the metal leg. He's a very important Scada, he's quite stupid, though."

"And what is Scada?"

"The bad guys. They don't like Keepers, and that's why they threw Mister and us overboard," Alice sighed.

"Oh some Scada like Keepers, Alice," Clancy countered venomously, maintaining a steady scowl on Hastings. "But not for the right reasons. Some are just such easy targets. Scada can't get enough of them—particularly the ones who get demented thrills out of mind games and seductions." His volume escalated with each syllable.

"Seductions?" Livesey repeated with concern. All eyes turned to Hastings, waiting for an explanation, a defense, anything.

But Hastings paid them no attention; he stood, staring curiously at the growing waves. Nature has a way of responding to inflicting forces—treating things such as opposition and infection with extreme prejudice, out of self-preservation and the instinct for maintaining balance.

When Hastings failed to respond, Livesey glanced back at Clancy. Clancy's mouth twisted into intense disdain, and he threw away all desire to control his contempt.

"Yes, Doctor, seductions. Seduction and corruption. That's her game! Never has an Arch Keeper been so stupid as to fall for her tricks and—"

"Quiet!" Hastings suddenly barked. Hastings's eye was focusing on an object battling against the combative waves.

His outburst and intense scrutiny drew the attention of young Alice, causing her to assume an equally curious stance beside him.

"What is that?" she pried. "A seal? Or a penguin? No, that would be silly. We're nowhere near snow. And it's far too big to be a small animal. Perhaps it's a shark? Ooh, or a mermaid!"

Hastings ignored her guesses, formulating his own. Whatever it was, it was struggling to stay afloat. The waves pulled it closer to shore, and now captured the observance of all of our unfortunate castaways. Water crashed and rolled onto its target, causing arms and fiery, dark red hair to splash frantically.

As it turns out, demons are not particularly skilled swimmers. In her defense, she had rather powerful forces fighting against her and had good reason to fear. Evidently, the Alden weren't the only ones who harbored strong feelings toward Korbl's mistress. Ava crawled desperately to shore, coughing up salt water and gasping for air.

Clancy's jaw dropped, Alice frowned in confusion, and Hastings's body tensed defensively.

"Isn't that...?" Jim whispered to Alice.

"Shhh," she hushed him with a wave of her hand as if his talking was distracting her sight.

Doctor Livesey's nature was far too inclined to heal to let a collapsing woman remain abandoned and in distress. It was an occupational hazard, it seems. Disregarding her involvement in their current predicament, Livesey rushed to her side and supported her weight as he helped her stagger safely beyond the tide. As they approached the onlookers, Hastings curtly addressed him.

"Drop her," he ordered.

Livesey looked at him strangely. "She can hardly breathe," he tried to reason.

"Drop her," Hastings repeated with authority. "She can do just fine on her own."

Reluctantly, Livesey obeyed and took a step away from her. She stumbled, unbalanced, to the ground, wiping her damp hair out of her face.

"Oh no," she coughed. "Are you going to kill me now, Keeper?"

Hastings's mouth tightened, but then shrugged. She played him like a fiddle, but now it was his turn. For whatever reason, he was now given the upper hand. "That would be far too easy and far less fun, wouldn't it?"

"Easy, eh?" she continued to clear her throat. "Someone's awfully cocky."

"Perhaps we should kill her," Clancy mumbled.

"Tie her up!" Alice suggested emphatically.

"We don't have rope," Jim countered. Alice looked at him as if he were a fool.

"We don't need rope, silly. Mister can do it with his magic."

"Because he's a Keeper," Jim assumed. She nodded, he was starting to learn. Doctor Livesey, however, remained in confusion.

"What is she to us, Mr. Hastings?" he pressed.

"The devil," Clancy muttered under his breath.

She chuckled before spitting the remaining salt water and sand out of her cruel mouth. Casually, she plaited her damp hair atop her head and secured it with a thin, torn section of her cloth skirt. "Hm, no. But we are quite close."

"You were working with that Spyros fellow," the doctor pieced together. "Why would he maroon you?"

"That is the question," Hastings ruminated. His voice was hoarsely contemplative, barely loud enough to be shared.

"Perhaps the girl is right," Livesey decided. "It may be wise to keep her restrained. And you have the...um, magic?"

Hastings subtly gestured for Clancy to step in, but Livesey's eyes did not move. Alice seemed so sure that Hastings held the key to their freedom and the power to control this fiend—yet the supposed hero did very little. Livesey's doubts regarding the magic aside, Hastings's disinterest and reluctance puzzled him.

Clancy hesitated. He knew what Ava was capable of and was perfectly aware of the contrast to his inadequate magic, should she choose to retaliate. But, taking a deep breath, he took Ava's hands without more than a grimace.

Before waving his own hand to bind her, he noticed something strange and froze at the sight of her bare wrists. The absence of Scada wristbands seemed strange to him. He actively avoided studying her, as a general rule, but he would have assumed she donned them just like all the others. Narrowly avoiding eye contact, and trying to ignore the corner of her lip curl, Clancy finished the job and quickly stepped back.

Ava sharply inhaled as though the straps were burning her skin upon contact. Constrained as she was, her smirk remained intact.

"What are you, Hastings? I do believe we deserve some answers," Livesey reiterated.

"He's the Keeper, of course," Alice chimed in, a bit exasperated that no one seemed to be paying attention. "I keep telling you. All will be well now. He put the jacket on, he's in charge, and now he will get us off this island."

"Will he?" Livesey challenged. "If indeed he has such magic, then why would he not do something as simple as binding the woman's hands?"

"Because he can't," Ava answered curtly. Her trademark smug little smile settled on her face while Hastings's eyes narrowed. "Can you?"

"Hey, stop that," Alice spat, careful to stay a distance away from her. Even constrained, this particular captive was capable of far more terrible things than she cared to see. "Mister has magic that can...do wonderful things."

Ava raised her eyebrows. "Yes, he does, doesn't he? But you seem to be the only one confident of that, little one. Not even the scribe is leaping to his defense—and he's probably read about how much raw, natural, awesome power this Keeper has. You and I...and the scribe...we all know that the only thing preventing the Keeper from harming me isn't inadequacy...it's fear."

"Or timing," Hastings voiced.

"Ah, and the fear speaks," she grinned, interlacing her fingers. "You wear such a convincing mask, handsome. Make believe you're in control, but inside you're quivering in a corner."

"Why did Spyros abandon you?" Hastings cut to the point, crossing his arms in front of his chest. He didn't give her the satisfaction of weakening his resolve. His expression was determined and absolute, not showing a single symptom of the fear she attempted to shame.

"Because he apparently prefers legitimate bearings to his little island."

"You gave him a false map?" Livesey interrupted. "Why would you do that?"

Ava ignored the doctor, keeping her eyes fixed on Hastings. "So, you see, you are not the only one who falls for my lies. You're not so special."

"But, what have you to gain from betraying him?" Clancy asked. He mirrored Hastings's crossed-arm stance, but added his own nervous flare by failing to hide his tense shoulders.

She paused with calm deliberation before responding, her eyelids flickering with subtle hesitation. "Relevance," she answered. "As long as I possess something they need....I'm indispensable. Since the rat sabotaged my assignment, as I predicted he would, I had to keep a hand on his most valuable resource."

"Why maroon? Why not just kill you?" Hastings suggested.

Ava clicked her tongue. "Now, Keeper. I can't give you all the answers at once—far too predictable and dull."

"Maybe he's not allowed," Alice mused.

She had lost interest in the interrogation and found a small pebble with which she drew swirls and doodles in the sand. Hastings watched the child briefly, considering her input, before turning back to Ava.

"Or he was afraid to," Clancy contributed as an aside to Hastings. "She's infinitely more powerful than Spyros."

"Just how well do you know each other?" Hastings questioned.

Clancy's fists moved to his hips while his tense shoulders squared. "Enough to know that if she wanted to stay on the ship, she would have. She wants to be here, Hastings."

"Or she's waiting for her colleagues to learn their lesson the hard way." Ava sat in the sand, listening keenly to every muttered word, and she was growing impatient. "Not everything is about you lot."

"What lesson would that be?" Livesey asked.

"That he needs her." Hastings stepped closer to her and crouched to her level. "You must be terribly important for Spyros to be so afraid of your involvement."

His assertive role in the interrogation excited her. She leaned forward, ever so slightly, with a wicked grin. "It doesn't take much to make a rodent scurry. Everything is a competition with him, but only I can win. He knows that—some just insist on living in denial. Such a sad way to live, isn't it?"

His lips tightened into a straight line as he studied her face. "Mm, if only he could get into Korbl's good graces the way you have. Something tells me he's not properly endowed with your particular set of...skills."

She shrugged. "Natural talent can't be taught, I suppose. He may try harder, but it's no easy feat for me. I know, I make it look effortless, but Scada are vicious, aren't they? Survival is much easier when your allegiance is limited to your own well-being."

Her mouth finally loosened with solemnity; her jesting seemed to be over, and her sense of self-preservation had been activated. But Hastings's penetrating stare would not yield. A game had now begun.

"What is it that Spyros is planning for the treasure?" Livesey pressed. Still, she refused to acknowledge him, only having eyes for the Keeper.

"I may be a favorite, but I'm kept in the dark, same as the others. This is his assignment, not mine. You were mine... before he spoiled things for me. It's a shame you were such a gentleman, or we could've ended this already."

She reached her bound hands to touch Hastings' face, but he abruptly snatched her wrists. His tolerance was diminishing quickly. She gasped softly in surprise at this sudden and sharp response. After waiting in vain for a break in his eye contact, she soon conceded.

Sighing in defeat, she went on. "There is something on Treasure Island. Something more valuable than the treasure itself. Whatever it is, he's using anything and anyone he can to get it. He's trying to best me because he's a jealous child."

"Now that part was the truth," Clancy pointed at her, his other fist still firmly planted on his hip. "I think we should set up camp. A watch may be wise to keep an eye on that one."

"Where could she possibly go?" Livesey questioned in confusion. There were no ships in sight, and her magical hands were visibly bound. Livesey doubted such precautions were necessary, but when Hastings nodded once in agreement, he conceded.

As the others gathered what few resources the island offered, Doctor Livesey volunteered the first watch of the prisoner. He stationed himself far enough away from her that she could not reach him without making quite an obvious effort. He did not understand magic, but he assumed that limiting physical touch would lessen his likelihood of being cursed. The ignorant have silly superstitions like that, I suppose.

"If Mr. Hastings is a Keeper who saves worlds and such," Livesey attempted to understand—based purely on Alice's ramblings, "then what are you supposed to be? A witch of some sort?"

Ava grinned. "I'm a princess. I've just lost my tiara." Her eyes flickered with a black shadow, successfully spooking him out of pursuing any further questioning. "But what about you, doctor? What's your story? Guardian of the little hero-in-training?"

"In a sense," he replied slowly.

"That's quite good of you. He's certainly impressive—and at the most impressionable of ages."

Livesey's face soured. His instinct told him she was dangerously prying. To her amusement, he brought an end to the answering of questions for fear she would find fault in his words and use them against him. Thankfully, once the fire was lit and the others gathered around it, Alice eagerly offered to be Livesey's replacement. He posed no argument; he would have given anything to avoid the discomfort of Ava's sneering gaze on him. She relished every eerie moment.

Approaching this curious new being, Alice sat with her legs crossed directly in front of the prisoner. Ava adjusted her seated position, jutting her chin inquisitively at the girl as if challenging her many unvoiced questions. Alice was unmoved by any form of intimidation. Instead, she squinted her eyes, memorizing what was before her.

"I finally read your story, a little while ago, Ava," the girl whispered so that the others couldn't hear. "Wicked people always have stories. Just like you. But I don't know why you helped me. On the ship, when Spyros was going to hurt me, why did you stop him? That wasn't so wicked of you. It doesn't fit."

Ava stared at her for a long moment. "You know quite a bit, don't you?"

"I know loads of things," Alice insisted, anxiously, "but I don't understand. I've forgotten quite a bit. That's why you must tell me."

"Not everything is to be understood. What's life without mystery, Alice? You can't tell me you understand everything in the Arkis—"

"No, but I know it all." Alice's tone was defensive and lofty, but it was her conviction that intrigued Ava.

"All of it?" she considered, leaning forward.

"Yes, of course, all of it."

"And yet, you ventured outside of the Arkis to try and understand things outside of your realm. Perhaps you shouldn't jump too quickly into the mystery. It may be contrary to your nature, but avoiding trouble is much safer for children," Ava warned with a foreboding expression.

"But I'm not a..." Alice started. She then looked down at her small legs and feet, remembering that, as far as Ava was concerned, she was, in fact, a child. She sighed in resignation. Scooting about an inch closer to her, Alice propped her elbows up on her knees and rested her chin in her palms. "I just like understanding things, Ava."

"Do you understand, then, why it is that your master never allowed you on an adventure like this before?"

Alice lifted a challenging brow. "I don't even think you understand that. Of course I do, though. I know exactly who I am—I've never once forgotten. Not ever. Not even for a little while."

Ava watched her for a moment, her head leaning to one side. "You used to be blonde. I like you better this way." She slightly shifted in her sitting position. "I've never much cared for blondes."

"You used to. I think you've forgotten quite a lot too. I never liked how you made your story. So let's play pretend, shall we? Let's pretend you were still kind. Let's pretend your story was different—"

"But it isn't," Ava cut her off.

Alice frowned. "What if it could be?"

Ava leaned closer to her. "Would it make a difference?"

"To you, it would. You would be very different. Except for your hair. I think we should still pretend it's red. I very much like red things. Sometimes I wish my hair hadn't turned brown but red instead. But, this isn't my pretend game, it's yours. Where would you be?"

"When did it turn brown?"

"When we got here. Clancy thinks it's because we're in trouble, but I always know better than him. I don't turn brown when I'm in trouble—I'm never in trouble. Clancy worries far too much. But, in any case, you haven't answered my question, Ava. Where would you be in your pretend? If you could be anywhere?"

Ava was already bored with this session of make-believe; she already had what she wanted, and the child's chatter grated on her ears. She leaned back into her lazy position and rolled her stained eyes. "Anywhere but here."

A short time later, when the turn finally fell on Clancy, he approached her with poorly disguised fear. Continuing to keep a relative distance from her, Clancy angled himself away from her.

"I won't bite you, scribe," Ava said derisively. "You've put me on a leash, remember?" She held up her bound wrists for him to see.

"Of course, I remember," Clancy mumbled. "There's no need to speak to me, witch."

Ava chuckled. "You know, for a scribe, you're awfully cheeky."

"You can't use your tricks on me, Ava." Clancy held strong, but a barrier was necessary for such resolution, so the scribe bolstered his legs as a makeshift wall between them, setting his forearms against his knees to further feign his confidence. "I know what you are. I've read about you."

Ava rolled her eyes. "It seems you're not alone."

"Alice doesn't understand as I do."

"That's not what she claims."

"I know what you've done."

"On paper," Ava shrugged. "But, this is your first time leaving that dusty library, isn't it?"

Clancy crossed his arms self-consciously. "Yes, things are a little different on paper. The smell, for example. But you won't be getting any information out of me, do you understand?" He pointed a scolding finger at her, and she watched as it shook.

"Oh of course. Because you are the soul of discretion," she kissed her pointer finger and then waved it away. "You know better than all those other people. You know my ways. You've studied up on the big bad villainess, yeah?"

Clancy tightened his lips and shook his head. But Ava needed very little feedback to entertain herself. So she continued...

"Villainess," she hummed. "Who gets to decide who the villains of the story are, eh?" She straightened her legs in front of her, removing the barrier between them, to more effectively encourage this battle of wits. "Anything that one individual deems disagreeable can be viewed as evil. It's all relative. One could commit what another views as a sin out of simple necessity."

Clancy shook his head once more, resisting the urge to correct her. Jim sat nearby and glanced at Clancy's movement. Livesey and Hastings were preoccupied assessing Alice's exhaustion.

"Who is to condemn the one for their actions when they consider themselves justified?" their captive went on. "Good and Evil are both so ambiguous. That's what makes the stories so fun."

"Good and Evil are perfectly clear," Clancy burst. She was employing a weapon he had in spades, and he could no longer resist. The barrier came down; his legs crossed and flattened, and his torso leaned forward. "It's humans who try to make them ambiguous. Blurring lines between right and wrong, regardless of motivations—that's what confuses people like you. Your confusion twists the stories."

"And there's nothing more perturbing to a scribe than when someone messes with his stories." Ava's eyes flashed with satisfaction. She finally had him engaged, however reluctant he was. "People like me become who they are because their stories force a level of understanding and self-preservation—your Keeper is an example of that. People like you live in a bubble where everything is pretty and perfect, and you all never come out of it long enough to see those lines start to blur. It's not the people that make it all ambiguous; it's the circumstances. And that's the ugly truth of it."

Clancy shook his head, vehemently. "Truth is never ugly. It's the single most beautiful thing there is. But of course you wouldn't understand anything about that, would you? And the funny thing about truth is, regardless of the general opinions toward it, it does not change. You may think otherwise...but that's what makes you weak." He pointed another stern finger at her.

"Hm," she hummed again, genuinely enjoying the conversation. "In a realm where moral ambiguity runs so rampant, what makes you think I would be seen as so villainous? Look at your little hero."

She jerked her head in Jim's direction and Jim quickly looked away. "A young boy, driven by his shallow desire for treasure; a doctor with the same motivation; and a squire who was so weak that the slightest flop in plans sent him drinking his sorrows away instead of fighting for what he wanted. And your so-called villain....he's merely a sailor who was once cheated out of what was rightfully his in the first place. He worked for that treasure, and now he's only doing what he can to get the payment he deserves. You think you're so godly that you can properly label who's in the right and who's in the wrong?"

Her argument was calculated and collected without a hint of frustration. To her intrigue, Clancy finally responded in kind. This was truly his battlefield, despite his efforts to restrain himself.

"No, I'm not godly. I just pay attention to someone who is. At some point, the motivations matter as much as you believe the actions do. It's not just about what's motivating you; it's what you do with that motivation."

"Do you think your Keeper sees things quite as clearly as you do?" she smirked.

Clancy's eyes flickered toward Hastings, who was supervising a refreshed Alice as she stoked the fire. Hastings wore the jacket, but was he indeed the Keeper? When Clancy looked back to Ava, she had already sensed his doubts.

"You know what he's done. He and I bear the same marks." She brought her branded finger on her right hand up to her face, lightly tapping her cheek. "And yet you sit here and condemn me?"

Clancy remained quiet.

"What? No leaping to the Keeper's defense?" Ava clicked her tongue. "Not very Alden of you, love."

"As if you knew," he retorted.

"More than you think. I know that black-and-white mind of yours is doing somersaults just watching him wear the jacket. All that magic he put on his shoulders..."

This time Jim's eyes flickered toward Hastings. The Keeper and his jacket. The man Alice believed in and Clancy so clearly doubted.

"If you had your way," she continued, "you'd still have hold of it, waiting for the next one. We don't all get what we want, though, do we? You know there has to be a reason—his potential, his natural ability, or...something else. But you're afraid he's going to fall again."

Clancy cringed as she said *fall*. He couldn't let her see his distrust; he had already said too much. "Perhaps he will surprise all of us," he forced.

Ava chuckled. "Wow, you really don't like when someone messes with your stories."

"Of course I don't," he conceded, crossing his arms. "And you mess with stories more than anyone else. Twisting and tainting to get your way. It's how you were created."

She noted the drop in his volume as he mumbled the last sentence. She also noted Jim's ears perk, but his mouth struggled to resist involving himself. "Some stories don't need my help, you know. Storytellers are capable of doing enough twisting without my involvement, love."

"Don't talk to me about Storytellers," Clancy snapped. "They're not the ones at fault."

Ava's eyes widened and brightened. Jim finally turned to face them. His shoulders were relaxed but eager as her smirk beckoned him closer.

"What have they done?" the boy asked. His eyes were almost as wide as Ava's, longing for more answers.

"They haven't done anything," Clancy fired, jutting his chin toward the she-devil. "She has. She destroys them because they frighten her."

"Frighten me?" Ava lifted a brow.

The slight twitch of her face made Clancy's muscles tense again. Fear and adrenaline often interlace to form a unique brand of reckless courage. The sound side of his judgment was telling him to stop engaging with a woman who could ultimately destroy him with the snap of her fingers, but his chords had been struck, and the resonating wouldn't cease until his point had been made.

"They frighten her...." he leaned in, his hands shaking slightly. "Because of what they started and the power they wield."

Thrilled by the endurance of his newfound nerve, Ava tapped her lips with her pointer finger. "Now, now, let's not confuse the boy, love. Storytellers are not Creators."

"Doesn't matter. You fear both. You're afraid their stories can go from creating hope and guidance to creating even more dangerous things...things that undo all the hard work you've put in. Or perhaps there's just the envy, seeing as you're incapable of creating anything. Is that why you killed her?"

Jim leaned forward, resting his arms against his knees.

"Her?" Ava tilted her head to one side. "Are we getting personal now? Did I kill your ladylove, scribe?"

"I know what you did in Neverland," Clancy swallowed hard.

"What happened in Neverland?" Jim pressed.

"Hm, he hardly knows. Neverland is a wild place," she winked at Jim. "Anything could have happened there. If your master wanted it left alone, perhaps he shouldn't have filled it with so many treasures. Seems he was just as careless in this little venture." Her eyes flickered toward Alice and then back again.

"What—what does that mean?" Jim pushed.

Clancy saw the fire behind Ava's eyes as Jim's question settled, unanswered. His body tensed, and his jaw clenched.

The sparring was over; he finally adhered to the fear that had been gnawing at him. "Be quiet, Jim. Go see Alice."

Ava clicked her tongue. "Looks like there are no answers for the little adventurer."

"I'm not little," Jim softly insisted. "I'm nearly thirteen."

"Go to Alice, Jim."

"Yes, go to Alice," Ava taunted.

Jim sighed and obediently rose to join Alice. Clancy rose along with him, ready to pass on the duty of watch to the next in line. Before turning to walk away from her, however, he pointed a stern finger in the witch's face.

"You won't get her either," Clancy threatened.

Ava gave one more sly grin. "Ah, good. So long as you and the little one have an understanding. It's a wonder he let either of you out...knowing the risk. He is a crafty one, though, isn't he?"

Clancy's jaw clenched. "Myk won't let you or your Assassin get to her—not like Wendy."

"Wouldn't it be nice if we all got what we wanted?" she released an airy chuckle. "I write the stories here, love. And it's never any fun when everyone gets what they want, is it?"

The she-demon was right, of course. We don't all get what we want. If we did, there would be no story to tell. Hastings would not be the Keeper, Clancy would not have left the Arkis, and little Alice would be who knows where having incredible adventures. I suppose there would be some story to tell....but, in any case, it is not this story. This story was made to take a very different turn.

16

NOT A PROPER ENDING

The night fell, and our heroes huddled more closely around the fire. Roughly every hour, they rotated watch, but Ava seemed uncharacteristically silent. Her scheming now continued from behind a closed mouth. As an outcast, she was kept a short distance from the warmth of the fire, but she didn't seem to mind. They all maintained a wary eye on her—now it was young Jim Hawkins's turn to keep watch, and the idea made him quite anxious.

Livesey honorably sat next to the boy, to put him at ease, while both kept their distance from the vixen and still in sight of our heroes. Clancy and Livesey engaged in idle and dull chatter, which was brief and painfully forced. All the while, Hastings stared at the flicker of the flame, his mind churning.

"We should tell stories," Alice suggested with zeal. "Let's play pretend! It's a great way to unwind."

"What sort of story?" Jim inquired. He very much loved the idea of a distraction. "More mermaids?"

Clancy cringed, dreading Ava hearing more of Alice's revealing stories. He sat as close to Alice as he could, shielding her from Ava's sight. Yet, unbeknownst to him, the attention of the villainess was pulled elsewhere.

Alice adjusted her posture to prepare for her grand moment. "Well," she began, hands placed gracefully in her lap. "I shall tell you one of my favorites. His name was Fulco, and he was great fun. Do you remember this one, Clancy?"

"Fulco did quite a bit, Alice," he reasoned. "And every story is your favorite. I'm not sure which you plan to tell."

"Alright, then I'll just start already. It's called....The Mage's Test." Her tone suddenly changed; the telling of sacred tales tended to put one in an immensely divine position, which Alice took very seriously.

And so she began her tale. It was from one of her favorite volumes in the Arkis: the exploits of the Keeper Fulco. He was a sorcerer in his own realm who came upon a king who sought to pay him for his wisdom and aid in a horrible war. Fulco claimed the kingdom and its ruler were unworthy of any help, and only offered his assistance if the king could pass three tests. He sent a peasant boy to work for the royal family, a disfigured young woman to apprentice with the court physician to expand her mind, and a virtuous knight to join the ranks of the king's ranks.

According to Alice's retelling, the peasant boy saved the life of the prince he served and was praised for his heroism. The disfigured woman caught the eye of a duke who valued her for her mind and heart. And the virtuous knight gave an honorable account of a sin committed by a fellow knight and was rewarded for such honesty.

The kingdom was therefore declared worthy of Fulco's assistance in the war.

With a wide grin on her face, Alice proudly looked to her audience for reactions. Hastings proved to be difficult to please, as he had not taken his eyes off of the fire, nor changed his pensive expression since her tale began. She was satisfied, however, with Jim and Livesey's encouraging smiles —they were a pleasant contrast to Clancy's deep frown.

"What is it, Clancy? Didn't you like the story?"

"Oh Alice," he shook his head. "That's not the proper ending."

The girl crossed her arms in defiance. "Why not?"

Clancy took a deep breath, she never liked his amendments. "Because, the peasant boy did serve the young prince, but the prince did not thank him for saving his life. He quickly forgot the heroic act and continued to treat him poorly."

Alice's nose wrinkled in distaste, but he pressed on.

"The scarred lady worked for the court physician and did learn an exceptional amount of healing and medicinal practices, but she did not get love. While administering medicine to the ill child of a duke, she was turned away by the Duke's wife because of her hideous face. She so repulsed the child and the Duchess that the Duchess insisted that the busy court physician administer the medicine himself."

Alice made a noise, but Clancy ignored her protests.

"And the knight...he did tell the truth and reported the killing to the king...but the evening after the guilty knight was punished, the other knights took the honest knight from his sleeping quarters...beat him horribly, and left him to bleed out...alone in the forest."

Clancy glanced to the ground, saddened by the truth of the account.

"When the king finally went to Fulco, he asked about the three tests—unaware that they had already taken place. Fulco told him that his kingdom was doomed. His people failed to recognize and appreciate beauty and value in the unlikely, bringing about their own downfall."

"Well, that is certainly a dreary alternative," Livesey commented, leaning back on his propped arm.

"It is a cautionary tale—and those seldom have happy endings," Clancy pointed out.

"Nonsense," Alice argued. "Any story can end happily if you want it to."

Clancy shook his head again. "No, Alice. These people did not make the right decisions, so things ended very badly for them."

Pouting, Alice placed her hands on her hips. "I like my story better. We can just rewrite your version. We can forget the original and move on with the happy one. It's much better anyway. Anything can change."

Hastings tossed another piece of wood into the fire, bringing the conversation to an end. "You might want to get some rest," he offered. "I'll take the next watch."

It had been quite a day, so our weary castaways did not take long to fall into a fairly deep sleep. Our Keeper and his prisoner were the only two who stirred. She had a suspicious lack of curiosity in Alice's fairy stories. For the duration of the storytelling, Ava had turned her head away, whispering to no one. While he couldn't understand her incoherent mumbling, he was too wise to assume she had gone mad.

As the others drifted off, Hastings stood and chose a seat closer to the shifty witch. The sound of his movement drew her eye.

Ava crossed her legs with subtle eagerness. Several scrutinizing seconds passed, consisting of stares and silent questions. At last, in her smokey, honeyed timbre, Ava spoke. “I am sorry...about Lorelei.”

“No, you're not,” Hastings countered.

She shrugged playfully. “Nah, you're right. But, I won't sincerely apologize for taking care of myself. I did what I had to do.”

“Hm, I can see that.”

Intrigued by his shortness, her smirk deepened. “You're very unlike most of them. And you're so...uncomfortable with the fit of that jacket. It does seem a bit small. Your broad shoulders are practically bursting underneath that leather.”

Her flirtation did nothing to sway him, and this piqued her interest all the more. She angled her chin upward, looking down her nose at him. It was his turn to study her, and she was up for the challenge. Boldly, she adjusted her chest and her gaze settled.

"You don't even want it." He broke eye contact as she spoke. "How hard did the scribe have to work to get you to put the blasted thing on? The opportunity for authority, magic, an unspeakable power to fight for such a cause—and you don't want anything to do with it."

His mouth teased a painfully entertained smirk, but he remained composed, molding a small clump of sand between his fingers. "Sometimes survival means minding your own business."

"Well," she chuckled softly in amusement. "Tell me, is it difficult to be so indifferent...all of the time? Must be freeing. No sides, no alliances, no cares. You answer to no one and have no expectations or obligations. No one is constantly pulling your strings...you're free..."

Ava trailed off, speaking more to herself than to Hastings. Catching herself, she cleared her throat and straightened her back.

"I suppose, after all the mistakes and misfortunes trailing behind you, it's just easier to be indifferent. I mean, how much disappointment and slaughtered enthusiasm can a man take before apathy naturally sets in? After all, you're only human."

"As are you," he related, tossing the clump of sand into the fire.

"Just a couple of survivors, aren't we?" Her eyes followed the clump of sand and then lingered. "I work for a serpent to continue existing...and you put on a magic jacket." Her gaze returned to show the flame they captured. "See? Not so different."

He shrugged. “Hm, perhaps. Still some fairly distinct differences.”

Ava wrinkled her nose and snickered. “Oh yes,” she clapped her hands giddily. “Let's compare, shall we?” With her right hand, she once again framed the side of her face, stretching her pointer finger and thumb along her jaw and cheek. On her finger, the Keeper could see two darkly tattooed rings, one on the base and another, the mid-section. “I think in pure numbers, I'm still winning...but you're catching up.”

She jutted her chin toward his right hand, which he quickly covered with the left. Her jab elicited the desired response: his jaw clenched, and his smirk hardened. She took the fun out of their little dalliance. He swiftly recovered, however, clearing his throat of regret and reclaiming his fortitude.

“Minor details,” he shrugged again.

It thrilled her to see the belittling of past sins. He hid it well, but spotting pain in others was a particular talent of hers.

She laughed softly. “Minor, yes. And you could easily remedy that...you do have too much of a hero in you, though. No matter how much effort you put into deceiving yourself, it's nearly impossible to destroy every ounce of hero. What you don't extinguish yourself, Korbl takes advantage of. It's how he works, you know? Even with reluctant warriors, like yourself. There was a sliver left in you...and Lorelei brought it back to the forefront of your thick shell. Women can do that. We're demons, and we're good at it,” she released a proud exhale. “I hope you've learned something—I'm sure you have; you're a clever one.”

He caught a glimpse of her ears twitching as if listening closely for the whispers which had presumably kept her company. “You're not so dull, yourself,” he returned.

She raised a brow. “Are you impressed?”

“I wouldn't go that far. Despite your venom, you seem to defy the Scada archetype. You're not as thick as the rest of them. No doubt thanks to your apparent mentor.”

“And what do you know of my mentor?” she encouraged, tilting her head curiously to one side.

“*Raw, natural, awesome power*,” he enunciated and leaned in. “You're not threatened by it, you're in awe. The two of you studied the same material. Mastered the same approach. You outgrew him and went on to study under the master himself. Not that I blame you—he was a novice compared to you. Easy to dispose of, too.”

“And they said you've stayed in the shadows all these years,” Ava narrowed her eyes.

“I have. Your methods are not as mysterious as they seem.”

She released a frothy chuckle before retreating, ever-so-slightly, and reassessing. “And what of yours? I remember hearing of you. The young Regent who slayed the dragon and saved the princess, all on his own. O'Leary had finally found his prized Regent. When do I get to witness it for myself? The slaying of a dragon. Guiding troops. Outsmarting a troll.”

“Oh come now,” he teased with a smirk. “You're hardly a troll.”

She laughed fully this time, but Hastings's eyes darted past her. Off in the distance, some ways down the stretch of the beach, he could have sworn he saw Ryder, his own personal apparition, waving his arms to the sea as if signaling a ship.

Hastings knew better than to assume he was mad, despite however many times he had heard it from others. But, in an altered state of mind, he had discovered a method which, when exercised, enabled him to see the face of one he had lost to war and carnage. His loyal batman on the battlefield, Patrick Ryder. The good die young, it is believed, but young Ryder's death was never confirmed.

He only ever appeared to Hastings, and he only ever sought to interact as Hastings saw fit. The sight of him flagging a ship and then promptly disappearing the moment his eyes met his was unsettling. He was tempted to call out to him, but he stopped himself.

Instead, Hastings's eyebrows wrinkled deeply.

Ava carefully followed the Keeper's troubled gaze, seeing nothing but noticing everything. Another devious smirk spread across her face, twisting whatever softness was beginning to set in.

"Ah, Keeper, your demons are showing."

17

Treasure Island

Upon acquiring the correct bearings, Spyros and Bastien sailed their ship of miscreants successfully to their intended destination.

Silver was rightly impressed by their seemingly divine knowledge of the realm. Treasure Island did not seem as foreign to them as it ought to have. They knew every curve of the coastline as the ship floated along the shallows when they neared the island itself.

To the surprise of both native and foreign personages alike, the island was not uninhabited. According to the altered writings of the realm, a reasonably significant individual is said to have taken up residence amid the wilds of Treasure Island, but there was never a record of mystical creatures.

The Wanderer approached large boulders resting in the shallow waters. They were members of the landscape that had never before shown themselves. And perched atop each rock was one or two beautiful women with long hair, beckoning eyes, and colorful fins instead of legs.

"Sirens," Bastien exhaled in exasperation. "Someone's cheating."

"Ah," Spyros snarled. "I knew they didn't belong. Myk's got his tricks, but we're gettin' to this island whether these fish like it or not."

And then they sang.

The sirens opened their smooth lips and out danced the most intoxicating melody these uncultured pirate ears had ever heard. Each crew member gradually fell under a spell, abandoning their duties to get a better view of the beautiful creatures.

A drunk fellow, by the name of Mr. Arrow, was so enticed that he attempted to climb over the railing of the ship, intending to swim to a boulder and embrace one of the angels. The fool fell into the water, and in his drunken daze, could not manage to stay afloat. The entranced Scada who remained on board showed no interest in retrieving their colleague and instead kept their smitten eyes on the sirens while Mr. Arrow flailed in the water.

Even Spyros failed to look away—though his resolve was somewhat lacking, so I suppose this comes as no surprise. Bastien, however, was only momentarily lapsed in his focus.

The lone siren who sat on the closest rock, with a metallic fin of silver and gold, and an air of authority, was the only one capable of capturing the brief attention of this broken Keeper—for his desires resided wholly elsewhere. Her golden hair spread wildly in the wind, lending a beguiling background for her perfectly sculpted face and deep grey gaze. She lured his eyes with her voice but captured them with her words.

"Another consumes your heart," the siren crooned. "But she has chained you, and your Master will pull you to your destruction. You need only prove power over yourself...before those chains tighten beyond hope of relief."

For a painful moment, Bastien dipped his mind into the siren's words and nearly drowned. The truth of them choked any words of rebuttal. Mentally coming to, Bastien drew his pistol and fired a bullet through the siren's chest. At the falling of their queen, the other sirens shrieked and lunged for the ship, but Bastien's dark magic flung them back into the crashing waves.

The wounded siren grasped for a grip on the giant rock, lifting her head to face Bastien one more time. Though dying, she was determined to strike his heart once more with her venom.

"You have brought a curse upon your soul, Bastien," she swore, her voice growing raspy and faint. "What you have done...there will be...no more light."

Her sirens' fading cries were silenced as she spoke her last word. A chill rushed across the ship, snapping all of the sailors out of their enchanted stupor. A few of them felt a sudden depression and regret, losing sight of the desirable beings, but Spyros's correcting cough brought their attention back to their leader.

"Well then," Spyros quickly recovered. "To the island. Get the Englishman."

Cold and removed, Bastien was unaffected by the crowd of hustling bodies moving past him to set foot on the island. He retrieved the cowering Regent and lugged him to land.

A flat rock protruded far enough from land to serve as a dock through which the crew would seek to enter their destination. The native crew members were elated; they could hardly believe they had finally reached Treasure Island. Even Silver felt a rush of excitement. He knew this island like the back of his hand, and the prospect of finally laying hands on his treasure consumed him. Captain Flint herself flew off of his shoulder to explore the familiar territory.

As the creator of the realm described the island best, perhaps I should paraphrase his own words. A large part of the island was flooded with greyish woods, peppered with pine trees and hills that ran clear above the vegetation in mounds of bare rock. The sand of the beach was yellow and rough against the crew's feet—only for a short distance, however; the tall trees lined the island, almost to the shores, burying the appearance of what one would imagine when picturing an island in the middle of the ocean. There were two muddy rivers, which perhaps gave the isle that pungent scent of something rotten and damp.

Unusually, there were also scattered sightings of large swine scurrying across the beach. This went unnoticed by all but Long John Silver, who merely wrinkled his eyebrows and frowned.

"Perhaps Hastings wasn't so mad after all," the pirate muttered to himself.

Bastien's eyes narrowed. "What's that?" he demanded, matching the muttered tone.

Silver's head snapped toward him, unaware his utterance had been heard. He grunted, adjusting his belt as he deliberated his next words. "Flint wasn't gonna share his loot with any man; we all knew it. He took a few men with him to bury it—for security. All of us suspected he'd kill 'em before he got back to the ship." He paused and stepped closer to the nearest pig. Something about the pig's big eyes felt familiar to him. "None returned. Not Flint, not any of 'em."

Spyros waddled up beside the two men. "What? What's happening here?"

Bastien watched Silver bend down to look the pig in the eye; his face settled as he realized the pirate's suspicions. "They didn't kill each other off. What happened to them?"

Clearing his throat, the pirate shook his head. "Well... there were no pigs on this island when I last came."

"What does that mean?" Spyros pressed, forcing his inclusion.

Silver stood upright and breathed deeply, placing his hands on his sides. "We left. There was a shriek....louder then yer little ears could imagine. The waves picked up, and the crew thought a storm was comin'...so we sailed off. No Flint and no treasure. And that was the end of it."

"Stay clear of the trees," an ominous voice hummed over the breeze, almost inaudibly, followed by a chilling shriek.

Bastien drew his weapon and took a few steps ahead. "You said Hastings wasn't so mad after all...."

"Hastings?" Spyros repeated, imitating his colleague and drawing his weapon. "What's the Keeper got to do with it?"

Remaining indomitable, Silver sighed again. He glanced around at his men and signaled for them to gather in closer to him—which took some time, as the ominous voice had struck such fear into their hearts as to render them frozen. The recognition of the ghostly voice terrified them. Their eyes darted to one another and then finally rested on Long John Silver.

"There's a witch on this island," was all the explanation the pirate offered.

A long pause followed his statement. Another shriek sounded, followed by a crashing in the distance. Using what limited knowledge he had, Spyros sheathed his weapon and rolled his eyes.

"Oh, please," he scoffed. "You lot stay here—Silver and Bastien, bring the Regent and follow me!" Then, in a lower, secretive tone, he added to Bastien, "It's just the marooned pirate who wants cheese."

"Pardon?"

"His old crew marooned him when he tried to lead them to Flint's treasure and couldn't find it again. Least in the original. Gunn, they call him. Ben Gunn. Been here ever since. He misses the taste of cheese."

Bastien stared at Spyros strangely, but Spyros moved forward. Silver cautiously followed the Scada leaders, keeping his wits about him. Spyros led them through the wooded terrain until he came to a small hill. Hiding at the top of the hill was the presumed cheese-loving culprit. He was a smallish man with burnt skin, black lips and a wild face. He seemed to have been there for years, as evidenced by his worn and tattered clothing.

"Gunn!" Spyros barked.

Silver raised his eyebrows and whistled at seeing what had become of his former crew mate. Gunn had always been talented at mimicry and had humorously spooked his old crew with the uncanny imitation of Flint's voice, seemingly from beyond the grave. He had been amongst the few selected to help Flint hide the treasure. Silver was kept silent by the notion that Gunn had somehow survived whatever curse Hastings claimed befell their other cohorts.

Gunn shriveled in fear when Spyros came into view, but even more when Spyros gestured for tall and intimidating Bastien to apprehend him.

"Curse you, Silver," Gunn bit hoarsely. "I knew yer greed would drive ya back here."

"Where's the treasure, scum?" Spyros demanded.

Gunn tightened his mouth in defiance. "I don't know what yer talkin' about." Suddenly, he released a loud squawk, as if Captain Flint herself was projecting her fowlish caw. "Where's the treasure?"

Bastien recoiled for a moment, suspecting the man had completely lost his mind, before he twisted Gunn's scrawny arm behind his back, exposing the scars on the palms of his hands. "Don't feed us that tale; we know you moved it."

"He moved it, did he?" Silver went along.

"They don't know wut they're sayin'," Gunn grunted in pain.

Just as Spyros's temper began to flare, Bastien bent Gunn's hands, so his palms were visible. His skin was burnt, and not from the sun like the rest of the man's skin. Bastien smirked, embracing the upper-hand he now gained. "You wanna try that again?"

Spyros peered at the burnt palms and moved his snarling face inches from Gunn's. "You idiot. You tried to pick it up, didn't you? We don't give a rat's arse what you did with the rest of the treasure. Where'd you drop that little beauty?" he nodded toward the evidence.

Gunn's eyes widened. "No one can move her rock," the poor man shook. "It punishes you."

"The witch?" Silver assumed, moving in closer to Gunn. He stopped inches away from his face, lowering his voice in menace. "What deal did ya make with her, Gunn. Why aren't ye a little piggy too, eh?"

Gunn struggled to make eye contact, perhaps due to the distraction Bastien was inflicting on his arm. "I-I warned 'em. Flint and the others...they didn't listen...they showed no respect...that's why she turned 'em..."

"You showed respect, did ya, Gunn?"

Gunn's eyes snapped to Silver's. "Yes."

Bastien lifted Gunn to his feet and patted him encouragingly on the back. "Then let's do the respectful thing and have you introduce us, shall we?"

With the phantom pain of Bastien's arm twist reminding him to keep true, Gunn obediently led the fiends through the rough island terrain to his new mistress's living quarters. Whether Ava had given Spyros the accurate map or not would have made no difference now.

This new witch's presence had altered so much of the land that it was hardly recognizable. Trees still dotted the landscape, leading them to a high plateau that shrouded them in bushes. They headed to the mouth of a river that ran near the plateau before ascending the plateau itself.

Pieces of richly colored jewels and gold coins seemed to pave their way through the grass to a snug encampment of a few wooden chairs that surrounded what looked at first like a fire pit. The closer they came, the brighter the Stone in the center of the shallow pit became. Directly ahead of them, at the head of the empty chairs, sat a woman draped in a light purple chiton gown. Her light brown hair was tightly curled and pulled to the side of her head. Beside her quaint throne was a wooden table with a large, blue teapot with a matching cup on a saucer beside it.

The woman wore a frustrated expression as she scowled at the teapot, but glanced up when she heard the group approaching.

"Hm, welcome, gentlemen," she waved lazily. She glanced at them again and, as if seeing something different this time, shook her head and sighed. "Oh, no, never mind that. You're not the welcome ones. See yourselves out." She waved again, but this time gesturing away from herself.

Spyros stopped his comrades with a determined arm and continued to step forward. "Circe," he thundered.

The woman lifted her head toward him again, raising her upper lip in distaste. "Do we know one another?"

Spyros centered his weight. "I'm Spyros."

A thoughtful finger went to her lips. "Hmm....Spyros?" She shook her head. "No, I don't believe we do."

"The Master stopped you from turning me into a rat," he seethed.

"Ah-ha!" she clapped her hands together. "The rat! Now I remember. That was quite funny, wasn't it? Allora didn't think so, but I got a good laugh." She chuckled to herself. "You were Cromer's little sidekick, weren't you?"

"We were equals," he corrected, his temper boiling. Bastien's stifled snicker behind him was not helping his shattering ego.

"Hm, I don't recall that being the case." Circe leaned back in her chair and refocused on her teapot, lifting the lid to check on the contents. "I remember Cromer...he had such intriguing eyes...like an adolescent wolf. Clearest blue I've ever seen. And then that fiery woman with the hair...Ava, I believe she was."

She raised a finger and waved it slowly in a stirring motion, watching the liquid in the teapot stir along with it. "Ah, she was a fun one. But you...I don't recall you making too much of a splash." Taking a small spoon from the table, Circe dipped it into the teapot and sampled her progress, only to release a chilling shriek of disappointment. "Not again!"

Bastien glanced at Silver and smirked as the sorceress returned to stirring with an expression of such determination that one would think her very life depended on perfecting the flavor of whatever beverage she was concocting.

"Just give us the Stone, woman," Spyros groaned in annoyance.

"You can't..." Distractedly, she looked up at them, ready to shake her head again. But she paused when her eyes settled on Bastien. "Oh, you-you could," she pointed. Given another moment of observance, Circe soaked in the stains on Bastien's leather vest, and then sighed and waved away her previous statement. "Oh no, never mind again. I forgot. This batch had better work." She went back to stirring but kept an eye on Bastien. "Honey, I don't know what O'Leary told you, but you can't pick up the Stone either..."

Bastien frowned at her assumption and watched her pause and consider.

"Hm, wait...honey. That could be good." And she waved her opposite hand, magically adding the sweet new ingredient in hopes of achieving perfection. "I would offer you some, but I'm not one for sharing."

"We don't want yer tea," Silver spat, shifting his weight toward Bastien.

Circe's glare bore into him with more force than a falling anvil. "Tea?! How dare you! I never drink that leaf water; I don't care how natural it is," she wrinkled her nose. She lifted the lid once more and took another sip. "This is Gingerbread Sap," she explained, smiling at her success. "My good friend Locasta brought some to me after doing some good deed for that fellow John Dough. The funny pastry gave her part of his leg."

Delicately, she poured herself a cup and sat the teapot back down to admire her work. "Locasta's all right," she went on. "I did much prefer the Witch of the East, though. Shame about that whole house incident. Unlike her sister, she could have been Avalon material. Tsk. But, as it turns out, the Great Elixir in this provides a constant supply of flavor for my sap. Simply needs to soak just right…." She took another satisfying sip. "Ah, so much better than leaf water. Keeps me happy and spry."

Spyros was quickly irritated by her lack of focus on the matter at hand. He stomped his metal leg and took another aggressive step forward. "We're here for the Stone and nothing else, so just hand it over, witch."

"Well you can't have it," she merely shook her head and sipped.

Gunn rounded the small pit and stood just close enough to whisper into Circe's ear. "They brought a crew, ma'am," he informed her nervously.

Circe shrugged idly; her eyes closed to enjoy the Sap properly. "Didn't do them much good last time, did it? I only spared some because I was given strict orders not to attack the ship with a Regent onboard."

Silver cocked his head to the side and breathed, "Hastings knew. The blaggard."

"We have a Regent this time as well." Bastien dragged the trembling Jackson to the center by the collar. The poor man wrung his hands together. He couldn't take his eyes off of the lazy sorceress. Non-threatening as her posture seemed, the presence of her wandering pigs maintained enough threat to fill his heart with dread.

"Do you?" Circe opened her eyes, lowering her cup only slightly. "I didn't sense a speck of Alden presence when you so rudely intruded." Her curious gaze found Jackson and his clear nerves, making her laugh. "Oh, honey, they don't make Regents the way they used to, do they?" she threw her eyes at Bastien as she said this, hoping he'd join in her amusement. "He can't have it either."

"He's a Keeper, isn't he?" Spyros pushed Jackson to his knees, closer to the Stone in the pit. "We brought him to claim what's his and we defeated the fish you had guarding the island."

"My fish?" she scoffed. "You are most definitely not Cromer and Ava. Much to learn. The sirens were here for the same reason I am. Though I must say, this whole sisterhood thing The Lady has set up for us seems to be generally beneficial for all. Favors done, favors returned." She lifted her cup slightly and took another sip. "No, they were the first line of defense, so I wouldn't have to interact with your kind. They must've been called away, because here you are."

Sighing to herself and pouring a little more Sap in her cup, Circe continued, "I suppose she knows what she's doing. She reminds me of myself when I was young, you know. Wisdom for the ages and such an authoritative presence. We women can be quite catty—give us the title of Queens, and suddenly we all have better things to do. But no one denies

The Lady. At least the pirates have been entertaining." She waved her arm toward Gunn and her wandering pigs.

"Just grab the Stone, Jackson," Bastien groaned. They were losing time; the longer Ava was left on that island, the less likely Bastien felt he could accomplish his assignment.

"Go on and try it," Circe challenged. "What harm could it do, right Mr. Gunn?"

Jackson's hands shook as he fixed his gaze on the Stone. The strange markings it bore set it apart from the stones surrounding it. It was above the ground, being previously removed from its burial place. Ever-so-slightly it glowed a subtle protective barrier around itself.

Jackson was in awe.

Finally, he had seen it. The Stone. The Soter Stone. The one thing a Keeper could use to dispel Korbl from any realm. The one thing that could bring physical weakness to the Dark Master himself. A power strong enough to weaken Scada magic, even without being wielded by a Keeper.

Its divine origin was evident and even a little blinding. This Stone is not the one dear Caverly wielded to defend many realms in his reign. This one was new and unique. Its power and purpose remained the same, but this one belonged to one Keeper and one Keeper alone.

"Pick it up," Bastien shoved the Regent.

Desperately obedient, poor Jackson closed his anxious eyes and very slowly reached for the Stone. The moment his skin made contact, however, his lungs released a loud and shocking yelp and he flew backwards. His back slammed onto the ground behind him. Spyros rushed to him, but not out of concern. His face was twisted with rage as he snatched the Regent's burnt hands and scowled with such deadly fury that tears began to sting in Jackson's eyes.

"What the devil is this!" Spyros howled.

Circe cackled, setting down her teacup and clapping her hands together. As she clapped, Jackson instantly morphed into a whimpering swine, wailing in pain and surprise.

"Fifteen!" she counted loudly. "Welcome to the island, Jackson."

With impulsive frustration, Bastien crouched down and reached for the Stone himself. His conspicuous eagerness bit him, as his skin was just as unacceptable to the Stone as Jackson's. Spyros continued to swear—first at Jackson, and then Bastien.

"What's wrong with you!" he spat at his colleague. "If this maggot couldn't do it, why would you?"

Stung by his overzealous hope, Bastien remained silent and stumbled backward. He didn't know why he would have been any different.

Circe continued to cackle; it was all too amusing. Her laughter reached an uncontrollable level. As she worked to catch her breath, Spyros advanced, rounding the pit to get to her.

"This is your doing," he accused, waving a threatening finger in her face.

"Oh please," she panted, steadying herself. "I told you that none of you could touch it. And yet both of them still tried. What made you assume that I could? I have no need for it anyway. Only the Arch Keeper can touch and wield the Soter Stone. Though it would be incredibly entertaining to me if you and your ugly mug attempted it yourself."

Spyros's entire face wrinkled tightly. "This is Ava's doing."

Circe sipped her sap once more, moistening her dry throat and recovering from her amusement. "I wager she didn't tell you your little plan was not well thought out. They don't make villains the way they used to either."

Enraged energy filling his frame, Spyros clutched the hilt of his sword—which the sorceress Circe did not take lightly.

"Don't go drawing weapons in my place of habitation. You're lucky I didn't turn your tall friend here into a pig too—go on home and don't come back until you've found the real Arch Keeper." Circe stood from her chair and grimaced. "Otherwise, you'll make lovely additions to my little tropical farm."

As the villains reluctantly retreated, grabbing Gunn as they went, they heard her return to her seated position and mumble, "I'm far too close to retirement to tolerate this kind of interruption again."

When they neared the beach, where the other pirates awaited their return, Bastien pulled Spyros's arm, keeping him away from the rest of the crew. "Looks like we're down to only one option," Bastien pointed out. "She wouldn't have withheld that without reason, Spyros. Even if that reason is simply that we'd have to go back for her."

"Oh, we're going back for her," Spyros promised, clenching his fists. "Because I'm gonna to kill her."

18

The Nidlings

It felt like days passed. In actuality, it was no more than two. The Keeper was growing fidgety. All of the castaways sat in a circle, discussing possible methods of escaping the island, and Hastings's hands shook like leaves.

Clancy and Livesey ignored it, passing it off as impatience or blaming the heat. They were too busy posing strategies.

But Ava knew better. She recognized the symptoms.

"Never knew how much you needed it, did you?" she hummed, escaping the notice of the two debating intellectuals.

He looked at her with cold, desperate eyes. "Need what?"

She raised a skeptical brow. "The way you downed that pint in Tortuga...you need it. Vices are a beautiful thing." With her bound hands, she mimed drinking a mug of ale while still wearing that reliable smirk. "You chose yours, didn't you, handsome? And you chose the one that wouldn't involve bringing anyone else down with you. Sweet, in a twisted way. Once a hero, always a hero, yeah?"

Hastings scowled, stilling his hands under his arms and pacing off the anxious energy that was ready to burst.

"We just need enough power," Clancy was insisting.

"If Mr. Hastings can't even manage to produce some mystical rope to bind a captive—what makes you think he can do this?" Livesey countered. "Or is he truly the Keeper? Who's to say you couldn't be the Keeper, Mr. Clancy? You seem to know what you're doing."

Thanks to unseen whispers of encouragement, Clancy considered this and almost responded, but he was overridden.

"Oh, no, no," Alice shook her head. "Clancy would be a terrible Arch Keeper. That isn't how this works, doctor, sir. We can't just pick them."

"I could say the same to you, Alice," Clancy snapped. "You can't just point at a man you vaguely recognize and declare him the Keeper. Myk chooses them personally."

Alice aggressively crossed her arms in front of her chest. "Myk did choose him! You just haven't paid attention."

"Was this a mistake then?" Livesey posed. "If your Myk didn't choose him himself, then perhaps we have no Keeper. And if Alice is correct and the selection was subtle, then why couldn't it be you, Mr. Clancy?"

Clancy placed his hands on his hips and cast a regretful glower behind him at the distracted Keeper. Unfortunately, Alice is right," he confirmed reluctantly. "I'm not *the* Keeper, but I am *a* Keeper. There has to be something *I* could do."

Ava shook her head. "Now, now, you know better."

His nose wrinkled. He hated that she knew so much about his power. He hated that she was there. And he hated her.

"We don't need magic," Hastings finally contributed, with his back to them.

"Now he's talking." The she-demon craned her neck to see his solemn expression. The ache of withdrawal made it much more of a challenge to keep tight control over his obvious distaste. She loved that. "What Keeper needs magic to get off of a silly island? You're above that."

"Shut up," he silenced her, loudly agitated. His head pounded, sparking an uncharacteristic bout of anger.

Suddenly, his eyes narrowed, and his stance shifted. Alice leapt out of her seat, kicking dirt into Jim's confused face. Clancy, Livesey, Ava, and Jim tried to follow the exciting line of sight to see a ship sailing in the direction of the island.

It was a large ship, with dark green sails flickering in the gusting breeze.

"It's Myk!" Alice cried. "He sent help!"

Smiles spread across the faces of the stranded, but Clancy and Hastings were not so quick to rejoice. For the closer the ship came, the better Clancy's view of its crew.

They were women, of varying races, ages, and sizes—and they all bore one thing in common in his eyes: familiarity.

"Hastings," he started. "That's—"

"Myk!" Alice shouted. "Myk did this!" She jumped up and down in excitement, tugging on Clancy's arm. She couldn't understand why he wouldn't be as enthused and pleased with the rescue as she was.

Hastings immediately stole a glance of Ava's reaction. It wasn't relief. It wasn't fear. It wasn't excitement. It wasn't hope. It was a strange contortion of complacency and impatience.

"Alice, Alice, Alice, calm down," Clancy shook her off. "That's not Myk's ship."

"Then whose is it?" she abruptly stopped jumping.

"Nidlings," he muttered through clenched teeth.

Ava stood and sighed, effortlessly breaking the magical bonds that once held her hands together. "No more need for quarreling, boys." She moved past them all and walked to the edge of the beach, waiting for the ship to dock.

"She summoned them, Hastings," Clancy whispered. "I know it. We need to stay on the island."

"And then get off how?" Hastings posed.

Clancy was at a loss. "We could go back to the Arkis, figure something else out."

"You can go back to the Arkis," clarified the Keeper. "And what of the rest of us? The boy and the doctor?"

"You only lack the—"

"Clancy, I know them," Alice tugged on Clancy's shirt.

The ship floated in the shallows and a single boat, containing four female sailors, rowed to shore. The men and Alice, behind her, watched as the apparent leader of the sailors gave Ava a subordinate nod. The leader then gestured for the other three to continue and seize their new prisoners.

"Looks like it's too late," Hastings mumbled to the scribe.

Several hundreds of years ago, back in the first era of Keepers, known as the Alpha Age, Nidlings did not exist. Korbl's battles were only fought and sometimes won by corrupt men. I suppose women knew better than to get involved with the likes of him before Penthesilea came along.

The Amazonian queen, hailing from a realm of the Ancient Greek persuasion, found herself owing Korbl a debt on the battlefield. Penthesilea was a rather ghastly woman—although Achilles seemed to have taken a liking to her—however, she excelled in combat. She was so impressive and skillful that Korbl took the opportunity to intervene before she met her fate by Achilles's sword. He was able to take a much more direct interest in the intricacies of his schemes at that time. He revealed to Penthesilea her fate, had he not stepped in and saved her, thus presenting her with a deal in exchange for her life.

Simple allegiance was how it began. She and her army of well-trained female warriors fought in every assigned battle, running errands and taking care of business as was required of them. Absurdly, these women, who were created to be so strong-willed and independent of any and all opposing forces, quickly became Korbl's personal serving girls after only one conversation with their leader.

It didn't take long for each of them to gradually fall into complete corruption; even humans as indomitable as women sometimes yield to the entices of dark power.

However, even in our current story, Nidlings are not required to partake of the Scada oath since they are bound directly by the original oath made by Penthesilea herself. Leadership changed as Nidling soldiers were recruited and killed, and very few remained the same.

Medea, currently chiefest among them, was one of the earliest Nidlings who still stood. Despite her receiving the Scada oath and her historical lust for power and affection, Medea still managed to be the lesser of the two she-demons who currently stand before us in our tale, both in authority and favor.

After receiving the instructive wave of Ava's hand, Medea clenched her fists as she obeyed. It was her ship, to be sure, but a higher queen had set foot upon it. Had she her way, these Alden prisoners would have been thrown in the brig and chained to a wall with the other one. To her chagrin, however, Ava demanded that all prisoners be given leave to walk freely about the ship.

Medea received little more than a flippant wave, while the honor of the first respectful form of acknowledgment went to a young woman of a familiar description.

Her amber hair was a mere two shades lighter than Ava's own rusty locks, giving the two women a striking resemblance. Her sandy brown eyes, however, were remarkably unstained. Their height and build varied slightly, as she stood a few inches shorter than Ava herself, but what most surprised the onlookers was their warm greeting. Ava placed an affectionate arm around the young lady's shoulders, taking her on the pedestal above Medea.

Medea scorned the woman, who clearly understood her own favor in Ava's eyes. The young woman stood with a confidence that was only empowered by Ava's careful encouragement.

"The journey wasn't easy; the sea was not on our side," the woman reported.

"I'm sure the reason is obvious," Medea put in snidely.

Ava turned back to Medea with raised eyebrows. "It is, is it? Don't pretend to know the sea, Medea. Very few of us really can, and you're not the natural here, are you?" She then looked back at the woman at her side. "Don't let it lure you. We'll be keeping as close to ports as possible until we reach our destination."

The Keeper's glare followed her until she entered the captain's cabin, where Medea sat brooding at her desk. When she heard Ava enter, her young red-haired friend trailing behind, her dead eyes didn't even lift to greet her. The tension in the cabin was palpable, but Ava was unmoved.

She had changed out of her male attire and into an ensemble worthy of the warriors who called this vessel home. Ava's small waist was hugged by a long leather wrap, securing her white peasant blouse tightly to her figure, with her bare shoulders peeking out of the top. A colorfully layered skirt draped around her, inconsistently covering her legs and the collars of her black heeled boots—some pieces of fabric even skirted along the floor behind her as she walked.

"If you're here to bark more orders...."

Ava's lips curled, as they do. "I know it's your favorite thing, Medea. If you were better at it, I wouldn't have to do it for you."

"If you're so skilled, how did you let yourself get caught? I shouldn't have had to come rescue you at all, O Great One," Medea mocked. But, Ava's arrogance did not yield.

"Hm, you amuse me," Ava sneered, waving for her friend to close the door behind her. "I need your room."

"And why's that? Your little dog-boy didn't even come with you this time—"

Ava silenced her with a dark flick of the wrist. "Marin," she acknowledged the redhead. "There are some things you should know before embarking on this maiden assignment of yours..."

Marin eyed Medea before taking a seat in front of the desk. "By all means."

"Why you would bring her with you on the high seas is beyond me, Medea. I thought you were cleverer than that," Ava muttered to the Nidling general.

"The Master said to keep her on hand. You're the one who called us to the seas—"

"Stay clear of the water, Marin," she cut Medea off. Marin nodded in understanding; she had heard this before and was always so careful to heed Ava's orders.

"She's not a fool, Ava," Medea rolled her eyes.

Standing directly behind Marin, Ava stopped circling and snapped her eyes to Medea's. "No, but you are. But don't worry, you won't be in my way for long." She cocked her head to one side, asserting derisive authority.

Medea could do little to argue. She knew her place—she didn't like it, but she knew it. It was a position she was unaccustomed to before becoming a Nidling.

A sorceress of royal blood, she married Jason of the Argonautic Expedition, was betrayed and left for another woman, and then killed her own children in a fit of rage. Yes, she was not one to surrender to anything less than complete control. And yet, here she was. She was an underling, a lackey, and fighting with one so powerfully dominant as Ava would get her nowhere.

"And I suppose you'll be keeping her with you now," she complied.

"Of course."

"Good riddance," Medea murmured.

"What is my assignment?" Marin grew uncomfortable with the conflict between them, her loyalty torn between her direct supervisor and the one she emulated.

Ava smirked, satisfied with Medea's submission. "Stay away from the Keeper," she said. "You've excelled in your training, but he's far too ambiguous for me to risk it. Stay as far from him as possible—he's more dangerous than you know and he can only bring damage to our...arrangement."

Ava rounded to the desk and leaned against it casually to face Marin. "I'll free you from Medea's useless influence, but you will not be venturing far on your own. You will be my shadow: close and consistent."

"Then what of the Keeper?" her pupil asked curiously. "Is he still your assignment?"

"In a sense," she replied. She pursed her lips and brought a contemplative finger to them. "I've been recently forced to alter my approach. But my influence remains."

"And how can you be so sure of that?" Medea challenged.

Ava laughed lightly. "An ally, of sorts. Nothing is more advantageous to me than the preexisting afflictions of another."

Before she could spit another word, her *ally of sorts* appeared in the center of the room. He was a young man, fair and lanky, with absorbent eyes and a tight mouth that held secrets. His skin was nearly translucent, while his crossed arms made quite clear his defiance.

Medea sat back further in her chair, soaking in the sight of him. "And who might you be?" she posed.

"Whomever you like," was the tart reply.

"Who is this?" Marin frowned.

Ava sighed, rolling her eyes back. "Someone who was supposed to show some patience for just a few moments longer." She took a seat behind the desk, tilting her head in Medea's direction. "He's nearly as bad as you are."

Right before she shot back a vicious retort, Medea considered. "This is your grand asset." She looked him up and down, not entirely unimpressed. "Why have we never heard of him?"

Ava shrugged, idly studying her wristbands and the burns surrounding them. “You were never meant to. But I don't believe in wasted talent. Every asset should be stationed where they are most useful. He can appear without being seen, so long as I allow it....and that's beneficial.”

“The ideal messenger,” Marin assumed. “That's a clever idea.”

Ava leaned back in her chair and beamed at her. “Of course it is. Naturally, he must be used appropriately and with great discretion. But you certainly are a reliable little errand boy, aren't you?”

The young man rolled his eyes. “I always am.”

“Where did you come from?” Medea posed, somewhat aggressively.

“His origin isn’t relevant,” Ava interceded before he could answer. “Only his skillset.”

The Nidling sorceress quietly considered the development and cleared her throat. “Always so resourceful, Ava. It's a wonder you don't put all of your assets to good use; perhaps you'd already have this assignment completed.”

Ava glanced at Marin, but contently settled. “Timing is everything, my dear. And the best work takes time.”

19

Enemies in Strange Places

Heroes band together. Clancy would tell you it was on principle; the heroes in the stories he spent years organizing always banded together to show strength. Now that he was forced into circumstances such as these, he would probably admit that it was just as much for comfort as it was solidarity. He and Alice clung to each other for hope and kept Livesey and Jim close at hand. They sat clustered on the steps where they were left to fend for themselves.

Hastings, however, stood to survey the ship.

"Be wary of this crew," Clancy warned them. "We're no safer here than we were on that other infernal ship. No doubt you're feeling perfectly safe here, though, aren't you, Hastings?"

"Leave Mister alone," Alice tapped Clancy's knee in reprimand. "You know better. Besides, I've read about some of these ladies. I don't think they're all bad."

"If they're all together, why don't they all have those... dark marks around their eyes?" Jim inquired.

"They're not all Scada," Clancy answered. "Only those who want the dark magic bother to take the oath and become slaves. But that doesn't mean they aren't dangerous. Sometimes the fence-sitters are only one lean away from destruction," he hinted in Hastings's direction. "Take caution, Hastings. Ava is likely leading us into a trap."

"We're already trapped, Clancy," the Keeper pointed out. His surveillance rested on one Nidling in particular as she left the captain's cabin to resume her duties.

Clancy grimaced. "Well, stay away from them, all the same."

Hastings chuckled to himself at the scribe's ignorance. "Clearly you've never been in a war." He leaned in closer to his handful of allies and lowered his voice. "There's something to be said for knowing your enemies. And being stuck on a ship with all these...fence-sitters...well that's the perfect opportunity to find one to lean our direction, now isn't it?"

"The man has a point, Clancy," Livesey added softly to Hastings's philosophy. "Perhaps he's not as incompetent as he seems."

"That's because he's not!" Alice insisted.

"Oh, Alice," Clancy sighed. "You hardly know the man."

"I wish you would stop pretending to know him. And I wish you could just be his friend, and sometimes I wish Myk would teach you a lesson." The little girl pouted, furrowing her brow.

"You have far too many wishes," Clancy waved.

She considered this, then shook her head. "I'm quite serious about these. But it is true; I have thousands and thousands of wishes."

"There's nothing wrong with thousands," Jim assured her. "Wishes can come true."

Alice shook her head again, prepared to once again correct the boy. "No, they can't, Jimmy. Wishes never come true. Wishes are just words you say when you want something. That's just lazy."

Jim looked to Livesey, who only shrugged and suppressed a laugh. "Well, that goes against everything I've been told."

"Wishes just don't come true, Jimmy. And dreams don't come true either. Plans come true." With this vigor, she looked Clancy right in the eye, challenging him to tell her she was wrong. "And Mister has so many plans; he's going to blow your mind."

Clancy conceded for the moment, remaining silent but anxious.

As for Hastings and his "mind-blowing plans," the Keeper sensed the orders Ava had so explicitly given: Marin did her best to avoid him as she moved about the ship. But her lack of eye stains caused her to stand out amongst the crew. That, coupled with her vague resemblance to Ava and the contempt she received from the crew, all made it remarkably easy for Hastings to track her movements.

"Will there be any audiences permitted with the captain?" he innocently inquired after cornering her below deck.

"No," she snapped in alarm, attempting to slip past him, but he stood his ground.

"It's curious, isn't it?" he went on. "As prisoners, we should have some sort of guard on us. What's to stop us from escaping?"

Marin exhaled, her lips tightened in agitation. "We're in open waters, and you're obviously not enough of a threat to warrant a guard."

Hastings shrugged. "I suppose that's true. I don't see a guard being too much of a burden though. There are plenty in the crew who could be used—even you'd do."

She rested the small crate she carried against her hip. She gave up any attempt to escape him and decided to let him speak to his satisfaction.

"I've been given other orders," she patiently explained, involuntarily touching the necklace she wore. "We won't be seeing much of each other."

Hastings made a face and note of the necklace. It was a simple golden chain, but on the end hung a small hourglass. "Hm, how did the great Queen of Deceit summon you lot anyway?"

"What was your name again?" she sighed in exasperation.

His mouth curved into a teasing smile. "She didn't tell you?"

She nodded once curtly and situated the crate on her other hip. "I've been ordered to stay away from you, Mr. Keeper. That's all I needed to know. And I intend to follow those orders."

"If you said that with a little more heart," he grinned wider, "I'd be inclined to believe you."

Her eyebrows raised at the challenge he posed. "Heart or not, I'm not the best source of information anyway. Whatever it is you want to know, whatever your reason for wanting anything from me at all, you should probably find someone more knowledgeable...and more willing to give you what you want. Maybe Medea," she suggested half-heartedly. "She likes handsome men—as long as you tell her she's pretty. And she hates Ava because Ava's just...better." Swiftly she moved past him and headed for the stairs to the deck.

"At what?" he followed.

She spun around, wearing an incredulous expression. "Everything."

Despite her effort to seem disinterested, Hastings had captured her attention. He leaned lazily against the wall and began to pry further. "You know, I've been around a very long time..."

"Funny, you don't look a day over thirty," she commented.

"...and I can't think of what sort of leverage she could have to keep a girl like you so loyal. She's heinous, sure, but what's the worst she could do if you defy her? Kill you?" he challenged.

There had to be more to this woman than blind obedience. She hardly seemed the sort to cringe at a raised blade, so Hastings suspected leverage of a more grievous nature.

Marin laughed blandly and fiddled with the hourglass around her neck. "You don't know her well, do you? Threats are not her only power."

Fascinated, Hastings raised a pensive hand to his jaw, scratching it as he deliberated. "I'm starting to," his smile eased. "Sometimes it isn't actual power but just the mere impression of power."

"All it takes is a small bit of truth to make the threat scary enough to believe," Marin sighed again.

She leaned her back against the wall, holding the crate securely in front of her with one hand. She visibly wrestled with the desire to continue the exchange and the urge to follow orders.

Catching herself fiddling with the hourglass, she dropped her hand. "Ava is awfully talented."

"She is something," Hastings agreed. He took notice of her obvious admiration and added, "Don't worry, I'm sure someday you'll be as great as she is."

Returning both hands to the crate, Marin realized she had been more helpful than Ava would have liked. She lifted her chin, aimed to put him off with a glare, and straightened her back to leave. "In the meantime," she resolved, "good luck with Medea."

Hastings stood there for a moment, snickering. No need to get Marin into trouble by immediately following her to the upper deck. He paced himself; he had what he needed, and she was wrong.

It wasn't Medea.

When Medea approached our heroes to deliver Ava's orders–the prisoners were to have special accommodations in addition to their free movement throughout the ship–the others quickly went to inspect their new quarters.

Hastings was not so quick to settle in relief. Feigning complete confusion, he took Medea aside.

"Are you not the captain of this ship?" he inquired.

Her lips pursed. "Presumably. Our ranks, however, go beyond the structure of a ship."

"Ah, and so Ava outranks you on land as well as at sea," he nodded in understanding. "It's a shame; you seem more than capable of running a crew yourself."

Marin only slightly exaggerated Medea's liking of flattery. The Nidling leader smirked at his assumption, almost forgetting he was a Keeper, but then stopped herself.

"She doesn't sail and never has. She and her little fish avoid it like the plague," she snickered as if revealing a great weakness. Her eyes darted across the deck, leading Hastings to assume she was referring to Marin as well as Ava. "She may not be as infallible as she believes herself to be, but orders are still orders, Keeper."

The day was closing, the crew was nestling into their nightly duties, and the prisoners were attempting to feel comfortable in their new quarters. Clancy was skeptical of the

Nidlings's every move—even the food they served them—but Alice kept telling him he was silly. The close eye he kept on Hastings suggested that the Keeper shared in his suspicions, however.

The Keeper was a silent thinker; his guarded stance and detached behavior lent enough evidence for Clancy to feel confident in his assessment. Hastings was cryptic during the meal, however. His stare was heavy upon the youngest Nidling, yet his expression was deep and contemplative. Clancy couldn't read him. When everyone on board went their respective ways, Alice dragged him, along with Jim and Livesey, to their cabin. She was a pushy child—else he would have followed the pensive Keeper to the quarterdeck.

Hastings lingered along the walls until everyone settled. Two women manned their posts on the various decks, but everything fell silent rather quickly. Medea's cruel orders struck enough fear in the crew to prevent any lolly-gagging or malingering. It was quite a contrast to the previous ship the Keeper and his gang occupied.

It didn't take long for Hastings to identify his target. She stood alone, leaning against the railing of the ship, facing the spray of the ocean. He seized his opportunity and approached the Queen of Deceit.

"Treating us as allies does nothing to lower Clancy's guard." His voice was low and steady, even delicately antagonistic, but he wasn't in the mood to pull punches. "Free rein, special accommodations...all these niceties have him on edge."

She wasn't the least bit alarmed by his sudden approach. Ava simply turned her head in his direction, wearing that little sneer of hers. "You're in higher spirits...and we don't even have rum aboard."

Hastings glowered briefly, but his smirk quickly recovered.

"The little scribe was on edge long before the niceties," she then gibed leisurely. "But I have nothing to gain from locking you heroes up the old-fashioned way. Detaining a prisoner takes so much energy. Besides," she added, turning her head back to the sea, "I have my ways of keeping an eye on my enemies."

She glanced at his reflective glare and chuckled lightly. His confident demeanor was laced with calculation, and she was amused. "And you're so caught up figuring things out in that pretty little head of yours, it's rendered you harmless."

Hastings noticed her hands; they were rubbing her burnt wrists tenderly. Before judgment could overpower instinct, he took her wrists in his hands and wielded magic for the first time since donning the jacket. Ava's stained eyes widened; the Keeper healed her, muttering incoherent words as he did so.

Once his judgment was awakened by her shocked expression, Hastings cleared his throat and loosened his grip. His heart pounded in his chest for a good long while in surprise. Her burns were gone, and he was careful not to touch her wristbands. He treated her wounds with such intuitive expertise it appeared to be second nature to him. She stared at her mended skin without lifting her eyes to meet his. He alarmed himself, but unlike Ava, he quickly recovered.

"It's a wonder you couldn't do that yourself," he cleared the nerves from his throat again.

When she finally spoke, her tone was exponentially meticulous. "Scada magic may be just as powerful as yours, Keeper...but it is not the same."

"You meant for that," he nodded to her wrists. She tilted her chin upward, casting a curious look across her face. "Getting captured and restrained. The burns were part of the risk, and you expected them."

"Ah, inspecting my motives," she clicked her tongue. "You really are clever, Keeper. I'm afraid you may give too much credit to my gift of foresight. Scheming around my colleagues would have been simple, but I nearly forgot the scribe's powers to restrain me—and I was certain I was in no danger of you using magic. As much as I would love to take this sort of praise, I must leave some things up to chance."

Hastings scanned every inch of her face, just now noticing the scars that tickled the sides of her eyes. The dark stains almost concealed them, but the white of the scarred tissue managed to poke through in the moonlight. "No, I'd wager you leave as little to chance as possible."

The green of her eyes flashed with frenzy, firing her next line of ammunition. Pulling back and aiming carefully, she released, "You've done your part to help me with that, handsome. You're ever so reliable, avoiding your duty like the plague and all. It's just curious—there's not many who can wield the sort of dark magic that you have and still maintain that which is fundamentally pure. Sparks madness in most. Which, I presume, is why you are now so afraid of your own magic."

He shrugged off the sting. "It's not mine."

"Of course," she sustained. "You would do well to remind yourself of that, I imagine. Make certain you never misuse it again." Ava fell quiet for a moment and rubbed the now absent wounds on her wrists. "Perhaps I did have some motivation to give you free rein of the ship," she suggested. "After all, Keepers heal by nature."

"Hm, you're not the type to cave just because of a little pain." The corner of his lips tugged into a knowing smile. Her scars and the obvious blackness of heart gave him reliable evidence of a high threshold for pain.

She grinned at this. "You're getting to know me too well, Keeper," she purred, shaking her head.

"No, no, not yet," he corrected. "You intentionally frustrated an ally, only to get closer to a man you deem a harmless adversary. Either this is all fun and games, or there's much more to your little assignment than fooling me."

She snickered under her breath, almost to herself. "A Keeper. *Men* are not adversaries. They are too easily beaten. *Keepers* are adversaries. And you are only deemed harmless until you've worked out all the puzzles. The tortured genius could only remain decapitated from the hero for so long before they'd yearn for each other again. Deny all you want, my worthy opponent, but it's working."

"*Worthy opponent*," he repeated with a nod. "Funny, we were so recently just a couple of survivors."

Ava shrugged. "Hm, those distinct differences, I'm afraid. You did put on the jacket."

"That I did," he exhaled, painfully acknowledging his stance. He turned and put his back to the waves.

"And you must admit, this is infinitely more interesting," she offered. "At some point, we have to move past simply surviving, don't we?"

Her voice broke when she spoke the word *surviving*. It was evident to him that surviving was the only ground that was level between them, for that was all Hastings had ever done.

In recent history, that is.

"It is more interesting," he confessed. "I almost forgot the fun of it all."

She looked at him and grinned. "And a compelling enemy is so much more entertaining than the do-gooders with their bookshelves."

Hastings couldn't keep himself from laughing at the truth of it. As much as he admired the Arkis workers he had encountered in the past, he couldn't deny their tendency for blandness.

Alas, I can offer no words of self-defense. Those constrained to keep within these enchanted walls with no hope of adventure are frequently limited in their social skills. The plight is easily remedied, however. Some are given the opportunity to trail after determined, young children with an overwhelming sense of discovery.

"Yes, how true." Hastings fiddled with the end of his sleeve. "And a discerning Keeper is so much more riveting than a rodent...or a dog." He teased a glance in her direction.

She chuckled. "Not everyone can be both attractive and compelling. But the dog comes awfully close." She then looked fondly at her fingertips before sneaking a side glance at Hastings. "I do believe we need each other, Keeper. Keeps things stimulating. Although, those similarities we share may pose a challenge to overcome."

Hastings frowned for a moment, then shook his head. "Oh no, I doubt it. I have this aversion to betrayal–should make it easy to maintain perspective."

"Ah, of course, you do. Things like loyalty and integrity are so important to you people. That is one inherently Alden trait you claim. You did just confess to being a Keeper, so this doesn't come as much of a surprise."

Realizing he had gotten carried away and referred to himself as such, Hastings fell silent. He turned once more, leaning his forearms on the railing and welcomed the waves again as a distraction from her deep gaze. The mental sparring was motivated by the desire to study and defeat. The instinct was so natural and gradual that he almost forgot to smother it. For someone so determined to stay uninvolved, he scolded himself for pursuing the enemy as he had. The thrill was starting to drain.

"This must be a recent development, though," she rambled. "Loyalty. You've convinced yourself you have no loyalties to anyone anymore. And now, all of a sudden, those Arkis imps show up with that blasted jacket and the most irritating claim that you're a hero. That's when you decide you care about loyalty again."

"That's enough," he simmered. "Alice means no harm to anyone."

Her eyebrows lifted. "What? No defense for the pocket scribe? His loyalty to you goes no further than the seam of the jacket," she flicked the Keeper's shoulder. "He doesn't trust either of us."

"Probably because he knows better." Hastings straightened his back and faced her fully. "People like us," he pointed, "you and me–we are so ensconced in the conflict, the thrill, the game...we lose sight of who should be heroes and who should stay out of the way."

Ava observed him before responding. "Aw, are you regretting the rush already?"

His shoulders loosened, the resignation he felt settling in. "Yes, well, the more I'm left alone, the less likely I am to repeat history."

Ava's contemplative finger lifted to her lips and tapped them gently. "You did quite a number on yourself, didn't you?" A grin began to stretch across her face. "That's why you've resisted for so long. Can't say that I blame you," she shrugged her finger away. "Once you choose a side, there's no going back."

"You're good," he chuckled. "Taking small pieces and talking them up like resolute facts while hiding the fact that you don't actually know what you're talking about."

"Oh, well said," Ava applauded. "I do love when you pick me apart like this. Except for this time I have a more reliable source. You had an enemy, as you are well aware, with whom I was once rather close."

Hastings narrowed his eyes. He noticed the murmur in her tone, and it was not one commonly used in praise or anything of the like. "An enemy?"

"Yes. And he still lives...right here," she leaned over and tapped his forehead. "It's what he does best, isn't it?

Hastings lowered his head slightly, understanding her inference. "You say that as if he's your enemy too. Quite a downgrade from *mentor*."

She considered this. "Sometimes enemies lurk in strange places. As it is, in my case, not all antagonists are enemies." She turned her head away from him once again, trying not to look him in the eye. "Thank you, for that."

"For what?"

"You could have killed me on that island. I betrayed you and you spared my life. Even healed my wounds. You probably shouldn't have. Myk would be so proud."

"I shouldn't trust you," he agreed. "And I don't. In fact... I don't even know why I'm still speaking to you." A teasing smirk flashed across his face.

"As I said, you're getting to know me too well. I'm not going to have any tricks left. I'll be telling stories you won't believe anymore."

"Oh, I'm sure you'll come up with something." They shared a moment of amusement, smelling the sea salt and allowing themselves to ease their guard.

"I certainly hope so. The unbelievable makes for the best stories."

He angled his body toward her inquisitively. "What is your story, Ava?"

His question seemed to startle her. She stared blankly into his dark brown eyes. "I...I don't have a story."

"Of all the stories you so carefully fabricate, you can't find your own?"

Her lips tightened, keeping her secrets safe but betraying their depth. Hastings frowned, studying her face. He saw an expression he had not seen on her since she'd been Lorelei. It was soft and vulnerable.

In the theme of such a sudden countenance, Ava quickly lifted herself on her toes and kissed his lips. Before he could react, she pulled away, her eyes darting everywhere but his face. Her jaw clenched as tightly as she inhaled.

Clearing her throat almost mechanically, she left him. He placed a balancing hand on the railing to steady himself. He exhaled deeply with deliberation.

She was trying to throw him off, he decided.

But then, the more he thought, the more he speculated. Her candid honesty was not entirely uncommon for a manipulator of her skill.

But the urgency and alarm she had just displayed...he hardly knew anymore. His trust remained safe behind locked doors, but he suddenly felt a strange understanding toward her. The conniving harlot had laid her cards on the table, and his mind went over and over each card, and each lying face until he had her memorized.

Despite the seemingly permanent barrier between them, his engrossment in deciphering her was now heightened.

20

An Elusive Asset

Silently, the vixen's lip curled. She could have congratulated herself heartily. A kiss from an Arch Keeper. It was quite a feat, and might have only been accomplished by one so efficient as to take advantage of moments of vulnerability, I presume. In all the years I've known Ava, I've never met someone as capable as she–her every action was highly motivated.

She idly rubbed her wrists as if the memory of his hands still burned. Her return to her cabin was mindless. When she heard footsteps, whether from ahead or behind, she paused, expecting the Keeper's voice. Instead, there was nothing. Curiously, she stepped backward through her cabin door.

"Ah, that fresh kill glow," a voice presumed.

Ava spun around, a blast of instinctive flame shooting from her hand. The shadow from which the voice came blocked her defensive blast with one lazy gesture.

"It's always so becoming."

He lit the large candle on the desk, illuminating what the darkness hid. Ava suddenly grinned wildly and with such excitement that she practically skipped into her lover's arms. Korbl kissed her passionately; they had not seen each other since she began her adventures as Lorelei.

"Just couldn't stay away," she hummed. "Did you enjoy the Aerest's execution?"

"Hm, thoroughly. Bastien did well."

"He aims to please," she sniggered.

Angling his head back, Korbl raised a knowing brow. "Yes, but not to please me, I think."

"You question his loyalty." It wasn't a question; she halfheartedly flashed a concerned frown, knowing the answer before it needed spoken.

Korbl released a dark chuckle and an eye roll, tracing her back with his finger, keeping her reined against him. "I question his priorities. I fear you did too good a job, dearest."

"Isn't that why you keep me around?"

"Hm...that's not why," he lightly kissed her eyelids. Korbl's dark, deep-set eyes burrowed past her fiery exterior.

"Just keep him on a tight leash."

Her grin grew devilish as she reached to stroke his jaw. "Shouldn't prove to be much of a challenge." She moved to the desk, smoothly escaping his grasp.

"Your last effort proved effective," he noted. Captivated, his eyes followed her to the chair as she reached to open a drawer and pull out another candle. It was not the light of the candle she craved but the flame. "I don't think he could ever be parted from you."

Her smug mouth and shrugging shoulders pulled together in arrogant unison. "It's what I do." She waved a finger over the wick of the new candle, igniting the flame and watching it burn. "But, I can't be given all the credit. It certainly helps that he's a hopeless sap."

Korbl slipped his hands in his pockets and relaxed his tall frame, gazing as the dark beauty's fingertips skirted across the burning fire, lighting her eyes with adrenaline and release. Slowly, he stepped toward her, not wanting to break her idle focus.

"A fool is easy prey to a pretty romantic."

Ava snickered, still watching the fire singe and absorb into her skin. "I must say...it's my favorite role. Tenderness and sincerity bear the most entertaining results. Although," she briefly inhaled the smell of the ash, "I've found a new thrill in haunting..."

Korbl lifted a brow. "Haunting?"

"Well, when presented with the opportunity for an elusive asset to move about to and fro at my bidding, I'd be a fool not to—"

"What elusive asset?" He abruptly stole her attention from her fingers back up to his eyes. They were earnest and demanding. "Who are you using, Ava?"

She paused but a moment before breathing easily and responding. "My love, your little sprite has been rendered dormant for far too long—why keep someone so valuable locked up where he's of no use—"

"I told you he was not to be used!" His shadow grew against the wall behind him, darkening what little light the candle provided. "I ordered you to leave him be," he hissed.

Swiping her hands into closed fists, Ava looked more intently into her lover's eyes. She didn't see the anger that was found in his voice.

She saw fear.

"Who is the sprite, Korbl?" she whispered. He didn't answer, but his brow deepened. "Do you even remember anymore?" she went on. "Who is he?"

Slowly, his shadow slithered back down to the appropriate height, his face softening. "No one of your concern," he promised her.

"I thought all of this was of my concern," Ava challenged. He may have calmed, but his Queen was just getting started. "Have I misunderstood how we're running things? Or have you forgotten that as well?"

He leaned over, placing a hand on each arm of her chair, and secured a rigid grip on her wrists. For only a brief moment, he curiously paused in hesitation at the newly mended feel of her skin, before lowering his voice with heavy resolution.

"Don't you dare question me; I taught you better."

Unmoved by his intensity, Ava slid her wrists out from under his grasp and crossed her arms in front of her chest. Her glower gradually eased his tight muscles. She didn't need words to pose her rebuttal.

"I needed him," she then stated unquestioningly. "This Keeper requires more than a pretty face and lovely words. He requires a more unique touch—remembrance, stimulated demons...the sprite has been invaluable. What would you have me do?" She steadily rose from her chair, causing him to take a step back. "Pull him out, now that I've come so far?"

Though he may have retreated, his stance remained immovable. The curious side of him that Ava had historically conjured allowed dysfunction but never cruelty. His flared temper could only inflict so much.

"He will be returned to his prison," he told her. Before she could rebuke him, he held a warning hand toward her. "If I am defied, Ava...dearest...not even you will be exempt from the consequences."

Sharply, his dark Queen swiped the flame and sat back in her chair. The grimace she now wore was focused fully on the candle before her. Her discontent left him unsettled. Korbl carefully moved to the back of her chair, lightly kissing her neck. But she hardly responded.

"If my hands are tied, how do you expect we best him?" she muttered, still toying with the flame. "I never lose, Korbl. But if you had your way, I'd fail terribly."

He kissed her head, letting his lips linger for a moment before murmuring, "You worry too much, dearest. You can't possibly fail. It's not in your nature."

Haughtily, she cleared her throat and straightened her back, moving her head aside to look up at him. "He has a Regent, a Storyteller, and a jacket. If he ever comes to accept it, this Keeper could do infinitely more damage than the ones before him. And you're arrogantly sitting around, limiting my resources."

"You can't fool me, Ava." Korbl lowered his head to match hers. "You've already arranged your contingency plan..."

Suddenly Ava's grimace faded into resignation. Her shoulders relaxed and her cheek welcomed another passionate peck. She released a throaty chuckle. "I always do."

She lifted her wrists, as if presenting her work, but upon finishing another kiss upon her neck, Korbl's focus remained on the issue at hand. He had little time for deviation.

"Who have you told about the sprite?"

Ava lowered her hands slowly; his frustration was unrelenting. "Medea and Marin were there when I last summoned him."

"Excellent," he grumbled in annoyance, smoothly placing a thoughtful finger to his lips.

"They fear my methods more than you do," Ava went on. "They wouldn't speak a word of it. But I certainly respect your need to maintain control of your ranks. That bit about my not being exempt from the consequences...that's a nice touch."

"I meant it, dearest," his eyes snapped up at her.

"Sure, you did," she pouted, examining her fingertips with abandon.

Korbl rubbed his forehead. "I don't know which I would have preferred. Your defiling of a highly confidential prisoner or your seducing an Arch Keeper."

"And aren't you just so glad that the last one didn't quite work out? No need for that jealous fury I find so attractive." His eyebrows raised slightly, but still she felt as though she could do better. "He's so deliciously different from all of the others. So complicated that not even a desirable woman practically throwing herself at him could be enough to tempt him."

Korbl straightened with a twinge of resentment. "Hm, I much prefer the straightforward type," he began to pace.

Ava smirked in amusement. "Does his complexity intimidate you?"

"Intimidate, no," he faced her. Now she had him. "Exasperate, most definitely."

"Come now," she encouraged. "The complex player is so much more fun. The last one was so dull. No dimension, very little challenge. This one's more captivated by the game rather than the attraction. Your sprite made that game all the more interesting, but it's still just as good, I suppose. Now there's no knowing which of our threats the Keeper will try to extinguish first. Will he fight to protect the Stone? Will he shield the little flower child from the Assassin's grasp? Or will he fall for my contingency plan?"

"Whatever keeps you entertained, my little flame," he chuckled.

Reminded of the fire in front of her, Ava leaned forward once again to resume her mindless game of taunting the flame. "I think, in a strange way," she continued to ruminate, "Bastien finds this adversary particularly relatable."

Stalling his pace near the door, Korbl glanced back at her, his face clouded in skepticism. "That's either a testament of the Keeper's weakness or Bastien's propensity toward treason."

"Whichever the case may be, the Keeper shouldn't be taken lightly." Almost entranced, she followed the flicker of the flame with a new fervor as she spoke. "...and I think he knows it..."

Her eyes moved from the flame to his face across the room. Korbl continued his stride, waving off her warning.

"Korbl," she made him stop. He turned to her and settled his stance, curiously cocking his head to one side. "You're being reckless. Even being here."

"There are greater matters at hand than a rebellious Keeper."

And so they had made their way to the subject of his own anxiety. Ready for the next matter of business, Ava intertwined her fingers atop the desk and waited for him to expound. When he took too long, she impatiently attempted to put an end to the issue.

"I've assured you that the Creator is not of current concern either. She's in her home realm—far from our reach, and therefore far from being our problem at the moment. She's a future threat, Korbl."

His mouth tightened. "And it is most certainly Caverly's wife?"

"How could it not be?" she raised her hands, almost insulted by the doubt in his tone.

"And you got nothing more from the O'Leary boy?"

She leaned back in her chair again, reminiscing the masterful work of her last assignment. "Only what I needed to. He was a foot soldier, darling. He knew as much about the Creator as we do. Perhaps less."

Korbl was silent for a moment, frozen where he stood. The silence intrigued Ava, but only for a few breaths before she grew impatient again. "He has her protected, you know."

Ava rolled her eyes. "Of course he does. Your brother is no novice."

"Even without magic permitted in Middangeard, intelligence should be gathered so we are better prepared. I've considered checking into it personally."

Ava stood suddenly. "No."

"No?" he repeated, advancing.

She stepped around the desk to face him head-on. "If Stella Caverly is the Creator, you can't be anywhere near her. I won't allow it."

"You won't allow it? Who's really in charge here?" he seethed. Aggressively, he backed her into a corner, propping his arm against the wall to trap her.

"You tell me," she defied.

"Is that a challenge?" He grabbed her arm.

"No, it's a defense," she flared. "You need to trust me."

Inhaling deliberately, Korbl looked her over. "It's so difficult not to," he resolved. "And you are simply ravishing when you're so concerned for my safety."

Ava's eyes narrowed as she grabbed his face again. "Well then, I must be the most ravishing woman in all the worlds."

"Oh you are," he grinned.

"Korbl..." she pushed his face away in frustration.

"Dearest," he laughed, "you needn't worry about me. I will send others to be my eyes. But I'll admit that I'm beginning to question the validity of our objective. If Caverly's woman truly is the Creator, then why hasn't Myk used her as such?"

His mistress sighed heavily. "Because it isn't her time. He's keeping her in the safest possible location—somewhere even you can't reach. The only explanation is her inherent value."

He didn't seem satisfied with her answer.

Ava sighed again. "She just lost her Keeper. No Companion can move on without being given time to recover and mourn. He's keeping her from you until she's regained her strength—that's when he plans to unleash her. And that's when we should worry. Not before."

Gently, he released her arm and relaxed his stance. "Then how do you presume we proceed, dearest?"

"Am I to think of everything?" she raised her eyebrows expectantly.

He chuckled, pressing his lips into her hair. "No, but I do so love hearing you talk. How did you get so brilliant?"

"My teacher is very attentive, albeit impatient," she hummed, letting herself grin again.

"Hm, I know. Good work takes time. As does thorough work..."

"Everything is calculated, Korbl." She kissed him. "Even our next step is in the works. Stop getting so needlessly anxious about the smallest concerns." In playful scolding, she tapped underneath his chin.

He tenderly lifted the chain around her neck, pulling the large, ancient key from under her blouse. He pressed the key to his lips and slyly smiled.

"I'm just restless without my little flame."

21

Crossfire

The Keeper did not sleep.

Hastings listened to Clancy's snores and Alice's soft singing in her sleep as he replayed every memory in his head. Every word that was spoken and every scrutinizing stare.

How much was to be believed?

How much was to be regretted?

Ava's relaxed expression the next morning was oddly comforting following the departure of her recent visitor; there was no trace of guile or mischievous agenda in their interaction. She gave a nod of acknowledgment during the morning meal, a small smile perhaps.

But nothing more.

At about midday, the Nidling ship came upon a familiar vessel. *The Wanderer* had been sailing for three frustrating days before Spyros received Ava's message from her otherworldly courier.

When the vessels aligned, linked together by two broad planks, Medea and Ava moved to *The Wanderer*, along with the prisoners, Marin and a Nidling by the name of Gerda–whom Alice recognized from a previous adventure, but I'm sure we'll learn more on that later.

Spyros stood aggressively with his fists on his hips, tapping his real leg against the wooden floor. His tall colleague, however, held back with arms crossed, eyeing the group with one part intrigue and two parts attraction.

"Ava, you slithery—"

"What, no Stone?" Ava held her hands up expectantly, mocking Spyros.

Medea moved past her, whispering something in Spyros's ear and then joined Bastien in the background. Spyros's branded wrist shot up, magically pushing Ava back, but ever so slightly.

Her response time was faster than he expected. She slammed him against the wall of the nearest cabin, slowly advancing. Long John Silver, who stood some distance away, perked up with keen interest. The vixen had revealed to him a beguiling truth, and he was sure to pay attention.

The fear in Spyros's eyes did nothing to stop his retaliation. He shouted insults and curses, which had no effect. "You should have told me, witch."

"Ah, but would you have listened?" she challenged.

Her eyes flashed with black shadows, but her face was playful and light. She was apparently not giving his threat much thought. He broke away from her, and she didn't bother pursuing. Like the rat that he was, he scurried around her, causing her to turn lazily, and stopped when he approached the Keeper and the Alden. Clancy leaned away from the smell of him, tucking Alice and Jim behind him protectively.

Spyros's target was not the children, however.

"What are you doing?" Ava asked, bored and a little inconvenienced.

Spyros grabbed Hastings, holding a dagger to his throat. Hastings frowned in confusion, looking to Ava for an explanation, but she merely rolled her eyes.

"Won't you beg me not to hurt the Keeper? Wouldn't want me doing your job for you, now would you?" Spyros prodded.

She shrugged. "I can achieve my assignment with or without a living Keeper. Can you?" For a moment, she paused, watching Spyros realize Hastings' role in his own mission. "By all means, go on and kill him; you'd be doing him a favor. Of course, you wouldn't be doing much of a favor to that Master of yours...he's not quite ready for the next one."

He stopped and considered. "You're lucky we desperately need him now," he grunted. "Now that you've meddled and sabotaged me."

"Yes," she agreed. "Forgive me for prioritizing the study of our greatest adversary over your simple retrieval of a glowing rock."

Hastings' eyebrows lifted at being labeled their *greatest* adversary, but Spyros indignantly moved past it.

"But you—"

"Sabotaged. Yes, I heard. We've both done our share of that here, now haven't we?" Her tone was condescending as if speaking to a slow child. "Tell me, Spyros, if we were both to be reprimanded...which of us would be quickly forgiven?"

His glare could have cut right through her, but her smugness was unchanged. Finally, he snorted loudly and shoved Hastings into Clancy, clearing the space between him and Ava.

"The Regent," he scowled. "Why let us waste our time with him?"

"They're talking about Jackson," Alice whispered to Hastings, as if he didn't know. She pulled at his sleeve until he looked right at her. There was fear in her eyes, the sort of fear that came with a profound loss–despite it being the loss of a man she hardly knew. It was a strange emotion for him to see in her.

Ava shrugged dismissively again.

"I like watching you run in circles. It amuses me. Even the purest Regent would have never done the trick. The Arch is the only one powerful enough to touch the Stone. As I'm sure you're aware," she looked almost pityingly at Bastien and his burnt hands, "the Stone is temperamental like that. Doesn't like being *touched*." She clicked her tongue at the word.

"Then why did we bother with him in the first place?" Bastien asked.

She scoffed and waved toward Spyros. "That was his brilliance, darling, not mine. But, it doesn't matter now. Our missions have aligned, so you will not taste failure, no matter how much I'd like to see it. It will all come much easier now."

"Yeah? And how's that?" Spyros scathed.

Ava turned on her heels, facing Hastings, Clancy, Alice, Jim, and Livesey. She made eye contact with Hastings but showed no hint of the vulnerability as she had the night before. She even cocked her head to one side with the arrogance of someone who was so clearly winning.

"Will you be fighting off Circe yourself?" Spyros challenged her. "We didn't seem much of a threat to her—perhaps she'd be much more compliant dealing with another irritating witch like herself."

"Circe?" Ava paused, placing a hand on her hip. "Hm, and I thought she was getting too old for all of this nonsense. In any case, she will be a minor obstacle. No need to fret. This Keeper will make it easy on us."

She stepped closer to him, speaking with thick perversion, her fingers tapping together excitedly.

"An adrenaline addict...who let his guard down just to taste that rush again. Even with your well-meaning and clear perspective, you couldn't help but engage. It's all right, Keeper. You can tell me I'm beautiful without selling your soul."

She smirked, and Hastings knew. *You can tell her she's beautiful without selling your soul.* Evidently, he was not the only one to have heard Ryder's voice in the tavern, clear as day.

"What are you talking about?" Spyros twisted his face in confusion, struggling to follow her revelation.

Clancy, however, was afraid he understood. "Hastings, what's she talking about?"

Hastings remained silent, his mouth tightening into a line of restraint. Swift and only seemingly impulsive, he swiped the sword from Marin's nearby hip and concisely moved the blade in Ava's direction. But her reflexes were uncanny. In less than a second, she had already drawn her weapon and blocked his attack.

The two parried and thrust until his aggression escalated. She toyed with him, casually blocking and poking playfully without any real deliberation. Just as her arrogance took the lead, his skill disarmed her, cutting the back of her hand. In the same motion, he pinned her against the wall.

With his face so close to hers, she inhaled suggestively. "Hm, that passion. I knew you couldn't control it. And so incredibly fit."

Bastien lunged nearly as quickly as Hastings attacked, aiming his sword in defense. Before he could make aggressive contact, Ava waved her hand, magically halting him.

"Stop, darling," she purred. "That won't do you any good. Hm?" She lowered her voice, making it hoarse and taunting so that only Hastings could hear. "He can't do anything to you that would cause more pain than you've already inflicted upon yourself." She lifted a brow when he didn't yield. "You've been good fun, Keeper. Just the right dose of pernicious and pleasurable—but too much pleasure makes one corruptible, now doesn't it? You're a thrill-seeker, handsome. As painfully attractive as that is, we all know the path it has led you down. And, unfortunately, our circumstances require you to stay safely clear of that path just a bit longer."

"I always have been one to play with fire," he acknowledged, in a tone far too calm for a man who just released this credible bout of anger.

Her eyes wandered to Clancy and Alice but were brought right back to Hastings's inquisitive glare. "Hm, and it is attractive."

Bastien stood down, but it was Spyros who interceded.

"Drop the sword, or these two'll be tossed overboard," he threatened, aiming a pistol at Clancy and Alice.

Alice's eyes were wide; she wasn't well familiar with guns, but she knew enough to fear when one was pointed in her direction.

"As much as I'd like to see the wretch with a few more scars," Spyros grumbled, "I need her alive."

Ava grimaced when he said *scars*.

Flashing a quick glance at Bastien, Hastings slowly lowered the blade. Never breaking his intense eye contact with Ava, the Keeper was arrested and his hands bound. He and the other prisoners were promptly thrown into the brig upon Spyros's orders. Ava watched complacently as Hastings was dragged below deck, picking idly at her nails without a twinge of conscience.

Marin, from the back of the crowd, stepped forward to get a better view of the prisoners assuming their rightful place in Spyros's brig. Hastings couldn't make out if her expression was of disagreement or appreciation. She caught a glimpse of his gaze as he was shoved down the steps, and he could've sworn she frowned.

Once the excitement settled down, Captain Silver convened with his sponsor to resolve logistical concerns. Spyros had assured Silver that he and his crew would get their treasure once they returned to the Island and when the assignment was ultimately finished–not before. As the meeting in the captain's cabin concluded, Silver hummed a stirring question.

"What is it about that woman?" he posed.

Spyros wrinkled his nose in disgust. "Why do you care?"

"Oh, I don't, sir. But she does seem to be stepping on your toes, so to speak. Why does she have so much power? Are you not the one with authority?"

"The Master's favorite can have as much as she wants," Spyros growled.

"Favorite, eh?"

"Yes," he hissed. "Only power of hers I can see is... schmoozing." He looked childishly at the map on his desk, pouting about his misfortunes seemingly caused by this she-demon.

"Well," Silver considered. "She does have charisma, don't she? Efficiency, intuition...and she manipulated that Keeper right well. Seems she has great reason to be your Master's favorite."

Spyros's lip curled. "You sound as though you admire her, Silver."

The pirate shrugged. "She's also well-endowed with feminine wiles. Any man can see that. That's her only advantage over you. I imagine you had to work your way up the ladder the hard way to earn your place as General, eh?"

He appeased the rat. Spyros grunted and sat a little taller.

"Say, how does one exactly join your Master's crew?"

Squinting his eyes in suspicion, Spyros replied, "Now you're interested? Well, I suppose there's always a spot for someone. Just prove your worth by getting us back to Treasure Island, and we'll see where that takes us."

Silver nodded and started to rise from his chair. "What's that magic rock do, anyway?"

Spyros sneered and released a breathy chuckle. "That's none of your concern, pirate. Stick to your duty without question, and you'll make a decent Scada yet."

22

Mutinous Whispers

Alice was thrown into a cell by herself. She didn't like being by herself. The brig was smelly and damp, and not nearly as welcoming as it was when she visited Jackson previously.

In the cell beside her, Clancy sat with his knees up to his chin and firmly held his nose between his pointer finger and thumb. Alice scooted closer to the bars that separated them.

"Psst," Alice beckoned. "Psst, Clancy."

Clancy sighed, still holding his nose. "Alice, you don't have to *psst*. I'm sitting right here."

"I know," she whispered. "But there are strangers, and I don't want them to hear me." Warily, she pointed at the slumbering prisoners with whom Clancy shared a cell.

"It's just Jim and the doctor."

"They don't know about the book," she shushed. "I think he should read it."

The Keeper sat brooding in a cell of his own, the third of the three cells, at the far end of the corridor.

"Does he have it?" Alice pressed.

Clancy rolled his eyes. "It's in the jacket."

"You should tell him to read it."

"I can't tell him everything he should do, Alice," he snapped. "He knows what has to be done. It's his fault if he fails to do it."

"But he needs to be told."

"Alice," he warned.

"But, what if he reads it and doesn't understand it?"

"Then he'll read it again until he does. If you don't learn something from a book, then you're not reading it right. He's clever enough to figure out that much."

Alice paused. "Why do you hate him?"

Clancy unplugged his nose and stared at her in surprise. "I don't hate him."

The little girl crossed her arms indignantly. "Well, you're acting quite rude, in any case."

"I'm not—" Clancy started, before catching himself in a shout. He inhaled and exhaled slowly before he continued. "He's gone and done it again, Alice. You saw how easily he trusted her," he waved a spiteful hand. "Even I would've known better. She had already lied to him once and he just let her right back in. He's a loose cannon—and if he can't keep it in check, then there's no hope for him."

"Clancy," she quietly scolded. "He's learning. Maybe he likes people better than you do."

The scribe chuckled. "No, that's definitely not it. He's just another one who falls for her tricks. More reason, I think, for us to find another Keeper."

"No," Alice pointed a stern finger at Clancy. "It's him, and there's nothing you can do about it, you silly boy. I like him, and Yonas likes him, and Myk likes him. So he's staying."

Clancy rolled his eyes. "You can't speak for Yonas and Myk, Alice."

"But they agree with me," she crossed her arms confidently. "The jacket wouldn't fit him if it wasn't for him."

"Just because it fits his frame, doesn't mean it's his."

Her aggravated squint turned into a glare at the scribe. "Stop it, Clancy. You don't know who he is."

"Oh, and you do?"

Alice sat her back against the wooden wall behind her and closed her eyes. "Of course I do. His story told me it's him. You just didn't read it right. You're not the boss, so it doesn't matter what you think."

The crashing of the waves against the side of the massive ship, combined with the extended length of the brig, prevented Hastings from hearing the exact words exchanged between the two, but he understood enough of Clancy's misgivings to be entertained.

Hours had passed, lulling the anxious prisoners into a tense sleep, but Hastings's mind got the better of him. The ocean was typically so calming to him, but he could hardly hear it. His mind was far too engaged.

Truth and lies have moments of confusion when they are dangerously close to the same thing. He and Ava knew that better than most. What was enticing was her expertly honed use of such knowledge. It was one of the most commonly useful tools in her arsenal and one which has brought about many a downfall. He anticipated Ava's encore performance—as he anticipated the physical obstacle of her guard dog.

Why else would he have allowed so much to get out of hand? He tactically exposed just enough for her to sense vulnerability and take advantage. She may have taken the bait, but she was swift to regain footing. Only when he shifted control, she masterfully took it right back.

And that kiss...so perfectly timed...

Easy, mate, he told himself.

He was becoming far too interested. He was flirting with a line that was continually shifting. Ava was right, as always. He missed the challenge. The enthusiasm he thought died long ago was creeping back to life, and he knew before long, if he wasn't cautious, he'd be seeing that jacket as a limitation. He suddenly felt very self-conscious of the jacket he wore. But more than that, he felt betrayed.

You can tell her she's beautiful without selling your soul.

He hadn't seen Ryder since they were marooned—and even then he was out of sorts and out of character. For many years now, he had been operating under the assumption that his late compatriot appeared in his mind merely to chide him for his drinking habits, as he had once done in life.

Could it be possible that Ryder was more than a haunting memory? If the Alden knew where to find him, perhaps the enemy had kept him under their observance for longer than he believed possible.

As productive as his brief musings were, Hastings snapped out of contemplation upon hearing the descending feet of Marin the Nidling.

They were quick and determined, minding Ava's explicit prohibition. She darted to the crate of apples stashed around the corner from Hastings's cell which doubled as extra kitchen storage. Marin attempted to walk on her toes, hoping to avoid catching the attention of the captives. She was not successful. Moving gracefully was not a strength that came naturally to her—losing balance, she fell into the wall.

"First day with the new legs?" Hastings muttered, shaking off his haunted nerves.

She turned curtly to face him, wearing a smirk that would make her mentor proud. "You'd better keep yours well-planted, Keeper. There's a storm coming."

Hastings raised an eyebrow and pressed his arms against the bars in front of him, getting a better view of the Nidling. "I didn't know mermaids could go as far as predicting weather patterns."

Her back straightened in surprise. "Mermaid?" she breathed, vainly lilting her voice in feigned shock.

"Hm, and one with legs," he pointed. "Traveling by ship instead of by fin....strange."

"I shouldn't even be traveling by ship," she commented distractedly. The wind was picking up, and she could feel the waves crash against the ship. Then, clearing her throat, she tightened her lips. "I shouldn't be talking to you either. Just came for Ava's apple."

She lifted the apple for him to see the proof of her mission.

Hastings shrugged. "She certainly can't have you going home now, can she? Bringing you along is quite a risk. Isn't she afraid you'll get thirsty and take a dip in the sparkling surf?"

"I prefer land these days."

"Hm, now I know who you're supposed to be," he grinned roguishly.

Her head cocked defiantly to one side. "Supposed to be?" she challenged. She was interested, even stepping toward him, and he was ready.

"You've traded quite a bit for that pair of legs, Marin. But judging by that sparkling, melodious sound of your voice, your deal was not with the sea witch."

Marin fell silent for a moment and fiddled once again with the hourglass around her neck. "I don't know what you think you know..."

"Is it true mermaids have no soul?" he posed.

"Some of us do what we can," she mumbled.

Her embarrassment prompted him to voice further suspicion.

"There has to be more than just those lovely legs keeping you with her."

And again she fiddled. The sand in the hourglass remained still, even as she rotated it between her fingers. Hastings nodded with understanding. Of course.

How else would one coerce a follower without completely robbing them of purity?

Promise them the very righteous thing they seek.

Hastings stuck his head a little farther through the bars of the cell and lowered his voice. “Her word is only valuable so long as you are useful to her. And her method will not be long-standing. You are meant for better.”

“What do you know of Ava's methods?” she questioned.

Her tone told him she would not be easily convinced, so he took a step back. “Believe me, Marin. When a Scada goes about taking advantage of a weakness, whatever is offered to fill the void will be temporary and weak. It's already apparent; whatever lie she's told you has already taken effect.”

“And you can see that,” she doubted.

He leaned forward once more, looking her straight in the eye. “I can see that. Such beauty and such evil; it doesn't fit. And when something doesn't fit...it fights itself until something dies.”

Her eyes fell to the apple in her other hand. Deliberately, she tossed it in the air and caught it. Letting the Keeper know he was right would be a dangerous thing, and Ava taught her better. And so, instead of pouting in agreement, Marin lifted her chin for her rebuttal.

Sadly, her vain argument was interrupted.

“Marin! Get up here with my apple!” Ava's loud voice barked, from above deck.

Crunch.

Ava sunk her sharp teeth into the juicy flesh of the fruit, satisfied. She sat on a stack of crates on the quarterdeck. She was pensive and quiet. Nightfall was her favorite time aboard any ship. The late hour provided respite from the chatter of idiots which constantly surrounded her.

Being on top can be a very lonely place.

Lonely, but never silent. Her mind never slowed, never rested. Amidst her internal debates and analyses, Ava began to hear the ethereal whistling of a melody in the air. She closed her eyes and soaked it in.

The whistling stopped just as a kiss came to the crown of her head, only slightly lifting the depth of her thought. It was a soft touch she recognized anywhere. Bastien's lips lingered for a moment on her head before he stroked her hair and pulled up a crate beside her. He couldn't have spotted curious eyes, or he wouldn't have taken such a risk. She rolled her eyes at his daring, but a smile still poked through.

"You're plotting," Bastien observed.

"I'm waiting," she corrected.

He raised his eyebrows curiously. "For what?"

Ava merely chuckled.

"I am a bit surprised you haven't succeeded yet with your...usual method."

She noticed a subtle clenching of his fist as he spoke. Her chuckles turned to giggles as she straightened her back playfully. "You amuse me. Relax, darling. He isn't that sort of man. He has a lot of weaknesses, but that isn't one of them. He wasn't the least bit tempted."

"How is it he is not smitten with you?"

"He is nothing more than a gentleman. A clever gentleman, at that. Those are the most dangerous. Not only does their curiosity stop at just exploring a woman's mind, but they know better than to take advantage of a chance under a lady's petticoat. He's a very different game. Scoundrels are much easier," she laughed again. "Unless I was just not nearly enticing enough."

"That doesn't seem possible, does it?" Bastien gleamed.

"Sweet. What's important is what I learned, not whether or not I succeeded in tempting him. For once, corruption is not my game. And that's exciting."

She almost took another bite of the apple but stopped herself. She examined it intensely as if learning its story. Another wicked smile formed on her lips, and she then offered the rest of the apple to the giddy fool.

Bastien reached for it but hesitated. His eyes narrowed on the apple, briefly, and then on his hands. The familiarity of the action and a brief remembrance of a familiar face awakened his disciplined instinct to resist temptation.

"This Keeper isn't affecting you, is he now? You've never been one to shy away from an apple." She raised a brow.

Resolutely, he snatched the fruit out of her hand and took a huge bite. As if proving his determination, he threw the apple core as far into the ocean as he could after polishing off every last bit of flesh. When he turned back to see her smile of approval, he suddenly noticed her picking at the back of her hand.

The cut Hastings had previously given her with his sword was now open and irritated. Almost dutifully, Bastien tore the bottom of his cotton shirt and took her hand in his. Carefully, he wrapped the fabric around her wound, absorbing the blood and covering the sliced skin.

Ava studied his natural movement with slight curiosity. He finished and almost shyly looked into her eyes. She gave him a sweet smile of appreciation and a gentle sigh.

He cleared his throat. "What is it, exactly, you're waiting for?" he asked softly.

"The next phase," she told him, a twinkle in her eye. "My direct involvement has ended. My previous plans have been...forced into alteration. It's now someone else's turn."

Bastien smirked. "That's a relief. Finally, a chance to enjoy the show."

Ava leaned forward with a mischievous grin as if sharing a secret. "I always enjoy the show."

Bastien smoothly closed the space between them and lowered his voice. "Yes, but I enjoy the show much more when you are not featured."

"Well then," she chuckled and moved in to steal a kiss. "Wish granted."

It was tender, albeit short—for they were interrupted by the uneven footsteps of their one-legged colleague turning the corner. Quickly, they both retreated to a safe distance from one another.

"Ah rats," Spyros swore, ironically enough. "I just ruined my chance, catching the two of you in the act. It really shouldn't be this hard—you're even sloppier than the last one. But we saw how that one ended. I'm hoping for a repeat performance."

"Oh shut it," Bastien growled.

"What do you want?" pressed Ava.

"We need a conference," Spyros demanded. "In my cabin."

In the captain's cabin, away from alert ears and prying eyes, our three despicable villains convened. There, they established their grand scheme. After so many fumbles, due to lack of trust and communication, the lead in the assignment finally thought it best to create a clearer and more practical means of strategizing.

Naturally, this involved giving credence to Ava's wise suggestions. Despite his many periods of denial and defiance, Spyros knew this assignment would fail without her contributions.

"I have already chosen a location, which you would do well to approve," Ava informed them.

She took Spyros's seat behind the captain's desk and propped her feet up, making herself comfortable. He scowled at this, but she gave no notice.

"Is that right?" he challenged, sitting on a stool from the corner of the room.

Bastien stood alert near the door, paying particular attention to Ava's input. "Where?" he inquired.

"My good friend, Montresor, has a rather notorious wine cellar. One which, if his realm proves correct, is home to the corpse of his late friend, Fortunato, along with a phony cask of Amontillado." She idly examined her fingernails as she so callously referenced the murderous tale.

"What does this wine cellar have to do with my assignment?" Spyros was growing irritated already. His patience for Ava's evasive answers was wearing thin.

"Come on, you bore," she held her hands up encouragingly. "Use that small brain of yours. Montresor built a wall in his cellar. A wall which kept his burning friend captive until he turned to crisp. This isn't just any wall. This one has enough rage and hatred woven into it to make things exciting. Just imagine the possibilities."

"And what makes you think the Keeper won't use the Stone against us when he gets it?" Spyros challenged with a snort. He deepened his stance with a stubborn crossing of his arms.

"Mmm, I wouldn't trouble myself over that," Ava assured him. "I'm in the process of acquiring the necessary leverage to ensure that doesn't happen."

"How'd you expect to do that now? He won't be falling for your charm now that he knows who you are," Spyros pointed out.

"Hm, you're assuming I intended to charm him myself."

"And did you not?"

"Staying predictable for your sake would be no fun at all," she hummed. "There's more than one way to take down a Keeper, my friend, and this one requires a much slower simmer before he's finished. There's a need for a slightly purer soul than my own to keep him...usable."

"What are you saying? The mermaid, Marin?" Spyros scoffed. "If I recall, you've forbidden her from even speaking to the Keeper."

Ava eyed Bastien with a glint of mutual amusement. "You can't even begin to understand the fairer sex, you poor thing." She angled her chin in a very mighty fashion, prepared to teach him. "The one way to guarantee a woman will pursue a man is by telling her he's forbidden."

Spyros grunted, unamused by their shared expressions of mocking his ignorance. "All right, so while the fish has fun breaking your rules, we shall continue with more important matters: getting that blasted Stone behind that wall."

"You're under the assumption that your silly little rock is the greater assignment." Bastien shifted his weight subtly toward Ava, preparing for her alliance in the oncoming debate.

Regardless of the forces standing against him, Spyros puffed his chest. "A stone that gives a Keeper the ability to wipe out our very presence in any given realm? Yes, Bastien, I'd say that is the greater assignment."

"Oh indeed," Bastien nodded, resting his elbow against the railing beside Ava. "A magic rock is an infinitely greater opponent than seven lost Galdere of almighty power, who've intermingled amongst mortals in a variety of unknown realms."

"Their mortal forms should be making your assignment all the more achievable—how hard is it to kill a mortal? Or does your struggle lie in killing the wrong mortals?" Spyros jabbed.

"Just because they're able to be killed, doesn't make the job any easier," Bastien raked his fingers through his hair. "They move around more than your little stone. And if you think my responsibility is limited to the Storytellers, you're —"

"All right, gentlemen," Ava yawned. The competition was growing stale. "Sheath the swords and duel later. The crew is getting restless."

"Ah, hang 'em," Spyros spat. "They'll all be dead soon anyway. I promised them treasure, not their lives."

"All of them, hm?" Ava went back to her nails.

"Not Scada, not my problem," he said decisively. "Just you remember, harlot—the Stone is mine." He lightly rubbed his wristbands, displaying his power by causing the ship to ever-so-slightly increase in speed. "You have your part, now sit back unless I need you."

"Which you will."

"Shut it, you. I only hope you don't ruin things and wind up corrupting this one."

Ava pressed her intertwined fingers against her lips. "Oh, this one won't be corrupted a second time. He's strong enough to prevent it, but with just the right amount of weakness. He's the perfect Keeper, really. Fun, but hateful."

During her arrogant assurance, there was a muffled twitch outside of the captain's cabin. Long John Silver's feathered friend flew to her owner on the other side of the deck and parroted the keywords Silver needed to hear.

"All dead anyway," she squawked. "Not Scada, not my problem."

It was enough for the pirate to piece together Spyros's contingency plan. All the man wanted was his treasure. If it meant suckering up to Spyros, that was his plan. But now, he knew where he stood, and he knew exactly what Spyros intended for the fate of the rightful owners of the treasure.

Whatever his other motivations may be, depriving Flint's former crew of what they had fought so hard for was far from excusable. The morally ambiguous pirate began to devise his own plans for the crew. He would not crumble because invaders of his realm felt their need was more significant than his. In his calm and discreetly manipulative way, Silver went to the brig and made nice with the good doctor and young Jim.

"Jim, boy, you'll be my cabin boy again. You've done nothin' wrong," Silver told the child. "Besides, it's best to keep you close. There's no tellin' what these intruders have planned."

"Intruders?" the doctor repeated. Clancy stirred in his sleep on the ground beside him but did not wake. "But, where are they from?"

Silver shrugged. "No clue, friend. But it's better to be on the right hand of the devil than in his path, eh?"

Livesey shook his head. "What are they after?"

"Well, our treasure, of course. Which they got no right to. I mean, it was your journey to begin with, eh doctor?"

"It seems they want more than simply treasure."

Silver pretended to consider what made no difference to him and unlocked the cell to let Jim out. Before he shut the door behind the boy, he looked the doctor dead in the eye. "I don't know about you, doctor, but if I had me crew behind me, I'd be turnin' the tables to save our skins."

Livesey knew precisely what Silver was suggesting, he just never dared consider it himself. Until now. The pirate meant to reclaim their quest to Treasure Island, and he had a very particular plan.

Mutiny.

23

Read The Book

Silver's schemes were no surprise to Hastings. Seeing the pirates return from their first trip to Treasure Island without their treasure was enough evidence for Hastings to draw conclusions. There was an uneasy, disgruntled tone that settled thickly on every corner of the ship. The whispers of the native crew members told Hastings everything he needed to know—save the one thing he needed the most.

Ben Gunn hid in his cell with his shirt pulled over his head as a makeshift cave to shield him from the world. Brig conversations had become Hastings's most common means of acquiring information, so in hushed tones, he beckoned Gunn to come out of his cave.

"Hey," he called. Gunn's cell was a way down from his own, but close enough for him to be heard. Gunn hesitantly poked his head back through his shirt.

"Wut?" he croaked.

"What did it do to you?"

"Wut?"

"The Stone they spoke of."

Gunn's eyes widened again, and he held up the palm of his hands to show his answer.

"So it's dangerous...?" Hastings prodded.

"It gone and burnt me," Gunn restated the obvious. "I couldn't move it fer anythin'. Not that she let me try again."

"It was protecting itself," the Keeper assumed softly. "Do you mean the witch from the island?"

Gunn nodded solemnly, his head beginning to bob from exhaustion. "I hid from her, but she said she weren't gonna turn me into a piglet because I was funny to her."

"Okay, okay," Hastings humored him. "But this Stone–do you have any idea what it does?"

It was too late for an answer; Gunn had already nodded off to sleep, returning to his shirt cave. In defeat, Hastings sat back and analyzed the little information he had gathered. Quickly, he ordered the next crew member who passed through the brig to call for Silver. The residual respect for Hastings's former position as quartermaster was enough for the pirate to obey, and Silver was standing before the cell within a handful of minutes.

"You called fer me, Hastings?"

Hastings cleared his throat and made certain that most of the other prisoners were asleep before he began. All but Clancy were now soundly dozing. "Do you even know enough to plot a mutiny?"

"Who's been talking about mutiny?" Silver innocently inquired.

"I can make it happen," Hastings went on. "If you tell me what they're after and why."

Silver narrowed his eyes curiously. "I don't care about the blasted Stone, Hastings."

"I'm well aware. But you're after more than just the treasure."

Silver slowly smirked. "And what more could I be after, mate?"

Hastings peered his head through an opening in the bars. "I know you, Silver. If you only wanted the treasure, you would have mutinied the moment you landed on Treasure Island. Spyros was never going to cut you in—and he's the killing sort. You're not as thick as he gives you credit for. You're after something else."

"Again, mate, what could I be after?"

Without words, Hastings subtly raised an eyebrow and glanced around the visible interior of the ship. Silver caught his meaning.

"This is no ordinary ship..." the Keeper baited.

Silver grinned. "Tis not. And you know more than ya let on, lad."

Hastings relaxed his shoulders. He had him. "You follow me through the mutiny, and the treasure and this ship are yours. I'll even tell you how to control it."

"Them magic bracelets of his." Silver gave a short grunt as he shifted his weight off of his wooden leg and leaned against the bars.

"Fair enough. Then you know what you need to fight for to get what you want."

"What is it you want, Hastings? The Stone?"

"I...I need it."

Those short words pained him. He could feel the jacket gradually overtaking him. He didn't want the Stone; he needed the Stone, though he didn't know why. Whether motivated by curiosity or his renewed sense of right, his need remained the same.

"Then it'll be yours, lad. It'll be yours." Silver shook his hand, agreeing to follow Hastings's lead when the time was right and then departed.

Sighing in relief, Hastings sat back against the wall. He looked over at the only conscious soul in the brig. "Clancy," he called reluctantly but with care. His tone was still soft and reserved.

Clancy's sandy-colored head jerked up to look at him.

"Why do I need the Stone?"

This time Clancy sighed. It was not a sigh of relief, however, but more of exasperation and resignation. His uptight back slumped with continual disappointment.

"Just read the book."

24

Change of Plans

The journal's pages have a funny crinkle to them as they turn—it's almost as if the magic is whispering to you as you read. And the enchanted words speak volumes. After all, words are merely vessels for the raw human emotion we all try so desperately to preserve. As Arkis scribes tend to be humans, you can imagine the amount of sentiment trapped between all of that parchment over the centuries.

The threat was made known, and the call was answered. Conall O'Leary came in the company of his Companion and three of their young Regent sons. In addition, the Arch was accompanied by a rather spirited Regent...

And those words were all that were needed for the bitterest of his emotions to reach the surface. Hastings slammed the journal shut.

There have certainly always been Arkis scribes who occasionally leak bias into their accounts—I, myself, don't bother claiming objectivity—but the words Hastings read upon following Clancy's instructions were perhaps as impartial as they come. It was the record of a tragedy no scribe wished to preserve. Mistakes are hardly happy memories, but such is the duty of the scribe to record the events as they happened.

Hastings had done his part to push the memories out of sight, and he despised Clancy for forcing him to confront them now. Once again, he had nothing more to learn from the journal. He knew the stories. He already knew the truth in the pages. No other page changed the story—it only repeated what he refused to read. Frustrated, he tossed the journal on the damp ground beside him.

He didn't deserve to read anything useful. Why would the journal trust him with guidance after all he'd done?

"Pester someone else," the Keeper brushed off what he assumed was Ava's twisted mind magic.

Nonetheless, his thoughts were completely his own as the pestering presence he suspected had, in fact, merely spied his responses rather than orchestrate them.

As if haunting the decks of *The Wanderer*, the unknown sprite drifted to the lofty crow's nest where the Mistress of Darkness awaited him. Curiously, she sat with a dark green book lying open on her lap as she pried out its secrets. Obedient yet reluctant, her spy informed her of the Keeper's reading of the journal, including the words he read.

Ava lazily turned a page as she listened. "I will miss this," she mumbled. He frowned and she sighed. "I'm afraid our partnership is coming to an end, darling...it appears I've been reprimanded."

"You?" he wrinkled his brow.

"I was just as surprised as you are," she shrugged, closing the book. "In any case, I don't believe in wasting resources, so let's send you off properly, shall we?"

The young man crossed his arms and leaned back against the mast. "What did you have in mind?"

Ava laughed as her grin stretched. "Oh, your favorite thing. I do believe a shift in leadership is necessary–and what better way to prove incompetence than an unexpected tempest to send one's plans crashing and burning..."

Sailors are a superstitious breed of human. Ava knew this. Their luck relies on silly traditions, and the avoidance of minute details that may or may not affect the outcome of their voyages. One of the most common of these was the presence of women on board a vessel. This particular night, a horrible storm attempted to thwart their journey back to Treasure Island.

While storms are not uncommon in sea travel, there was nothing common about the nature of the waves and gusts of wind that battled the ship from every angle. Water engulfed the deck, retarding the movement of the crew. Everyone on board was thrown back in shock as the elements fought. Even those in the brig could feel gallons of water spraying through every crack in the hull. Crew members toppled into the deep, losing balance or slipping out of reach of aid.

Marin nearly fell overboard herself, while lunging for a Scada sailor—and had Ava not yanked her back onto the deck, her legs would have returned to a fin and she would have been completely immersed.

Those superstitious souls took the storm as a sign. Either they were being cursed for allowing women to remain on the ship, or someone did not want them making it to the Island. Between the loud crashing, several voiced their concerns and theories.

The young, inexperienced sailors scrambled, panicked, and vomited. The seasoned pirates and Scada maintained composure and made it to their respective posts. Eventually, of course, the storm passed, but the mental damage had been done.

"It was a creature!"

"It was the sea gods!"

"It's those blasted women on board!"

Spyros took all of this into consideration. While the crew worked to restore the ship to its original state, he pulled his colleagues aside. "What in blue blazes was that? It couldn't be a monster of any kind, could it? Do those belong here?"

"I thought you were in charge?" Ava posed critically.

"Well, yes, but...."

"Try reading a book before you conquer a realm, milksop. There was no monster." Ava picked up an apple that had rolled away from a flipped crate.

"I'll tell you what unnatural creature it was," Bastien claimed. "Someone's cheating...again."

Ava took a large bite from the apple and chewed slowly, soaking in the suspense.

Spyros shook his head vehemently. "No. He wouldn't dare. He doesn't get involved anymore. It isn't his way. I say sea creature. He could've put one in here. Had it do his dirty work for him. That's his way–laziness. Besides, he already put sirens where they don't belong."

"What?" she stopped eating the apple and looked to Bastien, who then recounted their previous interaction at Treasure Island. "You shot her? The siren."

"Yes," Bastien nodded.

Ava chuckled heavily, with only a small dose of actual humor. "Well done, love. Quick and concise. Perhaps not entirely wise and effective, considering whose attention we've managed to catch. What did she tell you before you shot her?"

Bastien paused and looked at her strangely. "Does it matter?"

Softly, Ava lowered her head to reply, "It really does."

"Oi! I still think it's the women that are to blame," a loud-mouthed pirate loudly claimed.

Spyros didn't argue. In fact, he shrugged with acceptance. Looking at Ava, he said, "Perhaps he's not far off. We could probably do without them."

"Ah," Ava pointed her apple at him. "But then you would still be scratching that balding head of yours, wondering what Korbl meant by the word extraction. It is a long word, dear." She smirked, turning the apple in her hand. "Then where would you be? Certainly not about to complete an assignment."

"Yes, but the rest of us may have been in a much better place, wouldn't we?" Hastings offered.

During the manufactured scuffle with Mother Nature, no one had noticed the cell doors in the brig fling open. Nor did they pay mind to the Keeper making it to the deck to lead the charge in regaining control of the ship. Hastings's dry contribution to the villains' banter alarmed Spyros and prompted quick realization of his failure.

Behind Hastings, Clancy and Alice stood with their drenched clothes hanging on their bodies as if on a clothesline, and Gunn with his soaking shirt draped over his head. The pitiful man was still attempting to hide from this new, unsettling world he had reentered.

"Take the prisoners back to the brig!" Spyros barked at his crew.

"Wait, wait, wait," Ava waved off the advancing men. "The Keeper stays untarnished."

Spyros put a grubby fist on his hip. "Yeah? Then what does the wise one suggest?"

Ignoring the mock in his tone, Ava sized Hastings up as she had done many times before. "I don't see why he shouldn't have free rein of the ship."

"Free rein." Spyros shook his head.

The suggestion prompted Hastings to subtly gesture for Silver to stand down in his preconceived attempts to carry out the mutiny.

"You heard me," Ava assured. "There are plenty of your goons; he won't be unsupervised. And he's bound to do more harm to himself than to us. So let him wander freely as he pleases."

Before saying another word, she tossed her half-eaten apple into the ocean and strolled across the deck to the foremast where Marin was helping one of the pirates tie crates back together.

Scada may be foolish, but they know enough to understand self-preservation. This was a trait, however, which Marin occasionally let lapse. Too much hero still lingered in her heart. But never fear; Ava fully intended to chase the remainder away in good time.

"I never want to see you saving a drowning man again," Ava privately berated. Her immediate proximity on the forecastle deck didn't startle Marin—when filtered, Ava's suffocating presence tended to herald her arrival before she could be seen.

"I'm sorry," Marin conceded. "It was instinct."

"It was an instinct that could reverse everything you've fought for; I'll advise you to resist that urge in the future."

Marin nodded. She understood what was at stake. The hourglass felt a little heavier around her neck. "I'll be more careful. Let's hope we don't run into any more storms."

"With Spyros in charge, I doubt we'll be so lucky," Ava quipped.

Marin chuckled and shrugged. "You're probably right."

"I always am."

"You really are, aren't you?" Marin commended, looking her in the eye in acknowledgment.

Ava beamed at the compliment, but her beam smoothly became an expression of reproach. "There's a reason misfortune comes to Spyros when he doesn't heed my brilliant advice. He does not see the danger of this Keeper, but you know better. The Keeper has the freedom to roam for strategic purposes—but that only means you should take even more care. Even the useless Alden shouldn't be taken lightly. Never tempt yourself with an Arch, though, love. Their souls are not like the others. Galderean souls are always more difficult to defeat—not that the challenge doesn't excite me, but patience and care will be needed..."

Marin frowned. "Galderean? What does that mean? Immortal?"

A sly smile took its usual place on Ava's striking face, but her lips remained tight. "Just don't be a fool and stay away from the Keeper, love."

25

THE BLACK SPOT

The crew felt a rush of restored anticipation as they approached Treasure Island and hurried to dock their ship once more. Everything was set in motion—Scada were positioned, awaiting the orders to perform the massacre, and the mutineers were positioned to prevent it. Spyros gathered Ava, Bastien, and the Keeper, ready to set foot on dry land. Again. However, upon entering the island, Bastien froze with suspicion.

"What is it?" Ava asked.

Bastien scanned his surroundings before making any quick judgments. "The body. It isn't here. And there are no other sirens."

"That's because we scared them off when we killed their leader, Bastien. They wouldn't dare come back," Spyros grumbled as he moved past them.

Ava remained at Bastien's side, understanding what Bastien predicted. In idle humor, they both continued to follow Spyros and the bound Keeper he held at his side. Hastings observed Ava keenly; of all the monsters present, it was she who continued to maintain his intrigue and cause apprehension.

She, however, had more pressing concerns on her mind and gave no notice to his scrutinizing stare, else she would have no doubt made a sultry comment about the Keeper's interests. Instead, her eyes quickly flickered from Bastien to Spyros to the empty air around them. Her expression was calculating and cautious, yet she still managed to maintain her usual smugness.

When the small landing party finally reached the location of the Stone, they found the base of the tree lacking.

No Stone, no disrupted soil, no wooden chairs, no teapot, and no sorceress. Nothing but wandering pigs.

Ava and Bastien sighed, their expectations realized. Spyros frantically sought an explanation.

Ava chuckled lightly. "Few things could motivate her to leave her bacon behind. Her protection detail must have ended when you failed."

"It was here! It was here before! I swear it! Look at his hands," Spyros pointed to Bastien. "He tried to pick it up! Where could it have...?"

"So what does this mean? How are we to know where it's gone now?" Bastien posed the question on everyone's mind.

"Well, gee, I don't know," Ava surmised. "Perhaps our great mongrel leader can point us in the right direction."

The nincompoop was without words. The only sound that came out was a low squeak of confusion and shock. He looked to Hastings, who merely stared at the spot and shrugged. Spyros's eyes searched Ava's face for a hint of an answer or suggestion. Instead, she gave him a condescending pout and mimicked the Keeper's shrug.

"I thought as much," Ava clicked her tongue. "Perhaps we should regroup."

And so, the four of them returned to the ship empty-handed. The crew watched quizzically as they re-boarded. Silver waited for Hastings's nod but only received a shake of the head. The Stone had not been found; the mutiny was delayed once again. Hastings's bonds were cut as another act of good faith, and the three Scada generals met once more in Spyros's cabin.

Never had there been so many curious whispers. Dick Johnson, one of the native crew members, very softly asked his neighbor what this would mean for the mutiny, but both men fell silent as their feared leaders passed them. With no further orders given, the crew—heroes, Scada, and pirates alike—stood still, waiting for what was to follow.

The generals reconvened in the captain's cabin and allowed the tension to thicken like soup. The Keeper once again hoped the journal would lend some insight that the adversary was missing—half-heartedly, of course. There was only so much faith a burnt heart could maintain. He sat on the steps beside the captain's cabin and took another glimpse at the enchanted pages.

Marin crept slowly when she turned the corner, being careful not to startle him. Before she made a sound, something on his face stopped her. Glistening in his downward eyes and rolling down his cheeks was a portion of the human experience that a siren such as she had never before felt.

Tears.

The slight backward shuffle of her feet made him abruptly slam the book closed. He had only made it through a paragraph more than his last attempt. The story had not changed. But the handwriting had.

The retelling was different.

It was softer, gentler, and mournful.

He knew the author the moment he read the first sentence. The maternal memory of her overwhelmed him, provoking tears to fall. When he sensed Marin's presence, he wiped them away and put on his more sporting demeanor to avoid questions.

"What is that?" she softly asked.

"Nothing," he shrugged, tucking the journal back in his jacket. "Just a book."

"I've never seen a book do that," she pointed at his eyes. "Were those...tears?"

He had been caught. "You're not supposed to be talking to me," he deflected.

"They were tears, weren't they?"

There was no avoiding her persistence. Bracing himself, Hastings sighed. "Yes. Have you never seen tears before?"

Marin's dry eyes dropped to her hands and appeared almost embarrassed by the question. "We don't...we don't do that."

"What, Scada don't cry?"

"Mermaids don't cry."

Hastings frowned. "Why is that?"

Marin shrugged and leaned against the railing near him. "Tears are a means for humans to release pain. Mermaids just keep it all inside until it becomes unbearable and eats us alive. The release...it's one of the many reasons I envy you humans."

"And yet," he pointed to her, "you continue to smile."

"Well, there are other brands of hope out there. That helps."

Hastings stifled a chuckle, being sure not to rouse the attention of passing Scada. "That was the least Scada thing you could've possibly said."

Marin shook her head, hiding her vaguely playful smile. "Even Scada believe in something—not all of us see it as hope, of course. Just like you. I have my hope, and you have yours."

The Keeper rose to his feet. "And what is mine, exactly?"

Without stepping back from him, Marin posed her theories. "So many things. Your friends, your jacket, that Stone..."

He couldn't hide his hesitation; he made a face that caused her to raise a brow.

"Well, maybe we don't always have hope, but we have a reason to need it. Your reason looks like whatever you were reading about in that little book," she gestured.

He smirked. "You certainly are a shrewd little mermaid, Marin. What reason could someone so highly favored and carefully trained have to hope? What more could you need?"

"Come on, Keeper, I'm sure you've already figured it out," she humored. Resisting the urge to touch her hourglass, Marin exhaled. "An immortal soul, of course."

He grinned at his newly confirmed theory. "And you think there's an immortal soul in Ava's little magic sand-glass," he assumed.

"Well it wasn't going to come from a fickle prince," she snapped defensively.

"Hm, a jaded princess," he mumbled. "How original."

Marin narrowed her eyes—an expression she undoubtedly picked up from her mentor. "You're mocking me now."

Hastings nodded, "Yes, I am." Then, chuckling, he stepped to move past her. "And you're having too much fun breaking Ava's rules."

"The Master is not going to like this."

"What is this, your first day?"

Spyros slumped into his chair, his head hanging low. He glared up at her without moving his head. The she-demon had kept so much from him; he suspected she knew the Stone would disappear all along. "You knew, didn't you?"

Ava crossed her arms and smirked, reclining lazily against the nearest wall. "Did I know the Stone had a defense mechanism that causes it to change location? No. I assumed, but I did not know. I didn't anticipate The Lady would remain quite so…involved. The Keeper's slow rise to activity must've forced her hand." Gently, she swayed away from the wall and stepped to the desk with clear intent. "Which brings us to our fresh advantage. We may not have the Stone, but we have the next best thing."

"Which is what?"

"Perhaps you shouldn't have gone on assuming your assignment was the most important. It's quite clear you don't know what you're doing. Telling you would be a waste. You throw useful information around before analyzing its benefit to you—you kill the ones you need and hold on to the ones you don't. I'm not going to have you wasting resources."

"Oi! You are on my ship, and this right here is my assignment, woman, and you would do well to respect that." He pointed a threatening finger at her from across his desk.

"Spyros—" Bastien warned. His casual lean suddenly straightened in alarm.

Ava took another step forward, unyielding, and lifted her right hand. With a clutching motion, she magically shot Spyros back against the wall behind him, choking his throat and knocking his chair over in the process.

"Only one person in existence can tell me what to do," she enunciated, "and he's much better looking than you are."

Bastien cleared his throat, his shoulders tensing as Spyros gasped for air. "Ava," he murmured.

"This is no longer about a little Stone. Its importance has slipped to number three," Ava went on. The room, dark as it was, was cast with a new sort of shadow. It was a shadow Bastien recognized and Spyros feared. "This has become so much more. And you lost all authority the moment you sailed us into that storm. Your assignment was simple enough; the new Keeper shouldn't have been a monkey wrench—he should have been an opportunity. You couldn't handle it, so now I have to clean up your mess."

She stepped even closer, tightening her grip. "If you have a problem with it, cretin, you can take it up with Korbl." Her head cocked to one side, the corner of her smirk following suit. "Though, I don't see him taking your questioning of his decision lightly. So, we won't be having a problem here, will we?"

The small airway she left open released one breathy sound. "No."

"Good." She dropped him to the floor. Her black eyes briefly glowed red as dark smoke seemed to be sucked out of his wristbands and rested in her hands. Claim over the enchanted ship had been passed, along with the understanding of under whose authority it sailed. "Now, pay attention and watch how it's done."

She didn't have to touch the door for it to swing open and make a path for her reign to begin. Bastien swiftly followed before his support could be questioned while Spyros painfully recovered from his demotion.

If The Lady is Myk's equal in splendor and Light, then Ava is Korbl's equal in beastly horror. The Darkness she carried now spread throughout every nook of the ship, practically engulfing every being in sight. Alice's glow diminished to a grey cloud, her energy drained. Every step

Ava took on the deck of that ship clicked with dread and fear that struck into the hearts of all.

She didn't have to speak for her new authority to be understood. The native crew members were petrified, including Livesey and Jim. No one, not even the Keeper, would challenge her. Eyes were full, jaws were dropped. Some even trembled.

One brave soul, however, nudged his friend Dick Johnson to step forward. Contrary to Hastings's verdict, the native sailors believed mutiny to be a remaining and plausible strategy. And Johnson drew the short stick.

Timidly, the young man stepped toward the new queen of the voyage. In his hand, he held a small piece of parchment, neatly folded. Shaking like a leaf, he handed it to her. Without question, she took it and looked down at him with condescension. Casually she opened the parchment and saw what it bore.

The Black Spot.

The omen of death.

Their sign of mutiny.

As if it were nothing more than a mere nuisance, her fierce and deadly eyes aimed themselves at her audience. She held the parchment in the palm of her hand for all to see, and suddenly a flame burst from her skin, engulfing the threat.

"I had hoped for more than a dot on a piece of parchment," she clicked her tongue. Her voice spread through the body of the ship; every soul felt the vibrations in her taunt. "I do commend the amount of fight left in you. Your mutinous leader must have given quite the pep talk to get you this far." She took one step closer to young Johnson and leaned to whisper in his ear. "You were the brave one," she hummed.

Johnson released a low and eerie groan that resonated through the very wood of the ship, which sounded like death itself. It was appropriate, of course. Death needs a herald. The she-beast daintily lifted her hand, and the crew saw Johnson's feet slightly hover above the floor below.

Ava took one step back, getting a better view of the work before her. Eyes narrowed with focus, she deliberately curled each finger slowly into her palm, watching as her victim screamed in agony. Every organ in Johnson's body suffocated with the dark smoke that could be seen in Ava's eyes, being sorely crushed at the will of the monster.

Alice hid her face behind Clancy's arm, softly gulping back the horror. Commonly shielded from such terror while peering in the Arkis's Looking Glasses, Alice had forgotten the sort of destruction and cruel ruin the other side inflicted. The student had long become a mistress of darkness in her own right, and her cold methods reflected that of her master. The smoky fire in her eye ignited, fueled by the carnage.

Johnson's last breath was drawn, and his limp body was carelessly tossed to the floor. Ava kept her deadly hand held high enough for her petrified audience to remember to whom their attention was owed.

"I am not Spyros," she spoke crisply. "There will be no mutiny. You'll get the treasure you were promised; I don't believe in wasting good help. But, if anyone cares to cross me again, I will be more than happy to make time to extinguish the problem."

Her devilish grin returned, satisfied with the expressions on their faces. The pirates were unnerved. Those more familiar with the witch's wrath were certain to avert their eyes.

Hastings studied her from the moment she stepped out of the captain's cabin. He knew something had changed, and her swift murder of Dick Johnson confirmed it. It wasn't, however, Ava's tyranny that caught his attention, but Marin's mild disturbance. When Johnson's body slumped over, making that ominous thud, Marin inched closer to the Keeper. Something inside her twinged and wrestled with personal discrepancies, all of which caused an unsettling pain in her gut.

A very different conflict took place in the mind of one who stood only a few steps from her. Long John Silver, from whose scheming originated the plot of mutiny, was beginning to alter those plans entirely.

26

An Enticing Impasse

Duties were revisited in an attempt to normalize the air of the ship; yet the removal of Johnson's body and the memory of Ava's threat kept the volume of chatter unusually low.

"This is not good," Clancy murmured to Hastings in a corner. "This is very much not good."

Hastings leaned against a wall below deck and silently tightened his lips in contemplation. Clancy strained to glean some plan or hope from the Keeper's face, but no understanding was found.

"We need to do something," he went on. "We're completely at her mercy, and we don't have the Stone. How do we expect to find it—and what if she finds it first?"

"Clancy," Hastings shushed him.

"Well, what do you suggest then? Watching a Keeper do this is very different from doing it myself—this is your job. You should be coming up with a plan."

"And if you shut up, I will."

Clancy fell quiet, sighing in reluctance.

"We are not at her mercy..." Hastings explained, "...we're at a standstill. Yes, we're on her ship, but she's as lost as we are. How do you think they found the Stone's location the first time?"

Clancy thought for a moment and then shrugged. "For a short time—very short time—they were without an Arch Keeper to keep them from it. While Ben Caverly was alive, they only had his Stone to worry about, and he kept it close. With him gone, they had to wait for a new Keeper, but a Soter Stone always calls for its Keeper. You...you were drawn to it, and they were repelled."

He gradually slowed his words, realizing that the more the facts came through, the more he knew that it was truly Hastings on whom he must rely.

"They must have gotten clever enough from dealing with the Caverlys to figure out that they need to go closer to the toxin, not farther," he concluded. "It weakens their magic because it weakens Korbl's, so whatever they plan to do with the Stone must be quite significant—they're risking their powers....and their lives just by being near it."

"Fantastic," Hastings exhaled, clapping his hands against his thighs.

"Which part?"

Hastings shrugged. "Our plan is to do nothing, Clancy."

"What?"

"Nothing."

"What do you mean nothing?" Clancy squared his shoulders. "How can we do nothing?" The scribe lowered his voice. "Need I remind you of what she just did to a man without flinching? Ava's certainly much more vicious in person than on paper."

A soft whimper came from behind Hastings's legs. Alice had been hiding around the corner, hugging her knees and burying her face. Hearing Ava's name brought a sickly feeling to her small stomach. Her skin was still greyish and dim, not having recovered from the previous morbid performance.

"You see," Clancy gestured. "We have to think of something. Alice can't go on like this and keep sailing on an enemy's ship. She's wilting, and Myk is going to have my neck if anything—"

"I said do nothing," Hastings placed his hands on Clancy's shoulder, assuring him, and then moving him out of his newly determined path. "I'm working on it. Now, excuse me."

Ava closed the door behind her with finesse, presenting a victorious grin to Bastien, who stood leaning against her desk. His posture was contemplative and expectant, with arms folded and head slightly bowed. Ava cocked her head to one side, giving him a questioning pout.

"What's making that pretty face frown?"

Bastien slowly raised his head. "He visited you, didn't he?"

She sighed. "Of course he did. He does that."

His eyes closed briefly as he sighed in controlled frustration. "Shouldn't he be staying somewhere a little more...I don't know...secure?"

Ava chuckled and ran her fingers through her hair. In one smooth movement, she glided inches from him, dragging his attention with her from the door to the desk.

"Roaming a ship where a Keeper walks free is not the wisest move," he added.

"He just can't stay away from me." Her fingers danced across his back, prompting him to stand straight and slowly turn to face her. She perched herself on the top of the desk and dangled her legs where he once leaned.

"Well, I can't blame him there," he gave a small smile. The more time passed between them, away from prying eyes, the softer his expression grew. Gently, she tugged at the lapel of his jacket to pull him closer as he spoke. "Did he say anything about the Stone?"

"We are to clean up Spyros's mess, but the Stone is only a secondary problem."

"Secondary?"

"He's still heavily focused on that Creator. Which brings me to *our* next assignment," Ava's grin doused itself in concentration.

"Ours?" Bastien raised a brow. His voice lilted with the prospect of once again partnering with the wily beauty.

She, of course, chuckled softly at this and stroked his cheek—not teasingly but with surprising tenderness. He allowed his smile to stretch just a little farther across his face as he kissed her.

"Yes, darling," she said, pulling away slightly. "He seems...uncertain of your loyalty. And I...I need to change that." Her eyes lowered in regret.

Bastien sighed once more, with less control over his frustration than before. "Why bother?"

"Why bother?" she repeated, incredulously. "Darling, if he doubts–"

"Then he's not a complete fool," he scoffed.

Ava stared him in the eye so earnestly that he took a step back. "You took the oath," she whispered solemnly.

"Yes, but not for him."

He knew that she was well aware of his motives. Ava, above everyone, could accurately sense desires as if they were her own. He knew she could use every bit of his weakness against him and toss him to Korbl like a sack of meat. What took him aback was the desperation in her face as it fell. It thrilled her to be his greatest desire, but there was such a deep fear in her eye.

"You're afraid of him," he realized.

Her smile, losing its humor, faded completely. For a painfully long moment, Ava once again tugged at him to come closer before responding.

"Oh darling..." she started. "What can he possibly do to me? Nothing." She took his hand for reassurance. "But he can do plenty to you. So please, do as I say."

Bastien watched in wonder. "You truly worry that much?"

She cleared her throat and straightened her back. "I want you more involved, so you can prove him wrong. He's concerned that your current target is putting you at risk. You're too close to this Keeper—"

"Too close?" he scoffed. "I've never met the man before."

"But you know who he is," she pointed out, taking his both of his hands in hers. "And you know who trained him. If I didn't know any better, I'd say he had O'Leary blood in his veins–and if that doesn't make this assignment sensitive for you, I don't know what could."

He tightened his lips, despising the name. Men cut from the same cloth tend to have a certain sense for one another, but Hastings and Bastien had thus far operated in stubborn denial of recognition. Their times did not overlap, but great Keepers leave their mark on those they nurture.

"Not nearly sensitive enough to influence my judgment —save perhaps contributing to my aggression. Hastings is no friend of mine; I don't care who his mentor was."

"But he fell...as you did."

"No," he snapped. "I left. He fell."

A wicked grin returned to her lips. "That's right, love." Satisfied, she kissed him again. "You left for something greater." His hand still in hers, she lifted it to get a clearer view of his wristband. Upon the leather was engraved a series of runes, spelling the name of the Assassin's target. "We need to show him that you can still face the challenge."

Bastien's head lowered. "It's not his approval I aim to earn."

Ava dropped his hand and released a heavy scoff.

"Lie to yourself as you will, darling. But don't let your believed failure be the fuel for your lies. You didn't fail with the Caverly woman. She's been placed on hold for the time being, and Korbl doesn't want to see your talents wasted in the wait. The Storytellers are your priority. But, killing the little girl won't do much for getting that Keeper to lead us to the Stone. Heroes have a tendency to go to great lengths to keep that little one safe," she touched his chin and tilted it upward. "But perhaps watching and waiting will reap some benefits."

His forehead wrinkled in confusion, but she didn't let him pursue his next line of questioning. Instead, she kissed him lightly and mumbled, "Now, go fetch me that pirate."

Her legs were propped up on the desk, and her playful eyes were aimed at their next target. Long John Silver sat across from her with equally questionable intent. Bastien, the loyal guard dog, stood in the corner behind Ava, watching Silver's every move with suspicion, ready to kill if given the command.

In my experience, Korbl's mistress becomes a rather different sort of enemy when placed at the helm of the battle, with ability and intimidation to spare. Silver sensed this and had already plotted the benefits which could arise.

"You were certainly right; you're no Spyros," he concurred. "Where is he, anyway?"

Ava chuckled darkly. "Summoned for his scolding and reassigned. Korbl is not one to give second chances. The rat doesn't do well on his own; the more authority he's given, the more likely he is to fail. Take you, for example," she pointed at him. "He consulted no one before entering your realm, and look at how it ruined him. He came to you with an opportunity, knowing hardly a thing about you. He didn't bother learning about your wife, your time on Treasure Island, how you lost that leg of yours, where you plan to rendezvous with Mrs. Silver after you've acquired your treasure, or even your disarming use of friendliness and shallow flattery."

Silver adjusted his wooden leg, raising an impressed eyebrow to the vixen. "Don't you be using your seduction tactics on me, woman," he said, settling back into his chair. "I don't crumble as easy as the rest of the crew, givin' into some strumpet, no matter how well she fills a dress."

Ava grinned. "Oh, darling, I don't have time to seduce you. No, that would take too long, and I have business to see to. I'll be taking a very different approach."

Suddenly the grin straightened into a severe line as she swept her feet off of the desk and rose from the chair. Pressing her fingers against the top of the desk, she leaned forward to ensure his eye contact.

"You and I know human nature. In this sense, we are equals. You will get nowhere by conning me into being friends. And I will gain nothing by schmoozing loyalty out of you. Wasting time on outwitting one another would be beneath us. So let's clear the air. We've established that I am not the rat. I have no reason to cheat you out of what's yours unnecessarily," she assured him.

"You'll get your treasure—and then some—and you'll be left with your little wife to live out your life as you see fit. I see no reason for any other outcome. Unless..." she stepped around to sit at the edge of the desk, "...you should choose the oath. You'd be most welcome; I like you. And we are greatly craving intelligence. But valuable assets on the outside are also useful. Your decision doesn't matter; what matters is our understanding."

"You sure are refreshing, lass," Silver finally spoke. "I'll tell you what—you give me what I want, and you'll get nothin' but loyalty from me. I promise ya that. I'm assumin' you've got a new plan for findin' that little rock yer after."

Ava pointed to him and then pressed her finger to her mouth. "Hm, that brings me to that business I spoke of. Get out, and bring me my Keeper."

Silver smirked. "Of course, my lady."

Hastings followed Silver's direction and let himself into the captain's cabin without bothering to knock. Bastien was sitting on Ava's desk, leaning over where she now sat in the chair. They were in the middle of a hushed but heated disagreement, which ended the moment the Keeper stepped foot in the room. The two men glared intensely at one another, only breaking eye contact when Ava clicked her tongue and waved Bastien out of the room. The trained lackey was unhappy, to say the least. His dislike for Hastings being alone with Ava was evident and almost amusing to Hastings.

One lazy twitch of Ava's hand and the door closed behind Bastien. Her black leather boots were propped, once again, comfortably on the large wooden desk before her, her colorfully layered skirt draped over her slender legs. She had tightened the leather strap that wound around her waist a bit, creating a tighter corset. Her white cotton blouse now hugged every sultry curve it could find.

Hastings kept his scrutinizing gaze on her. As he studied, she hovered her hand idly above the open flame of the candle that sat on the right end of her desk.

The palm of her hand burned, kissing the fire enough to sear a layer of skin. She glanced at the smoke and smoothly moved her hand in a grasping motion, magically extinguishing the flame, only to reignite the candle's wick. Her wandering mind may have been unpredictable, but her nerve-numbing habit of self-destruction didn't particularly alarm him; it only intrigued him.

"You should have kept your guard dog with you," he recommended. "Though something tells me you don't need him."

"You see right through me," Ava grinned and gestured to the chair in front of her desk. "Have a seat, handsome."

Hastings remained standing, securing a defiant expression on his face, which intrigued her.

"Do I make you nervous, Keeper?"

He scoffed a little. "Why would you make me nervous?"

"Seeing someone torn apart from the inside out tends to strike fear in most men, and yet here you stand in attractive confidence when facing an adversary who could just as easily tear you apart."

The Keeper shrugged. "There's no need to try to impress me, Ava. You're already repulsive enough."

Ava laughed in arousal and dark amusement, standing to move around the desk to face him. If he refused to sit at her level, she would gladly rise to his. Resistance to a game such as this was futile.

"Is it repulsion...or is it inspiration? Nothing fuels a Keeper more than an unfair fight. It goes against the nature of your calling, but you can't deny being at least a little impressed." She didn't stop herself until she was standing so close to him that they could feel one another's breath. "You're not afraid of me...and I can't convince you that you should be...but hopefully you're finally motivated to up your game, Keeper, and make it worth my while."

Hastings didn't respond. Instead, he squared his shoulders, resistant to her taunting monologue.

"Come on, soldier, I know there's a fighter in there somewhere."

She swiftly reached for the knife in her boot and glided the blade against the skin of his cheek. Even more swiftly, Hastings twisted her hand away, disarming and restraining her against the wall, the knife now to her own cheek. She only giggled at his sudden aggression.

"Well there you are," Ava prodded. "There's that passion I just adore. My *guard dog* isn't here this time, Keeper—you don't have a reaction to gage."

He cocked his head to one side. "Reaction?"

"I'm not as foolish as my colleagues, Keeper. Understanding the enemy is quite helpful, and I must say, I do admire your methods. Without the handsome oaf in your way, you could kill me. Well, you could try. But you won't, will you? You wouldn't kill me...no matter how repulsive you claim I am. Perhaps I'm not truly so repulsive to you. Beauty can be quite distracting to a hero. Why do you think I've survived so long? You're still just a man, Keeper. And I'm just too beautiful to kill."

He slowly lowered the knife, observing every muscle in her face as she spoke. She was in her element and had a certain glow about her while provoking a Keeper. "Too beautiful, eh? Hm, it's a little hard to see past those."

He used the tip of the blade to gesture to her stained eyes. He stepped back again, throwing the knife to the opposite wall and out of her immediate reach.

"Mm," she purred, surveying him with those sultry eyes. "You're a challenge, you are. I've had challenges before, but once they're hooked, they rarely say no to anything—no matter how many stains their leather collects." She stepped to his side, now examining the jacket. "You see, some like to watch the colors darken. They get an unexpected thrill out of seeing lights go out and shadows take control."

Slowly, she circled him, grazing the tips of her fingers along his shoulders. "But you...you were so reluctant even to put the blasted jacket on, much less do anything to spoil it. For someone so indifferent, who knew you would cling to the Light so desperately? And I wasn't even enough to make you wonder what staining that jacket would look like." She returned to facing him head-on, the candlelight reflecting fiercely in her eyes. "I'll try not to take offense to that."

"Suit yourself," Hastings shrugged.

"Though you have found beauty on my ship, I think."

"Have I?"

"You're an artist. Beauty is something you crave, something you seek. It reflects in your sketches. Tell me, Keeper. Have you sketched that little mermaid of mine?"

Hastings narrowed his eyes. It wasn't quite the direction he intended to pursue. "I suppose I have found beauty on your ship. It's a rare thing here, but I managed without even looking."

An inquisitive eyebrow raised, Ava crossed her arms in front of her chest. "Well that didn't answer my question, now did it? But..." she tapped her lips "*...you weren't even looking.*"

"Hm?"

"That was the lie. You *did* find beauty. It *is* a rare thing on this ship. Well, to you. But you were inarguably looking for it. I, apparently, came as an utter disappointment to you, so you were forced to find it elsewhere. What was it the mad Keeper realized that would turn him against me so?"

"The madness told me you're no good," the Keeper lowered his head along with his voice.

"Is the Keeper digressing?" Ava grinned. "Slipping just close enough to the darkness to talk to the shadows haunting him?"

"Hm, no," he hummed. "Not anymore. After nearly a quarter of a century of keeping me company, the haunting shadow seems to have grown tired of me."

Ava took a step backward, wrinkling her brow. "Quarter of a century?"

"But you already knew that, didn't you?" he queried, noting her slight withdrawal. "The way you pull strings and play the game, I would have thought you would have all the answers. Then again, if you did have all the answers, I don't think you would have summoned me."

"Hm, cheeky devil," she smiled for a moment, recovering from her brief stupor. "I suppose you've brought me to the business portion of this little...dalliance. Not quite as fun but productive."

Like a child told to stop playing and come to supper, she retreated to lean against her desk, still facing him. "You're going to find the Stone."

"Oh? Will I, now?"

"You can't go on pretending not to care, Keeper. You have too brilliant a mind to let these riddles lie. Why did the Stone disappear? Where did it go? There's no staying out of this now—the tortured genius within you won't allow it. You don't quite know why, but you want the Stone. You *need* the Stone. And there is only one way to get it."

"One way that you can figure out," he jutted his chin in her direction, then crossed his arms expectantly.

She snickered and pointed slyly. "And there is the intellectual drive I was looking for. You've finally accepted your role as Keeper and chosen your side—let your mind weigh the possibilities."

"You have no bearings."

"And you have no ship."

"But, I do have this," he gestured to the jacket.

"Use it," she dared him.

She took the stolen pocket watch from a small pocket on her belt and opened it for a moment, skating her gaze across it as if intentionally reminding him of how well she previously weaseled herself into his head.

"I know Keepers better than you ever could, handsome. And they all have this...this tic," she clicked her tongue, "when it's time to leave an assignment behind. It only comes when the assignment is considered accomplished. You just recently discovered what your assignment even is, Keeper. Which means, as a naturally appointed hero, you won't be able to bring yourself to leave the cause behind and execute an escape plan until you're finished. At least, in my experience. I've never been wrong before, but it's certainly not impossible. So by all means, magic your way out of here, if you think it's within your power."

"And where would that leave you?" he offered a questioning palm in the air.

Ava laughed, snapping the pocket watch shut.

"If you manage to harness the magic afforded to you, then I would gladly watch you best me. But, since we both know what you are capable of and that you are already formulating alternative plans as we speak, allow me to make a contribution: an Arch Keeper can find the Stone. It calls to you. It may be harmful to me and my kind," she went on, "but you....you have the advantage, for obvious reasons. You don't need me to find it; you need me to get to it. Unfortunately for you, you have a handicap."

"Oh, I wouldn't consider Clancy a handicap," he said with subdued humor.

Ava grinned at his wit. "Sadly the scribe is not your most crippling asset. Consider its nature, Keeper. To touch the Soter Stone, you must remain pure. You know *I* cannot touch it," she placed a solemn hand on her chest. "I'm at your mercy. I need you to cling to that pathetic Light that seems to appeal to you. Why else would I give you such freedom? I've even kept my Assassin from his prey. And that little one glows much brighter when she isn't behind bars."

Her tone was less threatening, securely matter-of-fact. "Naturally, you and I are enemies, Keeper. But I'm finding it necessary to lower our weapons and join forces for the time being." In compromise, she laid her hands upward on the desk before her. Ava's manipulation had now evolved into outright negotiation. "We both want the same thing...so shall we make peace now, and then kill each other when we find the Stone?"

Digesting her monologue, Hastings slowly approached the corner on which she was seated. Her eyes lit as he neared. "You're not after the Stone," he noted.

"Am I not?"

"Neither is Bastien." He leaned closer to her, lingering long enough to snatch the pocket watch from her hand, simultaneously snatching her complete attention and ensuring she abandoned any immediate plans of interrupting him. "If you truly were, Spyros would not have failed. You would've seen to it that the voyage to Treasure Island was a success the first time around."

"Hmm, intriguing theory," she commented.

"I'm not finished," he held up a finger to silence her. "Scada never work well together. They tend to...sabotage for their own gain. No, you and Bastien have your own ends to meet. I'm guessing yours has everything to do with me."

He paused, allowing her to respond, but she merely smirked and waved for him to continue.

"You live for control, so you're certain to impose that on every other scheme around you, forcing them into your hands." Hastings slowly circled her and the desk as he mused. "Spyros is assigned *things*—he doesn't need any more resistance than a little lost-and-found scenario already offers. You're assigned *people*—the easiest objects for you to manipulate. But what of your mutt? Surely his assignment involves more than just pandering after you in your pursuits, eh?"

Ava crossed her arms in front of her chest, enjoying this. "He's assigned people. I trained him myself; naturally, that qualifies him to handle the most challenging of assignments."

"Which inevitably intertwined with your own."

"As it is," she shrugged.

He tossed the pocket watch in the air and caught it quickly. "Interesting," he paused again. "Could it be that he needs more assistance than Spyros? And that's why keep him so close?"

"Hm, no, no," she smugly shook her head. "Even dogs have their uses. They're often used in tracking and hunting, as a matter of fact."

"Ah," he pointed the pocket watch in her direction. "Best be careful, Ava. You sound awfully close to revealing something."

Ava grinned widely, propping her arms behind her and leaning back on the desk. "Don't let that stop you."

Hastings grouped his hands behind his back and leaned forward slightly, encouraging her. "And just what might a dog like Bastien be sent to hunt for?"

Ava inhaled deeply, standing upright, and pressed a teasing finger to her lips. "Korbl was not the only Galdere to fall," she started. Smoothly, she made her way behind the desk, creating a barrier between them before giving him a taste of the answers he craved. "Nor was Myk the only Galdere to stand against him. Interestingly enough, instead of keeping his allies close, Myk cast them out, forcing them into mortal realms to wander lost, vulnerable, confused...they've forgotten who they are and what they're capable of. Pity they didn't listen to Korbl when it all began. Perhaps they'd still have their full form."

Hastings furrowed his brow. "Full form...right. Just as he does," he nodded once, then paused and scoffed.

Ava's smirk soured, but remained lifted.

"So the dog hunts Galdere," the Keeper concluded.

"All of Myk's Lost Boys," the witch confirmed with an amused lilt. "Well, Lost Girls, in some cases. So many targets, so little time." Hastings's eyes wandered away from her, deep in contemplation. "If it's any consolation, Keeper, I reiterate my previous assurance: my little hunter's current target will remain untouched so long as you and I both get what we want."

His eyes snapped back to her. "He won't kill Alice."

Ava tilted her head. "Not without my say so. You see, I'm currently allowing our impasse to work in favor of cooperation. The moment you cross me, my dog will rip out the child's throat and move on to his next target. Goodbye, impasse. Take heart, Keeper. A peaceful resolution is within reach."

She stood firmly, and all jest dissolved from her tone. "Just get me a new map, and we'll both end this happily."

27

Desperate Collusion

When Clancy found the Keeper, his calmly calculated demeanor was somehow alarming. Anger and panic surged through Clancy's veins; he could only imagine what the Keeper might be feeling. But Hastings, instead, sat on a step sketching madly. Clancy stood before him, hands on hips, waiting expectantly for the news of his meeting with the enemy.

"Well?"

Hastings's eyes never left the grainy, weathered parchment on his lap. As Clancy watched, he began to recognize the Keeper journal in its defiled state. The rules have never been clear for the care of the journal itself.

Even Albert, when granted the journal, was instructed by Myk to consider the words. Interestingly enough, the parchment was blank and Albert was left entirely confused—but nonetheless, the eventual lesson learned was this: the information it held was infinitely more important than its tangible host.

"What are you doing!?" the scribe panicked. Hastings carefully tore the parchment at the seam, separating it from the remainder of the journal.

"I need a different angle," Hastings mumbled. His hands moved across the page with grace and accuracy, but all Clancy saw was desecration of holy parchment. His mouth hung open, searching for words.

"Did you try reading it before you decided to destroy it?"

Hastings waved him off. "Says the same thing over and over again—useless to our current situation. But it's fine; she gave me the answer herself. She knew what I would do with it." His voice was still low, speaking more to himself than to Clancy. "She knew exactly what she was doing. She's very clever."

"You sound like you admire her," Clancy said bitingly.

Hastings peered up lazily to correct him. "I admire the way she plays her game. Well-matched adversaries make it all the more fulfilling, Clancy."

"Oh yes? And what is this now? You're—you're allowing yourself to be played? She's inspiring you to vandalize a precious piece of the Arkis? That hardly seems well-matched to me."

"No, Clancy," he sighed. "She said I'm an artist. This journal, it's magic, yes?"

"...yes." Clancy still didn't understand.

"This parchment, my hand..." he continued to scribble. "We'll find it as they did before. How else do you find treasure, my friend?" Before adding a final touch, he peered up at the scribe with a satisfied smile. "A map."

Clancy was not impressed. "You're saying that she gave you the answer? You're working with her then?" he accused. When Hastings didn't reply, Clancy shook his head in frustration. "I—what—have you not seen what she can do?" he stammered. "She killed a man—just by lifting a finger!"

"Eh, she used a whole hand, Clancy—it's not that impressive." The Keeper seemed remarkably unconcerned, and Clancy was beyond bothered.

"You're playing with fire."

"I've always been the type to do so," Hastings lifted a brow.

"What exactly is your intent, Hastings?" Clancy's tone hardened. "She is the epitome of evil. She murders for pleasure and betrays anyone she has to to get what she wants —she's even betrayed you a number of times, if you recall! You don't understand: in this realm, she is at her weakest because of that Stone—and still she is unyielding! No Keeper in his right mind would consider an alliance with—"

"I told you to do nothing," Hastings refuted. He stood and held the map between them. "I knew she would come to me with a proposition. We were at an impasse, Clancy; she needed us. This map is our way to the Stone, and she is currently the means. You've convinced me that we need the Stone, and now we're getting it."

"But it isn't right!" Clancy insisted. "How victorious would we be, knowing we used the devil's ship to get where we needed to go? We're sacrificing the moral standing the

Alden have always kept strong. The end does not always justify the means."

"Ah, now really isn't the time to think of morals."

The scribe shook his head once more, this time slow and with conviction. "It's always the time to think of morals."

Jim Hawkins and little Alice gravitated toward the arguing duo, finishing up one of Jim's chores for Silver. Alice spotted Albert's journal in Hastings's hand and bounded toward him with excitement.

"You're reading it! That's fantastic—it'll be most helpful, and I think all of the answers are in there too. I'm glad he finally listened, Clancy."

"Oh, he didn't," Clancy retorted. "Not exactly, anyway. I'll tell you what he's doing though, Alice. He's working with Ava."

Hastings rolled his eyes in exasperation, but Alice did not respond immediately. She looked at him strangely, giving no indication of her approval or disapproval. Jim was the one to express his shared concern.

"Mister, she's...horrible," he said in a hoarse whisper, afraid Ava might hear. "Don't you remember what she's done?"

"Oh Jimmy," Alice put her hand on her hip questioningly. "You don't know half of what she's done. She's quite scary, but you mustn't pretend you know her." She then returned her attention to the Keeper. "I don't know about her, Mister. Clancy could be right; it isn't a wonderful idea. We should wait. Myk will help us. Now that you're wearing the jacket and reading the book, he can come to help you."

"Alice," Hastings sighed, tightening the rolled map in his hands. "He helps after the Keeper has done things on his own. Right now, this is on us."

"So we're to rely solely on you then?" Clancy objected, flicking his hand in Hastings' direction.

"You can leave," the Keeper suggested. "You've done your part, you've given me the jacket—none of it is your problem anymore. Go back to the Arkis."

Clancy exhaled sharply. "It's everyone's problem. And I'm in far too deep to just walk away and let you do more damage than good."

"You're just going to have to trust my judgment then, aren't you?" Hastings patted Clancy on the shoulder before walking off back toward Ava's cabin.

"For the record, I most definitely do not," Clancy called back.

Standing at the helm, Ava gripped the Keeper-made map. The Light magic of the parchment caused a subtle burn on her fingers. Her trademark smirk rested on her savagely beautiful face, which Bastien admired from a short distance. He leaned against the railing, watching her take the lead with such determination and elegance. Then his gaze settled on the map.

"Is this wise?" he questioned. When Hastings approached the deck, Bastien stepped to Ava's side and lowered his voice. "Encouraging an alliance will only lead to his corruption. That isn't what you want," he warned.

She sighed. "You don't know him, darling. He won't fall again. Not like this."

"He watches you like a hawk," he seethed in her ear.

Giggling, she leisurely caressed his cheek with her free hand. "Mmm...no, I think the Hawk has his eye on the Fish."

Bastien glanced down the deck at Marin, who wandered slowly toward them. "Aren't you concerned she'll corrupt him?"

"Please," Ava scoffed. "I highly doubt she's capable of that. She doesn't have it in her. Besides, if all works according to my suspicion, she'll only fuel his cause."

"And if they fall in love and she becomes the Haeleth Companion?"

Ava flashed a skeptical glare. "You really don't understand mermaids, darling."

"But I do understand a bit about Arch Keepers, Ava. Particularly this one. And a mermaid gaining the love of a Keeper is more powerful than that of the average mortal—she can hardly be immune to that sort of affection. Even the soulless can fall in love."

"Aw, look at you. Still believing in fairy tales, after we've worked so hard to destroy them." She stroked his cheek again, this time with condescension. "But, perhaps you're not wrong. We should keep a close eye on her. We want him pure —but a Companionship is not exactly ideal. That would be a bit counterproductive, wouldn't it?" she clicked her tongue. "Fortunately, the value of one's soul is too great a risk. I'm not entirely concerned."

When Hastings was close enough for their voices to be heard, they fell silent, exchanging only expressions of understanding.

"You've sped up our progress," Hastings observed, noting the pace at which the ship now sailed under her control.

"A perk of being in charge," she stated. "But I am beginning to doubt this map of yours."

Hastings stepped in line and scanned the sea surrounding the ship. Marin quietly stepped up behind them, joining their chorus of frowns. There were no islands in sight, as the map suggested. Instead, the ship grazed past wood and metal debris of damaged vessels. Large, sharp rocks protruded from the ocean floor, displaying the cause of the damage. *The Wanderer* weaved through the obstacles, coming upon large chunks of shipwrecked masses and dodging the rocks at Ava's masterful hand.

"The Stone can't be here," she muttered to herself in confusion. The map lied.

She could hear Clancy coming to the deck just behind them, with Alice and Jim's small feet following. Jim dragged Livesey behind him—he had spent the majority of the voyage back to the Island vomiting and attempting to gather enough composure to move about the ship without crumbling over.

"It isn't working, is it?" Clancy shot at Hastings, careful not to address Ava directly.

To his dismay, it was she who fired the first response. She tightened her gaze at him, mentally designing an explanation based on Clancy's doubts.

"Maybe it was just misread?" Marin suggested in subtle defense.

Ava gave a quick shake of her head, flicking the ends of her fiery red hair. "Oh no. It was carefully studied. After all, the devil's in the details."

"Sometimes, so is the angel," Clancy put in, softly and almost bashfully.

Hastings inspected the seascape in perplexity. How could Light magic fail? Whatever doubts he had in his own ability should not have hindered the effect of the magic the journal's parchment contained. The possibilities raced through his mind, but Ava's solution beat him to the finish line. She angled her head toward her second-in-command.

"Throw them all back in the brig," she ordered, concise and firm. "We're done here."

Her resolution was decided, and any trace of collusion between herself and the Keeper was now dissolved. Marin's face fell. The Keeper's foolish alliance was what she feared, and it was ending just as she expected. She knew the scribe's loud rantings would be proven right.

Ava's deals never quite held the way one would hope.

"Wait—wait," Hastings stuck his hand in Bastien's face, just as he moved to seize the other heroes. "I can get it to work," he swore.

Bastien saw it fit to apprehend Hastings personally, clutching the Keeper's arm with as much tenacity and personal aggression as would be expected. But Hastings resisted him.

Ava advanced, tossing the map in Hastings's face. "You can't do it. You've already proven that. Perhaps you're already corrupted. Whatever the reason, you're even less capable than I feared. I'm now left to find the Stone on my own. You led me to believe this arrangement would work in both of our favors—you deceived me. You were just desperate. Forget your freedom, Keeper."

She threw an additional comment Bastien's way without looking away from the bewildered Keeper: "No need to be gentle with them, darling."

"You won't find it," Hastings shoved Bastien's arm away. "Not without me."

"A-ha," Ava crowed. Raising a carefully aimed hand, she lazily threatened him to make another move. "Oh, I will. And you'll just be sitting around waiting until you'll be of use to me. Don't worry. I won't let you go to waste." She nodded for Bastien to continue the arrest. "Oh, and throw her in with them while you're at it," she added, jutting her chin toward Marin.

"She has no part in this," Hastings fought.

"Oh...I think you'll find the traitor does."

Marin's eyes widened. There was something to be said for Ava's discernment. Tainted though her eyes may be, the Dark Queen saw things otherwise hidden.

Marin knew what she had cost herself, and that terrified her. Her eyes were wary but dry. But the Keeper saw the pain. He pressed his body against the bars that separated their cells, reaching for her, but her bitterness kept her face angled away.

"Marin," he coaxed.

"You've made her desperate. You pushed her, promised her help, and then couldn't follow through. This is your fault," she boiled. "She lumped me with you because I was a fool who felt sorry for you. Can you even imagine what she could do to me?"

"Marin, she can't—"

"You have no idea what she can do." She glared back at him with intense fury, but all Hastings could see was her fear. "She warned me...she warned me about Arch Keepers and I disobeyed her. You charmed your way into making me care, and now I'm going to lose..."

"I know what you're afraid of losing," he stopped her. "Even if she takes that away, she is not your only chance. There is more than one way to change your fate, Marin."

The Nidling's eyes couldn't meet his. She knew what chances she had, but she had long given up on them. Ava was a guarantee, a guarantee she feared she no longer had.

Before another word could be spoken, Bastien lumbered back into the brig and barked, "Scribe!"

"No, no, no, no!" Alice screamed at Bastien—even pulled at his arm to stop him from taking Clancy from their cell. Bastien easily shoved her aside and shut the bars behind him, dragging a stone-faced Clancy down the brig corridor. Poor Clancy had no nerve to fight back but instead went as a hopeless beast to the slaughterhouse.

I try not to dwell on the details of the gruesome happenings of the Scada's treatment of imprisoned Alden. Ava was built for malice, and her techniques of torture are that of a particularly ruthless nature. With such an extensive arsenal at her fingertips, no brand of pain was off limits. Her aggression intensified when there was no specific objective to be seen. Clancy had no valuable information, nothing she didn't already know. This was merely for the satisfaction of besting them, further displaying her blatant control.

What was done may not be said, and what was heard by his friends in the brig was just as unspeakable. Clancy's screams rang through the ship, pulling Hastings to his feet to clench his fists around the bars of his cell. Alice sobbed, and Jim vainly attempted to comfort her. The child's body shook with fear.

"Alice." Hastings, while kept in a cell of his own, was in the center of the two cells housing Marin and the other heroes on either side. Hastings tried to reach for Alice, but he couldn't fit more than his arm through the bars. In surrender, he fell to the ground and bowed his head in sorrow. "I'm so sorry, Alice. This is my fault..."

Alice lifted her head and ran to him and grabbed his hand through the gap between the metal. She hid her face in his palm, sobbing into the skin.

"I should have listened to him," he breathed, his voice breaking.

"It's all right, Mister..." she whispered to him, wiping her tears.

He grasped her hand and cupped it in both of his, wishing more than anything that he could hush her fears. The child was lying, he suspected, faking optimism so the Keeper wouldn't lose faith. It was her duty, she felt, to help him keep his Light. The Keeper's assumption was misguided, however.

In any case, Hastings had known Alden like her before: the unwavering believers who will continue to fight if it kills them. As they sat there, another steadfast Alden fought for his life, without standing a chance.

It took two large pirates to carry Clancy's limp body back down to the brig, red burns tearing up his arms. They tossed him into the corner of the big cell, causing a deep groan of pain and a feeble twitch at feeling the cold ground. His friends rushed to his side, and even Marin rose curiously to see him. He shook violently like a small, burnt tree in a windstorm, taking short, uneven breaths with each movement.

Bastien, who had escorted Clancy's carriers down to the cell, immediately opened Marin's cell. “Come.”

“Bastien, please...” she begged, closing her eyes to the beckoning hand gesturing for her to follow.

“Just come,” he repeated, almost reluctantly, grabbing her arm.

Hastings tensed, watching closely as she was pulled up the stairs. This time there were no screams, only chilling silence.

The silence was more deafening than the screams.

When Marin descended and was returned to her cell, there were no burns on her arms—nor was there any sign of physical torture. However, her eyes were twice as wide and her mouth, twice as tight.

She couldn't face the Keeper. She couldn't face anyone. Her hourglass was no longer around her neck; instead it was clutched tightly between her fingers. Retreating to the corner of her cell, Marin stared blankly for several moments before reaching to tie the hourglass back in its place.

Bastien's expression moved from reluctant to smug as he neared Alice's cell. "Alright, little one. Your turn."

He flung the door open and grabbed the girl's arm. Clancy, weak as he was, could hardly lift himself to rise and fight in her defense.

"Bastien, you bast—!" Hastings shouted with fury.

"Oh shut it, Keeper," Bastien flicked his wrist once more, shutting the cell door behind them. "Your turn will come, I'm sure. Be patient." Bastien winked at him and carried Alice off.

Bastien lugged the petrified child into Ava's cabin, presenting her as the next victim. Alice sat on the floor, hugging her knees, as she watched Bastien lean over to mumble something to Ava, who sat cross-legged and comfortable on her desk.

Alice hid her face while he spoke. In all of her imaginings of exploits, being so close to the Dark One, or his mistress, was not something Alice had considered. The bone-shaking horror that overcame her was a sensation she had entirely forgotten since her last adventure.

"Tread lightly. Children are impressionable," he whispered.

"Don't let her human shell fool you, darling," Ava purred aloofly. "She's hardly a child."

She jutted her chin toward the door, signaling for him to leave. As the door closed, Alice's head peeked through. The two sat in silence for a moment, Ava allowing the anxiety to set in before words were wielded. To her surprise, it was the little girl who launched the first attack.

"You just wanted a happy ending," she said through her tears. Her voice was so quiet that Ava almost didn't hear it, but the clarity of her words was sharp and poignant.

Captivated, Ava cocked her head to one side. "In my experience, even in the happy endings, not everyone's end is happy," she smoothly posed.

"But this one will be happy," Alice whimpered. "I promise. You don't believe me because yours wasn't. It wasn't the ending you wanted. Sometimes people lie about things... even to you."

Ava's throat went dry. Her eyelids fluttered, but her highly-trained lips remained disciplined and still. In one fluid movement, she dismounted the desk and crouched to Alice's level. "You think you know me so well, child. Don't you?"

Alice was afraid to nod.

"Okay then, Alice...let's pretend..."

Alice screamed once.

It was blood-curdling and vibrated throughout the whole ship.

But that wasn't all.

As she screamed, a bright force blasted Ava against the opposing wall, shaking the ship and prompting Bastien to burst into the room.

Alice lay collapsed but conscious on the ground. Bastien lifted Ava from the floor and begged for an explanation. Ava's eyes were fixed on Alice, filled with apprehension.

No explanation came, only a sudden jolt of the ship.

28

An Unexpected Guest

Just as the crashing waves had once attempted to rid the ocean of the filth we shall refer to as *Ava*, another tempest posed a similar threat to *The Wanderer* and its new management. A new storm was crashing, striking the crew aghast.

This time the aggressive surf vehemently beat against the exterior of the ship to defend the purest bearers of Light. A hand had been laid on one with an extraordinary sort of protection–that much was evident. The ship was tossed like a ball. The crew scrambled, but it was all for naught. Sailors fought the waves, but many were lost in the indignation of the sea.

The thundering, cracking, smashing, and clapping of the storm splintered the wood, miraculously leaving the ship only mildly damaged, though the body count was high. Within moments, it all ended. The water stilled, the debris floating ominously, and the air was quiet. The lifeless corpses that remained were strewn across the decks, painting the ship with a morbid image of washed-out blood, cold faces, and silence. The few survivors were shaken and gasping for breath.

Hastings was the first to gather his wits. He had been scraped by wood and bruised by the crates and bodies that had been brutally thrust into him. Clinging to railings and masts for support, he moved sorely down the ship to find any survivors.

Livesey was the second to show signs of life. Still youthful and athletic, the doctor sprung up the moment his mind bounced back from the trauma. His first instinct was to find young Hawkins, who was nowhere to be seen. A flashing image of Jim's poor mother, fretting for her son's unknown fate, alarmed Livesey to the point of panic. He shouted Jim's name, moving across the deck much faster than the stumbling Keeper.

Silver's only good leg was trapped under a fallen sail; he reached his arms for any sort of leverage, resembling a wounded cockroach attempting to scatter. Incidentally, the closest object for him to grab happened to be Ava's leg, resulting in a swift kick in the face. Bastien chuckled, which sounded more like a snort, as he hadn't quite coughed all of the water out of his lungs.

After untangling herself from the ratlines, Marin heard muffled cries for help. She looked over the side of the ship and saw little Alice dangling from a torn sail, only inches from the water.

Marin frantically wrapped the end of the sail around her wrist and pulled, gathering the fabric toward her and lifting Alice slowly to the railing. With impressive upper body strength, Marin managed to heave Alice to safety—of course, once Alice was securely in her arms, they both collapsed in exhaustion and relief.

"Are you all right?" Marin asked her, moving Alice's hair out of her face with maternal care.

Alice wheezed in exertion. "I'm alright—I'm alright."

"Where's Clancy?" Hastings called to them.

Alice looked to Marin, who only stared at Hastings. "I didn't see him," the mermaid replied.

From the nearly blocked stairway down to the mate's quarters, Jim Hawkins staggered into sight, carrying the weight of Clancy's fragile frame on his side. Clancy was conscious, but his eyes were glazed over, and his legs could hardly keep him upright. Little Jim was somehow able to prop him upward and lug him to the first available makeshift seat. Hastings hurried to their aid and finished positioning Clancy comfortably.

While the heroes regrouped around Clancy, Ava bitterly stood to her feet and summoned their attention. She swept both of her hands outward, magically wiping the ship of the lingering water and mud. Instantly, the deck was cleared, and only the damaged wood remained.

"There's a port town a short distance from here," she simmered. "We will dock there for repairs and then continue our business."

"And what's to stop them, my lady, from escaping once we've docked?" Silver queried.

"That is a thought," she allowed. Stepping over the large, snapped mast that stood between her and the collection of Alden before her, her eyes darkened and narrowed on Hastings. "The Keeper may scheme and anticipate, but I do have rather precious leverage."

Without shifting her gaze, Ava lifted a finger and Hastings heard Marin flinch. Her hourglass was still active. No matter on which side Marin's sympathies lie, her hourglass still kept her bound.

"I don't think we're in any danger, do you?" the she-demon taunted.

Hastings seethed. This made Ava grin, naturally.

"Just as I thought," she sneered, patting his cheek. Derisively, she laughed as he jerked his head away from her cursed hand.

The upper hand was still hers.

Bastien's magic was sufficient enough to make minor repairs and clean the debris, though it visibly drained his energy. Scada magic, in its nature, was never meant to sustain life, and when utilized to do so, actively degraded. Ava offered no assistance, despite her greater capacity and tolerance for Scada power.

In any case, she saw to business on land, sending a message to her distant allies. Silver stayed with Bastien, observing his work. Scada magic was becoming more and more intriguing to him, but something about the distribution of power was intriguing to him. Ava had dismissed his suggestion of recruiting more men for the crew, assuring him that she was perfectly capable of powering and steering a ship with far less manpower than Spyros required.

Livesey sat as the unspoken lookout while Hastings attempted to heal Clancy of his lingering wounds. He kept a wary eye on Bastien and Silver. Bastien's hands moved in a calculated manner, his fingers orchestrating the work. Boards were rearranged and re-fastened, and holes were mended.

Scada magic cannot heal, only destroy—however, when properly applied, it can raise and move materials needed to imitate healing. Bastien coerced the ship, returning it to sailing condition, as Hastings more authentically healed Clancy, returning him to standing condition.

"You're doing it wrong," Alice scolded Hastings. His hand was gingerly placed on the open gash on Clancy's leg.

"How else is he supposed to do it?" Marin questioned. She sat on her knees, peering over Hastings's shoulder in concern.

"He's not saying the words." Alice wrinkled her mouth skeptically. "The jacket doesn't know who you are until you say its words..."

"I said them last time," Hastings murmured.

"You're not a Regent anymore, silly. It's a different jacket."

"You've been a Keeper before?" Marin questioned.

Hastings grunted in annoyance. "It's the same magic, Alice. I've said the words already—give it time to work."

Alice sighed. "It's not the same magic! I keep telling Clancy you're not stupid, but you need to help me show him, Mister. Of course, Regents and Arches can't have the same magic—or they would be the same thing!"

"Could someone explain these words to me?" Marin pressed, still sitting in confusion.

Alice sighed again, trying to be patient with the ignorant congregation before her. "A Keeper can't connect to his jacket without the words. Then he can use its magic."

"What kind of words?"

"Marin, I can't tell you the words. You wouldn't understand them anyway," Alice shook her head condescendingly.

"I've said them with this jacket before, Alice," Hastings softly retorted.

Jim turned his head to the conversation. "Have you? I haven't seen it yet."

"Yes," Hastings snapped. "I've already healed someone."

"And there she is...." Livesey trailed off, spotting Ava returning to The Wanderer.

"Ava?" Jim said in alarm.

"If it's any consolation, I regret it," Hastings grumbled to Clancy. "It was on instinct."

"What?" Livesey finally joined the conversation. "You healed Ava?"

"Interesting," Marin commented, leaning back and giving Hastings a judgmental stare.

In the distance, Ava went to Bastien, pulling him aside for a private conference while Silver helped himself to the bag of food she had brought with her. However, it was not the presence of the she-demon that caught the doctor's attention. Only a few short moments after Ava boarded,

Livesey noticed another dark figure slither onto the ship behind her and hide in the shadows.

Absently, Livesey nudged Hastings's arm.

"What?" Hastings bit. "What is it?"

Disregarding Hastings's response, Livesey bent his head in the direction of the newcomer until the Keeper caught his meaning. Before any of the others could react, Hastings hushed the doctor the instant he recognized the impostor. No matter how hard he had disregarded the lies of Lorelei, Hastings vividly remembered her various interactions in the jails of Bristol.

The sauntering visitor.

The large man with the dark curls.

The rough-and-ready sailor with class.

James, she had called him.

The lower hand he may have had, but Hastings was not entirely prepared to give up the game. Tricksters are a relentless breed. He was open to the possibilities of another being on board who could tip the scales in his favor.

"Let her figure it out on her own," Hastings muttered to Livesey. He watched Ava and Bastien make their way to the helm and begin to set sail. A smirk spread across his face, in spite of himself.

The enchanted ship propelled forward, leaving the port town to disappear behind it. Night fell gradually, and the impostor felt he was in the clear to move about the ship a bit more freely. He emerged from his hiding place and moved slowly along the sides of the vessel, his sights set on Ava's figure at the helm. He held out his hook in anticipation. Its silver curve glistened in the dimming light of the sunset, catching Hastings's eye.

The heroes sat resting against the wall below the forecastle deck, either dozing off or looking to the sunset for hope. Hastings, however, was alert; his stimulated mind rarely rested. He saw James move like a serpent along the walls leading to the steps.

"Hook, mate," John Silver greeted the interloper, having waddled down those very steps. He was sure to keep his voice just low enough that Ava and Bastien—standing two decks above them—could not hear the encounter. "Haven't seen you since Flint's days." His voice was steady, but one could see an apparent effort of masking uneasiness.

James Hook relaxed his shoulders at the sight of the one-legged pirate. "Old Barbecue," he whispered hoarsely.

He extended his hand of flesh and shook Silver's. Seeing as it is recorded in Hook's own history, it's only fair to tell you that he himself once sailed with the notorious Captain Flint.

Hook and Silver had a very tumultuous relationship, in which Hook claimed dominion, but as far as these new players were concerned, they were both out of their element and therefore shared common ground.

"I see your intent, friend." Silver noted the fellow pirate's stance and position of his chosen weapon. Hook's aptly named weapon was still aimed for a kill, but Silver didn't bother inquiring after the intended victim—nor did he care how Hook climbed aboard in the first place. Instead, he did what Long John Silver did best: he seized another opportunity. "You wouldn't want to do the wretch in without gaining some swag first, would ya?"

"And what are you implying, Silver?" Hook curled his weaponized hand back suspiciously.

Silver held his own hands out in compromise. "Whatever you have against the lady can surely wait. We'll have no real use for her after we get our treasure. It'd be mad to kill off our greatest asset before her value runs out."

"It's logic like that that made me like you in the first place, Silver."

Silver turned on his peg to the voice behind him. Ava stood with her arms crossed and her tall sidekick at her side. Hook was struck by the sight of her and impulsively plunged his hook in the direction of her heart. In expert anticipation, Ava moved Silver in front of her with the wave of her hand, providing a new target for Hook's aim. Silver gulped the blood that burst to his throat. When Hook pried his hook from Silver's chest, his mouth hung open in shock and regret.

"Oh don't look at me like that, handsome," Ava clicked her tongue. "He had it coming. As it turns out, I don't take betrayal lightly, and he was a little too liberal with his loyalties." She lowered her voice to the hoarse whisper Hook released before. "If it makes you feel any better, you would've missed my heart anyway, love. Haven't you heard by now: I don't have one."

Bastien did not take the assassination attempt so calmly. While Ava stood in serene amusement, he drew his sword and lifted it Hook's way. Hastings, however, slid between them just in time, blocking Bastien's sword with one of his own.

"Gentlemen, as thrilling as this is, it'll have to end," Ava interrupted, tossing her smoky influence in between them. In a low and reassuring voice, she turned to Bastien. "Put them all in the brig, and maybe we'll kill Hook later."

Bastien's reluctance was more than evident, though his glare narrowed on Hastings, rather than the Neverland pirate. As Bastien forcefully shoved the Keeper along, his glare was encouraged by Hastings spewing, "The scenery is getting a bit old down here."

"There's only two of them," Hook muttered.

"Trust me, my friend," Livesey advised. "We've been on this ship long enough; I recommend not testing them. She actually has us quite outnumbered." Content with the threat, Hook shrugged and followed suit.

Bastien forced each of them into the largest cell together. Alice helped Clancy take a seat on the filthy ground, assuming their usual brig positions of slumping against the wall, with the help of Jim and Dr. Livesey.

"Are you all right, Clancy?" the little girl whispered.

Clancy grunted as he reached the floor. His tender skin sparked pain throughout his body. "I don't think I'll ever be all right again, Alice," his voice broke.

Once they were settled, all eyes turned to Hastings.

"You didn't know it was her, did you?" Hook propped his knees up and rested his arms upon them, peering over at Hastings. "You were in Bristol. And you're still with her...."

"Who are you?" the Keeper fired.

"He's Captain Hook!" Alice contributed.

Hook cast her a dubious glance. "That I am. Captain of the Jolly Roger and the only one who could frighten Barbecue himself. Though that matters little now...."

"Barbecue?" Livesey repeated.

"Silver," Clancy explained quietly.

"They knew each other," informed Alice. "A long time ago—before Peter and such. He's a lot older than he looks."

"What is she?" Hook spat.

"Why was Ava assigned to you?" Hastings ignored Hook's frustration.

"He wouldn't turn," Marin offered. Hastings turned his head to her in surprise. His attention on her caused her to straighten her back with confidence. "Ava targets the stragglers. His whole crew must have joined the Master but him. Corrupt or kill....that's the way it is."

Hook scoffed and leaned his head back, fiddling with a ring on his finger. The very gaudy ring he had snatched out of Lorelei's grasp back in Bristol. "Ah, she thought herself so clever. I was a more challenging target than she must have expected. She had to come back for me several times. When the devil took my crew, he didn't anticipate my causing... problems. Although, I must confess that I was tempted by her long enough to let her bring me to this dismal realm."

"And what realm, pray tell, do you call home?" Livesey asked conversationally.

"Oh, it's lovely!" Alice interceded, her eyes lighting up with excitement. "There are mermaids and fairies and wonderful things!" Marin chuckled lightly at Alice's fast-growing energy. "And boys can fly there, and girls too—and Peter gives you pixie dust, and all you have to do is think good thoughts, and you'll just start floating! He teaches you to steer and miss all the trees that are all around—as long as you stay away from the crocodiles." Hook grimaced and stroked his hook at the word *crocodile*. "Though, I do think Wendy is a much better teacher. Peter can be quite annoying. He doesn't really stop talking, and Wendy is quite nicer."

"Those are the first agreeable words she has said since that brute locked the door," Hook mumbled.

"...and the mermaids can be quite rude to poor Wendy, but they're very kind to Peter," Alice continued. "I'm sure they'd be kind to me, though I've only seen them through the glass..."

"Mermaids would love you," Marin assured her. "We tend to like children."

Alice jumped to her feet. "You're a mermaid?" Marin nodded with a smile, caught up in Alice's excitement. "I'm sure that's why she sent the storms—they weren't for me. They were for you too! She wants you back in the water, and then we all could meet your sisters!"

"*She*?" Marin repeated.

"Alice," Clancy nudged the girl. "Alice, let the man talk."

His efforts were too late; Hook had already made up his mind about Alice. The eternally young and peculiarly wise would forever be an irritant to him.

Hastings took the journal out of his jacket pocket as the chatter went on and opened to the last page, where the folded map was tucked away.

"How did that survive the storm?" Marin whispered to him.

He sighed. "A miracle, apparently." He unfolded the map and shook his head in disappointment. "Not that it matters. It didn't even work."

Marin peered over his shoulder, squinting at the letters and markings on the map. Her bitterness toward him softened and her fears slowly dissipated. Alice's influence tends to have that effect. She now searched for words of encouragement instead of scorn, but something rendered her speechless. Those markings suddenly began to change. They danced around the parchment and settled in a very different arrangement, forming new images and new words.

"Where....where exactly is that?" Marin asked in awe.

Hastings lifted his eyes from the parchment to the pirate. Hook made eye contact and twisted his mouth inquisitively. No words needed to be exchanged for the question to be answered.

Just around the corner, they heard the patter of feet clamoring up the stairs to bring the new information to his leader.

29

Devil's in the Details

"You were right."

Ava's back was to him, staring blankly at the wall behind her desk. "Of course I was."

Bastien wrapped his arms around her waist and rested his chin on her shoulder. "How did you know it would work?"

"The scribe told me so."

He paused, considering her explanation. "I don't understand."

"The devil's in the details...but sometimes so is the angel. Keeper magic is light, darling." She reached her hand to caress his face. "Light and shadow cannot be in collusion; it tends to make the magic...complicated. That was my mistake and one I had to amend. He was having far too much fun. He needed to hate me again." She angled her head slightly toward him and lowered her voice. "Tell me what happened."

Bastien regaled all he had seen and heard until she slowly turned to face him. Her expression was complex. She was both satisfied and disheartened. "What does it mean?"

"Oh, darling." Her voice was gentle and coaxing, like that of a lover. "Remember when you wondered what I do while I'm away from you? We're about to return to whatever's left of my good work."

"I thought Spyros led that attack."

"The realm was protected. How do you think he got in?" she posed. "Battles are more than the weapons and carnage. There's an art to opening, and an art to finishing the details of debris and suffering." She reached her hand around his head as he pulled her closer. "Despite our victories, there will be something to fear when we arrive."

"You said you turned the realm, Ava."

"Contrary to what the others may believe, darling...a realm is rarely won in its entirety. I didn't have enough time with this one...I couldn't be as thorough as I would have liked." She bit her lip and sighed. "The survivors may be deemed powerless, but they will no doubt show significant resistance to our presence there...especially once they meet the new Arch Keeper. That'll be all they need to regain that repulsive fighting spirit of theirs."

"How did you know we'd be led back?"

"As I said," she smirked, "the realm was not won in its entirety." Gently, she tapped his nose. "There are one or two souls Myk would want reclaimed by his Keeper. A Keeper, a Storyteller, and a Stone. Quite a win, I'd say. And I'm sure they'll agree that dying will be an awfully big adventure..."

Bastien released an empty chuckle. "I'm sure they will."

Ava smiled, but the smile quickly tightened. "There is something I will need of you, though, love."

"Anything," he swore.

She took his hand in hers, breathing steadily. "It will be required of me to use...an inordinate amount of power...and strength. It'll leave me....drained and nearly lifeless. I will be most vulnerable, and I cannot have that."

His eyes grew intense with fierce loyalty.

"I need you," she told him. "I need you to protect me. To take care of me while I'm..."

He lifted her hand to his lips and softly kissed her palm. "I swear it."

Ava grinned with growing dominance. "Then to Neverland it is."

Part Three

To Fight & To Fly

30

Follow the Fairy

Just as the realm before it, Neverland had tasted the presence of the Galdere. Before the coming of the Stone, Myk and The Lady had every reason to visit a realm of pirates just as they had every reason to visit a realm of fairies and mermaids. With such heroic souls within, the two realms were never meant to be neutral territories.

In one, a young treasure seeker would befriend pirates and adventurers, leading him to a Keeper, a Scribe, and a Storyteller. In the other, a childish leader would be placed in the safety of the fairies to never grow up and create a protected haven for those he would gather.

As in nearly every story, all was ruined by an evil witch and her dark tricks.

The creator of the realm in which our heroes will now step foot understood the mind quite well. You see, a child's mind—or anyone's, really—is much like a map, filled with zigzags, roads, school recitations, favorite foods, family and friends' birthdays, and so on.

But there's a portion of their map that remains unexplored by everyone but the one whose mind it is. A portion filled with islands and treasures, magical shores and mermaids, pirates and frivolity. A portion of the mind that runs amuck all day long, fueled by folly and imagination. A portion called, by the respectable J.M. Barrie, *Neverland.*

Everyone's Neverland takes a different shape, of course, but there are resemblances between family members. Neverlands are never scary in the daylight. Children always have control of them then. It's at night, when all runs wildly out of their control–that's where nightmares are born.

Even so, not one single nightmare is formed out of nothing. The child, during the day, must have tempted fate and let just enough darkness into their daytime Neverland, even if only to make things more fun. Neverlands are untouchable and impossible to enter without the allowance of its creator.

All darkness needs is an invitation.

And an invitation to Peter's Neverland was all this trickster needed to unleash her Darkness. She had acquired much more with much less effort. The poor boy never saw her lies coming. Children never do. Once one Scada was permitted, all of her friends soon joined, bringing about the gruesome Battle of Neverland. Blood was shed, corruption was had, and the entrance of Neverland was forever defiled. It was no longer a sanctuary; it was a diseased battleground.

And so Bastien stood at the helm with the cause of his own corruption hanging lifelessly on his arms, drained of all the energy she used to walk back through the entrance.

Mighty as she was with Dark magic, her mortal frame felt the necessary drain. She nearly fainted but was held steady by Bastien's arm. The tenderness in which he held her would have been heartwarming had she been a less beastly woman.

"Look," he whispered to her. "You did it. We're here."

The jarring effect of the travel through the barrier shook the walls of the brig. Exclamations of discomfort were exchanged, particularly between Hook and Marin, as Hook crawled to the closest porthole. His face fell as he lifted himself to the proper height to see beyond the dust and grime of the glass.

"Well, mates," the pirate sighed. "The woman did it... somehow. We're making port...in Neverland."

"How did she get us here?" Livesey wheezed.

"Neverland!" Alice cheered. She stepped on poor Jim's leg to stand and appropriately express her excitement. "Oh, I love Neverland!"

"Not this Neverland," Hook promised. He looked at Hastings warily. "She's taking us south along the Lost Shores. Believe me, Hastings, that's not where we ought to be. What more could she possibly want from this cursed place?"

"To win the game." The Keeper helped Marin to her feet and returned Hook's wary glance. "We have to beat her to the Stone."

"And how do you expect to do that?" Livesey inquired. "She still has us caged like dogs."

Almost on cue, Bastien's heavy steps entered the brig. "Everyone off the ship!" he barked.

Hastings held a presenting hand to the stairwell to gesture to the serendipitous orders. As per his orders, Bastien shoved each prisoner out of the brig and onto dry land.

Ava led the way down the ramp to the dock Hook and his goons had built ages ago while Bastien brought up the rear. Hastings watched Ava's low energy as she limped to the beach. The transport from Treasure Island must have been strenuous indeed; her eyes were sallow, and her head was not held quite as high and proudly as usual.

When not a soul remained on board *The Wanderer*, Ava turned to face it. "Stay clear of the water," she softly advised. "And don't trust the stars." She sounded out of breath as if even speaking took considerable energy. "The closer we get, the more she'll intervene."

Apparently disregarding his guard duty, Hastings noticed Bastien go to her side and lent his arm for her support. To see someone so powerful become reduced to something so needy was shocking. But this was not what made our Keeper frown. Something troubled him; something didn't connect. With each step the group took inland, the more Hastings questioned Ava's plan.

If she wanted Hastings to lead them to the Stone, why had she not waited until she was strong enough to provide the necessary coercion?

Captain Hook cared little for the vixen's schemes and instead saw her weakness as an opportunity. As soon as they were close enough to a tree, he picked up a sizable fallen tree limb and thrust it into the air, bringing down a handful of other branches as it fell. They were well-aimed on Hook's part, landing precisely on his intended targets. Ava and Bastien were temporarily felled. Shouting his call to freedom, Hook ushered the heroes quickly past the trees, and without question, they followed.

Bastien scrambled to stand and stop them, but Ava had a firm grip on his arm. “Let them,” she rasped. Before he could protest, she added, “Trust me.”

The convoy of Alden followed Hook's lead, taking them farther north into the Never Woods. He occasionally glanced at Hastings's map and followed it expertly through the terrain.

Now, much had changed since the last visit of James Hook. War has that effect. Territories had shifted, and even the landscape showed signs of warfare. They trekked past the home of the Lost Boys, which seemed completely abandoned.

The magic of Neverland which Alice had anticipated was tragically diminished. The trees whose hollow trunks led to the legendary Peter Pan's home underground had since rotted. If the Lost Boys and their fearless leader were still in the realm, Alice supposed, they must live elsewhere. Though, she couldn't imagine anyone abandoning such an adorable dwelling as theirs had been.

“It's all much darker than I remember,” Hook muttered, almost mournfully.

“But what about the fairies? And Peter Pan?” Alice despaired.

Hook stopped cold and turned on his heel. "Don't keep your hopes high," he seethed. "Ava took Pan; he's no friend to Neverland."

Alice's eyes went wide, forgetting to whom she was speaking. Briefly she fell silent, but children seldom remain silent for long. Even when given strict orders, they often forget them within minutes and resume the chatter.

"The fairies should be here to help us," Alice whispered.

"Alice," Clancy shushed, dreading Hook's temper. "A lot has changed since you last read this story. Remember, Myk told you to read something else....well, I'd imagine this is why."

The young girl frowned. She never suspected that bad things had happened—she just assumed Myk wanted her to meet Dorothy instead.

"War," Hook confirmed. "Can't be certain what happened to the others after I left—nor do I care. Once she took my crew, there was nothing in Neverland worth fighting for."

"So you're saying you have no knowledge of who claimed the territory," Livesey clarified with a hint of derision. The natural healer he was, the doctor served as Clancy's crutch as they traveled but kept a free hand to dramatically gesture to the land around them. "We're entering at our own risk. I mean, what are we to expect?"

"Would you rather be in the brig?" Marin considered, moving past him.

Livesey almost forgot she was on their side. He looked at her strangely, still questioning why she hadn't stayed with her master but then smiled. The young woman had always had a look of goodness about her, so he agreed readily.

"That, I most certainly would not," he chuckled.

She smiled with commiseration before her eyes wandered to the unusually quiet Keeper. He was deeply contemplative and had been since they landed in Neverland.

The farther they traveled into the Never Woods, the more the shadows followed them. With very little sign of life or Neverland magic, Hook felt an overwhelming sense of being stalked. His eyes darted just a bit more frantically, and even his hook twitched. He had felt this sort of presence before.

Hastings noticed his strange behavior, keeping a curious eye on the pirate's fiddling hands. He hadn't vocalized any concern, but Hastings knew better. He knew Hook's sort to be cold and calculating; the kind of man who'd rely solely on his own intellect and resourcefulness. He wouldn't speak without knowing the facts and then formulating a plan from those facts. For better or for worse, Hook and Hastings were kindred spirits. Both men were receptive to their similar natures, lending, no doubt, to their immediate alliance.

The Keeper decided to stop for the night, as the sun was about to rest for the day anyway. "We've gone far enough," he declared. He glanced behind them, getting a sense of their progress. "By the state of them, I'd say neither Ava nor Bastien will be searching very long for us tonight."

Marin took Hastings's arm and quietly pulled him aside. "You're on edge. You think it's a trap?"

Sitting down on a flat stump, silently marking their temporary campsite, Hastings peered up at her. "You tell me."

Marin sighed, crossing her arms in front of her chest. "I'm being punished, same as you."

"Because I'm just so enticing, you couldn't resist," he suggested.

"We're on the same side now, Hastings."

"And she hung you out to dry, did she? Not a word of what her plan might be?"

His tone was not accusatory. He knew she didn't understand Ava as much as she claimed. Whatever she did know was not what he needed anyway. Without waiting for her to answer or defend herself, he continued to muse.

"Why not wait until she is fully recovered to release us from the brig? She moved us off the ship too quickly while she was still too weak to stop us from escaping. Nothing she does is without reason—therefore, our escape was by design. But, recover she must, so we do have time on our side. We're safe for the moment, at least."

Clancy took a seat near Hastings, his breathing still labored but not constricted enough to refrain from contributing. "We are all after the same thing. You said so yourself, Hastings: she can't find it without you."

Hook advised against starting a fire since it would draw attention. Instead, they attempted to regain some energy that had been lost during the transport through the barrier. As was his restless nature, the Keeper could not allow himself to sleep. His confidence had inspired trust from those in his company, for most of them slept like babies with the knowledge of the Keeper keeping watch.

Not all, of course.

Our poor scribe sat upright, with his back facing where the others slept, gingerly rubbing his healing arms. Keeper magic may heal the wounds, but the scars never fade quickly.

Hastings moved quietly to Clancy, facing the same direction alongside him, without saying a word. Silence is often the most effective form of consolation. Clancy was not accustomed to any bit of this adventure, however, and words were his comfort.

"He let me choose my age, you know," Clancy muttered the moment he felt Hastings beside him. "Myk did. When I reached manhood, he–he told me I could....progress at whatever rate I wanted. Progress...that's what he called it. I used to sit in the Arkis and listen to stories from the other scribes. There was one man, Mr. Mackenzie, told me of a civilization he knew that considered the physical signs of aging a manifestation of wisdom. Age and wisdom. And who wouldn't want to be wise..."

Clancy trailed off, looking down at his forearms, lightly grazing his fingers across the burn scars. "That's what I wanted...every grey hair and every wrinkle...I wanted it to come at the pace of my wisdom. I thought I had enough. I have read everything there possibly was to read in the Arkis. I didn't think there was anything else left...any other sort of wisdom. Apparently...apparently Myk still didn't think I was old enough..."

Hastings's silence weighed on Clancy. All this time, the Keeper had known what he had not. There was far more to understand about this war than what can be read on a page. He knew that now, and he was ashamed.

"I..." he started again. His voice was breaking, much like his poor heart. "I am not any good at this, am I? I'm sorry."

Finally, Hastings sighed and spoke.

"I once had a commander," the Keeper began, "who told me that scars make the soldier. Your scars are your badge of honor—they show your enemy that no matter what they throw at you, you've been through worse and you'll do it again. You have the scars to prove it." He placed an encouraging hand on Clancy's shoulder. "Even Ava could not break you, Clancy. I imagine few men can make such a claim, but you are one of them. And now you have a few more wrinkles to prove it."

Clancy released a breathy laugh that he didn't truly mean. "You know I'm not the one she means to break, Hastings. I'm not the threat. I'm only collateral."

Hastings paused and considered this, moving his hand from Clancy's shoulder and intertwining his fingers while he leaned against his knees. "Well, I've always found it a happy thing when the enemy underestimates my assets. Makes for a more interesting exchange."

The frustration returned to Clancy's sighs. "Is this all just a game to you?"

"Sometimes," Hastings shrugged. He vaguely noticed an irritated movement behind them.

"Why?" demanded Clancy. "You—you who actually seem to understand more of what's happening than I do—why would any of this be a game to you?"

A satisfied smirk stretched across Hastings's face. "Because Myk knew someone had to teach you how to smile, Clancy."

He playfully patted Clancy's shoulder again as he stood to look behind them at the source of the movement. Hook, who had been sleeping very lightly, was awakened by some pest. He swatted the air, with both hand and hook, growing more and more irritated. His wild movements, while entertaining to the Keeper, were soon disruptive to those resting. Marin, Alice, Jim, and Livesey woke abruptly to Hook's grunts.

Hastings squinted his eyes, straining to see whatever insect was being a nuisance. To his surprise, it wasn't an insect at all. It fluttered about like one but had a peculiar glow. Not like that of a firefly or anything you and I might recognize from our world, but instead it looked like a small, floating candle. Only when Hook caught it by the wings could Hastings identify it.

"Is that a—?"

"A fairy?" Clancy finished.

"A fairy," Livesey repeated. His tone was no longer incredulous; he had seen enough not to question the magical phenomenon.

Alice lept from her disturbed position on the grassy ground. "I knew it!" she exclaimed. She ran to Hook's side to get a better view of his prisoner. "It's Tinkerbell! Marin, oh

Marin—it's Tinkerbell! She's my favorite of all fairies. Oh, Marin, you'll just love her!" Alice took Marin's hand and dragged her to see their new friend. Hastings and Clancy also advanced, joining the others in their inquisitive circle around Hook and Tinkerbell.

The blonde fairy, with her leaf-green dress and her voluptuous curves, placed her frustrated hands on her hips and scowled at Hook's hand. Instead of words, her indignant protests were expressed through a frenzied series of bell-like tinkles. The pirate only groaned in irritation.

Alice whacked away Hook's grip on the fairy's wings, and Tinkerbell kissed Alice's cheek in gratitude. Alice giggled and watched the fairy hover around her energetically. Fairies often inhabit flowering plants and are drawn to little else. And Alice was not always a little girl...

"I'm her favorite, Clancy," Alice announced. For the first time since his trauma on the ship, Clancy forced a small smile.

"Of course you are," he sighed.

"What else is she saying?" Marin pried curiously.

Tinkerbell was now buzzing in Hook's face, tinkling like mad and successfully irritating the pirate. He tried to swat her away again, but Marin stopped him as Alice continued to translate.

"She says we should be fine as long as we stay out of the witch's way."

Livesey frowned. "She's seen Ava, then. Is she already mobile?"

Alice shook her head patiently, as if correcting a child. "No, no, doctor. Not Ava. There's a witch in the woods. She just likes to collect things, so she shouldn't bother us much."

"Ah." Clancy nodded, quickly receiving a questioning glance from the Keeper. "Baba Yaga," he explained to him. "Tinkerbell's right, she shouldn't give us much trouble. At least we know we're in the right place."

"How's that?" Livesey questioned. His head was beginning to ache from the abundance of new information.

"Queens of Avalon guard the Stones," Hastings chimed in, crouching to Alice's level as Tinkerbell landed on her shoulder. "And *the witch* who likes to collect things is a Queen of Avalon. Isn't that right, Alice?"

Alice smiled at him as she casually patted Tinkerbell's head. "I told you he'd read the book, Clancy. Tinkerbell says she got here just before we did. So she must have followed the Stone."

Hastings returned the smile. "Does the fairy know where it is?"

"She doesn't think we should find Baba Yaga, that's for sure," Alice claimed. "She's far too busy collecting for Timo."

Hastings could sense the eye roll Clancy attempted to hide as he sighed. While The Lady set the standard, not every Queen of Avalon measured up to such a standard. At least, not according to the Arkis scribe still learning his place. One man's battlefield debris was another man's high quality inventory–and no one seemed to be immune to the enticing prices Timo offered in exchange. The capitalization on such sensitive matters will no doubt arise more prominently later, so we won't digress too much now, dear reader.

Alice continued to listen for a moment and squinted her eyes, trying to make sense of it all. "She says we need to keep going north—the Indians are nicer than those in the south."

She then frowned suddenly. "Oh no...Ava offered Peter dark magic, Clancy. Oh, wait," she listened more. "No, he didn't take it, did he? He didn't. He said no. Oh dear. Peter isn't Pan anymore....I'm sure he doesn't like that very much. But who's Pan now? Where did Peter go?"

She took a very long pause to hear Tinkerbell's tale. Clancy tapped his foot lightly. "Well, what is she saying?"

"Shh," Alice held a finger up to silence Clancy. "She doesn't really know. No one can find Peter. But a new boy is Pan..." She wrinkled her nose. "She won't tell me his name... but how can Peter not be Pan anymore? That's his name."

"Pan is the island's leader," Hook mumbled.

"So it's a title," Clancy explained to Alice. "Peter wasn't able to keep everything Light, Alice, because he's not in charge anymore." He cast Hastings a wary glance; they both had a horrible feeling that Hook's claim of the damage done was not an exaggeration.

Alice's eyes flooded with tears. They searched through the falling dusk to find Clancy's assuring face. Helplessly, the girl fell to the ground.

"Clancy...the Lost Boys...they hunted the fairies. They thought it was a game..."

"She probably tricked them, Alice," Jim offered, kneeling on the ground beside her.

"She tricked all of them," Marin put in. Her arms crossed defensively, pulling Hastings's attention to her. "The Lost Boys, pirates, mermaids—probably all but the Indians apparently...if their lands are really *nicer* than the south."

Alice shook her head vehemently. "Oh no no no. Ava can't have mermaids, Marin. They don't listen to her because they know better."

Marin fell silent and looked down at her feet. Alice, however, paid no mind. She was momentarily distracted by Tinkerbell's continuation of her tale.

"Tink says the lands were split up—a nice part for the Indians and a very dark part for Pan. She survived because she knows all the best hiding places."

Alice paused and smiled at the fairy. "Well, thank you," she told her. "Miss Tinkerbell says she wants to help us fight Pan and the Boys because they hurt her feelings by trying to kill her. But she really wants to know if Peter's alright; he's been gone for a long time. There's no Lost Boy as lost as Peter is now." Earnestly, the child tugged at Jim's arm. "We have to help her find Peter, Jimmy. We have to."

Without a second of hesitation, Jim nodded and looked up at the two Keepers with surprising decisiveness. "We need to find Peter."

Hastings crossed his arms and glanced at Hook speculatively. The pirate was grimacing; his nose wrinkled the moment the fairy started tinkling. The Keeper gave the pirate a nod of confidence, easing his anger only slightly.

"Well then," Hastings decided. "Follow the fairy."

31

The Land of the Piccaninny

Ava and Bastien made little distance inland from the beach. No attempt was made to follow the escaped prisoners, and they instead stopped when they came upon the notorious Wendy House.

The small cottage was once built by Pan and the Lost Boys to be home to their new "mother," the young English girl Peter had brought to Neverland with the intent of having adventures and hearing the end of stories. Long absent from Neverland, Wendy's influence still haunted the island. The house remained empty, save the remnants of her stories shared within its walls.

Ava slumped up against the outside wall, Bastien loyally at her side.

"I hope you're right," Bastien said. He was on high alert, keeping his eyes keen on his surroundings as if waiting for something.

"Is there any doubt?" Ava rasped. She held her hand close to her gut, still struggling to muster the strength to breathe easily.

"Of course not," he absently rubbed her arm in assurance.

"You're worried about me," she sensed.

"Of course."

Ava chuckled and patted his arm limply. "Don't be, darling. I'm in good hands—"

Bastien held up a finger, quieting her and stood protectively in front with his sword drawn.

A shadow danced across the trees, summoning an overcast of darkness in its path. But the shadow was not all. A soft rustling was closing in on them, and small eyes could be seen dangerously reflecting what little light still shone through. There were several sets of them, each with its own level of ferocity, but they all curiously remained at bay, hidden in the shadows.

A single dancing shadow slowed its pace and settled a short distance from Ava's side. It stood as a young boy would, a cocksure young lad with his hands on his hips. Its faceless aggressive stance kept Bastien alert but merely annoyed Ava.

"Hmph," she lifted herself onto the porch and rolled her eyes. "Relax, darling. Put your sword away; they only require a firm hand."

All the eyes growled at this until Ava's presence soothed them into a light murmur.

"Is that right?" Bastien sheathed his sword and assisted Ava until she found firm footing.

With her mask of strength restored, she inhaled smoothly and held on to Bastien's arm as she faced the shadows. “Come on, you little beasts. Come on out.”

No movement came. Ava sighed in exasperation; a different approach could prove beneficial. “Alright...” she hummed. “Show yourself. Be a good boy.”

At the address of their leader, the little eyes blinked madly. Ever so slowly, each little beast emerged from the trees, holding his child-sized weapon downward in surrender. They were each no older than twelve years old, with mud on their faces and animal skins draped across their bodies.

They were not the Lost Boys Wendy left behind. I very grimly report that these children did not go home to England with the Darlings, as they should have. For just as war ripped the island in pieces, so did Pan's Boys gain a new perspective on mothers and adventures and growing up, while the Darlings themselves...well, their fates were not as written either.

Their naughty king's laughter shook the leaves, but he did not appear right away. His laugh triggered a broad smile on Ava's face, which empowered her to release her grip on Bastien's arm. No sparkling light, no fairy dust, and no sweetness inhabited this boy. This Pan was not the same as you likely remember.

Things were quite different when the Pan was Peter.

Still, he flew into the scene, winking at his Boys before landing playfully in front of the woman who summoned him. Loudly he crowed, announcing his entrance as if it was necessary. His small fists planted themselves on his hips. He was perhaps a year or so younger than Peter. His strawberry blonde curls were overgrown and fell in front of his large blue eyes, but his cocky grin remained.

"Ava," he acknowledged with a curious gleam in his eye. She seemed to incite both the prospect of a challenge as well as a strange interest in him. His grin was wide, much like hers. There was no trace of fear in him, the poor fool. She didn't need his fear. She was in need of something else entirely.

"Hm, I see you've thinned in ranks, dear," she pointed out. "Not that you need a great army; you're clearly capable of maintaining our territory on your own."

"That's right, I am." He puffed out his chest in pride.

"Yes, those pesky redskins don't stand a chance, do they?"

"No, they don't—do they, Boys?" he grew louder, encouraging the Lost Boys's cheers of agreement.

Ava chuckled. "Naturally. But you've had to dispose of a few of your Boys, didn't you, darling?"

The boy frowned, then shrugged. "Well, yes. They were starting to grow up."

"And we can't have that, can we?"

Pan shook his head. "No, we can't."

"As always, dear, you're right," Ava nodded. His ego was inflating by the second. "And I see you're learning the gifts you've been given. No more fairy dust. Didn't I tell you my magic was better than what your predecessor had?"

"No, I told *you*," he contradicted.

"Oh, yes, of course, you did."

"It lasts longer, I can fly higher, and those filthy savages are more afraid of it. They're no fun anymore, but they're afraid like I said they would be."

The boy hilariously misremembered every bit of his corruption. Ava was far too good at what she did. She merely humored him and allowed the arrogance of boyhood to continue to control him.

"And what of the Boys you have left? Are they good enough for you?"

Bastien tensed, watching the Lost Boys raise their weapons at the challenge. While there were a limited number of Scada sent to Neverland to win the realm, word of its success spread enough for Bastien to know what he was to face. Funnily enough, the allegiance of Pan and the Lost Boys —or any other recruited Scada—was not always reassuring to those already in Korbl's ranks. You cannot genuinely expect villains to be a trusting breed. Even toward their own.

What an uncomfortable way to fight a war.

Pan glanced idly behind him at his Boys, ignoring their tightened formation. "Sometimes our games scare them, but the scared ones are easier to kill. That helps."

"It helps to know which of your Boys to kill?"

"No, the redskins do that for me. That's why I only have five left. Five strong ones."

"Would you like more, darling?" Ava's tone was soft and coaxing, keen negotiator as she was.

His chest puffed again. "I don't need them, but more could be good, I suppose."

Ava smiled, moving toward him, as if sharing a secret. "First, show me how your flying is going."

Pan laughed. Little boys are arrogant; they leap at any opportunity to display their foolish tricks. The shadows followed him, fueling his flight as fairy dust once had. He flew around her, doing flips and spins before landing. Feeling so robust, he crowed again, planting his proud fists against his hips. His false sense of control soared higher than he did.

"You're doing so well, darling. It's working. You knew it would. The Darkness loves you better than the fairy dust ever could have—and your Shadow is so much stronger than the last Pan's," Ava praised. Pausing dramatically, she tapped her finger to her lips. "I do believe you deserve more Boys in your command."

Pan nodded proudly. "I do. I really do."

"Well," she began, "I brought a new one for you."

Zealously, Pan searched behind her for this new recruit. "Where is he?"

"Oh, silly boy. I can't just give him to you, can I? That wouldn't be near as fun as a game would." With disturbing ease, Ava's hand lifted, her fingers bent toward one another in a combined effort to pull the air beside her in a ripping motion. As she did so, the new Pan screamed.

Lightly waving her hand back toward her, she brought the Shadow she had ripped from the child's form closer to her face. Softly, but threateningly, she whispered to it before casting it away into the shadows of the trees. Her fiery eyes settled once again on Pan, who now stared in morbid curiosity.

"It'll be like hide and seek. Find the Shadow, find the Lost Boy. The Shadow will lead you to your prize. And you love prizes...don't you, dear?"

She was right, and he agreed. Ready for the new challenge, Pan turned to his Boys and rallied the troops. "I can catch him—can't I, Boys?" The little beasts cheered for him in blind submission.

"You are a cocky lad, aren't you?" Ava posed. "Get your Boy before the Indians do."

"They won't win again!" he crowed.

"That's right. Don't come back to me empty-handed," she warned him. "And don't forget my policy. Don't forget. And be careful. There's a Nidling with him. A mermaid. She's a horrible traitor, but I don't want you to kill her. Traitors can still be useful." Pan's eyes wandered, bored with the instructions. Ava grabbed the collar of his shirt and put her face close to his. "Don't kill her. Or the little girl."

Still too foolish for fear, Pan shrugged with reluctance. "If you say so."

How is one to recognize an ally in a land so overrun with the enemy?

Trust does not come easily, and an arrow aimed at the face does little to inspire it.

The crew of Alden followed the fairy safely and deeply into the lands of the Piccaninny Tribe. The air grew lighter, and the foliage moved more easily. However, Hook still feared for his life as a silver arrowhead and wooden stick stared him dead in the eye. He had just finished debating with Alice over the savagery of the Indians in Neverland. She was optimistically convinced that their goodness was unbreakable, while Hook held a starkly different opinion.

As he remembered them, they were feral simpletons who sided with that beastly child Peter and struggled to say even the simplest phrases in English. This sort of language barrier must have improved in the time the Scada began recruiting in the realm, for my record will prove a bit of a difference. Instead of "Me kill Hook," the young native woman who now threatened the sanctity of the captain's face more fluidly said,

"Don't move, or I release the arrow."

"It's Tiger Lily!" Alice exclaimed, jumping up and down. "I wanted to meet you! Don't hurt Hook; he's hiding from the bad guys too. Mister here is the Keeper now—"

"Alice," Clancy hushed and pulled her behind him. "Why don't we let Hastings handle this?"

"Well, I told Hook that the Indians wouldn't go bad, didn't I?" she whispered bitterly.

"Keeper?" Tiger Lily relaxed her shoulders. Her long dark hair was pulled back into a braid; loose strands fell around her face as her forehead wrinkled in confusion. Don't misunderstand: the confusion was not over the word itself. Not recognizing Hastings as *Mister*, she glared and examined Hook. "He is not a Keeper," she bristled.

"No, he isn't," Marin concurred. "He is," she pointed to Hastings. "But the pirate is on your side too, at the moment." Marin shot Hook a wary glance.

Tinkerbell fluttered in front of Tiger Lily's face, alarming her. Tiger Lily lowered her bow and followed Tinkerbell's flight with keen interest. "The fairy. You are still alive?"

Tink tinkled frantically, apparently rambling an explanation that Tiger Lily didn't need.

"She's been hiding from Pan and the Lost Boys," Alice translated. "And she was bringing us to you because you're nicer than those in the south."

"It's true," Jim spoke up. His eyes gleamed faintly as he watched the Piccaninny girl. Tiger Lily was, at this time, only a couple of years older than young Jim but was well on her way to womanhood. She was unlike anyone he had ever before seen, despite her deadly arrow being aimed in their direction. "We're not here to hurt you, miss. In fact, we'd love to help you...if—if you'll help us. Maybe refuge?"

Hastings raised a subtle eyebrow at Jim's attempted flirtation, but it seemed to have produced the desired effect. Tiger Lily softened her defenses but kept her eye on Hook.

"Refuge, I can give you," she finally spoke after a long uncomfortable silence. "Alliance is not my decision."

Tiger Lily signaled for her hidden soldiers to show themselves. There were over a dozen of them, all wielding defensive weapons and watching for their leader's commands. She gave them an order in their native tongue and then turned to Jim.

"Come," she told him and his friends.

The natives surrounded them as if they were their prisoners until they reached the central Piccaninny tribe camp. Nearly a hundred natives, in a variety of shapes and sizes, watched the scouting party escort their prisoners through the large cluster of teepees. Children peeked in fear until Tinkerbell's bright energy caught their eyes. They then giggled and chased after her. Her light shone more brightly around these old friends, and she playfully teased the children, buzzing past every skeptical onlooker.

If the fairy had brought these visitors to them, then how bad could they be? The somber expression of the fearless warrioress left some still in doubt, however.

Tiger Lily called to someone in the grandest tent, which stood tall in the center of the camp. The camp fell silent. Whoever was called brought a sudden and weighty tone before even making a physical entrance. The tent flap opened and out waddled a short, but widely built, older Piccaninny gentleman with small, laughing eyes. His greying braid swayed behind him as he advanced toward his lovely daughter.

Tiger Lily kissed his cheek and spoke to him, gesturing toward her captives. He only heard half of her explanation, for his eyes were immediately fixed on Hastings.

"Haeleth," was all he said.

Tiger Lily squinted to understand him. She followed his gaze to Thomas Hastings, the man whom she took only slight notice of before. Suddenly understanding him, her posture changed. Having her father's confirmation, she believed Alice's claim. She quickly knelt on the floor, respectfully bowing her head to Hastings. Despite their confusion, the rest of her tribe followed her lead until they all knelt before the Keeper. The chief, however, did not yet bow. He walked toward Hastings in amazement.

"What are they doing?" Hook mumbled with disgust.

"They're bowing to him," Marin answered.

"But why?"

"Because he's the Haeleth Keeper," Clancy said with a strange reverence that made Alice smile.

"Please," Hastings shook his head to the chief. "Tell them to stop." He was embarrassed, even ashamed.

But the chief shook his head with a laugh. "I will not, Keeper." He bowed his head delicately and took Hastings's hand. "Please stay. We very much need your presence at this time. I am the chief, and some call me Ahanu. The little Peter boy named me Great Big Little Panther."

"Ahanu," Hastings bowed his head, feeling uncomfortable with the amount of honor bestowed to him. "We only need safety and supplies. We don't want to impose on—"

"Keepers do not impose," Ahanu frowned. "They empower. My people have heard many stories about you. I have seen visions of you in your greatness; the Great Mykolas prepared us for your reign, Haeleth. Many of us are even of his kind." He nodded to Clancy, recognizing his Keepership as well as addressing his own. "You need many men for this fight, so we were given powers of the Great Mykolas to give you aid."

"Is that why you've survived?" Marin suggested.

The chief gave her a respectful and acknowledging bow, allowing her part in the conversation between himself and the Keeper.

"When the Dark One's soldiers attacked and took the pirates and Lost Boys, Peter was lost, and Pan became our enemy. War was waged between good and evil. Good always has strength, but sometimes help is still needed. The extinction of the fairies took Light magic from Neverland."

Tinkerbell stopped playing when she heard this. She perched herself once again on Alice's shoulder and solemnly concurred, hanging her head low.

"What little remained was fleeting," Ahanu continued, "the mermaids are often called away by their mistress to see to other duties..."

"Their mistress?" Marin pressed.

Ahanu's face lit up. "Ah, The Great Lady...she treasures those under her dominion—she fights for them and entrusts them with sacred callings. That is why hardly a mermaid is seen in Neverland as of late. They have much better things to do. The Great Lady's waters stretch across many realms, and their assignments are never an easy journey. But then, no Alden's is. This land was meant to be a haven for The Great Mykolas's kind, one the child Peter was chosen to lead."

Solemnly, Ahanu hung his head. "The fairies that The Great Lady sent him could only teach so much. He thought he knew better...he was arrogant and he began to rule improperly...and that's why the Great Evil came and the beast won. The Great Mykolas offered sanctuary and relocation to my people...but my home was my first assignment, and I could not surrender so easily."

Ahanu raised his chin with a sense of duty. Clancy understood his meaning. Keepers of any kind do not take failure lightly. They are fighters, by nature.

"Reclaiming a realm is no easy feat," Tiger Lily spoke up. "But you have another duty, Haeleth." As the chief's daughter, she inherited much of his intuition. "So, we will grant you a safe place and supplies."

Hastings bowed his head once more in gratitude. "And what would you like in return?"

Tiger Lily's lips tightened, but her eyes spoke volumes. She wanted so many things. She wanted her childhood friend returned. She wanted the Darkness banished. But she was a realist. Her duty to her people and her father were just as active as her faith in Keepers.

"When the time comes," she said deliberately, "I want you to do your duty and save a realm."

32

Calm Before the Storm

Reminiscent of our time with King Arthur and his knights, Ahanu and his people took every opportunity granted to throw a feast. The arrival of a Keeper is reason enough for celebration. There was dancing and cooked meats and vegetables.

Pan flute music floated through the celebrating crowds of natives and the foreign Alden, both peoples being now one in the same. The drums beat gleefully, and all was well. A warm fire in the middle of the camp kept the party alive even after the sun slept for the night.

Alice was simply delighted. Music, dancing, and food were three of her favorite things. While her uncoordinated caretaker sat with some of the less enthused men, Alice joined Tiger Lily in the lighthearted activities around the fire, dragging Jim along with her. He was only too happy to comply, keeping a bashful eye on the chief's daughter.

Alice pulled Marin's arm as well, but Marin subtly pulled away until Alice distracted herself with Tinkerbell's energetic tinkling. Marin stepped back awkwardly and resumed a more reflective stance.

Livesey, one of the less enthused men, sat beside the Keeper on a log. They were both spectators by preference, and thus bonded comfortably in their uninvolved silence, picking at the strange food they were served. However, Livesey's mind wandered in a direction only the Keeper could reconcile.

"Mr. Hastings," Livesey attempted a conversation. "The chief–he is a Keeper as you are?"

Hastings looked up from his dish of bizarre meat and cleared his throat. The smell of the food was peculiar, but he hated to be so rude as to insult the chief's hospitality. "Ahanu is a Regent Keeper, like Clancy."

"Hm, I see," Livesey considered. "Alice mentioned you were once a Regent as well. How does one become a Regent?"

Hastings swallowed hard. "Well...a wise Arch Keeper must pass on the necessary authority and magic. Keepers are always chosen."

"And are you such a wise Keeper?"

The Keeper cleared his throat. He knew the answer, but no part of him wanted to address it. His face was riddled with doubt, but Livesey didn't notice–he was briefly distracted by a rustling that came from the tree line behind them. Clancy, who sat across from the good doctor, shook his head when Livesey's eyes fell on him.

"It's only the witch," Clancy assured him. "If it were a threat, every bow in this camp would be drawn."

"Ah, right," Doctor Livesey nodded, turning back to the Keeper. "Baba Yaga. Collecting things. You were saying, Hastings?"

"You're not asking the easiest questions, doctor," Hastings eventually answered. "I don't think I'm really equipped to answer myself."

Livesey quickly looked at him in disappointment. "I think there are others who believe you to be wise."

"Alice doesn't count," Hastings chuckled.

"Don't let her hear you say that," Clancy uttered quietly. He was subdued, seemingly focusing more on dissecting the food in front of him than the actual conversation. "Regents are made as they are needed. And the Arch Keeper isn't the only one who can make Regents—Myk...well, he can do whatever he wants, I suppose."

"And Myk is your employer?" Livesey fished for clarification.

Hastings chuckled and cleared his throat in time to swallow a mouthful of food.

Clancy eyed him and then slowly proceeded to explain. "He and his father Yonas created the Keepers. His is the magic we use. He is our leader against Korbl—so, yes, in a sense, he is our...employer."

Livesey nodded. "And Korbl is the ultimate villain."

"You sound more and more Alden every day, Livesey," the Keeper commented.

"And what does it take to change from Alden to Regent?"

"Being Alden is honorable, doctor," Ahanu answered, tapping his ivory pipe against his hand. "There's never shame in that. If Myk believes you to be Regent material, he will make it so."

"Yes, Myk's Keepers know what they're doing." Clancy glanced sideways in Hastings' direction.

"That was almost sweet, Clancy," Hastings swallowed.

"Yes, well, also purely accidental," he resumed, picking at his food with a suppressed smile.

Livesey looked to Hastings as well, hoping the Arch would pass judgment on his readiness, but Hastings neglected to comply. Instead, he offered Livesey a bite of whatever Neverland fruit the Piccaninnies were serving. Livesey shook his head with a wrinkled nose.

"And when were you made a Regent, Clancy?" the doctor went on.

A spark returned to Clancy's posture. Clancy relished the chance to share a story—almost as much as Alice did. That suppressed smile became less so as he set his utensil across his wooden plate and wiped his hands on his pants to prepare for his tale.

"A very long time ago. I was raised in the Arkis, where Myk and Yonas live. When I was an infant, I was taken from my mother by an evil imp named Rumpelstiltskin. Korbl had already won my realm, but the Keeper still saw it fit to save me. Korbl wanted me for himself, to raise me as a soldier, as the ideal, brainwashed Scada, if you will. Myk outdid Korbl... as he always does. He saved me from Korbl and raised me in the Arkis."

"Myk himself was a Keeper?"

"Of course," Ahanu nodded.

"He put himself in a considerable amount of danger to save me, but he did it anyway," Clancy praised. "He is a great man. Great men always disregard their own safety to protect that of the helpless. He raised me in the Arkis and made me a Regent when I became of age."

"And you hadn't left since," Hastings pointed out. "Until now."

Clancy cleared his throat. "Yeah. Well, we all have regrets."

Hastings paused in thought, momentarily lowering his utensil. "Hang on...Clancy, you were taken from your mother who was married to the king of your realm?"

"So you are a prince," the chief chortled. A brief smirk passed over his face until he took his next puff of tobacco.

Clancy was bashful. He looked down at his food with a doubtful expression. "I mean, I suppose technically..."

"Of course he is," Hastings chuckled.

"So you are both a prince and a Keeper—I'm sure Myk finds that most advantageous," Livesey went on. "And you being raised by Myk no doubt provided you with the training necessary for any given assignment."

"In theory," the Keeper snickered, but quickly corrected himself. "I'm sorry."

The scribe shrugged. "I have my strengths," he answered quietly. "Some things require more than training."

"Which Mr. Hastings makes up for," Livesey assumed. "You were a soldier? You seem to be well-trained in going behind enemy lines and returning with valuable information. Are all Arch Keepers trained as such?"

Hastings nearly choked on his food. Once his throat was cleared, he avoided Clancy's presumptuous stare and chose his words carefully. "I happened upon necessary intelligence, sure."

"What, uh, what does that mean?" Clancy chuckled along nervously.

Hastings laughed at his perplexity. In spite of his rank and decorum, Chief Ahanu joined in the laughter. Young Jim Hawkins and Tiger Lily, followed eagerly by Alice, recessed from their play-fighting to refuel with some food before continuing. Alice saw Hastings's fun and grew overwhelmingly curious.

"What is it, Mister? What is it that's so funny? I want to know the joke," she pestered, pulling at his arm. He only laughed harder, for Clancy's face froze in gradual realization.

"I do believe Mr. Hastings got a little more intimate with the enemy than he should have," Livesey presumed, suppressing a smile and promptly taking another bite of food.

"What did you do?" Clancy intensely studied Hastings's reaction. "What-what did you do?"

Hastings paused his laughter and gave a sly grin. "Relax, Clancy. It was just a kiss."

"You kissed her! You kissed–you kissed the devil's mistress. Do you even know what this means?" he stuttered.

"Oh, now," Hastings defended and stifled another laugh. "Give me some credit; she kissed me."

"Good heavens," Clancy set his food on the floor and held a hand to his heart.

Jim watched Clancy panic. The boy furrowed his brow in contemplation. "Is that worse then?"

Alice looked down to him with a correcting hand on her hip. "Of course it is, Jimmy. She is the enemy, after all—remember?"

Jim frowned. Tiger Lily crouched to the ground beside where Jim sat. She took a piece of food from his plate and nodded in agreement with Alice. Now he understood. Kisses from the enemy were not the best idea.

"Was she in disguise?" Clancy rattled. "Was she Lorelei?"

Hastings shook his head. "She was not."

And Clancy then shook his head. "No, no, this is so much worse."

"Then why is Mr. Hastings smiling?" Jim whispered to Alice.

"I think he finds amusement in Clancy's heart palpitations," Livesey contributed.

Tiger Lily chuckled. "He is funny."

"Let's go back—I'm ready to play again," Alice pulled Jim and Tiger Lily's arms back into the center of the circle to resume play-fighting.

She then turned to Jim, who seemed to have grown since their arrival in Neverland. He stood to match Tiger Lily in height with the eager expression of a pupil waiting for his teacher. And so they sparred. As she moved, he moved, blocking her every attack. She stepped back and examined him.

"You are a great warrior, Jim Hawkins," she acclaimed, clapping her hands together. "A natural." She bowed to him respectively, taking him by surprise.

"Um, thank you," he shrugged awkwardly. His cheeks went scarlet, but he tried to hide it by wiping the sweat off of his face.

Alice and her short attention span ran past him, playing chase with the Indian children and Tinkerbell. Alice was faster than all of them, and she came closest to catching the fairy.

The frivolity was a beautiful thing to behold, providing the perfect refreshment from the ugliness that Ava brought to this tale. Yet, the ugliness of her tricks had left Clancy disquieted and on edge.

"Calm down, Clancy. She slipped up. Ava's aim is not to seduce me," Hastings eased him.

He playfully nudged Clancy's arm. Something dragged his eyes to our little mermaid, who stood pensively just outside the circle of laughing spectators, her arms crossed in front of her chest. She neither engaged in Alice's play nor did she watch the frivolity as Hastings and the others did. Her discomfort prompted him to act.

Clancy's eyebrows shot up. "I'd say it is. Ava never does anything without reason."

"Yeah?" the Keeper answered distractedly. He stood, brushed off his pants, and took aim for Marin. "Then what's the reason for her?"

As Hastings walked away from him, the poor scribe sighed. His voice lowered with his head while he turned his focus to his food and grumbled to himself, "I don't know, Hastings. Perhaps a distraction...undercover spy...professional assassin...or to make you look like a fool..."

"Don't like dancing?" Hastings's hands met behind his back as he swayed over to her.

"Hm?" she snapped out of her reverie. "Oh, no I love it. I just prefer to watch. My sea legs don't let me move very gracefully," she lied.

They stood together for a moment in silence, watching their jovial friends prance. Jim followed Tiger Lily's lead, wholly entranced, while Alice and Tinkerbell gleefully trailed behind. Small drums were beaten quickly, trying to outmatch the dancing feet, resulting in clumsy giggles. Despite the music and laughter, the silence between the Keeper and the mermaid lingered; Marin could feel Hastings's eyes on her. Slowly, she turned her head to him and lifted her brows.

"Is there something bothering you, Hastings?" she spoke suspiciously.

Hastings shrugged, hiding a smirk. "Alice got under your scales."

"No, she didn't," Marin crossed her arms tightly in front of her chest.

"She does that," he pressed. He knew from the moment Marin moved her eyes away that he was right. "Mermaids know better, she said. But not all mermaids care as much about what you're after..."

"But everyone's after something," she said curtly.

"But, The Lady..." Hastings considered. He mirrored her stance and pondered aloud. "Of all the forces to answer to, in my experience, she's among the most reasonable."

Marin pulled her arms tighter around her. "I wouldn't know."

"Ever wondered why Ava fears the water?"

Marin didn't respond; she didn't have to.

"I have a theory," Hastings mused. "Considering her ever-powerful counterpart claims dominion over the waters, logic dictates that the waves are where she's least welcome."

"Careful, Alice!" they heard Clancy call out. The little girl tripped over one of the younger Indians she chased, but only giggled her way back to her feet.

"You have such interesting theories, Keeper," Marin muttered before catching herself.

Hastings snorted. "You even sound like her."

Clearing Ava's words out of her throat, the mermaid shook her head. "She's not...she's not all bad..."

"Sure," he nodded. "Forcing you to deny who you are isn't all bad. But she knows the water can save you, and she can't have that, can she?"

"Mm," she debated. "I can't have that."

"Because Ava knows best."

Marin lowered her arms, prepared to defend herself. "Well, if it means survival, then you have to do what has to be done."

Hastings angled his shoulders toward her, keeping his arms thoughtfully crossed and his eyes properly enlightened.

"I'm beginning to see where she got her inspiration for Lorelei. Of course, she was running from a fictional criminal past, and you're fighting for the soul you don't have." The Keeper chuckled lightly to himself as he weighed the motivations.

"What's funny?"

"Nothing," he shrugged again. "I just...you care so much about living forever...living is not something humans always value the way they should."

"'They?" she scoffed. "You don't consider yourself human?"

"I do, I've just...learned. That thing you fear so much... ceasing to exist—I once sought that, even tried to help it along. I didn't want this, any of it, and I didn't want the ghost of me to live on either."

Then a quick and strange wave of emotion crossed over the mermaid. "You humans don't know a good thing when you have it."

He made a note of the empathy in her voice as her face fell. "Well, I've learned the value of life since," he assured her. "Immortal souls and human bodies are taken for granted–so carelessly treated because we all have them."

Marin intertwined her fingers together and let her hands fall loosely joined in front of her. "You're right," she nodded. "You forget what a special thing you have."

"And you? You wouldn't take it for granted?" the Keeper challenged curiously.

"Mm, no," she frowned. "I don't think I will."

"Stop–stop," Tiger Lily froze, causing a complete halt to the dancing.

Jim, who startled to a stop in front of her, spun around to see her staring warily at the ground before him. The sun had begun to set, and shadows were strewn across the clearing in which the festivities took place. As is reasonable, there was a shadow for each dancer, prancing behind its owner. However, Tiger Lily's eyes were snagged by something a little less reasonable. Stretched from Jim's feet were not one but two shadows following his every move. Tiger Lily slowly looked at her father, who then looked across the way to Hastings.

Ahanu nodded to him with a calm but expectant tone.

"He's here."

33

PAN

Every Piccaninny in the camp immediately stood with weapons drawn—weapons Livesey didn't even know they had concealed. The doctor watched the defensive stances and attempted to assess the unseen threat. Instinctively, he rose and drew Jim closer to him.

"Who is it, Clancy?" he asked.

Clancy didn't immediately respond, but instead stood beside him, drawing little Alice close to him as well.

"Perfect," Hook muttered. Upon seeing a second shadow fall along the ground beside the Hawkins boy's, he flicked his plate of food on the ground in annoyance. "It's the brat."

Pan suddenly appeared, as if on cue, circling them mockingly and then hovered over the clearing in the center. Hastings and Marin moved in, stepping in line with the newly formed perimeter created by the Indian soldiers. Gradually surrounding the heroes was the small assortment of Lost Boys with their weapons drawn. Their leader laughed, grating on Hook's nerves and making Alice sad.

"That's not Peter," she whispered to Clancy. Clancy put a protective arm in front of her. Her eyes welled and tears caught in her throat. "That's Michael, Clancy...that's Michael Darling..."

Suddenly, the flying child stopped laughing. With a furious flick of his head, his curly bangs fell in front of his eyes. "I'm not Michael," he insisted with a sinister glare. "I am Pan."

"No, no, you're not Pan," Hook declared. "The real Pan was far more clever and more irritating."

"How did you get like this, Michael?" Alice begged, trying desperately to step in front of Clancy. "Wendy wouldn't—"

"I don't need Wendy!" he hissed. "And I am better than the last one."

Pan quickly recovered, however, when Jim Hawkins caught his attention, bringing a mad smile across his face. An odd expression for someone so young as Michael Darling.

"You're Jimmy," he pointed. "You've been playing with these redskins."

Jim swiftly removed the feathered headband the Indian children had gifted to him. He cleared his throat and straightened his back boldly. "Where's the real Peter Pan?" Jim demanded.

Hastings advanced to Jim's side, prepared for the unstable flying youth to snap again. Instead, Michael snorted.

"The last Pan lost the name when he lost the Battle," the Dark Boy said.

Hook clicked his tongue. "If you're Pan now, Michael, you're the enemy, and this is all in bad form," he chided him. "Attacking us when you are so outnumbered."

The boy's fists were propped against his hips in that proud way of his. Pan scoffed. "I won't be for long, Captain Hook. And I could beat you even if it was me against all of you. I have more magic than Peter ever did, and I don't even need silly fairies."

"You see here—"

"Easy," Hastings warned. Hook fell silent, but his scowl lingered.

"Oh," Pan said, spotting Marin beside the Keeper. "You're the traitor Ava told me about. I didn't recognize you. Mermaids look so different out of the water."

Hastings moved in front of her, holding tight to his sword.

"It's alright," the new Pan assured him. "I'm not supposed to hurt the mermaid in this game. Even if she is a traitor."

"Game?" Hastings challenged.

"Game," Pan repeated. "But you'll be more fun than Hook. And even Great Big Little Panther."

Ahanu shrugged respectfully.

Pan pointed enthusiastically at Hastings. "You, sir, have more magic. Everyone else was getting boring anyway. I don't much like being bored. But I'm not here for any useless grown-ups. I don't even want Peter's fairy."

He stepped foot on the ground and looked directly at Alice's shoulder, where Tinkerbell's head poked through the girl's strands of blonde hair.

"Then what do you want?" Marin challenged. She tried to step around Hastings for a better view of their adversary, but he proved a somewhat stubborn obstacle.

Michael ignored her. He hopped directly in front of Jim and crossed his arms. "Is Hook the only pirate you know?"

Jim was cautious, but answered politely, true to character. "No, he isn't."

"Ava told me where you came from, Jimmy. Pirates are vicious and horrible, aren't they?"

"They can be."

"They're just like other grown-ups, only with swords and parrots and hooks for hands...." he flashed a grin in Hook's direction but shot back at Jim before he could see Hook's spiteful reaction. "Do you like being a boy?"

"Well, yes...it is how I was born..."

Michael's hands fell. "No, a child. Do you like being a child?"

Jim frowned. "Sure."

"Where you're from, children have to rely on grown-ups for help. You need a grown-up to feed you, tell you what to do. Mothers and fathers and Wendys and Johns–they're all so grumpy," he grimaced.

Alice's gut curled along with Michael's sneer. The youngest Darling had always been her favorite. His childlike wonder and wise potential...she was beginning to understand why Clancy hid the record of the Battle of Neverland.

Michael's exuberance and the Lost Boys' fun and games had been spoiled, and no child should witness such degradation.

"No more, though," Michael went on, proudly planting his hands on his hips. "No rules, no worries–not in Neverland. Just play and fly. Me and the Boys play games all the time. And I'm in charge. I teach them to fight and to fly, as Peter did, only I'm much cleverer than him and John ever were. We have magic too—free magic. We can use as much as we want, and we don't even need fairies. We can do whatever we want to do. No mothers making rules. How does that sound?"

"But I have a mother," Jim shrugged. Livesey stiffened as Jim confidently stepped forward. "And....if all you do is play....what happens when there's trouble? What happens when you're threatened? If there are no rules, no responsibilities, what happens when a tyrant takes advantage of you and takes over?"

Michael made a face, but Jim ignored him and continued.

"Who is the hero? If no one grows up, how are you to learn how to fight and stand for yourself? If no one grows up, how do you become heroes? Who is to defend you? Who fights for you? If you don't grow, you can't know how to fight for yourself. If you can't fight for yourself, maybe no one will. If you're just a boy...forever...you'll be in your own little world until evil leaks in without you knowing it. You won't even know it's happening because you haven't learned. And that evil will control you. You'll be weak. Perhaps that's why Peter said no to Ava."

Livesey's face deepened with respect. The young boy Hawkins–who came to him at the beginning, whom he swore to protect and lead to treasures untold—was becoming a man. Even Hook was rendered speechless by the young man's monologue. Michael, however, would not stand for it.

He yelped, stomping his foot like the child he was. "Peter said no because he was too scared of magic! You wouldn't understand. It's too powerful! Not even John could handle it and that's why I'm better!"

This startling rise in volume may have caused Jim to take a step backward, but it in no way shook the young man's resolve.

Boldly, he crossed his own arms and straightened his shoulders. "Well, now I'm saying no as well. No thank you, Mr. Pan. I don't want to be weak."

The response was unacceptable to Michael. Jim was on the cusp of manhood, and he had already done the unspeakable. Jim had grown up. From the moment Peter brought the young Mr. Darling to Neverland, he knew growing up was the worst possible sin. His face contorted in disturbed fury as Michael remembered Ava's words.

Don't forget my policy.

And he hadn't. If you can't recruit them, kill them. The new Pan's eyes darkened and his lip twisted in distaste.

"Okay Boys," he signaled behind him. "Jim doesn't want to play. We have to end the game now." Before he could wave the kill order, Alice frantically pushed Clancy's arm away.

Seeing the girl's sudden movement, a Boy called Damien lunged for Hastings. He was tall for his young age, so his knife managed to lightly graze the Keeper's neck before the attack was dodged and Damien stepped back, tightening his grip on the blade.

But Hastings did not reach for a weapon, nor did he use any magic to defend against the Lost Boy. No, he did nothing more than stare at the threat incredulously. How could he do more when facing a child?

The Piccaninnies on either side of the Keeper matched Clancy's equally surprised expression, but not in the defense of the child. A boy with a knife doesn't often match up to a Keeper with military training.

Marin, however, saw things differently.

"No! Stop!" she cried.

Curiously, Michael crossed his arms in front of him. "Alright," he wagered, "I'll make you a deal." Aimlessly, he flew around quickly and returned to the earth. "I won't let Damien kill the Keeper if you tell me the scariest story you have ever heard."

"Hang on," Clancy scoffed. "You really think a child stands a chance against Hastings?"

Marin lowered her voice. "If this Pan has Ava's magic, then yes, he absolutely does. You've seen her—could you imagine the danger of giving power like that to a child who hasn't the faintest idea how to control it?"

The scribe exhaled with an understanding, "Ah, you're right."

"Thanks for the confidence, though, Clancy," the Keeper muttered.

"Go–go on, then," Clancy then encouraged, nudging Hastings's side. "Tell him a story."

Alice tugged persistently at Clancy's arm. "But I'm better at that," she insisted. He merely brushed her aside, pulling her further behind him.

Our little mermaid, emulating the confidence of a keen negotiator, stepped forward past the Hawkins boy and faced Michael with shoulders squared. "Tell him to stand down first."

After a long stare, with neither party wavering, Michael finally sighed and waved Damien back into the rest of his ranks.

"All right, now tell it. Tell me the story. And make it a good one."

Marin inhaled for strength, wrinkled her brow for consideration, and finally settled on the more earth-shaking story she could conjure. "It's a story...about a mermaid..."

"Of course it is," Hook murmured, rolling his eyes.

"Quiet," Livesey shushed him.

Ignoring the pirate, Marin went on. "This mermaid was cursed by a sea witch. Cursed with no voice and...she had to find someone to love her or she would cease to exist. One day, she walked on land and met a handsome prince...but he didn't love her. He chose to marry another. The morning after his wedding...the mermaid would be turned into sea foam and disappear forever."

Eager interest widened Michael's eyes. He even sat himself down on the ground with his legs crossed to properly soak in the bedtime story. "So she lost?" he stammered.

"No, she didn't," Marin shook her finger. "Because the night before she was meant to die, a woman came to her. The mermaid thought she could be a witch. The woman promised her that she could help her live forever." Marin inhaled once more, touching the hourglass around her neck. "But the mermaid didn't believe her."

"Why not?"

"The woman even broke the curse and magically cut out the tongue of the sea witch who cursed the mermaid and gave it to her...but she still didn't trust her."

"Her tongue?" Michael raised his eyebrows, impressed.

"Nothing Ava said would convince the mermaid, until —"

"Ava!" Michael exclaimed, rising to his feet. "You think Ava is scary? Pirates can be scarier than her! She's a mother who is very kind to me, not a sea witch. I think you'll have to try a little harder."

Marin held her hands in the air. "But you didn't let me finish," she answered steadily.

Alice attempted to squeeze past Clancy once again, grunting softly, "I can tell a better one—I can do the story, Clancy. I can do it!"

"No!" Pan shouted. "The game is over!"

The atmosphere darkened as if an energetic cloud finished the work of the sunset and brought on the night.

"I can't go back to her empty-handed—come on now, Jim!" the boy demanded.

Before Jim could vehemently decline once more, Tinkerbell frantically fluttered in front of Michael's face. At first, he swatted her away, until she loudly tinkled her compromise. Livesey leaned into Clancy.

"Don't, Tink," Alice begged. "Don't."

"What's she saying?" he whispered.

"I'm afraid to ask," Clancy replied to him. "But I have a feeling she's sacrificing herself."

"Tootles," Michael called to another one of the Lost Boys, who stepped forward with a small cage, made of twigs tied together with rope. The new Pan always traveled prepared, should he have the chance to claim the one fairy he couldn't seem to win. Tootles gripped Tinkerbell by the wings and shoved the fairy into the cage, slamming the door shut in victory.

"Catching a fairy isn't coming back empty-handed," Michael inhaled arrogantly, content with his capture.

But a promise from a child is not always well kept. Whether it's innocently forgotten or the gravity of such a promise is misunderstood, the very young can be very fickle.

After receiving their Pan's signal, three of his Lost Boys defied the fairy's wishes and fired the kill-shots in Jim's direction. Livesey, with impulsive heroism, lunged in front of Hawkins, welcoming the three arrows to his chest so long as they spared Jim.

In a panic at his failure, Michael and his Boys disappeared with Tinkerbell in a flash of smoke while Jim rushed to Livesey's side, tears already streaming down his face. He cupped his dying friend's head in his hands. Hastings and Clancy joined him on either side of the doctor.

"You have to save him, Mr. Hastings, you have to," Jim begged.

"No, no," Livesey lulled, taking his hand. "No, Jim."

"Livesey..." Hastings started, reaching for the arrows.

"No, don't, Hastings." Blood was beginning to fill his mouth, but the doctor swallowed hard and pushed out words. "Jim...I told your mother...I told her I'd protect you from the moment you left her inn. I...couldn't let her down...she will be...so proud to see the man you've become."

Clancy took Livesey's hand and held it firmly. "Great men always disregard their own safety to protect that of the helpless, my friend. I told you that. You are a great man."

"Ah," Livesey struggled to correct him, "I am not great...and Jim is far from helpless. I want you to live long enough to continue proving that, my boy."

Hearing Jim's sobs break through, Alice pushed past Jim to put her hands on Livesey's wounds. Desperately, she sought for the right words to heal him. She may not have had a conduit jacket, but that hardly mattered to her. She couldn't let a hero such as this fall.

"No, no, no," Alice whimpered. Hastings lightly touched the young girl's shoulder, stopping her.

"Alice," Hastings exhaled heavily. "Let him die a hero."

Jim's eyes were red and puffy. Since his father's death, Jim always had Livesey looking out for him. Losing him had never once crossed his mind. Of course it never does, does it?

Those we hold dearest are the last we expect to ever be without.

Out of respect for the fallen hero, Ahanu's people gave him a proper burial with the highest honors. It was just as the doctor deserved. Tiger Lily draped a consoling arm around Jim during the ceremony, and Alice held tightly to his hand. No one spoke a word during the burial. Nothing needed to be said.

The most silent of all was our Keeper. The imagery of mentor and student in their last moments was far too jarring. Hastings's brow furrowed and his hands balled beneath his crossed arms.

Ahanu and his Piccaninny Indians, Jim and his two biggest supporters, with Marin holding Alice's other hand, all stood reverently around the fresh grave. Hastings stood some distance behind them; the only one out of the Keeper's sight was our poor scribe.

"How do you do it?" Clancy spoke softly, approaching from behind him.

Hastings made little effort to face him and instead aimed his sights forward as he responded. "What is it that I do?"

"Watching the fall of a comrade. All this loss and pain...I don't think I can tolerate it, Hastings."

This provoked a glance. "We're not meant to tolerate it, Clancy. We're meant to fight it and then graciously accept it when it's out of our hands."

Clancy cleared his throat, perhaps swallowing a few controlled tears. "It was hard for you...not saving him," he observed. Clancy was no fool. Nor did he maintain his stubborn pride any longer. “Maybe the soldier is not as detached as I previously thought.”

“You didn't read my story very closely, Clancy,” Hastings croaked. Self-consciously, he rubbed his thumb against the dark ring of skin around his right pointer finger. “There's a reason I failed my first time around...and it had absolutely nothing to do with detachment...it had to do with reckless audacity...”

While Clancy absorbed this, making a note of the movement of Hastings's thumb, the Keeper put his back to the burial. “What are we going to do?” Clancy inquired.

“I'm leaving.”

“You're leaving,” Clancy repeated in alarm.

Hastings's eyes darted over their surroundings. Michael had long left Indian territory, but the Keeper's mind was actively assessing the flexible strategy of the child’s master.

“She's altered her plan. She let us escape and then sent a flying child after us instead of facing us herself. She doesn't delegate, Clancy. She engages. She plays her own game—she doesn't let someone else play it for her. I need to know what changed. I need to find her.”

“You need to find the Stone,” Clancy commented. His voice was not as berating as it once was. He slowly weighed Hastings's logic and sighed. “All right. But how will we track her?”

“You're not coming.”

“What?”

"I'm taking Marin with me. She knows Ava, and she's useful. And I'll be taking Hook—something tells me it's wise to keep him some distance from Alice; he doesn't have a liking for children, and she can be quite a pest to a man like him, eh?" Hastings chuckled.

"I'm going with you, Hastings." Clancy grabbed Hastings's arm and forced him to look back at him. "I'm going with you."

"No, you're not," Hastings replied firmly. "I need you here. Alice needs you here."

"Please," Clancy pleaded, his hand subconsciously touching the burn scars still forming on his arm. "I...I have to help."

Hastings's face fell. "You...you have helped. You've done your part."

"No," Clancy's breath staggered. "My part is not yet done. I can't leave you now...not now that you're finally doing so much good. I am still standing by you...my friend."

A slow smile stretched across Hastings's face. "And at last you trust me."

"I think so," the scribe smirked.

"Then please trust me when I say that you are invaluable here. I need to ensure Alice and Jim's safety while I'm away, and you are the only one I trust."

"What about Ahanu?"

"I don't know Ahanu," the Keeper enunciated, lowering his voice. "He hasn't fought beside me all this time, he hasn't risked his own safety to protect Alice as you have, and he hasn't been through what you have."

"You're right," Clancy agreed, "he's probably been through much more."

Hastings held eye contact, expressing such earnestness that Clancy's protests fell silent. "Clancy, please. I need this from you. You must keep Alice and Jim safe; I can't have harm come to them, and without Livesey...Jim will be lost. He needs you. And I don't think you need me to tell you how much Alice has always needed you. Please, stay with them." Hastings held out his hand, gesturing for Clancy to swear his obedience.

Fighting his urge to contradict, Clancy was touched by the sincerity in the Keeper's plea. Inhaling sharply, he took Hastings hand and shook it devoutly. "I will."

34

The Price of a Soul

The Queen of Darkness failed to recover with time. Her color was gone, and she struggled to stay upright as they trekked farther through the forest. Bastien's concern increased faster than Ava declined.

"I'm fine," she continually insisted.

"No," he argued. "You're not. We're stopping to rest."

"No we're not, not here," she sighed and pointed. "There."

Her finger was aimed at a crooked stone structure in the shape of a peculiarly small mountain with a small cave toward the top. It was not natural to Neverland but instead fabricated from foreign magic of a darker kind.

Ava grunted and inhaled deeply.

"At least let me carry you," Bastien offered. He couldn't bear the thought of watching her struggle any further. Without waiting for consent, he slipped his arm under hers.

Ava sighed but leaned her body weight against him anyway. "You know, of all my sins, you are my favorite," she stroked his cheek lightly before letting her hand fall into his.

He began to carry her, stifling a smile.

They were not the only discoverers of the spontaneous rock formation. Only a short distance behind them, Hook had led Marin and the Keeper to the very same landscape. Hook knew it didn't belong, and he also knew that Ava's master rarely took advantage of local resources when he could just as easily muster his own.

"He's in there," Hook pointed, following the same aim Ava had moments earlier. Marin and Hastings looked at each other and then at the small mountain.

"You're sure?" Hastings questioned.

Marin stepped ahead of them and confirmed the pirate's claim. "She'll go there to recharge."

"Recharge?" Hook made a strange face.

The Keeper began gathering thick branches, placing them together in a small pile. "She's been drained too long," he said. "He has to tend to his lady, or she'll be rendered useless."

"What are you doing?" Marin watched.

"I think he's making a fire," the pirate suggested. "Are we not following them?"

Hastings ignored them both for a moment until he had a small fire started in the pile of branches. "No, I'm following them. The two of you are staying here until I get back."

Marin placed her hands on her hips and glanced at Hook incredulously. "Is that the best idea?"

Hastings considered this as he brushed his hands on his pants. "Yes, it is. The fewer of us caught following her, the better."

"You're assuming you'll get caught," Hook put in.

Marin shook her head. "Odds are, she already knows we're following her. There's no point in splitting up."

Hastings adjusted the pack he had been carrying on his back and squared his shoulders. "Neither of you stand a chance if she decides to face us."

"Getting a bit cocky, aren't you?"

"No," he corrected. "I'm just the only one I'm willing to sacrifice."

He walked past her, leaving the mermaid and the pirate behind to look at each other in confusion. Hook shrugged and sat down beside the fire, accepting the break from tracking.

Korbl was there.

She knew he would be.

He waited for her, leaning against the inside of the cave. The moment she entered the mouth of the cave, he stood straight and hastened to her side. At the sight of him, she finally allowed herself to collapse, nearly falling out of Bastien's arms and onto the ground before her. Her lover waved her lackey aside and lifted her from the ground, carrying her to a more comfortable space inside.

"Stay," was all he spoke to Bastien.

Like the trained dog he was, Bastien stood guard just outside the cave while Korbl came to Ava's aid. His shoulders tightened; Korbl took Ava and carried her deeper into the cave, out of Bastien's sight.

"Hm, and here I thought Korbl was the cuckold," Hastings chuckled quietly from his hiding spot behind a smaller boulder. He was well out of earshot and had found the ideal vantage point from which to play spectator to Bastien's painful humiliation.

"What's so funny?" Marin came up from behind him. He jumped slightly, then sighed. He couldn't blame her for her disobedience, and part of him expected her to follow him anyway. "Don't worry; Hook was too comfortable by the fire to come with me."

"All right," he conceded. "Just stay quiet and out of sight."

She nodded in Bastien's direction. "She left him alone outside?"

Hastings chuckled again. "Something tells me Korbl isn't the fool here."

"You'll have to get through him if you want to get to Ava," Marin posed. She leaned her back against the boulder, facing the opposing direction of the Keeper, but looked him in the eye with sincerity.

"Hm," the Keeper hummed, tuning into a sound he swore he heard from behind them.

"You think I'm joking? He'd take more than a bullet for her."

Hastings didn't disagree, but his narrowed eyes told her she didn't quite understand the full picture. "He's hardly the threat," he assessed. "She keeps him around because he's useful. Someone to carry the bags. The only real threat is in there with her now."

Marin spun around to see the cave and the fallen Regent who now stood guard. "So Hook was right," she mumbled. "Korbl really is here."

Korbl held Ava against him as they sat on the cave floor, stroking her hair and face gently. With every touch, her strength grew, her breathing steadied, and the fire in her eyes glowed. Even the vilest of creatures can attach themselves to another individual in such a powerful sense that their very presence invigorates them. For as Korbl gently kissed her head, her power returned.

"An entire ship," he mused softly. "You managed an entire ship...and you're still standing. Hm...you astound me, my little flame."

Ava's eyes closed as she buried her head into his chest. "Did I not tell you I had things under control?"

Korbl grinned. Her evidence of control thrilled him. She was his greatest success, and so her every victory gave him such exhilaration as if he had done it all himself. "And the Keeper's Stone? It's here."

"Can't you feel it?"

He sighed. "Will you need me there, dearest?"

Opening her eyes, she lifted her head and hand to caress his face. "I always need you," she kissed him. "But I'd rather see you a safe distance from the Stone, love. It's best if you let me handle it and get yourself out of Neverland as soon as possible. Besides, I'll have help."

Korbl's gaze moved directly to Bastien, whose shoulder could be seen through the mouth of the cave, and went cold. "Be careful with your affection for the dog—you have a duty that does not require genuine attachment."

Ava released a breathy laugh. "You're jealous, darling..."

Korbl grinned, kissing her head tenderly. "Curb your amusement and rest, dearest." And after one more kiss, he finally set her carefully against the cave wall and rose to leave Neverland.

Korbl confronted Bastien as he exited the cave, and their distant spectator did all but applaud his exciting entrance on the stony stage.

"She will be fragile for a time," Korbl told the guard dog.

"She was already fragile," Bastien fired back. "Are you saying you've done her little good?"

Korbl tightened his lips into an ironic smile. "You're rather fortunate she likes you," he menaced. "Remarks like that could get you killed."

"I'll take my chances," the rival challenged.

An impossibly strong hand gripped Bastien's arm; Korbl forced him closer to better illustrate the gravity of his following words. "I know the reason you're still with me, dog," he cautioned.

The tighter his grip grew, the deeper the muscle in Bastien's arm burned. The very touch of the Dark Master was enough to kill a mortal man—but killing Bastien was not the intent. He needed only proper intimidation.

"It's because of her," the Master seethed. "I don't know what you're hoping to gain–and I don't care. But if you let anything happen to her, what you've wanted will no longer matter. You will not exist long enough for any of it to matter. And I'll be sure to make your demise slow and painful enough so you won't even briefly forget what you did to deserve such obliteration."

The zeal was gone. Bastien's clenched jaw quivered slightly, struggling to maintain his previously bold threats.

"Her flame has been restored," Korbl concluded. "And you'd be wise to see to it that it doesn't go out."

Almost simultaneously, as the Beast spoke these words, a light rain draped itself over Neverland. The raindrops dissolved the dark smoke in which Korbl disappeared. Bastien's hand went to his invisibly cauterized skin as he inhaled, trembling with rage. That rage was soon tempered by the visage of Ava, refreshed and revived to her former energy.

She kissed him and smiled.

"Now...let's check on our little boy."

When the show was over, Hastings nudged Marin and led her back to where Hook was still waiting for their return. After unpacking a small meal the Piccaninnies had provided them, they retold what they had seen and attempted to evaluate what they had learned.

Marin was not content. Nothing was seen that she hadn't already known. Ava was a unique Scada, and a part of what made that so was her direct link to Korbl's power—it was only right that she would return to him when she found herself in need of strength.

Hastings, however, seemed more than satisfied with what he had seen.

“They'll reunite with Michael,” he said simply. “She'll learn he failed and then reassess her strategy.” Hastings stoked the fire idly; his focus on the subject seemed to be fading.

“But what exactly was her strategy?” Hook questioned. “Why use the boy in the first place?”

“Distraction.” The Keeper fiddled with a small branch in his hand.

“Distraction from her need to restore her power, sure,” she agreed.

Hastings continued to fiddle as she spoke. Briefly, he lifted his head toward the woods behind them, hearing a snap. Before Marin could ask what he heard, he suddenly pointed the branch at her. “Did you really love him?”

“What?” she stared.

“Your handsome prince. Did you really love him, or did you love the human soul he would have provided you?”

Hook frowned, munching on his food. “What does that have to do with—?”

“You told Pan your story,” Hastings pointed out.

“Yes,” she exhaled.

“So did you love him?”

Marin paused a moment to consider. Her expression was grave, her response short. “I don't know.”

Hook sniffed loudly and wiped raindrops from his forehead. "So it was for the soul," he judged. Marin's eyes dropped down to her palms.

Hastings tossed the branch in the fire and intertwined his fingers, resting his elbows on his knees. "That's what made it so easy for Ava to win you over."

"She didn't win me over," she retorted defensively. "I didn't trust her."

"But you do now."

Marin cleared her throat. "She broke my deal with the sea witch and let me survive the night...before she even made me swear loyalty. I didn't have to put all my hope in a man who may or may not ever love me. The immortality she offered was guaranteed—"

"Right," Hastings humored. "For a heavy price." Marin fell silent. She couldn't counter that. "As cliché as it may sound, there is always another way." He stood and crouched by the fire to stoke it. "But if you truly understood that, she would lose all power over you."

"Yes, we've established that. The only other way is to gain the love of a human."

"See," he looked up at her. "I told you there was another way. And you're not out of the realm of possibility yet. The prince was just one man. Marin...one man was all it took to shatter your faith in the more freeing alternative. That's what she's counting on. I'm told falling in love is much easier than eternal servitude to the devil."

"Painfully true, yeah," Hook agreed with a mouth full of food.

Marin cleared her throat again and laid out the blanket that was rolled in her pack. "Thank you, Hook, for that inspiring input, but I think we should put this topic to rest."

And with that, she turned over and shut her eyes to seek out an escape from the great conflicts tearing her insides apart.

35

The Tale of the Storytellers

Clancy paced.

He paced so much that he nearly wore down an inch of depth in the ground where he walked. Alice played, so carefree, with Tiger Lily and the Piccaninny children. Jim picked Ahanu's brain while collecting firewood and performing various other chores. All were content with the wait because the setting was considerably more safe and comfortable than the brig of *The Wanderer*.

Even so, Clancy paced.

Finishing up his share of the tribe's chores, young Jim carefully approached our fretting scribe with a mind racing with questions. He had so patiently waited for what he was gradually learning, but he was still unsatisfied.

"Um, Mr. Clancy?" Jim spoke, trying not to startle him.

Clancy didn't even flinch. He was unusually aware of his surroundings as he paced. "Just Clancy is fine, Jim. What is it?"

Jim twiddled his thumbs for a moment before posing his question, aligning himself with where Clancy stood. "Mr. Hastings and the others...are they searching for Peter?"

The scribe looked at him and shook his head. "No, Jim. Don't trouble yourself until they get back. Hastings is just gathering information."

"All right," Jim nodded, pretending to be content with that answer. He turned away, but before he could leave, his impatience urged him to turn back and dig for more. "Who were you talking about with Ava?"

Clancy frowned. "What do you mean?"

"Storytellers," Jim reminded him. "Storytellers and Creators."

Sighing, the scribe turned to face where Alice and the children played, prompting Jim to turn and follow suit. "Storytellers are the sages of the Alden," Clancy told him. "They use stories to spread peace, hope, and guidance as necessary."

"Is that what Alice is?" the young man guessed. He watched Alice impatiently try to tell the other children how to play her game as she made up the rules.

Clancy chuckled. "She certainly is. One of seven."

"And Wendy Darling? Was she like Alice?"

A faint smile tugged at Clancy's lips. "Wendy Darling was one of the greatest Storytellers."

Jim crossed his arms in front of his chest uncomfortably before speaking the villainess' name. "Did Ava kill her?"

Clancy exhaled. "I honestly don't know. It would certainly fit if she did. Storytellers..."

"What about Creators?" Jim pressed, slid his hands into his pockets.

"Slow down, Jim," Clancy looked down at him. "There's only one Creator in an era. The Storytellers are greater in number." He then paused. "Regarding accessibility, at least."

Jim swallowed hard, his gaze fixed on Alice now. "And they'll kill them all?"

Clancy followed his eyes to their little friend, sensing his fears. The scribe's arm wrapped around Jim's shoulders and pulled him closer. "Not according to anything I've read," he assured him.

Jim's eyes earnestly met Clancy's. "And what have you read?"

The corner of Clancy's mouth tugged, teasing a smile, but then tightened into a straight line. "There are seven of them," he said.

"You said that," Jim countered.

Clancy sighed. Another child eager for answers, but not at all patient. "Well, there were originally fifteen in the High Council, but I won't confuse you with the math. Korbl and his Fallen Four believed the seven to be lost. For just after the war broke out, they were scattered. They traded Galderean forms for mortal shells so they'd be hidden until the time was right."

The black of Jim's eyes widened. "Alice is one of the Galdere...she's like Myk?"

"One of the oldest and most revered, in fact. Which is why Myk and Yonas will no doubt scold me for allowing her to come here. She was safe in the Arkis, and I let her walk right past the Assassin intending to end her."

"But you said he won't kill her," the boy pointed out.

"None of the seven have ever been successfully killed. Which is promising. By design, they're nearly as difficult to kill as Creators." Clancy's shoulders eased for a moment, before he continued. "I once sorted a collection in the Arkis that said the Lost Kin, or the Authors or Storytellers—they have a maddening number of titles—but they're meant to be gathered...eventually...and do their part again, standing against Korbl as they once did."

"There are so many stories and prophecies with this war," Jim threaded his fingers through his hair, overwhelmed.

In the short distance, Alice had stopped their game and insisted on learning how to build her own teepee, so the other children watched as Tiger Lily taught her.

"Try archiving them sometime," Clancy laughed. "But this is one you'd do particularly well to remember. It's the reason Alice ran away, allowing us to find you in the first place. Storytellers are drawn to Myk's people–past, present, and future."

Jim straightened his back again. "Alice found me?" Clancy nodded, and Jim immediately excused himself to go to her. Clancy simply shrugged and returned to his pacing and fretting.

"Alice!" Jim called.

He broke her concentration, and the three sticks she had tried so hard to hold together fell apart. Tiger Lily had gone to help her father, while the other children got distracted and left little Alice alone. To amend his intrusion, Jim grabbed the three long sticks and held them together while she attempted to tie them.

"I wanted to tell you that I decided on my three wishes," he told her. "Well, not all three of them, but—"

"Jimmy," she shook her head as her fingers fumbled over the rope. "We talked about wishes. Wishes and plans are different. You should really think about them—if it's something you truly want, you need to make a plan and not a wish."

"If a mermaid hypothetically granted me three wishes of whatever I want...I know my first wish...."

"Well go on then and don't you dare make me guess."

Jim grinned. "I wish to meet Myk."

36

A Dance with the Devil's Mistress

The night was loud with heavy rainfall and restlessness. All the great pretenders throughout the forests of Neverland feigned sleep—whether to avoid further discussion of guilt, to quietly digest a hearty meal, or to await the opportunity to slip away.

There was one mighty pretender who did not feign sleep, however. No, she sat upright, beside her loyal protector, discreetly stewing.

Though her energy had been returned, Ava's mind was far from at ease. One could only imagine the wheels turning behind her deadly eyes. Bastien slept anxiously, his hand on her thigh for subconscious assurance that she was still safe. Korbl's threat haunted his sleep.

"Korbl certainly knows how to motivate," the Keeper muttered aloud.

Ava leapt to her feet and instinctively shot a flame in his direction, which he masterfully dodged. The sound of the rain successfully masked the footsteps of her enemy through the trees, and her preoccupied mind had neglected the possibility of a personal confrontation.

"You just can't stay away from me, can you?" Ava kept her hand raised, scanning her surroundings. "All alone," she observed. "None of your little friends followed you."

He shrugged, advancing. "Didn't need them."

Ava broke into a sneer, helping him shorten the distance between them. "You're a dangerous one, Keeper. And women love danger. You'd better watch yourself, or you'll be making that poor girl fall in love with you."

Hastings smirked. She knew why he was there. "What are you to her, exactly?"

"Hm...you could call me her...fairy godmother, of sorts."

"So many roles," he bitingly praised. "Fairy godmother, leader, lover, strategist, deceiver...all so masterfully cycled through as needed." He circled her slowly before resting in front of her. "And I thought Lorelei was good."

She giggled darkly. "Hmm, Lorelei...yes, she was awfully useful. The name of a siren who lures men to their deaths. I admit I was a tad arrogant in choosing the name. But my arrogance did not create stupidity—if the make-believe siren should fail, I was in need of a backup—"

"After Ryder failed," the Keeper corrected.

For the first time since they started their little game, Ava froze. "Ryder....?"

Hastings hummed as he continued to circle her. "I suppose I should have assumed I'd have someone's eyes on me when I left."

"Since you left O'Leary..." she supposed, her own eyes narrowing. "Delegation can be tricky, particularly when there were so many other casualties of that little flop to track."

"Hm, yes. Your reach has slipped into every possible world and you just couldn't let go. I knew you were good, but Ryder...Korbl's power must truly be growing if the dead are now within his control."

Ava pursed her lips for a moment, her confusion nearly betrayed, before she sighed. "I don't fail, Keeper. My methods simply adapt. Haunting is only effective for so long before the haunted get wise. That is why I introduced the real Lorelei. And you seem to like her much better than me or the ghost."

Hastings shrugged again. He watched her mouth, noting the tense curl of her smile. It was forced, but still taunting. "I think you know your hold on her is loosening."

She raised a brow. "Well, you're wrong. But don't frown —you are far too pretty to let yourself frown."

"Oh I'm not frowning," he assured her. "I'm not the one losing."

Ava laughed humorlessly and took a step backward. "I win every game, Keeper," she held her arms up challengingly. "But don't let that discourage you from trying."

Seeing her retreat as confirmation, he once again advanced, this time stopping only inches from her. "Have you ever lost before?"

Unmoved by the closeness, Ava glanced down at the cocky Keeper's right hand. "Not as you have, handsome."

Hastings's marked hand instantly clutched hers and held it for her to see, taking her by surprise. Showing her the stained skin around his pointer finger, he compared it to those same rings which circled her own fingers. One on her thumb, one on the middle of her pointer and one on the base. "This is not how I count losses," he told her.

She grinned at his grimace. "Ooh, love. But it is, isn't it? For that's how I count my wins. See, you have already lost it all—a new jacket does not erase the past. Your effort may be noble, Keeper, but it's weak. Saving one little mermaid from my evil little schemes will not redeem you of what you once failed to save."

Hastings's jaw tightened, and he released her hand. "I didn't..."

"Didn't you?" she crowed over him. She felt the victory drawing near. "Your actions spiraled because of your recklessness, you lost an innocent and destroyed—"

"I know what was lost," he cut her off. "But that wasn't your win. And neither is Marin."

"She has more to lose than you do, Keeper. It doesn't matter how much you think she cares for you; the odds you'll mean more to her than her immortal soul are quite slim."

"And you told her you were the only way."

Ava cocked her head to one side, stepping backwards to restore distance between them. "Hm, and what did you tell her? That there's always another way? That you can never find what you're looking for if you're counting on a Scada?" Her chin lifted to display her arrogance at its best. "I'm no ordinary Scada, Keeper, and I think you know that. And...if you've noticed...her eyes don't have a single stain. That should be comforting for the both of you. She is not doomed in our arrangement; she can only benefit from it. Besides, the only other way is for her to gain the love of a human. Are you telling me she is gaining yours?"

Hastings didn't reply; his smirk returned, and Ava's chin slowly lowered.

"Hm," was all she could say for a moment. "Well...this is certainly a development. I suppose this would make me irrelevant then, wouldn't it?" she vacantly mused. "It appears you truly are winning." Her smugness fell into acceptance.

"She will be free of you, Ava," he promised her. "And there's nothing you can do to stop it."

Her stare went beyond him. She was no longer sizing up a Keeper, and that much was apparent. He had been adequately studied. Her uncharacteristic silence told him the weighted standoff had leaned back in his favor. But there was no retaliation, no flare of anger, no not even a biting retort. Instead, Ava seemed almost...impressed.

"Don't let her fool you, Keeper," she finally broke the silence. "She's in love with your soul—and I don't mean that in a romantic sense. You are simply a means to an end. She is no better than I—although, I must say she is a little less efficient."

He scoffed lightly. "Not all are as doomed as you are, Ava."

"And if you're wrong?" she posed. "If she can't be saved and I win this wager? What then? You'll give me your firstborn?"

This time, the Keeper stepped back with challenging arms extended. "If by some miracle you manage to best me, it's all yours."

Ava shook her head. "Cheeky devil," she purred. "You're mad, you know...but, at least you look good."

"Best of luck to you." The Keeper chuckled and gave her a mock salute as he gradually withdrew back to his camp.

It was when he left her alone with her thoughts and the rainfall that Bastien finally uttered, "What the devil is he doing?"

He had stirred awake the moment Ava moved his hand from her thigh to confront the Keeper, but feigned sleep to observe unobtrusively, as Ava suspected.

"He's playing my game," she replied, still staring at where the Keeper had stood. "They're not usually this clever. Not even the posh one," she whispered to herself.

Bastien rose; she still wouldn't face him, and this concerned him. "Does he love her?"

"Hm, I don't know," she continued to stare. "That's certainly what he wanted me to think. He is clever—whether he truly loves her or not, my believing that he does means admitting defeat. If he believes that I believe he has defeated me, in his mind, he has the advantage. Oh, this is such a fun game..."

"You don't seem concerned," he noted. "If he gets her an immortal soul, you've lost her."

Absent-mindedly, she took his hand which dangled near hers. "You're assuming she knows his feelings. If she doubts his sincerity, his love is meaningless, and she won't claim it, whether it's real or not. We haven't lost anything. He's only toying with us. He's a fighter who's been without a fight for far too long."

"So you're giving him one," he assumed, hating Hastings for the fire he incited.

Realizing his hand was still in hers, she lifted it to her lips and kissed the darkly stained ring around his pointer finger. "Poor unfortunate girl isn't as fortunate as I am."

"In what way?"

"She can only dream herself worthy of the kind of loyalty and devotion that I have in you."

His return to their makeshift camp was done in such anxious energy. Not out of uneasiness, mind you, but adrenaline and anticipation. Marin stood the moment she heard him approaching. Hook had been snoring comfortably, but she couldn't bring herself to sleep since discovering Hastings had gone off on his own again.

The Keeper's expression was determined and eager but softened when he saw her sitting upright. "You should be sleeping," he said.

"You shouldn't be pursuing her alone," was her reply.

His shoulders relaxed. "Marin, I figured it out—"

Marin leaned closer to him. "What? What have you figured out?"

He held up a hand to silence her, and his eyes snapped around him.

"Did she follow you?" Marin whispered in a panic.

She followed his eyes to where Hook lay sleeping. A strange shadow had slithered across the trees surrounding them and landed behind a bush that seemed to have appeared out of the darkness; she couldn't remember seeing it before.

"Hook, look alive!" Hastings shouted.

Hook startled awake, instinctively wielding his long dagger and waving it around him in blind defense. "What is it? What is it!"

He whipped his weapon around quickly enough to block the imminent threat: a sharpened arrow aimed for his heart. The one who wielded it had no bow, just a tight fist around the shaft and a heart filled with rage.

He was a young man with golden brown hair falling in front of what used to be the comprehensive, eager eyes of a potential English gentleman. He had dirt on his face, muddled into his short beard, but no mother or sister to brush it off and mend his torn clothes. Hook grabbed the young man's arm and threw him on the ground.

"Pan," he seethed, pressing the sharp hook against his opponent's throat.

"No," the young man grunted through his teeth. He pushed the hook away, but the pirate pinned him down with his other arm, returning the hook to his throat.

"Let the boy go," Hastings ordered, approaching them.

"Hardly looks like a boy to me," Marin muttered to him. "He must be at least twenty."

The Keeper crouched down to the young men's level, ignoring Hook's disobedience. "Where have you been hiding, Peter?"

"Peter..." Hook repeated, withdrawing the hook. He almost couldn't believe the aging of his previously adolescent enemy. His baby fat had dissolved into a strong, clenched jaw line. His neck had widened, and his shoulders broadened.

He was a man. But he was not Peter.

"I'm not Peter," the young man grunted.

Hook recognized his enemy, but Peter Pan was not his sole adversary in the glory days of Neverland. The pirate held eye contact too long for comfort, for the young man jolted aggressively again, this time toward Hastings, vainly continuing his assault. It took no more than an added pressure of his hand for Hook to hold him down.

The pirate frowned and raised a judgmental eyebrow. "Years of hiding have made you dull, Darling."

The boy couldn't help it. To fight and to fly. That's what Peter once taught his Boys. They were rarely ones to back down from a fight, and this one's recent crisis of faith did only minor damage to his endurance.

Hastings looked up at Hook strangely. "That's oddly affectionate, Hook."

"This isn't Peter Pan, Hastings," the pirate removed his hand from the young man so the Keeper could view him completely. "This is John. One of the Darling boys."

"I'm not Peter or Pan," John seethed with a hint of sadness. "And I'm not dull."

"He's not going to hurt you; none of us will," Marin promised, trying to put him at ease. She stepped forward, and John immediately dropped his arrow.

"Neither will Ava," Hastings added, noting the way John's eyes widened at the mermaid. Her resemblance to Ava did John's nerves no favors, Hastings assumed. He pushed Hook aside and offered a hand to the Lost Boy.

Hook looked from Marin to Hastings and back to John. "What did she do to you, lad?" he asked in a subdued tone, dreading the answer.

John stood upright, still uncertain of Hastings. He couldn't take his eyes off of Marin; he stared warily at her. "Why is she with you?" he jutted his chin at her. "She took our mother and killed the fairies."

"You know Wendy wasn't actually your mother," Hook pointed out. "She was as much a child as you." The pirate fell silent as soon as he received another warning glance from the Keeper.

"I am not Ava," Marin corrected. Her tone was defensive, but the way she slowly stepped closer to John was gentle. "I'm nothing like her," she assured him. "In fact, I'm a mermaid...The Lady sent me back here to help you reclaim Neverland."

John's tight mouth loosened, along with his tense shoulders. "The mermaids left. They're all gone."

Marin shook her head slowly. "No, John. The Lady called us away. But we're coming back."

Hastings observed as the mermaid lulled John's defenses with her words. The Keeper's eyes narrowed in on her while she took John's hand.

"Because Neverland cannot be lost," she added. "Not to Ava."

"She already won," John pulled his hand away, glancing guiltily at Hastings. "I–I made a mistake. She said she was a storyteller...like Wendy..." his voice shook with both anger and nerves, "...and that she had powerful magic...." John balled his fist in remembrance. "I was clever enough, she said. And I believed her...I wanted magic. That's what heroes do, in all of Wendy's stories—and all of the stories end happily."

The Keeper placed a stable hand on the young man's shoulder. Pulling John's attention away from anyone but him, Hastings looked him directly in the eye. "Did you accept Ava's magic, lad?"

John's eyes crashed to the ground. "It didn't work," he croaked.

"What do you mean it didn't work?" Hook frowned. "It seemed to work on your little brother just fine."

Hastings's attention never once strayed from the Lost Boy's fallen face. "You were too clever, weren't you? Too clever to keep it. You changed your mind and she got angry."

John's ice blue eyes welled with regret. "She killed so many...and then Peter rejected her, and she killed more..."

"She killed because you said no?" Marin raised her eyebrows. She had heard many versions of what had happened in the Battle of Neverland, however, all involved the dethroning of Peter Pan and the extinction of the fairies. She hadn't considered the Darling boys were ever particular targets.

"John, what's your father's name?" Hastings asked him.

The young man cleared his throat. He glanced up to read the lines on Hastings's face, but they only brought intimidation. "George Darling," he eventually said.

"Why so uncertain?" Hook poked.

The Keeper watched John's mouth twitch. "Because Ava told you something else, didn't she?" he assumed.

"What are you getting at, Hastings?"

"Peter Pan was not the reason Ava came to this realm," Hastings clapped his hands together, brushing any remaining dirt from his palms. "She was tracking a straggler. I couldn't have been the only one to run when O'Leary..." He stiffly cleared his throat. "When things fell apart." More to himself than the others, he muttered, "He has Neil's face."

"What do you mean?" Marin asked slowly.

The Keeper gradually moved away from them, giving her the impression he had already decided his next move. That distracted yet calculated expression she had begun to recognize was returning.

"What did she tell you about your father?" He threw the words over his shoulder toward the boy.

John's brow wrinkled. Swallowing hard did nothing to ease the struggle of the answer. "She said he was a natural. She told me I could be the same...I would be the best Pan, because it was in my blood...to wield her magic..."

"Hastings, what does any of this mean?" Hook pressed, growing irritated.

"I'm still figuring that out, but I have an idea," Hastings turned back to face them. "John, how'd you like to be a hero?"

37

HOMECOMING

Clancy eagerly awaited the Keeper's homecoming; amidst the safe relaxation of Jim and Alice and the Piccaninny tribe, the inherent lack of visible effort made Clancy anxious. He knew, all that time, that Hastings was somewhere with the pirate and the mermaid tracking the enemy and gathering necessary information. Meanwhile, he was left to fret about progress. The sight of the returning scouts walking back into camp was a long-anticipated relief to the scribe.

"What did you learn?" Clancy pressed, hurrying to greet them.

"The game," Hastings walked right past him. "Ahanu," he called.

"What does that mean?" Clancy asked Marin, who merely shrugged.

"I honestly have no idea," she sighed and watched Hastings's energy grow as he quickened his pace toward the chief.

He was visibly deprived of a good night's sleep, and he insisted on all in their small party rising early enough to make it back to Indian territory by nightfall.

"Erm, Hastings—Hastings!" Clancy cried as he quickly followed him to the chieftain's side.

Hastings was already taking the journal out of his jacket pocket and ruffling through the pages until he flipped to the end where his map had been sitting idle. Ahanu stood and bowed respectfully as the Keeper approached.

"Do you trust me?" he asked Ahanu.

Ahanu shrugged at the silly question. "But of course, Keeper."

"Why–why does he need to trust you?" Clancy inquired anxiously. The scribe glanced around, looking for answers, and finally noticed the new stranger standing beside the pirate. "Wait, Hastings, who's your new friend?" he asked, the anxiety increasing.

Alice released a girlish giggle and bolted towards the newcomer as she embraced John's legs. "John Darling!"

John staggered backward, barely avoiding falling to the ground. Between Alice's confusing enthusiasm and his immediate eye contact with the fair Tiger Lily, the poor boy was progressively overwhelmed.

The Piccaninny chief was the first native to step forward and welcome one of the island's fallen. "Master John," he bowed once respectfully.

Whether motivated by the envious exchange of eye contact between John Darling and Tiger Lily or impelled by an ingrown sense of duty, Jim Hawkins marched his way to the Keeper, sure to correct the nonsense that was no doubt happening.

"He's the traitor," Jim grabbed Hastings's arm, demanding his full attention. "Tiger Lily told me. He ran and hid instead of defending Neverland."

While not quite as accusatory but equally inquisitive, Clancy tugged at Hastings's other elbow to no avail. The Keeper was more focused on the map in his hands than the complicated reunion unfolding before him. Schemes were forming in his mind, and no amount of pestering would distract him.

"Neverland's been lost," John confessed. Alice gave his legs another squeeze and shook her head emphatically.

"But Neverland did not lose you," Ahanu echoed the words behind Alice's head shake.

John's gaze was still on Tiger Lily. Her expression was so apprehensive that he was afraid she'd draw a bow and finish him off in moments for his betrayal. But she didn't. She stared in silence, waiting for her mind to be made up.

"I have nothing," he went on, more to Tiger Lily than the chief. "She destroyed it all."

"And so you ran like a coward?" Accepting Hastings would do nothing, Jim boldly stepped around the Keeper and faced the traitor himself.

"*I'm not a coward,*" John snapped. Alice spun around, releasing his legs, and gasped at Jim's assumptions.

"He's not a coward, Jimmy!" Alice defended. "John is wonderful and he was just trying to be safe. He was in terrible danger. You can't even understand, you silly boy. He couldn't let Ava find him."

Before Jim could launch a retort, he heard Clancy sigh. "That's why you brought him back, isn't it?" the scribe muttered to Hastings. "Because if it is, I could have told you he was probably safer in hiding than he is now."

"Shh," Hastings waved at him, turning the book again, searching for a different angle.

Finally, Tiger Lily moved to the center to face John herself. Her mouth gradually formed a smile, and she bowed her head in acknowledgment. "John Darling. Welcome back."

"I don't know about this, Hastings," Clancy protested, grabbing the Keeper's arm this time. "Have you read his story? His real story. He was susceptible to Ava's influence from the beginning. Not the straightest arrow. Can we really —"

"Neither was I," Hastings whispered harshly. "Do you trust me?"

Clancy stopped himself before answering, then sighed. "Yes...yes, I do."

"Then trust him," the Keeper challenged.

The scribe sighed and watched the prodigal Neverland hero accept the Piccaninny welcome. "He'll be quite mad after this. Ava's Darkness has that effect."

Looking up for just a moment, Hastings flashed a glance at the boy and smirked. "His family's always been prone to a little madness anyway, Clancy. He needs a chance to get ahead of it before Myk relocates him. He needs to be a hero, even for a moment. Besides, he knows the lay of the land better than any living soul on this island."

"I do," John chimed in, suddenly right next to them, with Alice still at his legs. Hastings's whispered confidence had carried to John's ears and managed to capture the attention of the nearby Piccaninny listeners as well. "And I know all the best hiding places."

"He does," Tiger Lily supported, still a few steps behind. "And he is a great warrior," she slipped her hand into his.

Hastings raised his eyebrows and looked at Clancy with a smile. "A great warrior, she says."

Clancy crossed his arms in front of his chest. "Yes, but the Darlings are a proud sort. Can he stand behind a Keeper without stepping on toes?"

John looked down at his feet, then back up at Hastings before taking a few steps back, being sure to not step on the Keeper's toes. Hastings laughed and pointed for Clancy to see.

Clancy rolled his eyes. "I meant…the Keeper is our leader. He is to be the greatest hero in this fight. Are you capable of respecting that?"

Before Hastings could argue with his assumption, John was down on one knee. His head was bowed in deep respect; the Lost Boy sparked a ripple effect. Tiger Lily almost immediately joined him, kneeling at his side. Then Ahanu knelt, followed by the rest of his tribesmen. Finally, with a satisfied grin, Alice pulled Jim's arm down with her, following suit.

Clancy puffed up his chest, beaming with pride in the Keeper he had finally accepted. "I suppose that answers that."

Hastings snapped the journal shut and clutched it in his hand. "No, no," he insisted. He then began to pace his new stage, eyeing every knelt follower before him. "The real question isn't whether or not you'll follow me," he told them. "It's whether or not you feel you can stand against Ava and Michael, no matter the cost."

He then zeroed in on John.

"When they see you rise from your defeat, you will become even more of a target than before. Death is a very real possibility. You know Ava. She is focused, calculated, and dangerous. She knows who you are and she'll do whatever it takes to stop you. She'll remind you that you failed—she'll beat you down, fill you with crippling guilt, making you believe Neverland will never forgive you for what you've done."

John's eyes were wider than the morning sun rising behind him. Though he had the face of a man now, there was a child frightened by nightmares of a siren of fire and destruction. Seeing the poor boy's terror, Ahanu slowly rose to his feet and then turned to lift John.

"You have power, Master John," Ahanu assured him. He held his hands in his, patting them gently. "Power and instinct. It is not the forgiveness of Neverland you must seek. It is the forgiveness of yourself."

Briefly comforting though the chief's words may have been, John's despair quickly returned, and his eyes fell.

"I can't fight her," he said with certainty. "And I can't fight my brother. I can do a lot of things," he straightened his back, "but I can't kill them. None of us stands a chance. She has magic and fire, and pirates. She wins every game, and she will win this one..."

As far as battle rallies go, this was one of the least effective I've witnessed. John spoke with the conviction of one attempting to inspire his troops, but his foreboding message brought the natives' smiles to their knees. John's gaze settled on them, every face of every survivor. The Battle of Neverland was not exclusively his. His tragedy was their tragedy.

Now I realize, reader, that this particular moment feels to you to be the beginning of a conclusion to a battle you never witnessed. Commonly, in this portion of a story, the beleaguered hero rouses his soldiers for one last victory to resolve the conflict in a somewhat satisfying way. Every story's ending is another story's beginning. Stories are funny that way; they're always overlapping and toying with one another's characters as they see fit. John's story may have begun in an otherwise shelved record, along with Peter's and Wendy's, but I can assure you, reader, that theirs are far from over, regardless of Neverland's fate.

Looking at the survivors of Neverland, John felt the guilt of his story pulling him forward. None of them felt it was the end, nor did they accept it was. Ahanu and Tiger Lily shook their heads with conviction, gradually changing the tribe's frowns into solemn expressions of hope.

"But, I suppose..." John dropped his shoulders and lifted his mouth into a small, forced smile, "...dying would be an awfully big adventure."

Smoothly, Alice placed her small hand in John's. "And so would living," she beamed up at him.

All of Neverland seemed to stand and cheer, rushing to embrace their prodigal comrade. In all the excitement and exclamations, Hastings pulled Ahanu aside with a hushed tone, barely competing with the volume of the newly roused natives.

"My people and I need to find the Soter Stone," the Keeper started, stepping even farther away from the crowd. "That's what the enemy's after. But I need you and your people for something else." Ahanu nodded. "We will go to the Stone, and I need you to follow two steps behind us at all times as reinforcement. When the time comes...I need you to do exactly what I tell you...whatever I tell you."

"The Darkness may lose, Keeper, but the fire siren will win Neverland," the chief warned him, furrowing his brow.

"It doesn't matter; winning a battle isn't winning a war," Hastings grinned in spite of it all. "Are you with me?"

Ahanu returned the grin and nodded once more.

"Um, Hastings, what is this about?" Clancy persisted, having lingered nearby.

Hastings placed his hands on Clancy's shoulders to calm him. "My friend," he said. "Relax. Trust me. Get Alice and Jim ready. We leave in the morning."

Hastily gathered and puzzled beyond belief, our reunited group of heroes traveled in a southeastern direction, nearing the Coves. Their leader divulged very little detail, but his schemes were beginning to unfold.

Alice practically pranced at the opportunity for adventure while Jim followed along submissively, sure to keep a reasonable distance between himself and the cowardice of John Darling.

Poor Clancy found Marin less than informative and seemingly distracted. He didn't even bother to give the pirate a chance to explain what might be happening. Over the ridge of the cliffs, Hook spotted familiar sails flying into the shores of Neverland.

Hook's sudden howl of anger was alarming.

"What is wrong with you?" Hastings shut him up.

Hook pointed his hook violently toward the distant shore. Coming into the Coves was *The Jolly Roger*, in all her glory. The pain in Hook's face was agonizing. All he had once fought for was now taunting him. "That devil," he swore.

John stepped in line beside him and shared his expression of disgust. True to form, though numbered amongst the Lost Boys, John Darling did tend to favor piracy.

"She has all your men in there, Hook," John grimaced in commiseration. "Didn't realize she took your ship, too."

Hook snarled, "They're probably scuffing the decks."

Alice tugged the pirate's coat. "It's all right, captain. Myk could just get you another ship. A better ship. He'll know what you should have—just wait 'til you meet him. You don't need that silly boat anyway. Sometimes what we want isn't what we need."

"Oh shut up, you, or I'll—" he brandished his hook aggressively, but Hastings caught it with his sword.

"You'll get over it," Hastings finished. "If we sit and grumble, we won't be getting very far ahead of Ava and Bastien, now will we?

Hook twisted his hook away from Hastings's reach and muttered something incoherently. "Are you so sure she's following us?"

"If she's as clever as she thinks she is, then she will be. And she is as clever as she thinks she is. She hasn't forgotten about the Stone, even if she's gotten a little sidetracked. And she can't find it on her own. She knows we have the map and that we'll be going for it. She'll be following us all the way to..."

The map had changed. Hastings could have sworn the map was leading them farther south, but it was now moving west.

Hook peered over the edge of the parchment and smirked. "Hm, it doesn't seem to be working very well, Hastings."

"It was," Hastings mumbled.

"What happened to it?" Jim asked curiously, careful not to get too close to the feuding men.

"Maybe it's you," Clancy accused, wrinkling his nose.

"Me?" the Keeper challenged.

"No, not you. Him," the scribe pointed to Hook.

"I beg your pardon!" the pirate huffed.

"Well," Clancy considered, "the map's surroundings tend to render it ineffective if there are unworthy souls among us."

"Maybe it's the coward," Jim muttered. As with any pubescent young mind, the sensitivity toward his romantic rival was running rather high for poor little Hawkins.

"It's not me, and I'm *not* a coward," John seethed, shooting daggers in Jim's direction.

Clancy sighed impatiently. "Last time the map stopped working was when we were cooperating with Ava." He fired Hastings an arresting glare. "The magic is hindered when Darkness creeps in. It's the only explanation."

"Unless the Stone itself changed location again," Marin offered.

"Or maybe it's you."

"For heaven's sake, Clancy," Hastings exclaimed.

"She's a Nidling, Hastings," the scribe enunciated. "That is, by definition, the enemy. Maybe the map still sees her as a threat. I certainly do—where are her burns?" He lifted his sleeves to remind Hastings of the horrors of *The Wanderer*.

"Ava dubbed her a traitor, Clancy." Hastings's tone was deep and cautionary. "If Ava herself has cast her aside—why would the map wait until now to stop working, when she's been with us this whole time?"

Clancy's nose wrinkled. The Keeper made an excellent point, to which he had no reply. Alice sat on the ground and cupped her chin in her palms.

"Maybe it's not working because you're all bickering," she suggested glumly.

"I feel quite attacked by you, scribe," Hook protested. "Why label me a threat? Have I not been on your side from the beginning?

"You are a villain," Clancy sighed. "A villain is a villain, whether you're a willing Scada or not."

"But he *has* also been with us this whole time," Marin defended. "The map is being affected by something new. Some change. Perhaps it's your every criticism suddenly returning when there's the slightest rise in panic. How could any of us possibly measure up to your expectations of what Alden should be? If the map feels as you do, it's a wonder it ever worked in the first place."

"The map responds to purity, and you're all tainted," the scribe shot.

"So self-righteous," Hook exhaled.

"Self-righteous? I'm just trying to put lipstick on a pig here—do you know how hard it is to convince a washed-up has-been to accept his calling as a Keeper?"

"Washed-up..." Marin straightened her back menacingly. "Well take it from him then, Clancy. Why don't you claim the jacket for yourself? Clearly, you would be so much better suited for all this. Perhaps that would get the blasted map to work!"

"Your bickering is entirely too loud." Alice's softly uttered observation prompted the Keeper to remove himself.

As the quarreling went on, Hastings continued walking, ignoring the volley of insults in various directions. Gradually, starting with Alice of course, our heroes came back to their senses and followed him, as they should.

Clancy matched Hastings's step and attempted to apologize for his cruel words, but Hastings refused to let him finish.

"It was panic talking," he kept telling him. "It wasn't you, Clancy."

"Well part of it had to be," Clancy admitted regrettably. "But it was unnecessary—the part about the... washed-up has-been..."

Hastings chuckled. "Oh? And what of the part about the vicious Nidling?"

Clancy lowered his voice to avoid Marin overhearing. "You did defend her so vigorously," he pointed out.

The Keeper's chuckle softened into a more severe response. "I can't lose this one, Clancy," he uttered.

Clancy glanced back at the mermaid. Alice had taken her hand and proceeded to fill her in on the fun games she missed out on while she and the Keeper went on their adventure with Hook. Marin smiled and listened patiently, but her mind was elsewhere.

"Is this you proving me wrong then?" Clancy suggested. "I tell you not to mess with Ava, so you decide to target and save the innocence of her little protégé?"

"She threatened me with a challenge," was the reasoning.

"Marin threatened you?"

"Ava."

"Ava threatened you? She was flirting with you."

“Of course she was,” Hastings almost smiled. “I don't think she knows how to speak to a man without flirting. But she's not winning this one. Marin is too important to lose.”

Clancy watched his face, waiting for the playful jest. But none came. The stakes were too high. The mermaid was stolen from their side once already, and if anyone could get her back, it was Hastings.

“She won't be lost,” Clancy pledged. “Not while you're fighting for her. And, as long as you're certain, I'll still fight beside you.”

The moment Spyros's metal leg set foot on Skull Rock, Neverland felt his presence. His Darkness contributed to the shadows that already inhabited the island. He paced in frustration across the beach, barking orders to his crew to await the message he had yet to receive. He was not a patient man, and he knew the speed of his messenger was nothing less than bias. When he finally arrived and faced him, Spyros growled.

“Take my assignment...what am I, a piece of useless meat? I've completed more assignments than she can even imagine...and then the nerve to call me back...I'm not her little dog boy...thinks she's doing me a favor...”

Just as he grumbled, Spyros noticed a stir in the water behind him. A long tail splashed, quickly hiding behind a rock amongst the small waves. He was being watched. With spite, he spat in the direction of the mermaid, cursing her very existence.

"Very distinguished," she muttered. She propped her arm against the rock and lifted her head for him to see. Her piercing eyes saw right through him. Her dark, damp hair framed her small face, and her mouth was turned upward mockingly. "I know why you're here," she said in a sing-song voice intended to antagonize. "When she fails, you're gonna be just as much to blame now...won't you?"

"I'd watch myself, fish," he gnashed. "I'm not afraid to kill your kind." Now that was a lie she knew all too well.

"Is that right? I don't think you could, though. Because I can swim faster than your fat, crippled self could waddle." She flicked some water in his face, lifting her eyebrows once quickly in instigation.

As she intended, he was infuriated and bent over to pick up a large stone. He threw it in her general direction but missed. She flipped backwards and disappeared beneath the waves, but her laughter could be heard ringing in Spyros's ears. He shook his head trying to rid himself of the annoyance.

"Mermaids," Spyros cursed.

38

COUNTERING PARTS

The she-demon and her pet traveled a considerable distance before reaching their rendezvous point. The flying Boy was expected to find their peculiar red flare amidst the trees to report his progress in his assignment. The blanket of rain that now covered Neverland was merely a petty attempt to smother Ava's flame.

Though Ava's strength had returned, she still stretched lazily across Bastien's lap, indulging in his desire to tend to her every need. He sat against a thick tree, which did its part to shield them from most of the rainfall, and lightly brushed his fingers through her red hair.

Contrary to what he would've preferred, her thoughts were not of him. She was plotting, strategizing, analyzing. When Michael finally arrived, she despised him for interrupting her meditation.

“Well? Where's the boy?” Ava held her hands up expectantly, standing to receive his results. Bastien, as trained, rose as well, keeping a cautious eye on Michael and his Lost Boys. Damien stepped in front of Michael as they approached Ava, and promptly received a scolding flick from his supposed leader.

"He didn't come," Michael reported, now disregarding Damien's insubordination. His tone was so matter-of-fact that the poor fool had no idea what awaited him.

"So..." she pressed. "Where's his body then?"

"We don't have it," Damien spoke up, glaring at Pan from the corner of his eye. "He failed. Jim is still with the Keeper, the Nidling, and the girl Alice."

"Alive," Ava assumed, rearing up to respond characteristically to his carelessness.

"Right," Michael nodded. There was no fear in him, as there should have been. "But, I did bring her back." He signaled for Tootles to hold up the twig cage which held Tinkerbell captive.

Ava's expression was alarmingly bland. There was no smile of approval; even more terrifying was her equally expressionless tone. "Oh good. I've always wanted a fairy."

Bastien took the cage from Tootles, following his unspoken cue to act, and then returned to his place behind Ava.

"You weren't a good boy, little one," she began the scolding, like a parent to a delinquent. "I told you to get the boy or kill him. The Pan magic certainly didn't pass on the old one's keen focus, now did it? His fixation was a trait I would've dearly loved to exploit." She circled him this time, keeping her pace slow and deliberate so he could soak in her every word. "Tell me, darling, do you like flying?"

"Well, yes," he nodded with a strained smile. He didn't much like hearing himself compared to the former Pan. "I do a lot of it."

"Do the Lost Boys like flying?"

"Of course."

"Did you teach them properly?"

"Of course—I taught them to fight and to fly." He was a bit resentful toward the implications. Damien scoffed lightly.

"Are the Lost Boys obedient?"

He considered this. "Yes, mostly," his eyes snapped at Damien. "They have to be. But sometimes they mess things up. They missed the boy Jim when I told them to kill him."

Ava clicked her tongue in disappointment. "I'm relieved they're obedient. I am. Maybe it will help them survive. Allow me to help you enforce that."

Without a moment's hesitation, her hand was raised in a clutching movement toward Damien; gradually, she squeezed the air in her hand. Just as poor Dick Johnson before him, Damien's organs were crushed before he could breathe a protest.

"Do all Lost Boys find death so adventurous?" she whispered coldly.

Smoke leaked from his mouth and eyes, dragging the life out of him as it fell. When Damien's body crashed to the floor, Tinkerbell tinkled so loudly and so devastatingly that it's a wonder our heroes didn't hear it from a forest away. Perhaps Alice sensed the despair, but it could have been perceived as nothing more than a shiver.

To the fairy, her own life had been squeezed out of her. He was no Peter, but he was once a beloved Lost Boy like all the rest. A child looking for a home. And for a time, that had been a pleasant home in which Tinkerbell belonged.

Now there he was, broken in front of her.

They all hated Tinkerbell in the end, but that could not erase the endearing affection she had had for her dear friends. Her light dimmed as the sorrow engulfed her, so much that she thought she would die. The Lost Boys cowered in overwhelming horror, hiding their faces from her behind the trees; their stupidly fearless leader's jaw hung open in repulsion. Even Bastien's face twitched.

"A child." His words were so quiet that Ava almost didn't hear.

"Oh please, darling," Ava chided. "He failed, just as any other Scada could have. I'll treat him the same as he deserves. They've never just been children, have they?" She then pointed to Michael, who flinched. "Take the Lost Boys to shore to meet up with our reinforcements. If any of them get scared and find themselves straying, *kill them.*" Michael's eyes widened, and Ava corrected. "Or have the moron do it."

As Michael and the Lost Boys slowly disappeared into the trees, Bastien inquired, "When are we expecting Spyros?"

"He's already arrived, but it hasn't taken him long to find himself foiled in his progress. He needs aid."

"About time," Bastien commented. "He's not one for speed."

Ava's fingers curled into a fist, her jaw clenched. Her mouth and eyes were too tight for him to read, and that worried him. He was accustomed to her cryptic demeanor; only heaven knows what genuinely passes through the mind of the Queen of Darkness. However, she smirked no longer, and her playful antagonism was fading.

"It'll work, Ava," he promised her. "All your plans do."

"Yes, I know it'll work," she said sharply.

"You think they'll head east?"

Ava twirled a strand of hair between her fingers, clenching her jaw. "I think their map will fail them and the Keeper will rely on memory..."

"The map will fail?" Bastien frowned.

"Someone will be deemed unworthy by the piece of Arkis rubbish. Just look at the lot of them. Between the pirate, the traitor, and the self-righteous scribbler, it's a wonder the map was ever really a success at all."

Tinkerbell, sitting miserably in her cage beside Ava's leg, tinkled some crass response to Ava's comments. Whether or not Ava understood the snide remark is irrelevant, for Tink merely reminded her of her presence.

In a smooth, callous sweep of her head, Ava opened the cage and grabbed the fairy, instantly crushing her into silence with her smoky hands until only fairy dust littered her palm.

Ava brushed her hand clean of the fairy residue. "I don't believe in fairies...particularly the blonde ones."

Bastien's mouth opened slightly, but he was beyond surprised. He had seen Ava's cruelty, but her recent sadism lacked her usual reasoning. She never acted without purpose, but her schemes were becoming much less apparent to him.

He didn't dare question her, even though he imagined Tinkerbell to have been quite useful to them.

"Now, that felt personal..." a voice resounded through the trees.

Ava shot up to her feet. "We must move, darling," she murmured to Bastien.

They walked only a few steps before Ava felt her closeness. The air was different. Bastien saw Ava's hand slightly raised, keeping her magic at the ready. She was prepared for war, so he followed in kind, wielding his magic while keeping a hand on his sword.

They had traveled close enough to the shore to hear mermaid fins splattered in the distance, serving as an unnecessary herald. The silence that followed was unnerving, but Ava's senses searched for more than just an audible sign of her enemy; her fingers twitched as her pace slowed.

Raindrops fell steadily around them, building with each thick breath they took. Bastien was suddenly reminded of his great kill in the previous realm. He shot the siren in cold blood and left her body to rot or disappear, as the case may be. He remembered her haunting words he had tried to erase: *You have brought a curse upon your soul*. He hadn't given it much thought, but his sudden remembrance was alarming.

"Does something feel familiar, Bastien?" the voice floated to his ears.

Bastien stiffened.

As if materializing out of the deluge itself, a willowy figure appeared before them, cutting off their escape path. Her golden blonde hair was twisted behind her head but draped down along her shoulder. Those fierce eyes made direct contact with Bastien's.

The siren.

The Lady.

How had he not seen it before?

The Lady herself had cursed him, and now she stood before him, determined to steadfastly hold ground between them and the Stone.

Steadfastly at her side was another woman Bastien recognized. Though not aligned with this particular realm's standards of what a fairy is expected to be, The Lady's companion was not easily misidentified. She had a sparkle in her eyes and on her cheeks which–while previously darkened by her notorious pettiness and vengeance–associated her with the fairies a casual reader would recognize as those who once blessed a beloved infant princess with all the desirable gifts she could imagine.

This fairy might not have bestowed the most desirable of gifts, but she made her mark on the life of the Princess Briar-Rose nonetheless. Far from the antagonist she once was, the Dark Fairy Seraphina's brown hair was now fastened atop her head, almost as tightly as her gaze was fastened upon Ava.

"Your fear wouldn't be so overpowering had you heeded my warning," The Lady spoke, shifting her gaze to her adversary. Bastien might have been frozen in apprehension, but she was not so easily shaken. "Tsk, whenever will you learn, Ava."

Ava stepped closer, superseding her currently useless colleague. Her hand was still lifted, but she first employed her more frequently used weapon: her silver tongue. "Did Myk extend your leash for the day? You've been awfully nosy as of late."

The Lady curled her lips. "The better of us have no need for leashes."

"Hm, I'm sure," Ava muttered. "He keeps you in line in other ways, no doubt. Can't have his Lady going rogue."

Seraphina cast a hesitant glance toward The Lady out of the corner of her eye, to which The Lady responded by bringing her hands delicately together in front of her.

"If that's the sort of limitation Korbl has put on you, Ava, then I am sorry for you. Brothers they may be, equals they most certainly are not."

Ava shrugged her mouth and looked lazily at Seraphina. "Hm, I imagine she rationalizes like that quite often. *I might be stifled, but at least he's not Korbl.*"

Seraphina released a light chuckle before catching The Lady's warning expression. The fairy cleared her throat. "There's still time, Ava. This is meant to be a peaceful negotiation."

Ava's eyes shifted back to The Lady. "Is it?"

The atmosphere between them was thickening with conflicting forces. A skirmish between Myk and Korbl is a sight to behold, believe you me. A battle between their fiercely female counterparts...now that is terrifying.

Physical altercations were rarely in The Lady's nature, despite how much Ava may have commonly instigated them. In any case, with two beings so evenly matched, a battle of magic would be fruitless and wasteful.

Ava sighed in exasperation. “So, this is the part where you solemnly say '*Oh sister, my dear sister—why must we fight?*' and then promptly blast me against a wall in that way you do.”

The epitome of peace, The Lady made no aggressive move of instigation. Instead, she stood with her arms open, welcoming Ava's assumptions.

“But, you must be tired,” she merely suggested, almost with a hint of concern. “You've transported your entire ship through the realm's barrier. That can drain an extreme amount of power.”

“Yet here I am,” Ava fired curtly.

“Here you are.” The Lady moved closer to her, but Ava didn't so much as flinch at her proximity. If anything, she seemed rather annoyed. “He keeps feeding you, and you just keep coming back,” she observed.

The Lady studied Ava's eyes with intent as if searching for something. The fire within them flickered fully and wildly, but that wasn't what saddened The Lady. “We've mourned you, you know,” she spoke slowly and softly, as if Bastien and Seraphina had disappeared and it was only the two of them. “Bastien is not our only loss. You've done such damage...and you are dangerously close to being lost forever... but some still believe there's hope in you.”

“Your undying patience for me is getting a bit old,” the Queen of Darkness rolled her eyes. Her posture was listless; she made little effort to challenge The Lady's tenacity. “Why don't you show me your power—remind me who The Lady is? Show me why Myk's afraid to put you on a leash—and actually be intimidating so we can accomplish something here?"

"I don't have to compensate," The Lady tilted her head to one side. "Some of us don't need our men to be weaker than us to feel powerful. Some of our men are deferential and persuasive enough to convince us not to kill you."

"Ugh," Ava groaned. "There's that patience again."

"Don't you dare mistake me for having patience, Ava," she quipped, sharply enough to make Seraphina flinch. The Lady's jaw clenched, and her mouth tightened. "I am no Myk. Patience doesn't come quite so naturally for me, and you have the great misfortune of testing it."

Neglecting the chord she struck, Ava exhaled. "Yes, yes, banter is such fun. Could we make this hasty? There's a little beacon of light just aching for my shadow. Just warn me to stay away from your Keeper and be gone."

"So anxious..." The Lady remarked, jaw still stiff. "And what leads you to believe I'm here for the Keeper?"

"What are you here for, then?" Bastien, at last, contributed from behind them. His mouth had thawed from the shock and terror she provoked.

"Yes, please, continue your monologue," Ava groaned under her breath.

"Welcome back, Bastien," The Lady's lips sloped upward again. She moved past Ava, after flashing her a glare, and focused her deep gaze on the fallen Regent.

His resolve was sustained, but only just. The confidence in his stance was balancing on the edge of a knife, and had his lover not been standing before him in such arrogant apathy, he would have so easily fallen off of that knife.

"Arch Keepers are in the least need of assistance. Thomas Hastings doesn't need me. I have other assignments. Besides, Keepers typically don't fall under my realm of responsibility, do they?"

Ava turned her head. The Lady's eyes were still on Bastien, but Ava knew that the reminder was for her benefit. "Then why don't you go to her already?" Ava suggested venomously. "Leave and save your little fish instead of taunting us. We all have better things to do."

The Lady of Light closed her eyes for a moment. "I'm not here to taunt you, Ava," The Lady finally said. Her heel turned slightly, angling her body back toward her Dark counterpart. "I'm not even here to threaten," she assured her. "I'm straying from our natural patterns...I'm here to warn you."

Seraphina cleared her throat again, this time pairing it with an agreeable nod.

"Warn me?" Ava faced her completely. Her fiery eyes narrowed in on their target as if bearing into her soul.

"You have to know what is coming, Ava. You can feel it."

The eye contact between the two women made both loyal onlookers uneasy; it was lengthy, and it held as steady as the silence. Ava's previous impatient indifference had quickly vanished as detrimental disdain took its place.

"You are mistaken," Ava enunciated.

"No," The Lady shook her head. "Neither of us is, sister."

Ava cringed at the word. "I will burn this world to the ground…and breathe in the ashes…and you won't stop me."

"Tread lightly. There's a war inside you, and when it bursts–when your flame ignites, martyrs will be made," The Lady admonished. She held her hands up, relenting for the moment. Before dissipating into the mist of rain, she declared, "You know what martyrs are, Ava…heroes immortalized by your own hand…and there's nothing more damaging to a villain than an immortal hero."

39
Mortal Heroes

Our mortal hero was damaging enough—to himself as well as his nemesis. The map still failed them, and it was beginning to frustrate.

"Why don't we eat some food? Food solves everything." Alice's declaration was well-received.

John showed Clancy and Jim the ideal place for collecting firewood while Hastings and Hook stoked a fire, with Marin contributing as she could.

Alice sat herself down with the small packs of food they had been carrying, searching for something to hold her over until the meal was made. Eventually, she found a tantalizing piece of Neverland fruit that looked relatively normal. Satisfied with her choice, she took it from the bag and bit into it.

Hook idly glanced in her direction while he stepped back to give Hastings and the flame some space. When he saw her eat the fruit—the fruit he had set aside for himself—his face twisted into a bitter scowl. Two bites in, Alice became easily distracted by some silly thing Marin had done long enough for Hook to come to the remembrance of a certain vial he kept in his vest pocket.

Hook has a rather soft spot for poisonings as he once attempted to poison Peter Pan, but his plot was foiled when the fairy Tinkerbell sacrificed herself and drank the poisoned medicine instead.

But this is a different story.

And Alice no longer had the fairy Tinkerbell at her side. This vial of poison was not to be given to a selfless fairy. Hook tapped the vial twice, releasing two drops into the fleshy part of the fruit. When Alice turned her attention back to the fruit, Hook watched eagerly for her sudden death.

Little did the pirate know, the Keeper was too wise to take his eyes off of him. Bitter though Hastings may have felt toward Clancy, he knew the scribe's claims had truth to them.

While Marin and that window of opportunity kept both the attempted murderer and his victim occupied, the Keeper's blade was gripped and ready—and thankfully faster than Alice's appetite.

Alice screamed, and Clancy and the others ran as quickly as they could. When Clancy saw what Hastings had done, his arms fell to his sides. He was speechless. Crouching over Hook's body, Hastings's jaw was tight. He looked to Marin, afraid of what he'd see. Her expression was the most complex blend of pain and relief.

John stared blankly, with memories of Peter attempting and failing to kill his nemesis running through his mind, as well as newly founded feelings of regret. Jim, however, looked as though he would be sick, seeing death yet again. Alice raced from Jim's arms to Clancy's, sobbing and begging Clancy not to be cross.

"You killed the man." The words escaped Clancy's lips, but not with scorn or criticism. Hastings couldn't look at any of them for more than a few seconds at a time, ashamed and conflicted. "You killed...I'm sorry. I'm sorry you had to do that."

Hastings inhaled sharply. "He was a threat to Alice from the beginning," he confessed. "I shouldn't have ignored it."

He rose and brushed the dirt off of his pants. His jaw still clenched, he went to work in fueling the fire; considering his end, Hook would not be granted an honorable burial as Livesey was. Everyone followed Hastings' instructions without question, helping him place Hook's body on the fire.

While the Keeper seemed the hero defending an innocent, Clancy knew that it was much more than that. Heroism comes naturally to some, but to others, there is a constant struggle. The second a hero transgresses, he must fight to maintain high footing.

"Hastings..."

"It's fine," Hastings snapped, visibly shaken but masking the regret. "It's fine, Clancy..."

He cleared the guilt from his throat and pulled out the map to see if Hook's death changed the purity of the company. Certainly, a man with murder in his heart was to be blamed for the tainted directions. Seeing that the map had not returned to its original image, Hastings abruptly tore the page out of the journal and threw it on Hook's burning body.

"But the map!" Jim shouted. Clancy put an arm out to stop him from lunging to retrieve it.

"It's all right, Jim," Clancy said softly. "He remembers the way. Don't you, Hastings?"

Marin and Alice watched the Keeper warily as he took too long to respond. Marin could wait no longer; she stepped in line with Hastings and smoothly took his hand.

"Of course he does," she said with confidence. She looked up at him until his eyes met hers. "You remember. We don't need the map. Because you're the Keeper." She squeezed his hand.

However laboriously, he inhaled and looked at John. "We're almost there."

"Yes, we are," John nodded in agreement. He could feel the landscape changing, though he didn't understand how it drew him in the way it once had.

"Follow the water," Hastings said.

The sudden and constant rainfall had formed a small stream of water that ran downhill toward the coves themselves. The Keeper held onto Marin's hand and guided her and the others down the hill to wherever the stream led. They all followed eagerly, but Jim had to be dragged by the hand by Alice. His confusion was unsettled. How could the Keeper know without the map?

Accepting that he understood very little, Jim looked upward and trusted Alice's guidance. Suddenly, something in the sky caught his eye and made him stop toward the edge of Mermaid Lagoon.

"Hey, a shooting star!" he pointed. "Make a wish, Alice."

"I don't have to," Alice squealed. "She's already here!" The child jumped up and down gleefully.

Jim looked down to see what Alice could be talking about—and that's when he saw her. Leaning against a large rock, with her mermaids surrounding her, as well as a tall brunette with legs instead of a fin, was The Lady.

Alice ran to her, weaving through the rocky terrain, prompting The Lady to stand and lift the little girl into the air for an embrace, and then rest her on her hip. Seraphina and the mermaids beamed at the young girl.

"Who let you out?" Seraphina chuckled.

"Clancy did," Alice assigned the blame, causing Seraphina to snort in her laughter.

"Ava has her work cut out for her, Thomas," The Lady hummed as the Keeper and his crew approached.

Hastings stopped in his tracks. He didn't need an introduction; the Companion of his former mentor was so closely connected to The Lady that they could not be strangers.

"My Lady," he bowed his head respectfully.

"Myk kept telling me you had things well in hand...not that I doubted him. She did, though," she gestured vaguely to Seraphina.

"I did not," the fairy muttered. "I merely had questions."

The Lady smiled at her friend before returning to Hastings. "You've always impressed me." John hid behind the Keeper, hoping to avoid eye contact with The Lady. "As have you, John."

John cleared his throat and stepped back into her sight. "I do my best, ma'am."

The Lady nodded. "Yes, you do. And in time, you will do even better."

"Are you going to give us the Stone now?" Alice asked her, still hugging her neck.

The Lady laughed. "The Keeper's already found it." She moved aside to reveal a small glowing Stone embedded in the boulder behind her. "You didn't need my help, little one. But I am here to help someone."

Alice's head snapped to Marin. "I think she's going to love you," she whispered in The Lady's ear.

"I certainly hope so," The Lady whispered back. "But she has to believe me first."

"Why wouldn't she believe you?" Alice frowned.

"Sometimes the truth is a hard thing, Alice."

"Not for Marin," the child stated proudly. "Tell her, Clancy. Marin is very wise and wants to be happy."

Clancy's expression and shrug told The Lady what she already suspected. The mermaid was conflicted.

"Well then," The Lady set the girl down and held out her hand. "Introduce us, Alice."

Alice beamed and took The Lady's hand, leading her quickly to her new friend.

"Marin, Marin," Alice beckoned the mermaid to meet them halfway. Marin stepped forward warily. "Marin, this is The Lady—she's very nice and quite powerful. She can help you get whatever you want, but you have to listen to everything she says. And this," she tugged at The Lady's hand, "is my friend Marin. She's a mermaid just like your other friends."

Alice briefly waved to the mermaids that sat along the shore, including Navena, Spyros's previous antagonist. Navena winked and returned the sentiment.

"Tell her how she can be good," Alice nudged The Lady.

The Lady smiled. "She has to understand her story first, Alice."

"I know my story," Marin contended.

The Lady raised a gracious eyebrow. "Do you now?"

"Yes."

"I'm sure Ava told you a good one. She's an excellent storyteller. She always has been."

Marin cringed at Ava's name, raising a hand to her hourglass. Noting this, The Lady called over her shoulder.

"Seraphina, fetch Baba Yaga, won't you?"

Clearing her throat once more, Seraphina nodded obediently and slipped away toward the nearby forest to search for her elusive fellow Queen of Avalon.

With her other flight risk now dismissed, The Lady stood close and lifted Marin's hourglass herself. Between The Lady's fingertips, the hourglass seemed far less threatening. Marin stopped staring at the sand and focused on The Lady's eyes. They weren't like Ava's. There wasn't a shred of guile or trickery. They were clear and bright like a sparkling ocean.

"The farther you come from Ava, the more the sand falls," The Lady revealed. It was nothing Marin didn't already know, but the Keeper and the scribe suddenly understood. "Look how it's moved already, Marin. You're drifting from her, and you're still in one piece. She can't hurt you—"

"I'm not afraid of her," she straightened her back.

"Then what are you afraid of?" The Lady knew the answer, but she watched as it tore Marin apart. Marin cut her eyes away and put her back to The Lady, walking far enough away from the heroes that she could breathe. "The true resolution of your story was withheld from you, Marin," The Lady called to her.

After a long pause, Hastings stole the focus from the disturbed mermaid. "How was her story meant to end?"

"Her fate was not to lose existence because of the choices of another. Her fate was to grow from the disappointment and receive an additional three hundred years to obtain an immortal soul, based on her own merit."

"Oh good!" Jim commented, receiving his own interrupting smile from The Lady, which silenced him.

"There are two truths Ava stole from her. Our own actions decide who and what we become, not the inability of others to see our value. You know that, Thomas," she turned her smile to the Keeper. "And sometimes sea foam doesn't dissolve...sometimes it transforms into spirit. While the lack of a body is limiting, Myk would argue that some of the best work can be done in spirit."

"And he's usually right," Clancy threw in.

"Yes, he is," the Great Companion agreed. "He is always right—though we shan't tell him that," she winked.

While The Lady spoke to the others, the mermaid Navena swam down the shore to where Marin stood. She recognized her expression—without the ability to cry, an expression of pain could only be seen through the tension and twisting of facial muscles. Poor Marin's face was so twisted that Navena flicked some water in her face in an attempt to wash it away. Marin swatted away the spray and glared at Navena, but her face softened at Navena's sisterly smile.

"She's been right so far, yeah?" Navena offered. She jerked her head in the direction of The Lady.

Marin inhaled deeply before turning around. Shakily, she walked back to the other heroes. The Lady had a fair hand held out, waiting for her.

Marin almost put her hand out to take it but hesitated. After a long moment of deliberation, she cleared her throat. "I need certainty," she shook her head slowly.

That pained expression now spread across The Lady's face. She inhaled sharply and promised, "If that's what you seek, then certainty is what you'll find."

40

Neverland's Last Stand

Earth has a peculiar smell when it's being scorched. Ava doesn't believe in empty threats, nor is she the sort to exaggerate her intentions. Each step she took singed the soil beneath her boots, building the scent of ash and ruin. The realm behind her was being razed to the ground, but Mermaid Lagoon awaited her visitation.

The Lost Boys and Spyros had met up and began surrounding the area, while the Keeper's Piccaninny allies followed suit, falling into formation around Hastings and the heroes. The standoff appeared to be The Lady's cue to leave, for once the heroes noticed the enemy advancing, their divine guardian had disappeared along with her mermaids.

The battle for the Stone was beginning.

"That didn't take her long," Hastings mumbled.

Ava was ready for that fight; her hands were raised as the flames grew behind her. Bastien had given up tempering her rage or understanding her distracted expression. She was both parts cryptic and terrifying. The Lost Boys stood at her right, beside Bastien and Spyros, while Havelock and her remaining followers were at her left.

Her aim was set.

The entire Piccaninny tribe leapt down from the tops of the hills and caves to stand with their Keeper. Tiger Lily took her preferred place beside John Darling, while Jim and Alice stayed behind Clancy. Clancy, however, was steadfast; he did not leave Hastings's side, no matter how much fear those flames inspired. He stood firm, never yielding. Though his hand shook, his voice held steady.

"What is your plan?" he asked Hastings under his breath. "I'm assuming you have one."

"Just follow my lead," Hastings muttered.

He grabbed the Stone from the boulder and turned back to face the enemy. Clancy sighed, but the terror of Ava outweighed all irritation.

Ava moved smoothly ahead of her troops, quickening her pace to engage in battle. But a battle did not begin. Just as she neared the Keeper, Hastings made one quick gesture with his right hand.

Catching his meaning, Ahanu shouted in his native tongue for his soldiers to lower their weapons. One by one, each Piccaninny dropped their swords, their bows, their arrows, and yielded any readied magic.

"Um..." Clancy breathed. "Hastings, is this a great battle strategy?"

Hastings grinned as he watched Ava's face fall. There was no resistance, no aggression. "How else are we to win the game?"

Ava's breathing staggered as she tried to regain composure. Her blood boiled; testing the Keeper's resolve, she resorted to lifting a hand and snapping the neck of the nearest Piccaninny. Despite the gasps and outcries, the Keeper merely flinched.

No call to battle.

No promise for vengeance.

John Darling, however, felt differently. Prompted by a side-glance from Hastings, John stepped forward.

Ava soaked in the sight of him, having last seen him as a child. "My, you look more scrumptious than you did when we last met, darling...albeit filthier," she commented, her eyes scanning the dirt on his face and the torn clothes he still wore.

His chest still puffed with aggression, John took a step closer to the Keeper, doing his best to mask his terror.

"I see," Ava exhaled.

Behind her, Bastien eyed Spyros and exchanged an uncertain frown. Ava was not one to share strategy, but even her ignorant allies could see her expectations unraveling. Often, by now, there would be at least a bit of bloodshed, some battle cries, perhaps a few demands of surrender.

Before our slightly rattled villainess could start for the Keeper, Marin stepped in front of him. "Ah, little Marin," Ava sighed.

"You're done with this one, Ava," Marin said firmly.

"Oh am I?" Ava's eyes flashed dangerously. "Well, all is fair in love and war and all that nonsense...but it isn't really, is it?"

"He's not going to be easy to defeat, and he already has the Stone," Marin bravely pushed on.

"Because heroes always win, yes? Good trumps evil, and all that. I'm sure that's what he's been feeding you. He'll say anything to save you, love. That's what Keepers do." Ava lifted a hand toward her and Marin inhaled sharply, sensing what was coming. "Tsk, I would take care, Marin. Your time may run out faster than you think."

"You can't control me with empty threats," Marin decided. Her back straightened as she said this, supporting the declaration. Before Ava's fingers could move the sand in her hourglass, Marin tore the necklace from her neck and threw it on the ground before Ava.

"Ava..." Bastien cautioned.

"Shut it," Ava snipped, staring at the hourglass in the sand. All of the sand had moved to one side. It was done. Marin had left her. "Impossible," she whispered distantly.

"Heroes can always do the impossible, Ava," Alice poked through to the front. "Impossible things..."

"Alice!" Clancy tried to stop her.

"...such impossible things, like—"

"Like drowning a fish," Ava finished in derision. Her raised hand clutched thin air, magically lifting the mermaid into the air. Slowly and painfully, Marin's lungs filled with smoke. "I don't think you quite understand what this means, Marin," she chided, "what it means for us to be parted in the way we are now."

"Ava!" Hastings barked.

As if she had forgotten the Keeper was even there–or as if she had suddenly been pulled out of delirium–Ava looked at him in surprise. "Oh, but her jolly sailor bold—you can save her, Keeper. You can save anyone now, can't you? Go on, save the fish from drowning. All it takes is handing over that Stone, and I'll let her drop."

Hastings rolled the Stone from one hand to the other. "Let her go."

"I told you the terms, darling. It's not difficult. Give the rat here the Stone so he can feel he's accomplished something, and you can have your little ladylove back." Spyros stood beside her with a small chest, opened and ready to receive the Stone. "You're the Keeper," Ava went on. "Go on then, hero. Save the damsel in distress."

"I am the Keeper," Hastings confirmed. "But I'm not the hero."

He stretched his arms to gesture behind him. The strong backs of every Piccaninny soldier straightened with pride. They had stood against her once, and they would continue to do so until they were reduced to ash.

"How disgustingly inspiring," Ava groaned. "Are you going to leave the fate of the Stone to the native cretins then? Or will you be the one negotiating for our little mermaid's life yourself?"

Hastings tossed the Stone in the air once, then caught it. "You're not getting the Stone, Ava," he swore emphatically. "It doesn't matter what you threaten us with."

This hardly satisfied her need for thrilling resolutions. No battle. No retaliation. Just simple words. What were once her most expertly wielded weapons were now the only thing standing between her and the conclusion of her assignment—well, the conclusion of Spyros's assignment. As weak of a defense as a string of words may appear, it was enough to cause hesitation.

Feeling the anxiety channeling through Ava's magic, Marin wheezed a debilitated laugh as she choked on the smoke. "You've been saying he's not like the others," she gasped.

Ava squeezed her hand tighter, increasing the flow of smoke into Marin's lungs. "Don't try to speak dear," she fumed. "You can't even begin to understand heroes as I do. Letting you die is the most heroic act a Keeper could muster. The life of one woman is a small price in the perspective of the damage done if I had my hands on that Stone. No, the Keeper is proving he is just like the others. Congratulations, handsome, you've found your place amongst them."

In one sharp exhale, Ava released her hold on the mermaid, letting Marin fall to the ground. Hastings lunged to lift her to her feet and pull her from Ava's reach.

To no one in particular, both of Ava's hands flicked flames outward, as more of a discharge of rage than an actual attack.

"It seems the Keeper has chosen, boys," she glared at Marin.

"But he was willing to watch her die...I don't see how —" Spyros started.

"Shut up," Bastien snarled.

"I don't think he's leaving us much choice..." Ava ignored them both. "If they won't be bothered to resist...and the Keeper refuses to surrender the Stone...they'll all just have to burn with their realm."

"Go on then," Hastings encouraged. "You'll only make martyrs of us all."

That expression of cryptically detached rage returned. Ava tightened her jaw; his philosophy was obnoxiously familiar.

"Oh dear, Ava," The Lady's voice sounded amongst the sound of the crashing waves. "He's figured you out. The Keeper has learned how to best you...play your game and then take the fun away. Now isn't that refreshing...?"

"Face me, you harpy," Ava whispered.

The Lady suddenly appeared where the water met the shore. Her hands were joined in front of her, ever so peacefully, as she tapped her fingers together.

"Hmm....go on, Ava," she lulled. "Go on and make those martyrs—take the easy win. Korbl would be pleased by the conquest, but all the fun would be gone, wouldn't it? Either way, it appears you'll fail."

Absorbing the sight of The Lady did not dampen the blaze–it ignited something much worse. In the moments of silence that followed, Ava's face hardened. Her eyelids closed. She inhaled slowly, her muscles tensing as they attempted to harness the chaos that grew inside of her.

"Make no mistake," she hummed, however hoarsely. Her voice, like The Lady's, rolled along the landscape, striking the hearts of all who could see her. "I do not fail."

That's when Ava lost control.

When Ava's eyes caught fire, the Scada were the first to flee. Pan, the Lost Boys, Havelock—all of the underlings left Neverland and disappeared in smoke. Bastien never left his love's side, no matter how the flames burned against his skin.

The fire roared around them, radiating from Ava's body and spreading like an unquenchable life. The moment Ava had ignited, The Lady brought a vast wave from the sea behind her to engulf every Alden on the shore, wiping them away and transporting them to the Arkis for safekeeping.

All who remained were Hastings and Marin.

As the wave pulled the others to safety, a flare came dangerously close to hitting our Keeper, causing him to stumble backwards and drop the Stone.

Spyros lunged, but was delayed by another flare, which shot from Ava's hand, presumably aiming for the Keeper. Spyros returned fire by shooting a deadly glare her way, to no avail, of course. Her eyes were as aimless as her flame. By the time he turned back to his target, the fire had grown uncontrollably. He hastily scooped a glowing rock into his small chest and disappeared in smoke like the rest of the Scada.

Stuffing the true Stone into his jacket, Hastings started for the water. The Lady's hand appeared in his, and he turned to see her beckoning him back to the Arkis.

"You must come now," she pleaded. Hastings's head shot back to where Marin once stood, but she was nowhere to be seen. "She'll manage, Thomas. You must come."

And with a flap of a mermaid's fin, they were gone.

Epilogue

Montresor's Cellar

The casks of wine rustled a bit at the dark influences which surrounded them. Their owner yielded to the Scada leaders' wishes, giving them full access to his cursed cellar. The wall he had built himself, to hide his sins, was temporarily cracked open for their particular purposes. Only Ava, Bastien, and Spyros initially entered his home.

"Well, go on," Ava pressed in a husky tone. Spyros held the chest containing evidence of their success in Neverland. "Put it behind the wall."

Spyros wrinkled his nose at the rotting corpse hidden amongst the casks of Amontillado. He grunted as he placed the Stone behind the wall, intending to seal it with an enchantment. Korbl watched intently, awaiting the finality of the assignment. He didn't often come to the conclusion of his minions' assignments, but this new era was requiring increasingly more of his oversight.

"Wait, wait," Bastien stopped Spyros.

"What? You want the honor?" Spyros challenged, suddenly more aggressive with his Master watching.

"Perhaps we should ensure our success is certain before our arrogance gets the better of us," Bastien suggested.

Ava, lingering in the far corner, shifted slightly to get a better view of the chest. Spyros humored Bastien's suspicions and opened the chest. Where they expected the glowing, cryptic sight of the Soter Stone, however, they instead saw a dull, ordinary cave rock.

Korbl's eyes flashed. "Well, where is it?" he demanded.

Spyros stammered. "I don't....I don't understand. Ava—you little witch! You did this–you sabotaged me again, and now it's cost us the Stone!"

Ava's face was expressionless. Coldly, she responded, "Of course. Because nothing would be more advantageous than letting a Keeper win. My petty need for you to fail was just far too overwhelming and went against my better judgment."

"This is no time for jests, snake! Tell the Master you did this—tell him!"

"Perhaps you should take responsibility for your own failure," Korbl rumbled.

Spyros fell silent, but only for a moment. He then suddenly grinned. "You were distracted, weren't you, Ava? She wasn't right, Master. She's not much used to losing, now is she? He took your little fish, and you didn't like that. Someone finally beat you."

Ava's hand shot up, magically choking the accusing rat who stood at the opposite end of the room. Spyros gasped for air but maintained his victory. He was confident he was right.

"See," Spyros wheezed. "She doesn't care about the Stone—it's all about her little pet."

Korbl waved Ava down, and reluctantly she surrendered her grip on Spyros' throat.

"Is this true, dearest?" Korbl asked her, turning his back to the other two. "Where is your mermaid?"

"I don't know," she leaned back against the wall. "But I'd be more than happy to hunt her down and find out for myself."

Something about the lack of sport in her voice made Korbl tighten his lips. This was not the Ava he left in Neverland. The thick hatred that dripped from her words had stolen away all trace of the seductive game she usually played. She was ready for something new, he decided, something fresh and fun.

"Well then, Ava," he deliberated. "Are you prepared to face a new challenge?"

Without a smile, smirk, or cocky shrug, Ava straightened her back and looked Korbl dead in the eye. "You have no idea," she hoarsely proclaimed.

END OF VOLUME II

EXCERPTS FROM

The Alice Archives

The Tale of the Dragon's Keeper

The Tale of the First Beast

The Tale of the Child Thief

The Tale of the Dragon's Keeper

Dragons are one of my favorite things. I once had my very own dragon egg, until they made me leave it behind. They're scaly and fiery little friends. Lots of heroes like to fight them, but they're not all bad. The best dragon I've ever read even got to meet the O'Leary boys, and they're such fun.

He didn't have "such fun", Alice.

I suppose you're right; he liked their friend much more. But I should probably start at the beginning of the story.

That might be helpful.

Well, Neil and James O'Leary were sent by their father to take care of something, along with their friend...actually, I don't think I remember his name.

That's all right. It might as well be stricken from the record.

But it isn't, Clancy. I'm sure I've read it in so many places, but I can't seem to remember. Timothy? Theodore? In any case, the three of them were a fun and wild bunch. James was the tame one, but even he did wild things.

It's in the O'Leary blood. At least his skewed righteous.

He was the lovely one. Neil isn't quite so lovely.

He has redemptive qualities, to be sure. Reckless, but not horribly rebellious.

Yes, well, back in those days, everything for the naughty

Scada was about either stealing children or gathering beasts. Cromer was much better at gathering beasts than Ava was at stealing children—but I suppose Myk did fight against her quite a bit more.

Considerably. Children are much more defenseless and innocent than beasts.

But not all beasts behave beastly. Some are tricked, like the dragon—and Cromer was quite good at tricking. He's tricked the cleverest of men and beasts. Sometimes men need more work, but everyone likes magic. If you promise a dragon magic, he'll love you forever. Or at least, for a long time.

Before the king of the realm even began complaining about the dragons in the mountains, Cromer promised the dragon powerful magic. He was the sort of dragon you could talk to about your day during a tea party and tell jokes. He was just like a person.

Cromer gave him the magic as a gift and told him to make sure he practices using it often, or he'll lose it. But practice doesn't help Dark magic. It finds a home to live in, and it makes a mess. Practice only makes it worse. And when a beast uses Dark magic, it goes mad. Mad animals become wild, and then it doesn't matter how many jokes you tell them or how many tea parties you've had.

Rabid is the word. Beasts with Dark magic become rabid, viciously animalistic.

And when rabid beasts lose their minds, they become dangerous and terrorize villages. The king finally had something to complain about. So he called for help, and Conall O'Leary sent his Keepers.

And his best ones, too.

James led them to the dragon's mountain, and they all

spouted their ideas. Neil always liked brute force—weapons were his favorite things.

So why not attack the dragon with the best weapons they could find? A dead dragon can't terrorize the kingdom.

Well, Neil was sometimes silly. The knights of the kingdom had already tried every mortal weapon in the realm—they managed to kill the poor dragon's wife, but not him. The Dark magic made him far too strong.

James—I liked him best—reminded his brother and their friend that the dragon used to be...oh, what was the word. You know, the type of dragon you can have those tea parties and jokes with—

Anthropomorphic.

Yes, that. And so, since he was almost like a person, perhaps he'd be capable of reason. So James wanted to simply talk with him and try to make him like a person once again. There was no need to kill the dragon if they could get him to choose a side on his own.

Then they asked their friend...Timothy...

Thomas.

...what he thought they should do. But he only shrugged.

He wasn't the sharing sort.

No, he was the thinking sort, Clancy. James decides to use both of their ideas—first, they'd try to have a conversation with the dragon and come to an agreement. If that didn't work, Neil could try and kill him with Keeper magic, as a last resort.

Seemed reasonable enough.

It was only fair. But when James tried to be charming, and even offer the dragon some food, the dragon only got angry and blew fire at him.

He barely escaped with his life—and the bottom of his

Keeper vest even got burned! Neil thought that this meant it was his chance to best the beast. So he grabbed his sword and prepared his magic to attack, but was stopped by Theodore—

Thomas.

—who told him to wait until morning, when the dragon wasn't already on guard. So the Regent Keepers made a small camp a little way down the mountain, out of sight of the dragon's cave, and they slept for the night.

Well, James and Neil slept. Tobias didn't sleep much. He was always restless and energetic and bored. So, while offering to keep watch, he decided to go on a walk.

Strolling around the mountain was a little dangerous, but Terrence loved danger—

Alice, I told you it's...never mind.

The dragon's cave was dark, but when he came closer to the mouth of the cave, he could see the dragon curled up tightly in a corner, whimpering in his sleep. Whatever Cromer did to corrupt this dragon left one of his back legs weak and crippled. It was as if it was rotting away, like some dead thing.

A common physical manifestation of Scada corruption. Reflective, I imagine, of the effect it has on one's soul as well.

Well, Tristan doesn't like seeing living things suffer. So, instinctively, he waltzed into the cave—that's just how he walked, with a confident sort of swagger, like every brave hero—

You mean, like every arrogant fool.

Clancy, stop it. He's the hero in the story, so let me tell it.

He walked into the dragon's cave and healed the dragon's leg. By the time the dragon felt the Light magic and woke up, Thaddeus was already on his way out. The dragon rose from his corner to attack the Regent but soon realized that his leg no longer ached. He was able to stand without pain or falling over.

A little way down the mountain, James and Neil suddenly awoke and noticed that their friend was gone. He was a wanderer by nature, so they decided to look for him and make sure he hadn't gotten himself into trouble. At first, they supposed he wandered down to the nearby village for food. When the villagers saw that the Regents were searching for their friend, they decided to help them, and soon there was a great big search party looking for him.

Only after about an hour did they think to look near the dragon's cave. They got to the cave just in time to see the dragon rise against their friend—but then the dragon stopped...then he turned around to glance at his leg...and then turned back to the Regent.

All the while, Thurston simply watched, without so much as a flinch when the dragon stepped closer to him. He was possibly the bravest Regent Conall ever had, and the O'Leary boys weren't the least bit surprised. The dragon began to bow his head to his healer, and the villagers were in awe. The hero had tamed the dragon.

But then, all of a sudden, the dragon's leg began to itch. It grew irritated and even a bit painful. The dragon clawed a couple of times at the leg and then flashed his eyes back at Nicholas—

Well, now you're straying to a different part of the alphabet entirely, Alice.

—he was so confused.

I'm confused.

Confused and afraid, but not scared of the Keeper. He thought he had been healed, but now the Dark magic only returned. And this time, it was even worse. The Light magic that healed him now fought the Dark magic that remained, and that is always painful. They fought each other until the dragon didn't stand a chance. The dragon flashed his teeth and growled at Samuel, as a warning. The Darkness was about to win, and the dragon couldn't stop it.

The beast was about to become beastly.

Within seconds, his fire breath enflamed and encircled the Keeper, causing the O'Leary's and the villagers to all gasp and cry out. Neil and James lunged forward to try and save their friend, but the flames were too big and too dangerous. Neil kept shouting while James tried to keep his brother from jumping into the fire.

To everyone's surprise, when the fire died down, their friend was still standing there, holding up a single hand to keep the fire at bay. He was completely untouched. The dragon sighed in relief, but the beast in him was ready to try again. He breathed in deeply and aimed for the Keeper once more.

But Timothy just kept standing before him—

And...we're back to Timothy.

—shaking his head slowly and looking at him with sadness in his eyes. When the dragon exhaled, spewing another fiery force, the Keeper's magic hand curled just a little, guiding the fire and redirecting it to consume the dragon instead. Wounded and pained, the dragon staggered back into the cave—which, with a flick of Theodore's wrist, caved in on the poor creature, smashing it with heavy stones until there wasn't a breath of life remaining.

Then the O'Leary's friend became the most renowned and powerful Regent of his time.

His short time.

Yes, but, in the original story, that poor dragon was only supposed to be tricked into getting trapped in a cage, not filled with magic that could hurt him. Sometimes, Clancy, when people are tricked, they get scared. And sometimes, even when they are nice again, they're still stuck and scared.

Not everybody's story has to end either. Maybe if it isn't happy yet, it's not the ending. There's still more of the story left.

I do believe you could be right, there, Alice.

I know.

The Tale of the First Beast

There are plenty of old stories out there. A lot of them are very much like the ones we have now. Other people, from other worlds and such, have their own ideas of how the stories go—and when their ideas are bound with particular leather binding, those ideas become new worlds anyway. It makes for a crowded library, but sometimes the different ideas are refreshing.

Well, very few stories are truly original.

Except for ours.

Some would argue we are a variety of repetitions from the past as well.

We're the best ones, though.

Notwithstanding, our story sounds very similar to previous lore and mythology. It's all a matter of which account is considered older—ours, the Greeks, the Romans, Egyptians, Asians, Norse...

Those were the first to come to life, Clancy. When the Council woke them all up.

Which made them the first targets.

Yes, of course. The first round of battlegrounds. It's where Korbl and his best friends decided to invade right away. Although Korbl only ever had one best friend. The others only listened to him. He didn't like them the way he did Cromer...until he betrayed him too.

Korbl betrays everyone eventually, Alice. Even his own best friend.

This story is before the story of Korbl's betrayal.

Yes, this is the story of Korbl and Cromer—

And the wolf.

Those mythologies from the other old worlds had the biggest and baddest beasts. And Cromer loved beasts. He was always trying to capture and recruit them. They all listened to him and liked his ideas. The biggest and baddest ones were more likely to join him—but he tried the good ones too. Only a couple of those fell for his games. It was mostly the bad ones who were so foolish.

A long time ago, the Norse gods, according to their stories, thought that the world would end with a monstrous wolf killing one of the greatest of them, Odin. They feared the giant wolf so much that they imprisoned him.

Not the most effective tactic. Sometimes pieces of influence and magic can still escape and cause problems.

They tried their best, Clancy. And Fenrir isn't Korbl—he doesn't have magic that could leak out. Chaining him up worked for a bit.

I only meant, imprisonment rarely lasts forever. The wolf was bound to escape someday.

Oh, that is true. Especially when Korbl and Cromer love looking for disgruntled people and beasts. They were always very good at it, too. Disgruntled means weak and dangerous—two of Korbl's favourite things.

Fenrir is a giant wolf. Not like a big dog, but a giant wolf. He's taller than two men together—tall men, not men Clancy's size. And he didn't trust people anymore. Especially people claiming to be like gods. All they ever did was chain him up. They never played with him or fed him treats. They only feared him and locked him away.

But Korbl and Cromer wanted to use him.

They told him all sorts of lovely things about how powerful he was and how useful he could be. Cromer loved beasts, but Korbl wanted to find the next Creator. And dogs are wonderful at finding things.

The first Creator of all, named Ingrid, was gone now. It was time for the next one, and Korbl wanted to get ahead of her. He couldn't quite remember who she'd be. He once knew all seven of them, and that the leader of them would come last. But he had a difficult time remembering the faces of the remaining six.

Well now, he may have remembered. He only knew they'd be sent in different forms under different names.

No, Clancy, I'm quite sure his memory was fading. His memory started fading the moment he left. Trust me. You weren't there, were you?

Whatever you say. I think the truth is that no one can honestly know how much Korbl remembers. We can only be sure that he aggressively seeks out truth and memory so he can exploit it.

And now he wanted to exploit the next Creator before she could start undoing his work

He wanted to kill her.

But he couldn't. That's not how Creators work.

On with the story then, Alice. He didn't even know who the next Creator was yet.

Yes, yes. He thought he knew the bloodline—since all Creators are of Galderean flesh. All he needed was a beast with a particularly good sense of smell to help him track it.

He and Cromer were the most powerful, of all of the Four Fallen who left Yonas' Council. They knew it would be easy to free a wolf from his chains. They would just use magic. Cromer wanted a pet who would make him a better hunter—so he could find the Creator for Korbl as he did before. He was already the greatest hunter, and a loyal wolf would make him even greater.

But, even Korbl knew they'd need Fenrir to agree to work with them, or they wouldn't be able to do much of anything for him.

That's the rules, you know. One of the only rules Myk and Korbl *both* follow.

Storyfolk have to welcome them.

Like a vampire entering a homestead. A Galdere has to be invited, to some degree, before help or damage can be done.

Precisely. But when Cromer and Korbl came to Fenrir, offering to free him from the large chains, he was skeptical. Everyone always is, at first, I think.

That's true. Every living thing has an innate doubt toward corruption, initially. Sadly, many overcome that gut instinct and surrender to the offers of power or freedom.

Or both. Wolves don't care much for power, though. Especially wolves as monstrous as Fenrir. He was already powerful. When Cromer mentioned freedom—that was the only thing Fenrir cared much about. However, he knew the gods who imprisoned him, and no one can easily undo a god's work—much less a dozen gods put together. That's quite a bit of power to fight.

But the Galdere aren't mere gods.

I know. Let me tell this part, Clancy.

A witch told Odin, one of the Norse gods who trapped the wolf, that there were gods from another land coming to free him. I think the witch was Baba Yaga, but I can't be sure—and Clancy isn't allowed to interrupt and tell me. The important thing is that Odin decided he couldn't let anyone free Fenrir.

When Odin showed up to face Korbl and Cromer, Fenrir doubted the two strangers could stand much of a chance against the Norse god of wisdom and death and sorcery and every big thing. Odin threatened to summon the rest of the Aesir gods—his friends who helped him put Fenrir in chains.

But this didn't bother Korbl or Cromer. They both chuckled and smiled at each other. Storyfolk didn't scare them. Not even the ones who were meant to be the most like them. They thought it was more irritating than frightening that an army of gods intended to stop them from getting to the monster wolf.

"Interesting," Korbl snickered. "Nearly a dozen of you must band together to capture a wolf. Yet, it takes no more than four of us to topple and conquer an entire realm."

He was right, of course. Korbl was powerful enough to do anything with only the four who left with him. They were among the highest-ranking Galdere, to begin with—really, only two of them were needed to conquer a realm. Other stories prove that to be true.

Naturally, two of them could handle freeing a wolf. It was easy enough.

Even if Odin's magic gave him control of ravens and wolves and such. Even if Odin summoned Loki. He was Fenrir's father...somehow. I never quite understood how that could be since he looks like a man and Fenrir is a beast...

Not all mythology is for a child to understand.

Shh, Clancy. I'm getting to the next part.

Hm, very well.

Loki was the Norse god of mischief. Sometimes they call him the Trickster God. I suppose Odin thought he'd have more control of Fenrir than the Galdere—or at least succeed in tricking the impostors.

But silly Odin didn't know that Korbl was the King of Tricksters. He was the first Trickster, since before Loki's story even came to life. And since then, he gathered and led other great Tricksters, like Cromer. He wasn't the greatest trickster of them all like he was a hunter, but in this story, he was Korbl's best partner.

It doesn't matter, though. Odin never got the chance to summon Loki—he only threatened with a lot of words. The poor man didn't know who he was dealing with, for just as he moved to summon Fenrir's father, Cromer flicked his wrist the way Korbl taught him, and that was that.

When Cromer turned back to Fenrir—

You have to explain what he did, Alice.

It frightens me, though, Clancy. Perhaps you'd better be allowed to interrupt and explain it yourself.

If you wish. It's not too terribly frightening, though, Alice. He took Odin's power—withdrew it from his body, as it were.

I suppose it looked scarier than it was.

That's not to say it isn't something to be feared in some degree. If you were one as powerful as Odin or Cromer, then it's certainly something worth dreading and actively avoiding.

Oh, this is what Korbl uses later on, isn't it? With his friends.

Sort of. But that was a little different. The Galdere are a race superior to even the most powerful storyfolk. That makes stealing magic and powers much more manageable. Myk would never do that, of course. Nor would any Galdere Alden. But Korbl did this sort of thing regularly.

And so did Cromer.

Yes. But Odin's memory was left intact. He's no Galdere, after all. A Galdere's powers are attached to their soul, you know. That works a bit differently.

So Cromer didn't rip Odin's soul from his body; he only robbed him of magic.

That's right.

And that's how he was capable of controlling wolves and ravens and such. Like Fenrir. He could control Fenrir.

More fully, at least. I'm sure it wasn't too far beyond his natural skill-set as it was.

And the poor wolf thought that now he was free. Cromer told him to break his own chains, and he did. Fenrir thought he did that himself, breaking away from his prison and gaining freedom. But it wasn't him, was it?

He did what his new alpha commanded.

Cromer let Fenrir believe he was strong enough to leave Odin and the others in the realm and join Cromer in his hunt. Hunting appealed to Fenrir; he was a beast, after all. And this was only the beginning for them.

The beginning of the hunt.

Why is it, do you think, Myk doesn't use beasts?

The enemy prefers the weaker minds he can control. Myk commonly uses the strong who can act independently and fight with their own acumen. Not to worry, though, a beast's level of accountability is most certainly taken into account on Myk's part. Even if Fenrir was a kind beast, he yields to a master.

If Fenrir had joined Myk instead, he could have worked with so many lovely Keepers and Companions—and perhaps protected a Creator or two instead of hunting them. It seems beasts tend to join Korbl first, though. It's unfortunate.

Well, that's not to say some beasts don't reject Korbl and join Myk instead, Alice. There are plenty of creatures who are Alden. Mermaids, gryphons, some Greek bears, Medusa—

Mermaids and Medusa are not beasts, Clancy. That's horrible of you to say.

That entirely depends on your definition of "beast", I suppose.

Ladies are not beasts.

I could think of a couple of exceptions to that.

But you're right. I can give you a little credit, Clancy. We hear too much about the bigger and badder beasts who were easily fooled by fake promises.

Perhaps you should focus next on one who was good enough to reject Korbl and those fake promises.

Perhaps I shall. Unless I get distracted. There are an awful lot of stories in here, you know.

The Tale of the Child Thief

If I had to choose between a normal, ordinary baby and one who seems as if he was broken, I would most certainly choose the broken one.

Broken is a matter of perspective, Alice.

Yes, but broken and bent things are much more interesting than perfect things.

I don't think I could disagree with you there. Not that I would dare try.

Some people do. Some people would trade the broken baby for a perfect one. I think I want to tell the story of the hunchback boy today, Clancy.

Very well.

His story was changed, and that was unfair.

Not technically, now. His parents are the same; the circumstances simply changed a bit. Some would say for the better. If you had read his original story as I asked you to, you'd see his written fate was not at all pleasant.

It was incredibly long...

Yes, well, continue with the shorter version then.

It has one of my dear friends in it too. The other one doesn't.

Every story has one of your dear friends, Alice. Do you mean Ben or Stella?

They're lovely too. But just pay attention, and you'll see. The parents who wished to trade their broken baby were Regents. Their names were Eden and Gunari. They had travelled far and wide with Ben and Stella from the moment they met them in *The Three Musketeers*. Although...no, that's not right.

They weren't in their native realm when they met the Caverlys. They were never in one place for long—that's the nature of gypsies, Alice. Very suited to the lifestyle of a Keeper, I must say. It probably contributed to their great success. They were probably among the most efficient Regents in history. I mean, they undoubtedly had changes to make, straying from certain habits...

Not all gypsies steal, Clancy. That's unfair. Let me finish the story. They used to travel, but now they were back, and they were living in their native realm. They went home to have a baby.

Wait, wait. You skipped a critical detail. Don't look at me like that—go back. It wasn't just the two of them who returned, now was it?

I was coming to that part, Clancy. I'm a Storyteller, and you must let me tell the story, or else it will be no fun at all.

Fine, fine. I'll stop interrupting.

Eden and Gunari were a bit older, but even so, they loved exciting adventures. They always asked Ben to send them on dangerous missions, because they were the most fun. But some time ago, they were given an assignment they thought was painfully dull.

Taking care of a baby.

But not just any baby. The stolen baby.

They called her *cursed.*

Sometimes they called her the *devil's child*, which is terribly unkind. But their job was to protect her. So they did. And they were quite good at that. Tavie (that's what Stella named her) was never harmed or found by Scada.

She was safe. Safe, but wild. Her hair was quite unruly all of the time—unless Ben and Stella were supposed to visit, of course. She had dirt under her nails and holes in her clothes. Her large green eyes were always so full and curious—almost like mine, except mine are clear, not green. She loved to run and jump and dance. She was much happier than I think the devil's child truly would be—but they thought differently.

Eden wasn't the motherly type. Not like Stella. Sometimes she and Gunari forgot Tavie was even there. Then they'd just roll their eyes and leave her to play alone until they moved on to the next world, and she trailed along after them.

She could walk and talk on her own before long, so she didn't need much minding. But even so, she would have had more fun with someone to play with. It's a shame I had to stay here.

When they became pregnant with their own baby, they decided to go to their home realm. Since Eden loved adventure and thrill, she wasn't so careful during her pregnancy. And since they were older, the baby did not grow easily. When he was born, he was quite deformed. His face was twisted downward, and he had a little hunched back.

Babies are always cute, even if they become ugly adults. But not everyone believes that. Eden and Gunari were disgusted and ashamed that they could have a baby so hideous and horrifying.

And worse yet, he was an infant. A helpless infant in need of minding. Tavie was more infant than they ever wanted—and she had finally turned five years old and stopped needing them to mind her. She was almost six years old, I believe...or was she seven? It doesn't matter.

That's hardly a reassuring claim. I suppose being a Regent Keeper and Companion does not make one impervious to deep, thorough flaws.

I'd mind Tavie, no matter how old she turned.

I know you would.

In any case, babies require far too much attention and slow down the travel while seeing to Regent assignments. So they devised a plan—a terribly sad plan. They would sneak their baby boy into town and leave him with a young family in Paris.

But Tavie was smart. She was clever and was an excellent listener. She heard their plot to abandon the boy. She loved the little broken baby. Their parents called him *Quasimodo*, but she couldn't say such a long name, so she simply called him "Quasi".

He was her brother, and she loved him dearly, so she would never stand for him to be traded for another baby she didn't even know.

While the Laskos weren't looking, Tavie crept into the little tent and swiped her broken brother right out of his crib. She wrapped him up in linen, covered his head and whispered,

"I'm going to take care of you now, Quasi."

The Laskos turned to grab the baby and make the drop, and they suddenly realized the baby was missing. And because they couldn't find Tavie either, they thought perhaps she was causing trouble, as she often did.

Lucky for them—or, I guess, it's not so lucky—Stella has magic, and part of her magic is sensing trouble.

I think you mean intuition—particularly when her favorite children are involved.

No, I think it's magic.

Stella knew the Laskos were being quite naughty, and she probably suspected the children were missing as well. So she and Ben stopped by *The Hunchback of Notre Dame* for a visit.

Stella was right, of course. They walked into the Lasko tent and saw there were no children. Stella was furious, so Ben told her to calm down and take a walk while he reprimanded the Laskos himself.

So she did.

Stella strolled around the village—well, she didn't stroll. She was not at all having a great time, and people only stroll when they're relaxed.

She tried her hardest to remember how the book went. She didn't know the Laskos would be Quasimodo's parents, but here we are. She's a little sad about that. She's even sadder about Tavie being missing.

While she anxiously walked, she tried to think of what to do with Tavie and Quasi when she finds them. She didn't want them to stay with the Laskos; Myk told her that everything would happen as it should, and Ben assured her that he knew what he was doing.

Stella passed by some old building and spotted Tavie hiding in a rather large gutter sort of thing in a small hill, and she was holding something tightly. Stella coaxed Tavie out of the gutter and noticed that she was holding baby Quasimodo.

Little Tavie told Stella that she was not allowed to touch the baby. No one was allowed to touch her brother.

Stella asked if she can hug her instead—she can keep the baby, she just wants to hug Tavie. Tavie told her that was perhaps alright.

Stella pulled her out of the gutter and put her arms around her. Tavie insisted she was not going home, but she would let Stella walk with her if she wanted to. Stella had a trustworthy face, so she confided in her that she was taking the baby somewhere safe.

"Where are you taking the baby?" Stella asked her.

Tavie shrugged. "No one else wants him but me. But I'm not big enough. I'm a clever devil, but I don't know the first thing about babies."

"A clever devil?"

"That's what Gun says. But Quasi isn't a devil, so churches would like him. They take babies all the time that no one wants."

Stella made a tight face and frowned. "Not this church, sweetheart. You don't want to leave him with this one. There's a mean old man in there who would only mistreat him."

Tavie wrinkled her mouth the way Stella does when she doesn't like the sound of something. She thought hard to herself for a moment and then sighed. "I guess I'll be his mother then," she said quietly.

Having a five-or-six-or-seven-year-old for a mother would be ever so much fun, but I don't think she would have been big enough to fetch food from tall shelves and hold the baby once he started to grow. But Stella thought Tavie was awfully adorable anyway.

"Well," Stella tapped her chin and tried not to laugh. "Why don't I take care of him for you? I always wanted to be a mama. I wouldn't be able to take care of both of you, though."

"I don't need a mama," the little girl shook her head. "I'm big enough. I'm six now."

Oh, she was six years old, Clancy.

Yes, you weren't too far off.

"Every kid needs a mama," Stella frowned again. Hearing those words probably broke her heart just a bit.

"I mean...I have a Eden," Tavie shrugged.

"Eden's not your mama."

"No, but she's big enough to reach tall food sometimes. And she's not like some other mamas—with big dresses and crowns and sharp shoes..."

And what?

She got distracted.

Well, that certainly sounds familiar.

But she remembered that she was saying something and she looked back at Stella to finish.

"She does have magic," she added. "It's not always nice magic, but at least she's not a witch with warts and smelly clothes and bowls with dead things in them. I've seen those before—well I know stories about them, and they're not so nice. Some of them even eat kids—those wouldn't make good mamas at all."

She reminds me of someone.

I don't think you've met her, Clancy.

Someone I already have met. I think she enjoys hearing the sound of her own voice. And telling stories. Perhaps another chatty child.

No, no, Clancy. Tavie is clever and fun, but we are quite different. I know a lot more than she does. And I would never steal a baby. Tavie is much sneakier than I am.

You're probably right. You wouldn't steal a baby—you'd correct the Laskos with imagined authority and get yourself abandoned with a French family.

I don't imagine authority, Clancy. Myk would agree with me that no one should dump babies.

I can't disagree.

Anyway, Stella eventually walked Tavie home, where Ben had properly scolded the Laskos and taken away their Regent belts. When Regents are horribly naughty, they lose their magic. But not their duties. If Myk tells you to do something, the only one who can end that assignment is you.

That's not entirely true, but generally yes, you must reject the assignment of your own free will. There's a reason it was given. Technically speaking, they had honored their assignment to the first child. Regardless, losing their magic was well-warranted for a crime against their own child.

Well, losing magic was the least of their problems. If they ever messed up again, Ben would probably turn into a dragon and breathe their heads off.

I think you mean "bite their heads off".

No, if he's a dragon, he'd breathe fire, and it would burn their heads. He's quite scary when he's angry, and fire can be more frightening than teeth, Clancy.

I suppose that's a matter of opinion. But I will say, rarely is Ben Caverly so riled. He commonly left the invoking of wrath to Stella.

He told the Laskos to take Tavie to Middangeard where there was no magic to get to her. And if any harm came to her, he would personally see to their punishment. He even threatened them in front of Tavie and Stella. He certainly meant it.

Well, they chose to use Myk's magic, to fight his cause, and taut heroism. Understandably, any form of abuse would be horribly punished. And with a child so involved, it's understandable that even a docile Keeper would become aggressive.

Why didn't Tavie just live with Stella? She likes her a lot.

I'm surprised you don't have an answer for that yourself. Myk tends to have a broader perspective; you know that.

I know. I've told him that he's sometimes wrong.

And I'm sure that went over well.

He told me to skip to the end.

And he allowed you to do that?

Of course, he did. It ends in the loveliest way, but I still don't like seeing Stella sad all the time.

None of us does, Alice. None of us does. But that should put you at ease since you know so much more than I do.

That is true.

The Laskos are only human; they seemed repentant. The Caverlys kept a closer eyes following this incident, even living next door. They were chosen for a particular reason; I have no doubt.

Eden is very good with a slingshot, you know.

I'm sure it's more than her slingshot abilities.

I only mean it could come in handy. I can't remember what happened to Quasimodo, though. He must have gone with Stella and Ben to their next adventure and was raised to be a mighty Regent. He has such a good heart.

No, Alice. Well, yes, he does have a good heart, but he was not raised by the Caverlys either.

That is irritating.

Then tell Myk he's wrong again. Quasimodo is the Laskos', by blood. He was part of their chance at redemption as well.

At least Tavie can be his mother. She's good at taking care of people.

Well, she's six, but her heart is in the right place, I suppose. Regular reports on the children's condition were given to the Caverlys when they checked in on the Laskos—collected weekly by Stella herself, in fact. So, rest easy, Stella had a rather significant hand in the rest of Tavie's childhood. She saw quite a bit of that little rascal.

Yes, yes, I'm just very impatient for the rest of the story.

Mhm. As are we all.

About The Author

Renée Tamsin was raised in various parts of the Southern and Midwestern U.S. The one constant in her ever-changing environment was her stories. When not writing tales of adventure and intrigue, she's busy reading them. Things As They Were is Tamsin's debut novel, aiming to pull emerging adults back to the classics. She's currently working on continuing the saga of The Arkis Tales.

Like what you've read? Support Renée by leaving reviews and sharing her stories with friends and family.

www.ingramcontent.com/pod-product-compliance
Lightning Source LLC
Chambersburg PA
CBHW060756310726
48980CB00002B/110

* 9 7 8 1 9 6 1 8 7 2 0 3 5 *